# Uncle Tommy Squatch

## By

## Michael Henry

*Michael Henry*

A-Argus Better Book Publishers
New Jersey ***North Carolina

A-Argus Better Book Publishers, LLC

For information:
A-Argus Better Book Publishers, LLC
9001 Ridge Hill Street
Kernersville, North Carolina 27285
www.a-argusbooks.com

ISBN: 978-0-6158234-3-0
ISBN: 0-6158234-3-2

Book Cover designed by Dubya

Printed in the United States of America

## Dedication

Dedicated to the characters in our lives that have passed on to their next adventure. It's just not the same without you.

# Chapter One

Somewhere in a dark room, confined by walls of shadow and stone masonry, five single flames danced over a table covered with open books lying in disarray. These books were thick and musky; some bound by leather, others were nothing more than etched tablets of slate. And among these books lay what appeared to be hides of animals, folded over and resting on long, thin thongs of leather to the left. The last hide lay open to the right, blotched with line after line of deep, red markings, and curled at the ends—as though it had been rolled together like a scroll for a thousand years or more. The bizarre writing seemed to crawl across the hide under the wavering candelabra as a shadowed silhouette hunched over that last page like she had been writing in her spiral notebook for years. Unexpectedly, she sat upright in her chair, dropping her pen to the notebook as she stretched. She then folded that last hide gently over the others, and she turned to the beginning of her notebook to read what she had transcribed. And this is what she had written:

\*\*\*

Long before the notion of time, as the last regeneration of a seemingly dying world began, we descended from far beyond the reach of the hungry eyes of Earth. To the scattered remnants of this condemned world, we were frightening phantoms of animated light and glimmering dust that darted and swam across the dark skies in a chaotic search of hiding victims. We were something new, and unknown—alien by definition—but yet the Earth was as much a part of us as the native survivors were a part of the Earth.

We plunged into the surface, gathering the elements of a planet's decaying skin, and we formed into machines of flesh and bone. We were magnificent creatures, standing eight foot-lengths tall, on two, rather large, but very agile, feet, and we were shrouded in hues of beautiful, brown hair that flowed long and thick from head to toe. Our Earthly bodies were incredibly strong, but we were nothing more than energy, a free thought roaming throughout the universe, chosen and sent to this dying planet by our own consciences to restore balance to a lopsided, dark world.

A balance of light and dark is all there really was, and all that there ever will be—one as fast and strong as the other, and both pushing against each other in an endless struggle. Everything else is just a consequence of that effort. It can be no other way. Our responsibility was to cultivate and nurture new life, terra-form a balanced world, and we were to bear a race of disciplined guardians that would live in unbiased silence, resisting knowledge, as any other balanced creature that we created. Any other way would cast shadow upon the Earth. It was an inconceivable burden for anyone to bear.

\*\*\*

Enslaved in my body of flesh, I carried my burden across unknown lands in quiet conformity with my brother. I had many brothers, and sisters, but there was only one who I referred to as 'my brother' and I trekked for centuries, dispersing seed that clung to our hair, dispersing hair that clung to the briar, and watching as the sun returned to its harmonized rotation with the darkness. A deluge of new life scampered throughout the sprouting gardens of Earth. But I will confess, even with so much rapid change, the years would have been unbearable without my brother's silent company.

Then came that one, brief day that fate plucked from countless sunrises – or in this case, a sunset. We had been walking across the long, grassy plains between the vast inland sea to the left, and the great desert to the right, and we came to a broad river delta late in the day. We should have settled in for the night, but the opposite riverbank beckoned us with the sweet smell of fruit, and the allure of the other side. The grass was thick and tall, and filled with lurking eyes and blood-stained teeth. Our feet sank into the soft mud under knee-deep water, but we trudged on, toward the falling sun. The sun sat right down on the horizon before us, and a blinding glare shimmered across the water. And that's when a ghastly noise skipped across the river like a stone. Our hands went to our brows as we peered into the burning sunlight. On the distant shore, was a figure – an erect figure, pacing back and forth along the water's edge on two feet. It had to be one of our own, but yet, this creature appeared to be much too small, even with our corroded vision from across the span of water.

We curiously—but cautiously—watched as this figure frantically searched the unbroken surface of water, occasionally blasting a high-pitched sound that could only be described as anguish. But the old-world stalkers were cinching in on us from below the plain of water. It was only a matter of time before one of them grew confident enough to bite. We were prone to meet this stranger, ready or not.

The burning, red sun had fallen halfway behind the horizon when we reached dry land, but our eyes still remembered the glare of the water. The stranger was nothing more than a shadow, covered by a bright light that only existed somewhere behind our eyes. Our vision soon cleared though, and we ascended the riverbank. This peculiar being bared its teeth, and began aggressively jumping and thrashing about while squalling the most appalling sounds. Although bipedal, and covered in hair, it was clear that this beast was not the same as us. But she was beautiful, and she was alone – no doubt a surviving victim of the river.

My brother quickly continued on with his journey, leaving the beast to her misfortunes. But I stayed. My brother looked back just one time, our stares embracing in confusion. Then he turned his back, and disappeared with the sun. And for the first time ever, our bond was broken.

\*\*\*

As the seasons passed, I often thought of my brother, and wondered if he ever thought of me. I could feel his disapproval when I envisioned him, and after I had intervened in the destiny of my seventh child – a daughter, born from the womb of my beautiful beast, and of the purest generation to ever inhabit the Earth – I knew I could never return.

Ill fate had left my young daughter mortally wounded, by the sabers of a lion, and my own will to uphold my brother's constitution. I was her father, and she was so much more than just a piece of me. What happened next was inevitable. I carried my dying daughter deep into the forested mountains, and climbed above the clouds to the brim of the highest peak. The wind howled across the peak with a bitter bite, and blasted us with snow and ice, but the lake of fire lighted the night and warmed my determination. I gently placed my daughter to the soil, and covered her with the richest dust on Earth. I then looked to the skies. The stars wavered brightly, so close that I reached out for them. My mouth fell open, and a sound crackled from deep in my gullet. The sound strengthened into a strong, mournful moan, but soon my thoughts started to contort my tongue and tighten my lips. And imagination was heard for the first time. I had no idea what these sounds were, or where they came from, but my heart hurt too bad to care. All I wanted was for my daughter to live.

Over and over I repeated the sounds until they mashed together into a melodic blur. Eventually, a light beamed down from a single star and covered my daughter's body, pipelining sparkling dust upon her. It was working. My heart nearly stopped, hesitating the sounds, but only for a moment. I quickly resumed and called upon the stars all night, every night, until I collapsed with exhaustion on the third dawn.

\*\*\*

Four days later, I watched the sunrise as I descended the mountain peak, with my famished daughter leading the way. I nervously studied the sun and scanned across the skies. There was no darkness – not even a shadow. Nothing had happened, other than my daughter had been filled with life. The sight of her freely strolling down the mountainside brought me so much joy. My mouth opened again, and out came the sound of love. I had named my daughter. She smiled and mimicked the sound. And then, she called me...Enki.

I was proud of my name, but used it quietly. As soon as we returned home, I cleared a section of forest and built a wall around my family – no malice, just the work of idle hands. But still, I stood in the middle of my fortress and looked to the clear, blue sky. Again, nothing happened, and my family was protected from the vicious world.

My imagination exploded. I couldn't stop it. I named the rest of my family, and together, we named everything else. And we sketched pictures of everything we named. I enjoyed listening to my children speak even more than listening to myself, and I communicated with my family freely, and often. Basic tools soon followed, and some of those tools innocently progressed into weapons at the expense of a lion that inadvertently sealed its own fate by setting eyes on *Enki's* child.

I was doing no harm to the world, and it was my given right to make a better life for my family. But there were others who disagreed, and down from the night sky it came, a light so bright that it stifled the stars. This strange light scattered my frightened family to the walls of our protection as it settled over our fire, extinguishing the flames, and leaving only smoldering logs. There was something more – something inside the light. I could feel it, but my eyes could not penetrate the light. I charged, and leaped through the air, but the light slapped me to the ground like a mere fly.

My skull was ringing with bewilderment, but I managed to raise my eyes to my children. The light already had them. All seven were convulsing at the end of what resembled bolts of lightning that reached out from the light. The knowledge that I had taught them was being sucked from their brains while their beautiful hair fell into a pile at their feet. I called out to my children as I stumbled to my own feet and ran to them. But the light had finished, and released them to the ground, quivering uncontrollably.

My precious little daughter was the first that I reached, but she cowered at the sight of me. I could see it in her eyes. She had no idea who I was. I cradled her up in my arms, but her hairless skin seared my flesh like fire. I could not even hold my own children. Something happened inside – something more than the instinct to protect my children. I grabbed the pole that I had crafted with a chiseled, stone point, stained with the blood of a lion, and I hurled it into the light. I heard it strike. And I heard a never-ending gasp. But before I could act further, the light had me in the same manner as it had my children. And I was floating up into the air, with the light.

I struggled with all of my might, but resistance quickly proves futile when suspended in the air. I called the names of my children as I looked down upon them. They were naked and stupid, shivering on the cold, hard ground, as they were at birth. My welling eyes drifted to the other side of our family fortress, and there, pinned to the wooden wall by my spear, was my beautiful beast.

*** 

What happened next was a blur of consciousness. There were many lights, most flashing by quicker than my eyes could follow, and it felt as though my bones were being pulled from my flesh. When I awoke, I was face down in wet sand, staring at the morning sun that glared above the silhouette of a weathered, stone landscape. The sound of breaking waves beating against a shoreline echoed from behind. I knew that sound well, and didn't want to look.

But how could I not? It was the ocean—blue as far as I could see—a sight that I have stared at in wonder many times, but this time was different. I didn't know where I was, and I saw the sea in a sickening new light. I turned inland, and rushed up the barren rock slope toward the rising sun, hoping to find forest just over the break. All I found was another beach below me in the distance, and more blue water as far as I could see. I lost my composure, only for a moment, as I roared out across the sea. But there was not even a single bird to hear me.

I returned to the beach and sat in the sand, under the sun, watching as it slowly drifted across the sky and slipped into the ocean. That's where my children were – under the sun, and completely helpless, as was I. Looking out into the nothingness of the ocean, all I could see was my children in the rolling waves, as I last saw them. I tried closing my eyes, but then all I could see was that spear, in my hands. The dried lion's blood continually seeped down the handle, and into my hands. But it was not the lion's blood on my hands. It was not my fault.

I called to the stars for help that night, but the words would not come as they did on the peak with my daughter. I tried and tried. All I spoke was jumble. But I refused to give up, and never repeated the same mumblings the next night. Even if I would have gotten it right, I don't think the stars were listening anymore.

That first full moon, I scooped an arms-length mark in the sparkling sand with my hand. Each full moon thereafter, I scooped another mark, each mark half a step from the last. It helped to keep a grip on reality, and created a search grid of my prison – not that there was anything to find. I nibbled on the stale lichen that clung to the rocks, and sipped on stagnate pools of trapped rainwater. Occasionally, the unidentifiable carcass of some unfortunate sea creature would wash up on the beach. It was amazing how easy it was. I was not as far above the lowly scavengers of Earth as I thought. I was so hungry.

Eventually, the faces of my children, and my first love, were replaced by a glare of light. I couldn't escape the light. Day after day, the sun blared down hard, interrogating me, trying to conform me, and bleaching my beautiful hair as white as the sands underfoot. I had wandered under the perfection of the sun until I found a mark in the sand. It was my first mark, the place of my beginning. And though I was essentially tracking time, I had no idea how many marks I had scooped. I stopped. What was the purpose? Everything has a purpose, and mine was not to dig marks in the sand on some barren island. Something felt different inside. I could see things more clearly, inside and out, and I could hear the rolling water and the ocean breezes talking, as clear as I once heard my family. Freedom was a gift of the light, and it must be so. What right did the light have to take it away? It did not, and could not.

***

That night, when the sun was at its most distant, a ball of fire blazed across the star-spangled dome overhead and impacted on my island, as if I had summoned it from the night sky with my contempt. It happened so fast and so forcefully. I found myself pitching about on the swelling waters of my confinement, my ears ringing, and my eyes burning from the flash. I must admit that I was quite shaken, but also very excited. When isolated in nothing, even death is something.

When I made it back to shore, I found my little knoll of weather-washed rock had been blasted into a near vertical ring of jagged wall. A long-missed exuberance returned as I scaled the cliff, and descended into the crater. Once inside, I felt a vibration – first with my feet, then my fingers tingled in the air. It grew stronger, faster, and so intense that it hissed in my ears. I became disoriented, and looked to the stars for stability. But there was nothing there. Every direction I looked, nothing but black. It was as though a cover was dropped over the crater after I had entered.

Suddenly a flash of light caught my eye. I wheeled to my right, and there it was – the projectile that had fallen from the sky and wreaked havoc on my island. It was about waist high, but certainly most of it was embedded deeper into the rock. And it was clean, and clear, much like the crystal of Earth, but this was no ordinary crystal. Within it twitched a frenzy of grotesque lines of shadow and light, each line wincing away from the touch of another, and the vibration became almost unbearable. But the hiss slowed into an enticing whisper. I held out the palm of my hand, obviously careful of extreme heat, but oddly enough, it seemed as cool as the night air off of the ocean. Even stranger, it pulled at my hand. I eased closer, with absolutely no intention of actually touching it. But yet, somehow, there was my hand, lying flat against the crystal meteorite, while excruciating pain jolted up my arm and swallowed my head like it was on fire. I frantically jerked away with everything in my power, but the crystal had liquefied around my wrist and was flowing up my arm. I was looking right down over my shoulder, watching the horrifying beads of molten crystal seep up through the hair on my arm like snakes. The longest stream of crystal slithered up onto my shoulder, and I turned away, flailing my free arm wildly, grasping for anything. My heart pounded faster and faster as the snaking crystal crawled up the back of my neck, and curled up into a pool on the very top of my head. It was as though I was completely upside down, but I could feel the freshly shattered rock digging into my feet as I pulled away. The pool of crystal thickened and started oozing down over my head, forming around my eyes, molding with the bone beneath my skin. My brain thrashed inside, and my skull felt as though it were shattering like glass. I screamed out in terror, but what sounded like two worlds colliding overwhelmed the sound of my own voice. Then, everything flashed black and silent.

***

I regained consciousness to a strange murmuring sound, and I opened my eyes to the glaring sun, straight above me. My head ached so badly that I just lay still, and I closed my eyes anew to block out the burning light while trying to pinpoint the direction of the sound that I was hearing. I concentrated on clearing the haze from my thoughts, listening closely to the murmur. It was voices, engaged in conversation. My eyes jerked back open and my head startled from side to side. And then I remembered the crystal on my head. I leaped to my feet and lifted the solidified crystal from my head, tossing it away. The crystal shrieked as it danced across the jagged rocks, but it refused to shatter, or even scar.

I just stood there, not knowing what to do, and staring at the crystal from my head. It was a skull—my skull—only larger, and molded to fit perfectly over my head. And though it had spun to rest on its side, it was looking directly at me. I had to break away from its gaze, and survey my surroundings, remembering the previous night. But everything was quiet and dead, as always on the island. The meteorite appeared to be just another shiny rock glistening in the sun, and the voices had disappeared. I felt like I was being watched as my eyes searched the rim of the crater. I had to get out of that hole.

***

I sat on the beach, looking out into the sea for the rest of the day as I tried to make sense of the bizarre night. There was no question that the crystal held a power that I had never known – a deadly power. But yet I survived. And, out of the entire world, what were the chances that a meteorite would fall on this tiny island? This tiny island that shouldn't even have survived the impact. Someone was helping me.

As I sat, lost in thought, the sun drifted across the sky and hovered over the far horizon of water. And like every other sunset, I envisioned my children, alive and well under the sun. Without hope I had nothing. What did I do to deserve such torture? That was the moment that I decided. That crystal was my way off of that island, and I was taking it. But the sun loomed in my face, watching my every move. I waited for night, my only ally.

The sun plunged under the waves, slowly dragging the light down with it, and the dark crept along behind, whispering a low hum into my ear. It came as no surprise, but still, my withered-up stomach tied itself into knots. I didn't even turn around. I just patiently sat there, waiting, as if the sun would slyly peek back up over the water's edge to catch me trying to escape.

\*\*\*

I waited until the last star winked open in the night sky before I left the beach and eased up and over the sheer crater walls. The humming whisper was much louder inside the crater, and the skull came to life with its chaotic dance of light and dark streaks as I approached. I picked it up, staring at arm's length. It whispered to me, at least to part of my brain that was unfamiliar to me, like I was a third party stranger in my own body. And the mask wanted on my head. That was its design, like an exquisite mask, custom crafted for my face.

I spun the crystal mask and lofted it over my head. It hovered, stone solid in my trembling hands. Everything that was me screamed "no", but everything else—the starless dome of black nothing over the crater, the crystal mask, and the foreign me—assured that there was nothing more right. So I closed my eyes, and relinquished my futile resistance. The crystal mask gently lowered onto my head. There was nothing abrasive, or forceful, as was the night before. It was much like the touch that I had so missed.

But as gentle as the mask was, there was nothing calm inside. A thousand voices rambled over one another in my head, and even though my eyes were closed, I could see everything in the universe, like I was rocketing through the stars as countless images flashed by – images that I couldn't comprehend, and images of an Earth that never was. I was tumbling completely out of control. All I wanted was to get off of that island, so I concentrated on that thought. I envisioned myself, moving from the island to my children, and the clamor of voices softened, as only one voice floated to the top. I let the voice flow from my head to my tongue, and the words poured from my mouth and fell upon my tingling hands and feet. The prick of the stones eased from my bare souls, as if my feet were going numb, like I was lifting from the ground. I opened my eyes, and looked down. How could I have not lost my concentration?

I just stood in the still of the crater, rubbing my hands and digging my toes into the solid rock. The crystal mask was inanimate as the rock underfoot, as if pouting over rejection. What was I afraid of? That was the only clear answer – spending one more day nibbling on lichen in total isolation under the scornful gaze of the sun.

I imagined my escape again, this time with my eyes open. The crystal mask surged to life, and the words came, much easier than before. I let the tingle spread throughout my entire body until I became light on my feet. But I didn't look. Instead, I turned my eyes to the top of the crater, and I floated up to the rim with the ease of a fragrance on the wind. I then looked out over the ocean, towards home, and away I soared, skimming above the black, rolling waves.

\*\*\*

Home was not the place that I remembered. The river had dried into a lifeless gorge, and the grand trees of the forest had been replaced by mounds of arid sand. And there was no sign of my children. What had happened? I couldn't have been gone that long. Maybe my memory was at fault.

My children were still alive though – that I could feel without the mask. So I set out to search the land, always staying in shadows, with the night as my only companion. In time, I found my lost children, and quickly realized that my precious seven had long since left the Earth. But their blood had lived on through many generations. I had many grand-children, and I loved them as much as my own, but I was robbed of my family.

My children had persevered, and had spread out across the land, but they were huddled together in the dark – naked and cold, hungry and frightened. They were no more than the simple animals that they lived among. Then and there, I vowed, "no more", and I cloaked myself as their image. Out of the darkness I carried to them a torch of fire. They cowered before me, even though I looked as they, but I could see a spark of wonder in their eyes. Their imaginations were not completely dead. All they needed was someone to start the cogs of thought.

I taught my children nothing, but I led them into their destiny. And they followed well. Soon they could not imagine life without fire, were making weapons, and they used those weapons to replace their stolen hair, and for meat to feed their hungry minds. Their survival rate doubled, and they stepped into their place as the future of Earth. They were my children, and they loved me, but they did not see me, their father. I had escaped my prison island, but I could not escape my condemnation. And for some reason beyond logic, I took to the night skies again, and returned to the is-land. It was the only place that I felt I belonged – the only place that I could freely be me.

\*\*\*

That dawn, I stood on the rim of the crater and faced the sun as it leaped up over the ocean and stretched its neck out to look down on me. Blood surged through my body, and anger exploded from within. I cursed the sun, spat at it, and hurled loose rocks out into the sea. The crystal mask gleamed with as much intensity as the sun, and the light and dark lines inside of the meteorite thrashed about so violently that the entire island quaked. I turned my head back to the sky, with my arms spread wide, and I roared a blast that I had never heard before. Shadows raced from my mouth like a swarm of bats flying out of their cave at dusk, circling up into the skies above, forming a whirlpool of darkness. A thick bolt of electrical current ascended up from the meteorite and spread across the bottom of the swirling, dark clouds in every direction, launching single strikes of lightning down to the sea all around the island. The watchful eye of the light was gone. I finally realized then, that I no longer had to hide from the light. I was as powerful as it, and it could no longer stop me.

***

I stayed on the island and better acquainted myself with the crystal mask. I realized that it was just a tool that needed to absorb the energy of light as much as the energy of the dark to function at its full power, just as any other thing in the universe. It was the hand in which the tool was held that determined the implications – a responsibility that I well understood, and held very close to my heart.

The crater became my laboratory where I spent countless days exploring the reaches of my own brain. It was all there, and always had been. The mask just parted through all the chaos—the restrictions applied to the genetic skeleton of all Earth bound life—and allowed my desires to become tangible thought. And even now, as I write this, and with all that has happened, I lack the experience to even imagine the possibilities.

Like it or not, the crater was my home. In fact, the sheer rock walls somewhat reminded me of the wooden walls that

I had built around my family that were mysteriously buried under unfathomable amounts of sand. All that the crater needed was a little imagination, and some ingenious craftsmanship, and it would be a fortress of the likes never before seen.

The mask revealed a hidden dimension of numbers and lines that everything on Earth unknowingly obeyed. The rest was just a matter of chiseling away what didn't fit, and filling in where it did. I toiled for several seasons, although the mask did most of the work – slicing through solid rock with concentrated beams of sunlight, levitation of massive blocks of stone, and melting stone to reform with impossible precision. And when all was done, my fortress walls were ominously beautiful, and indestructible.

I had built a tower within my fortress, around the meteorite, that stretched far above the walls. I could see nearly everything below, and nearly halfway across the sea in every direction. I loved sitting atop my tower, taking in the view while recording everything that I had learned about engineering into journals – journals other than this, which are presently are lost to me – but I realized there was nothing to see, and no one to see my beautiful fortress. And the mask began to think.

I raced down the tower, and blasted a hole straight down, as deep as I was tall, just outside of the tower abutment. From there, I tunneled out in four directions to the sea, flooding the entire system and bringing the ocean water inside my fortress walls. I then took an egg from the great white lion of the sea and rearranged its genetic skeleton, adding some calculated mutations. The soft vibrations of the meteorite incubated and nurtured the egg, and it grew. It stretched out the four tunnels until it reached the sea, thickening by the day. Eventually the entire top on the island separated from its bedrock, and the rubbery cartilage of my creation spread between the tunnels, intermingling into the jagged crevasses underneath my fortress like the roots of a tree. And as the third full moon climbed up into the sky, we slid from the bedrock and out into the sea.

\*\*\*

It was a magnificent sight, my fortress slicing through the rolling waves and leaving that prison island to a watery grave. My creation stretched its sleek fins wide to the sides and flapped them through the water like a bird in flight. Its long, spiked tail slashed from side to side, shattering the waves into a million glints of wandering moonlight. I stood atop my tower with my own arms stretched wide, my mind as one with the greatest creature to ever roam the Earth, and I set my eyes to the land of my children. And with a mighty shriek bubbling up from the sea, we parted the moon glow across the great plain of saltwater and raced the night straight into the future.

By the time I reached the shores of my children, the sun had run me down from behind, but it seemed to stall directly overhead, watching with the utmost curiosity, and concern. My children were doing the same, without such a sinister agenda though. My famished creation ravaged the coastal swallows and reefs, fish and crustaceans disappearing into its mouth from under the waves. A creature that big needed plenty of fuel, and to my children, it was a beast, devouring their livelihood. I could hear them from the shorelines, calling my fortress a sea beast. This did not anger me. I rather liked the name, and I knew that once my children got a taste of what I offered, they would learn to think more logically.

\*\*\*

I carefully approached my coastal children, without a cloak; as I am. And they ran. They had seen my kind before, watching them from the shadows of the forest. Even if my white hair was brown, and I was without the crystal mask, I still believe they would have been defensive. I knew that I would have to bring them to me, but they had everything they needed – except maybe idle time. An easier life?

I kept my distance, but stayed just close enough. Out of the soil I grew food of plenty, from the seeds of Earth; and I mutated the will for freedom, from the tastiest of creatures to the fiercest. Every night I feasted on delicacies and sipped on sweet wine as the wind carried my irresistible life to my children. Afterward, every night, I left the shadows to the eyes of the wolf, and I floated music on the breeze. Soon, they came, and I was so happy to be accepted by them, but they were not the only company I had. I could feel the eyes of my brothers. I feared that it was only a matter of time, and I refused to be robbed of my time again.

***

I left progress to the mass of my children and returned to my fortress, taking to the sea with seven of my youngest. We explored the globe, traversing every bay, penetrating each river, and we mapped every remote shoreline. And every shoreline was filled with strange and curious eyes. But even at half a world away, I could not escape those familiar, unseen eyes. My brothers even trekked across the vast lands of ice to spy on me in the land apart.

The diversity of the lands and life was amazing, and my young apprentices became as hungry for the unknown as I. But even more necessary than learning, was remembering. We needed a more sophisticated language – more than just sounds associated with images of memory, or crude artwork. Together, we developed a system of symbols and sounds that would become a worldwide language, and we chiseled it all onto tablets of stone.

During the long days at sea, we recessed within the secluded reaches of the fortress tower and studied the hidden secrets of the crystal. We found things that, even now, I have yet to understand. We logged everything that appeared

thing that we felt – every genetic mutation,
1, and all of the energies hidden within the
There was so much, the stone of the tower
ed over by row upon row of journals and
 – specimens of our mysterious journeys, and our
secretive experiments. My grand tower became the central
nervous system of an exciting new world, and my sea beast
bore the weight of that information. My apprentices, old of
mind but young at heart, rewarded the beast with the affec-
tionate name of Atlas.

I sculpted a crystal skull from the meteorite for each of
my young apprentices. Not to wear as I—they would have
never survived such an intimate relationship with the crystal—but rather a solid skull, much the size of their own, and
yielding only power that my children could manage. I af-
fixed each skull atop an ornate staff of alloy, and each of my
apprentices not only matured with age, but as one with the
power of their own crystal skull. And when they were ready,
we returned to the civilization we left behind.

\*

Once home, my young masters served my vision well.
They engineered a race of master craftsmen—my size several times over—all of which could precisely see only one
plane on which they crafted, and all in servitude to the crystal skulls. And there were quite a variety of wee ones as
well—some with delicate wings that carried them to dizzy-
ing heights, others as small and nimble as rodents—all toting pouches of the shiniest stones and alloys found on Earth,
and decorating the most intricate details. The glimmering
city in the morning sun of a new age, Kalimera, arose from
the coastal bedrock, and through the generations, it stretched
wide along the shoreline, and reached far out into the sea.
Great tracts of soil were cleared inland, where seed and
stock were cultivated, and long canals supplied unsalted water to the masses. It was a magnificent city, filled with beautiful architecture and art, music and literature, and countless

children, with more and more sifting out of the surrounding landscape every year.

It was a triumphant age of enlightenment, but my children were not the only creatures on Earth that were growing stronger by the generation. Many of my brothers and sisters had returned to the stars, but they too had children's children, still suppressed by the light, and watching from the shadows like monsters. I was not concerned though. The light no longer had domain over me, and my brothers would do nothing, no matter how disgruntled – the light forbade it.

\*\*\*

But then it happened. The light poisoned the Earth. First, the underwater world beneath the city died, and the disease spread outwards through the seas. I had to take to the open ranges of the ocean, swimming nearly non-stop just to find enough food for Atlas – separating me from my children. Then, the skies hazed over, dimming the sun, and slowly thinning the vegetation, year by miserable year. With not enough vegetation, everything withered, including my children. From my crystal-powered tower, in the nothingness of the sea, I countered against the poisoned atmosphere, but the light only darkened the sky more.

With my children weak and alone, the light delivered blow after blow against innocence. The sun warmed the Earth beneath the dark skies, melting the lands of ice. The oceans deepened, and Kalimera slowly sank. Colossal migrations of my children poured inland, retreating into the countryside. They were confused and desperate refugees with nowhere else to go. Every thin animal, every green bounty of the soil, fell to their hunger, and those who did not eat, were eaten – mostly by the craftsmen that lumbered close behind. It was horrible, what was done to my children. And there was nothing that I could do, but watch it all happen through the eyes of my crystal mask.

When it seemed that no more harm could possibly come, in the blackest of nights, a scream rang out from high above the ocean air, more powerful than all of the water in the sea. As I cupped my hands over my ears, fire flashed over the entire sky, only for an instant, and then, a moment of silence that almost sucked me into the sea. A blast of fire and water came quickly after, tossing me from my feet and slamming me into the battlements atop my tower. Atlas shrieked in pain from the slicing concussion of the impact, leaving him quivering helplessly in the smooth plain of water.

I was stunned, lying still, looking into blackness, not even sure that it was the sky that my eyes were fixed upon. Suddenly, the tower pitched hard in the dead silence. I reached out, grasping for something to hold onto as my back pushed hard into the stone. Gravity was my only sense of direction, and my fortress was being tossed upward. My mind frantically clawed to get out of the forsaken darkness, but I was as helpless as the dead stone that carried me. Then the upward thrust weakened, and the battlement wall pushed me in a different direction. The tower straightened, hung in suspense, and pitched hard the other way. It was though I was weightless. We were falling. Atlas shrieked again, his mouth unnaturally out of the water. I braced for an impact. It seemed that we would fall forever.

But the impact never came. The tower just abruptly leveled out, and glided across the glassy sea. The rogue wave, nothing more than a ripple from the fireball that plunged into the ocean, tossed Atlas like he was a mere water skipper. And it raced toward land. There was nothing I could do. It was so fast. And like it was the hand of Earth herself, the wave reached far onto the shores and pulled everything into the sea. Kalimera was leveled in an instant, and swept away like it never even existed, taking thousands upon thousands of straggling children with it. It was the only time I ever removed the crystal mask. I did not want to see.

It was clear that it was all a tactical strike by the light, but not against me – against my children. I was so naïve to think such evil did not exist. But my lesson was only beginning.

\*\*\*

I somberly receded into the tower. The crystal meteorite immediately sparked to life, casting its eerie, pulsing glow throughout. With the crystal mask in hand, I slowly descend the spiraling steps, staring blankly at the stacks of journals and specimens along the wall, hoping the answer would fall out at my feet. But what was the question?

And like the mask had heard my thought, it vibrated. I stopped, and slipped the mask back over my head. I looked over the edge, down through the corkscrew of stone steps and terraced information, and there it was, hovering over the meteorite – the question and the answer.

I leaped over the side and floated down to an image of the Earth. Each plane of energy that holds everything in place for every moment in all of time briefly flashed through the image like a blade, and every point of intersecting planes glowed brighter with every intersection. It would have went on for eternity – each plane existing only once, for the briefest moment, making an infinite number of planes – but several points of intersection gleamed bright and steady around the globe, making a planetary pattern. It was almost like the fingers of two universal hands, holding the Earth firm, and navigating its course through time.

The slicing planes faded away, and each glimmering point dulled to reveal a tiny image of massive structures. Each structure had a wide foundation, and tapered to an exact point at the top. And on those exact points sat a small round crystal. The crystals all vibrated, in complete synchronization with each other, feeding from the energy of the points in the absence of the full sun, and pulsating waves of sound outward until a bizarre anomaly circled around the planet. The pieces were starting to fit, and I swung at the image. My fist glanced away. It was a system of protection. The light would never pummel the Earth from unknown reaches again. But there was much work to do, and limited time to do it.

*** 

My seven masters immediately set across the land to begin construction on the first pyramidal structure, their crystal skulls homing in on that exact point in the sand. The wee ones had already fled into the forests – there was no need for useless trinkets anyway – but the giants with an eye for craftsmanship slogged right along behind the seven skull masters, anxious to work. And work they did, reaching a new height of craftsmanship, and altitude, every day. Many of my children worked as well – workers received small rations of meat when available, usually from a beast that had tugged its last pull. Up from the sands of nothing, rose a mountain of ingenuity, and my unknown enemies that hid in the recesses of the universe were soon to be forever disabled.

But I was quick to find enemies hiding right here on Earth. It all started small – strange howls and screams in the middle of the night, and rocks thrown to scare more than to strike. Then, midnight raids through the refugee encampments, destroying shanties and scaffoldings, stealing tools and food stores, what little there was. My children were frightened, but there was no place to go but to huddle closer to the pyramidal structures where the workers and masters slept safely within. And when things escalated to abductions in the night, as harmless as they were, panic set in, and riots broke out. The refugees tried to force their way in, and the workers were forced into violence against their own. It was chaos, which was the intent of my brothers.

I was deeply hurt. I knew they did not approve of my freethinking, but I never suspected that they would cause harm to my children. I did what any father would. I protected my children. The bloodstained spear had not been to mind for ages, but I remembered how simple it was, and how easy it killed. We made hundreds of spears, only these blades were not of chipped stone, but forged from the minerals of Earth. And I forged seven more weapons, by the design of my seven skull masters, with a core of crystal within a shroud of the hardest alloy on Earth. Some were spears, some blades, but all were indestructible weapons of invincibility that led my children to become brave, ironclad warriors, standing guard along the shadowed edges, and ready to strike, bringing a manageable nervousness back to the construction site. But still, they were out there, watching, in the distance, where their silhouettes blended with the shadows of night.

\*\*\*

A new urgency lingered heavy in the air, and I divided my children, sending them across the land to other points of construction. The grid of defense had to be completed. The light had thickened the dark clouds even more, and the crystals would have surely dispersed the gaseous blanket overhead, as well as protect us. But transporting the cumbersome craftsmen around the world proved all consuming, and vulnerable. They became the targets of my brothers, and were easily separated from my warrior children. Although they used their tools as formidable weapons of total annihilation, the giants toppled near effortlessly, and fell hard. Many were left behind, in the hands of the enemy, diminishing much grandeur from further construction.

I took two of my youngest skull masters and as many of my children as Atlas could bear, and we set to sea, leaving the others to deal with their turmoil. They were capable. We ferried the length of the inland sea and skated across the rolling ocean toward the land apart where we would lay the final stones of our fortress around the planet, and claim the isolated and wild landscape as the land of my children. And upon completion of the defense barrier, Atlas and I, along with chosen young from all the lands, would build a new city, half a day from shore, over the flooded plains to where the sea floor plummets beyond reach – the most powerful point of intersection on Earth.

We lightened Atlas's burden by half on the lower shores of the land apart, and as my children were swallowed by the heavily forested landscape, I couldn't help but feel as if I were sending my loved ones into the gullet of a great beast. Fear burned bright in their eyes as they looked back before they disappeared, but above all else, I had to reveal faith in my own eyes.

Atlas slowly backed away from the shore, and swam up along the coastline, through the mighty currents, past my future, floating city, and along beautiful beaches and sandy bluffs, headed toward the final point. But beyond those beaches, and atop of those bluffs, in the forested shadows, were watchful eyes – more than I had ever imagined. And those eyes followed us up the coastline. Occasionally they were seen, briefly running across an opening and vanishing into the shadows before my children could focus on their large, hairy frame. It was a warning, a tactic to frighten, and it worked well on my children. But I could feel it in my heart: this time was no bluff.

We veered away from the beaches, and Atlas, as well as my own thoughts, drifted aimlessly in open waters. There was no turning back, and what lay ahead could not come to what was inevitable, but I couldn't just pitch on the rolling waves like a piece of driftwood forever. My brothers had backed me into a corner, and left me with no other choice. But no matter how small, there's always a chance of resolution.

For two days and a night I huddled in the privacy of my tower, studying the drawings of the flooded coastline, and waiting for another solution to come. When the sun slipped into the ocean for the second time, I forged my own weapon. It was a thick staff of solid crystal, honed to a fine, indestructible tip on one end, and a small skull beset in a crest of the finest blade on the other. Even with the advantage of numbers, and the leadership of the invincible sword in the hand of my young skull master, my children would need my help when diplomacy failed.

\*\*\*

I stood atop my tower as the sun rose over the dark clouds that hovered above the land where my brothers watched with anticipation. The staff was icy cold in my hand, and the mask whispered insanely in my ear. The time of waiting, and watching was over. A line had to be drawn, that none could cross. There was no other way.

I held my staff high and roared out over my somber children below. They roused to their feet and returned the roar, led by the skull master and his lofted blade of crystal. I turned and thrust my staff toward our destination with another roar. Atlas lunged forward, shrieking his own battle cry as his mouth raised above the plain of water from the thrust. My children cheered bravely.

Atlas's fins sliced down through the waves so powerfully, I wondered if we would take to the air. We swam with the warm current, moving quicker than ever before. Faster than my brothers could run. And the low-lying basin of two freshwater rivers that combined to pour into the sea was surely flooded into a wide bay. My brothers would have had to circle around, inland, across soggy ground, through heavy forest, while we sailed up to the next river inlet.

Our small inlet had also deepened into a sizable bay, and Atlas raced inland farther than I had expected. We shored up in the deep waters where the river met the bay, and I quickly led my skull master and my warrior children inland. Most of the females and young stayed with Atlas, but the rest followed behind, carrying weapons and tools, gathering food and water – the essential support for my argument.

We pushed hard through the forests and wetlands. My brothers were relentlessly fast as compared to my children, but we had quite a lead – I quietly hoped that it was enough. We reached the water's edge of the first bay when the sun glowed dimly through the clouds right over our heads, and we turned upstream, pushing on toward the river and a crossing. The support was falling behind, but we couldn't wait. We could see across the narrowing bay, and there was no sight of my brothers moving through the trees, but they were over there, catching up fast.

\*\*\*

We made it to the river before my brothers, and we drew our line. The river was wide, but only knee deep and slow moving. It was the most logical crossing. My warriors filled the trees along the steep riverbank, crouching in the shadows and watching the other side. The support straggled in the rest of the afternoon, a few at a time, collapsing in the trees well behind the line and out of sight of the river.

As the light faded on the opposite riverbank, tree trunks darkened, and shadows seemed to grow up and out from the ground. On my side of the river, anxiety was the only thing growing. Leave it to my brothers to wait until it was dark. The more we watched, and the darker it became, the more my warriors started to see movement on the other side. They were scared and jumpy, barely holding their nerve. I lay down my staff and walked to the river's edge where all of my children could see that I was not frightened. I could feel the presence of my brothers, and they could feel mine – there was no since hiding. But still, they did not emerge from the other side. In an act of diplomacy, I waded half way across, my crystal mask glowing in the darkness for my children, and I waited, and waited, in the middle of the river. Still nothing.

Just as I was about to turn around and leave the cool water to check on my children, a sharp, quick scream rang out and echoed up and down the black river. I wasn't sure where it came from, but it was the sound of my children, and it was too far away to be a warrior on the line. But my brothers would have had to swim across the bay to have cut us off from Atlas. Near impossible, even for my brothers.

It felt as though the water was holding on to me as I high stepped toward the bank, my feet plunging into the water in seemingly slow motion. A few more screams cried out in the darkened distance. I listened carefully, over my splashing feet, and under the sporadic screams of terror. The deep, black riverbank ahead was filled with feet blindly shuffling through the leaves, and metal blades frantically slicing through the air at nothing. Feverishly pounding hearts and quick, heavy breaths wafted out of the night from everywhere, peppered with grunts and moans in a desperate struggle with fear for the freedom to scream. I called out for bravery and control, my mask glaring brightly to anchor my children.

Then, a light exploded above the crest of the riverbank. Under it was my skull master, holding his staff high, the crystal skull illuminating the blind night. He brandished his powerful blade with the confidence that I trusted in, and other warriors joined around his clearheaded bravery. I finally leaped out of the water, calling for a calm, defended retreat to Atlas as I struggled up the bank with the river still holding on, clinging heavy to my legs.

But suddenly, a sound sliced through the night like the tip of my crystal staff. It was the sound of a never-ending gasp, filling an Earthly body as the life poured out of it. And it was a brother. Everything stilled, and the sound was washed away by a rogue bolt of lightning that raged across the sky under the black billowing clouds. My stomach sickened and twisted. Murder was not as easy as anticipated, and a new, unexpected fear for my children collided fiercely with my determination.

I pushed on through a seemingly endless black void, as if my innocent children were lost in an unreachable dimension, like I was helplessly trapped in a surreal nightmare. The chaos erupted again in the dark, only this time it was different. The sounds of anger, revenge, and desperation filled the air. Even I was terrified. The ground began to tremble underfoot, and the winds began to howl in anguish, carrying screams from my children, and the smell of blood and death. My brothers were consumed by jealousy, and were lashing out with vengeance, casting more darkness upon the land. And the Earth was angry. Lightning bolted across overhead again, and up from the ground, splintering trees on all sides. There was splashing in the river that I had just left, but the confusion of screams, footsteps, pounding hearts, and stolen breath was so intense, I couldn't tell if it was my brothers attacking, or blind children in the grip of panic. The night had grown even thicker with darkness, darker than black. Even the sharp glow of the skull and mask seemed nothing more than a tiny star, lifetimes away.

With staff in hand, I pulled my skull master and gathered warriors inland, into the dark pandemonium. I called to all of my children, but even I could barely hear my voice. The shimmering crystal was a beckon to my bewildered children – that was my only hope as we snaked through the dark trees and the sounds of death. The sounds of my children's pain and fear cried out in the darkness to the left and right, ahead and behind, and my brothers flashed by all around like a shadow in the corner of your eye, or the chill down your spine.

Then out of the black and into the light of my crystal mask was my brother – the one I called so. Our eyes locked onto each other, and I froze in his stare. He was standing still, almost in shock, with blood dripping from his hands onto one of my children at his feet. She was completely innocent, only there to help feed those who vowed to protect her family. And my closest brother murdered her. How could he have, and why? I had never felt pain like that before, and even now, I still carry the burn. But in that moment, I gave up. My brothers had dragged me into a place I did not want to go, and I swear, it was though my energy, my thoughts, had left my Earthly body. And so did my staff. It left my hand, and flew through the air like it had the wings and eyes of a hawk. The tip parted my brother's hair, his flesh, breastbone, and pierced through his heart before impaling the ground several lengths behind the hole in his back. My brother's eyes never left mine, even as he collapsed to his knees, with blood spewing from the hole in his chest, and even as he gently fell over to his side a moment later.

Suddenly I returned to my body, my senses, although there was no conflict, no sound – just those eyes, as they lay motionless on the blood soaked leaves of the forest floor. Reality seemed so unreal. But the gathering silhouettes of my other brothers were very real. They were all around, standing at the very edges of the light, flogging me with blame that was not mine to bear, and demanding their demented idea of justice.

I leaped over my oldest friend, and my staff dislodged from the ground, finding my hand across the distance. My brothers stood solid, determined to seal off the escape of my children. I cut down two with a swipe of my staff while the crystal blade lunged by and into the bowels of another, my young skull master holding onto the handle with all of his might. The rest of the warriors followed the lead of their skull master and his invincible blade, and we all broke through to the black forest that lay before Atlas.

We ran through the trees so fast, there was no time to look back. Rocks trembled up from under millennia of fallen leaves and erosion as the Earth quaked violently, and the wind toppled trees in front of us as lightning split the thick darkness with deafening explosions. But we never stopped running, not for an instant, even as we caught and passed by other children that were fleeing ahead of us. My brothers were in pursuit, and my children were disappearing into the black monster that chased at the edges of the light. Their murderous revenge was ripping the world apart with darkness.

Finally, the light of Atlas poked through the fleshy black of the night. The meteorite was glowing bright inside of the tower, and the brilliant white was beaming from the windows around the top of the tower, marking the blind edges of land and sea. Atlas was guiding us home, out of the storm, and my eyes had never set on a more welcomed sight.

*

A shriek bubbled out from under Atlas as I broke free from the grip of the forest, and my seemingly deserted fortress came to life with scurrying children. The heavy fortress doors swung open under the blustering torches perched on the walls above, and out poured the old, the weak, and even the young, all carrying what they were able to defend their returning family.

I stopped in the openness of the wide beach, turned, and faced the darkness while my skull master led my children aboard. Builders and warriors, and occasionally a female straggled out of the darkness one or two at a time. I had to make an instant decision whether it was child, or brother, and I was forced to strike several times. But I could feel something off in the distance, out in the dark. It was something relentless, strong, and it was coming fast. I ordered Atlas to swim, and he pushed away from the shore, circling toward open seas as my children rushed inside the fortress walls.

I slowly wiggled my feet down into the sandy grass as the tip of my staff honed in on the unseen monster that was about to charge out of the darkness. While softly pleading for Atlas to swim faster, I looked so hard into the black that it hurt. I couldn't see, and all I could hear was the thunder and rumble, and the wind screaming in my ears. But I could feel it coming. Not a brother, one generation younger. I had just killed his father, my closest friend. And he was more machine than creature of Earth. I could feel those fearless, brown eyes racing through the dark above the touch of my children, and those large, bare feet silently skimming across the trembling, forest floor. He was so strong and brave that he carried nothing but his bare hands, and his long, brown hair wavered behind from his legs, forearms, and face as he sliced through the shadowed forest, bounding over downed trees and heaved up boulders. My eyes were blind, but my senses, my imagination, could see him as clear as if he were in reach at midday.

***

I leaped from the ground, and flew through the air to Atlas, barely making it over the walls – my mask weak without the energy of the sun. My children, only half of what I had, were frightened, and silently looking to me for answers, direction, but I had neither to give as I recessed into my tower.

The crystal mask rejuvenated with light inside, but even the meteorite would soon exhaust its energy. I didn't know what to do. I was so angry, but so lost. I climbed the spiral of steps, again searching my brain by blankly staring at information. The tower tossed about so much that journals fell out of their pockets and landed on the steps at my feet. I scaled the remaining steps and wandered out onto the deck. The wind scooped up droplets of water from the ocean and blasted me so hard that I had to hold onto the battlements, and the lightning stretched from bottom to top and danced sideways across the sea. I looked down over the edge, and the smooth, rolling plain of water below was chopped to pieces, as though the waves were rolling in opposite directions and clashing together. My brothers had brought about so much darkness that it was choking the Earth, and the Earth's rotation was slowing to a standstill.

Then a chill bit into the back of my neck, and zipped down my spine. I turned, looking back, and there before my eyes, was the very image painted by my imagination. My nephew launched out from the dark timber, raced down the wide beach, and plunged into the ocean. I chuckled at such a foolish notion, at first, then realized that Atlas was struggling in the mash of disrupted ocean currents, and open seas was not coming as quickly as expected. Even so, what chance did my daft nephew have? The infuriated ocean tossed him about like he was a mere acorn that had fallen into a raging river. But yet, he also seemed to be tossing our way, as though the insane waves were passing him from one to another, sweeping him out to be devoured by the sea.

Atlas pushed and pulled his wide fins against the waves with all that he had, and I pleaded for more. We would thrust forward, rise and hang in suspense, and slide back half the distance we gained. My nephew was closing the gap between us, as if we were to be sloshed about until we came together by some mysterious law of nature.

Atlas lashed out with his long, barbed tail, striking at his pursuer like a whip with tremendous force. Over and over Atlas's tail plunged under the waves that never left my nephew still for a moment, until his tail emerged in my nephew's grip. Atlas shrieked with frustration as he flung my nephew through the air, and dunked him deep under the broken surface. But my nephew held on impossibly, pulling himself closer, hand over hand. Atlas whipped his tail side to side like a serpent in the sand, but still, my nephew refused to release his grip.

My nephew slithered up onto Atlas's back, head hanging low with exhaustion, and as the sea water poured from his matted hair, he crawled to the base of the fortress wall, out of my sight. I leaped from the tower, down to the top of the fortress wall, to dispose of this nuisance. I walked along the top of the wall, balancing myself with my staff as the world ground to a halt with a massive jolt that pushed me to my knees. The wind seemed to spin in a circle around us, slowly pulling the waves and lightning with it. I looked down to my children, huddled under the erratic shadows cast by the volatile torch flames, silent with fear, as when I first found them. It was the end of all of us. Unless I could rid the Earth of this overbearing darkness. I rose to my feet, and pushed on toward the back of the fortress, where my mad nephew was hiding.

I anchored my grip to the top of the wall, directly above the base of Atlas's tail. But when I looked down to my nephew, he was gone. I raced around the top edge of the wall, the entire length of the fortress. My nephew was not to be found. If I could have been so fortunate that he was swept into the sea.

The eruption of terror among my children betrayed my fantasym though. As I look down upon my children, my skull master stepped out of the shadows, with his invincible blade, crystal skull beaming brightly atop his staff, and he faced my menacing nephew, who apparently had no plan further than getting aboard.

The hidden crystal of the blade sliced through the air with such speed and agility that it left my fortress littered with long clumps of soggy hair. But as the blade swung wide, my nephew dropped to one knee and blocked the skull master's wrist. The blade ripped from the skull master's fingers and spun into the shadows, clashing against stone as it struck the fortress wall. The skull master immediately thrust his staff, but my nephew simply jerked the staff out of his hands.

The skull master hung his head before his towering opponent, hoping death would be swift as I focused in on my nephew's broad chest from atop the wall. I hurled the staff with all of my fury, and it sliced into the night. But my nephew flinched and lunged backwards, and the staff sailed right between his ribs and his startled arm. Suddenly the tower sank, and the walls catapulted up, tossing me headlong into my children below. Atlas's mouth lifted from under the water, blasting a shrill, horrible scream, and bright, red sea water spewed up from a hole where my staff should have been.

I must admit, I was bewildered by how quickly fate betrayed – family betrayed. It was his fault. That smug spawn of darkness, so self-righteous that he was completely unaware that his hand alone stopped the world. I scrambled into the shadows for the crystal blade, and I attacked furiously. From the left, from the right, I slashed again and again, my nephew miraculously defecting the blows with the shaft of the skull staff in his hands. But I drove him back with each clash of alloy – back into the shadows, back against the quivering fortress wall. My poor Atlas moaned with terminal sadness.

My nephew stood, back against the wall, with the crystal skull staff held out at the ends of both arms. His brown hair, darkened and matted by water, made him all but invisible against the dusky stone – all but those big, gleaming eyes. They were so focused on the moment, on me, and unafraid, almost as though they were not of the natural world, but of someplace, something, beyond the grasp of my imagination.

It was time to close those eyes forever. I swung the crystal blade back and heaved it over my head, bringing it down upon my nephew with a strength only bested by Atlas's tail. But my nephew spun the staff vertical, and thrust the crystal skull forward. The blade and the skull clashed in a fury of blinding light and deafening noise.

\*\*\*

I opened my eyes to a light that was as bright as the clearest day, lingering throughout the fortress. My head was ringing inside the crystal mask, and I felt the rubbery touch of Atlas's skin on the palm of my hand. I sat up, blinking my eyes frantically to stop the spinning. Red sea water gushed out of the hole and onto my leg in unison with Atlas's moaning heaves. My nephew sat crumpled at the base of the wall, shaking his head. The crystal skull had a gash along its crest. I lifted my hand, looking at the jagged chip in the indestructible blade, then I looked back toward my nephew. Our eyes locked in a stare of will.

Suddenly my nephew was on his feet, and rushing past me. Around the tower he disappeared. My children erupted into panic and poured around the other side – those behind trampling over those in front. I staggered to my feet, and chased after, rounding the tower just in time to see my nephew thrusting the skull staff down into Atlas along the front wall that stood between him and Atlas's eyes. Atlas thrashed and contorted in every possible configuration, shrieking desperation. My nephew held on to the embedded staff, shoving it deeper, and deeper. Atlas frantically rolled side to side, and his tail flung up over the back wall as he lashed at the murderous pain at the base of his head. Stones began to crumble from the top of the walls, and a large section from atop the tower broke free and plummeted down upon a crowd of my children. Everything was chaos, and death. My children were scattered throughout, running and screaming aimlessly. And although Atlas may have been the most active entity on the planet in that moment, he was lost. My nephew, so focused, heartless, shoved the staff deeper yet. He well accepted death before relenting from his determination.

Crystal blade still in my hand, I grabbed the skull master by the arm and leaped over the wall. I was so caught in the confusion that I had forgotten about my children's touch. My hand blistered terribly, and I dropped the skull master my length twice over to Atlas's fin. He landed with a thud and rolled across the pitching fin, right off of the end and into the sea. I quickly sliced off the tip of Atlas's fin with the blade – a section large enough to keep both of us afloat – and it fell to the churning water. I held onto the blade and reached out to the skull master with the handle, pulling him out of the deadly waves.

We lay on the fin, silent and still, rising and falling on the black waves, listening to Atlas shriek and thrash, listening to what was left of my children scream out into the darkness. Both near breathless, it was almost as though we were hiding from reality.

Eventually Atlas quieted, and stilled to an occasional twitch as he settled deeper and deeper into the waves. Although the meteorite still gleamed brightly inside, the tower no longer beamed out beacons of hope, but rather a tilted, wide beam pushing through the crumbled rooftop and flattening abruptly on the bottom of the rolling, spinning, black clouds. And the blustering fire of the torches faltered as dim as my children's hopeless cries as more and more of Atlas slipped under the waves. My beloved tower sank so slow, but was gone so quickly.

***

Everything was lost – we were lost, my children, the crystal, Atlas, civilization, and even time. We drifted in silence, across the dark waves, for two days, maybe three. The lightning had exhausted itself, and the wind had weakened into a familiar breeze. There was movement in the Earth again, and the currents flowed through the sea once more. I was not sure if it were real, or hallucinations, but then, the sun appeared in the sky one morning. Although quite hazy, and rising on the wrong side of the planet, my mask assured me that it was very real. I did it. I paid everything, but I returned the sun to the sky. No matter the cost, I will always protect my children.

By midday, land appeared on the horizon. Again, was it real? There was only one way to find out – we paddled. And the closer that our vision of land came to our grasp, the more the land disappeared as the sun fell before our eyes. But in that returning darkness, we felt the rugged harshness of the shoreline in our hands.

Stones pricking the souls of our feet, and mud pressing between our toes had never been appreciated more, but we were still hungry, thirsty, and still lost. We hadn't drifted far. I could feel my family near, and everywhere, but brother or child, I could not distinguish. I took the blade – its crystal core revealed by the fractured alloy, but still as fine an edge as ever honed – and I slashed the cold, rubbery fin into many pieces. I was hiding our tracks. Maybe my relentless brothers would have presumed that I lie at the bottom of the sea with Atlas, and my nephew. But before we faded into the dark interior, the pieces of fin started to move. They came to life, every one of them, and all swam away, under the waves. It was an amazing and unexpected surprise, and it brought me a moment of joy that my Atlas may not have been as dead as I presumed.

***

The bright glow of the crystal mask faded into the black night around it, and we crept inland through the dark forest like serpents – unheard, unseen, and whichever direction my senses lead me. There were eyes and ears scattered throughout the standing dead and uprooted timber, and a few close enough to smell. Some were hiding in fear, others were hiding in ambush, but none could reach us.

The morning sun climbed up into the sky at our backs, and a weak, thin beam pushed through the bare canopy overhead and warmed my hand. I had relished the freedom from its menacing gaze, but that morning, I welcomed its touch – only for a moment though, before retracting my hand back into the shadows.

We left our lurking kin behind and rushed through the endless forests of this land apart. We waded two rivers thick with silt, corralled by waves of brown grass and barren rock, and trekked across countless rolling ridges that spoke a history of a once magnificent society rich with bountiful trees and a diversity of life to match any other place on Earth.

Then we reached the mountains – old mountains. So old their secrets were ancient even to me. And amidst these mountains hid the intersection of planes for which we searched – an invisible point in the woods, but where else could we go? The crystal mask led us over the rubble of several mountain passes, and up and down the sleeping valleys tucked in between, until we came to an immense ridge that shot up from a valley floor. The sides of this ridge were so sheer that only the youngest trees in the forest could dwell, and so rugged that huge boulders were falling out of the sides.

We were close to our point of destination though. I was sure that it hid somewhere just out of sight, above our heads. We searched the edge for a suitably safe place to climb, but all that we found was ourselves farther away, instead of drawing closer. So we returned to deep, narrow gorge that we had passed on the side a canyon that cut into the ridge and ended as abruptly as it started. Cold spring water tumbled and sloshed down the gorge, back and forth, falling from someplace unknown and leaving behind what resembled a grotesque set of steps that climbed to unseen heights.

We climbed. And steps or not, it was a tough, slippery climb, and the frigid spring water bit into our feet like the prick of countless thorns until we could feel no more. My young skull master was at the end of his endurance, body and mind. He wanted to turn back. Back to what – starvation, imprisonment?

Finally we reached an offset, much like a ledge, where the water pooled in a pocket and we could rest our feet on dry rock, letting the blood return. Another treacherous climb of steps that faded away into the gray sky laid ahead, maybe even steeper than below. I looked back from where we came, out over the deep canyon from where we started to climb, and that is when I could see it. The opposite canyon wall was the same as that of where I stood, that we knew from our earlier search, but on that opposite wall was also a ledge, as level across as I could perceive. It stretched straight and true for all that I could see across the canyon, and though my sight was limited to the gorge in which I stood, I had to be looking at the very same ledge as I rested upon. And the gigantic boulders that jutted from the sides—they weren't being dug out by erosion, or being pushed out by an unfathomable weight bearing down on them from above. They were placed where they lay. I couldn't grasp a pattern, but what I was viewing was close enough not to be coincidence. The top was unnaturally flat and level, and as far above the ledge, as the ledge was above the canyon floor. This mountain was built.

As the grandeur of what I was seeing set in, the obvious question arose; who, or what, had built this? It was not the randomness of nature, and much too chaotic and ambitious for engineering. This was something in between, but greater than both. Then, the chattering stream of water called for my attention, like it spoke out loudly and clearly from a wall of bland noise to answer my question. I turned and stared at the water as it forever tumbled down across the rocks. It was though it had eyes and knew exactly where to go, with no hesitation, no regret, all while carving out this hidden piece of art. Or maybe the water was just to keep the steps clear of the forest debris that accumulated heavily over the rest of the structure. There were no answers on the ledge though, and the other side of the canyon assured me that we were only half way to the top. And resting on the ledge was no rest at all – only growing weaker.

We pushed on for the top, and the farther we climbed, the less the steps could be referred to as such. The skull master even slipped, and nearly slid to certain death. He held out his hand for help, but I could not take it. I thought that I was going to have to leave him behind. He moaned pathetically, as if he were about to choose death. But eventually he used the crystal blade to regain his footing, and he crawled upward.

The gorge deepened, and the grade of the steps lessened as the stream curved up to the top. Finally I stepped out of the water, and looked out across the plateau. The forest floor was smooth and flat, and quiet still for as far as I could see. And the stream stretched across the plain as straight and steady as the edge of the crystal blade, and disappeared into the deepness of the trees. The trees were broad enough to hide a giant craftsman, and they seemed as though they touched the clouds. I had seen nothing like it before, anywhere. This place was special, humbling.

My feet started to sting as blood reclaimed them from the cold of the water, and I looked down at my wiggling toes. My feet were plump and wrinkled, and whiter than the hair that draped over them, whiter than snow falling from the sky. They had never been so clean and pure. Maybe the water was to cleanse the feet of those who dared to enter.

I followed the stream into the interior, leaving the skull master to his desperation along the edge of the plateau. If I didn't find him nourishment quickly, I would not have had his company long, and it was clear that I would find no other in these woods. The trees were deep in sleep—or dead. There were no scampering creatures, not even a buzzing insect. I couldn't even tell if the water in the stream was moving. All there was, was a steady, pleasant breeze blowing through the trees, and I found myself speaking to it, as if the currents of air would carry my voice to an ear out there somewhere.

The straight line of the stream ended, or rather, it began, with a perfect circle. Nothing flowing in, or bubbling out of the ground, just a perfectly symmetrical ring of water about as wide as my shoulders lying perfectly still on the forest floor. I reached down into the water until the icy cold climbed up to my shoulder, but I could feel no bottom; just smooth, vertical sides. Within the circle, the ground was as level as the rest, but elevated slightly, with a gigantic, gnarled-up oak firmly rooted directly on the point of intersecting planes. The oak wasn't nearly as tall as the others, but the broad crown well reached over the ring of water with its long, crooked branches that stretched out to ancient fingers of wood. And a deep, dark, triangular hole twisted around with the thick bolt of the tree, much like a piece of leather that had been wrung of water. I couldn't have twisted this tree more with my imagination, but then, if you're reading this, you have seen – seen that even the strongest, the most pure, are twisted by such intimate knowledge of energy and power.

*

I searched this lonely plateau for days after, looking for answers, or another passage up, and I found neither. By the size of this place, and steepness of the walls, it must have reached the stars. And whether it is unfinished, or destroyed remains a mystery. Or maybe it is neither, and the secrets hid inside. I fear that I may never know. Some things are forbidden to know, by the laws of the universe, maybe to keep us from the fate of the oak.

I did find several carcasses of deer though—reduced to carrion again. The memory of my prison island is strong in this place, but we will rebuild. We will finish. I will use the energy of the point to re-forge the invincible blade into the crystal needed to complete the grid, and I will place it in the twisted oak. My children will come to me again, and we will build a new city right here.

But I fear that we are not as alone as it appears. My brothers are still out there, and I can feel their malice creeping closer and closer. That is why I am writing this, in the event that I fail to balance the never-ending darkness. These crude scrolls will be here, hidden, waiting for you, so you will remember, the truth, and you will carry on. I will put my whispers on the wind, every day, and every night, and you will hear. You will come, eventually.

\*\*\*

Back in the shadowy room of stone, the silhouette slowly closed her spiral notebook and carefully leaned back in her chair. It was as dead quiet as a crypt, other than the sound of the candelabra's flames rippling on the breeze of fresh air that secretly drafted into the dark, secluded room. The mysterious young woman gently lifted from her chair and leaned over the table, slowly pushing her face into the draft of air. As she drew closer, the light from the candles painted her blank, shadowed face with plump, red lips and long, sultry black eye lashes upon a symmetrical canvass of tight, snow-white skin, all nearly swallowed by long black hair that wrapped up tightly atop her head. The reflections of fire shimmered in her deep, green eyes as the draft of air, warmed by flame, caressed both rosy cheeks and tickled her ears with flipping hair. She listened closely to the breeze, the sounds that it made, for the first time. Her ears grasped at the hum, the hiss, the toneless whistle, as the flames snapped and crackled like a blustering flag.

Suddenly she jolted upright, knocking the chair backwards to the floor with her locking knees. She stood motionless, listening even more closely, as if her very life depended on it. Her eyes darted back and forth, chasing the flashes of wavering light into every dark corner and across every shadowed wall, still listening for what she thought she heard. Then, as abruptly as she launched to her feet, she rolled the animal hide parchments together, cinched them tight with the thongs of leather, and shuffled around the table and across the floor with the parchments tucked under her left arm and the spiral notebook in her free hand. The notebook hit a cabinet shelf first, the hides stuffed on top, and the steel cabinet doors slammed shut. She snapped the padlock closed on the cabinet and hastily receded into the black beyond the reach of candle flames, where a heavy, oval-shaped, iron door screeched shut with an imprisoning rumble.

# Chapter Two

Half a Lifetime Later

The never-ending winds have roamed the planet since there has been a planet to roam, picking this up here, and dropping that there, witnessing everything, and telling all to the six senses of Earth. Sometimes soothing and warm, other times bitter cold and hateful, there was no place to hide from the wind, as though it were a great, cunning beast with boundless faces afore countless snake-like fingers, racing across every ancient, wilderness plain, and slithering into each secret room. And those very same winds still insanely followed the very same path thirty-eight years later, as if five thousand years earlier. Forever they howled in from the west, and up over Rocky Ridge, tumbling over and over for a moment above the crest of the mountain, before screaming down the east side and veering south with a vengeance.

Down the valley the winds roared – searching, listening, and hissing secrets. It scorched across vast, snow-swept fields, and flooded through endless tracts of trees frozen by a timeless winter, before swallowing a small, quiet town. Day after day the unbiased wind sliced a quiet community in half by furiously wedging in between two parallel rows of houses and scoring down the street. And on this afternoon, caught in the whispers of the chilling winds, were two teenage boys, riding their bikes through town as though they were two charioteers racing around the Circus Maximus to win the hearts of the mob, and their freedom.

\*

"Let's just go to your place," Jeff whined as he and Andy pedaled across Main Street, veering toward the old picnic grounds and away from Andy's house. Andy pretended not to hear and raced down the pitted, uneven slabs of concrete that formed the only sidewalk in town. He did not enjoy the ridicule any more than Jeff, or the social clusters. And he sure didn't idolize anyone just because they had money, or a driver's license, but missing a Friday night at the ball field was socially defunct. From all across Little Cove School District, and occasionally a few neighbors from South Braddock, every teenager with a car, or a friend with a car, gathered on the long abandoned ball field every Friday evening. And every underclassman within peddling distance gathered to listen to the promised adventures that await them out of town. But there *was* another motive that beckoned Andy as well, and he cut around the mailbox at the Falling Rocks Post Office and pedaled for the old ball field with Jeff reluctantly tailing close behind.

"Don't park beside Charles," Jeff yelled up to Andy. "You know he'll just embarrass us."

Andy ignored Jeff again and pedaled right to Charles's passenger window. Most of the cars were a generation old and swapped between parents so their kids didn't have to drive hand-me-downs, but Charles sported a brand new '87 Ranger, customized with a thick, black roll-bar lofting two round spotlights above the cab, a three-inch lift, and oversized Sidewinder tires. Charles's family owned the paper mill, and in one-way, or another, everybody in town. But Andy only envied Charles for one thing; Sally McCormick.

"She don't even know you exist," Jeff whispered from the farthest reaches of the building crowd. "She's always cold, and keeps her window up anyway."

As usual, Charles was bragging and showing off for his own personal crowd of cronies on the other side of the truck. He loved throwing his weight around as the less fortunate jockeyed for social positions in the encompassing crowd. Charles's girth lay all in his surname though, and his wallet. He only weighed about 130 pounds, but he was wiry, like a lean piece of gristle, with thin beady eyes and lips upon a pointy, chiseled face. If not for a mop of curly blond hair, he would have resembled a snake, and in fact, he was as mean and ruthless as a copperhead.

Suddenly Sally rolled down the window and leaned outside, as if to get a breath of fresh air, or farther away from Charles. Her long, brunette locks were untamable, and never quite looked the same as the day before, but Sally wouldn't think of disheveling her hair with a warm cap, leaving her icy white face blotched with flushes of pink – confused between the outside cold and the dry warmth of the truck. She stared at Andy and Jeff with her mesmerizing blue-gray eyes, as they gawked back at her. Both boys straddled their bikes, knees locked, feet flat on the frozen grass, white knuckles wrapped around the handlebar grips, and mouths hanging ajar – both paralyzed with fear. The corners of Sally's mouth curled ever so slightly with amusement, and a hint embarrassment. No one in Falling Rocks was a stranger, especially these three, but in that moment, these three may as well have been from opposite corners of the planet.

Jeff finally broke the awkward standoff by goofily nodding his beanie-capped head up and down, and he said, "Hey."

Sally grinned. "Hey." Then she looked at Andy.

Andy had a million things that he wanted to say to her, and he had rehearsed the words a thousand times over, but he couldn't remember a one of them. "H...Hi, Sally."

"Hi, Andy," she replied, her grin growing into a dimple-releasing smile.

"Hey!" Charles shouted as he pushed through the crowd like he was wading through chest-deep water. He stormed around the front of his truck, scolding Sally with a hateful stare. "What are you two dorks doing?"

Jeff's eyes widened with the increasing distance between him and Charles's truck as he backed his bike away to give Charles a wide berth. Andy stood his ground. Andy was two years younger than Charles, but he was bigger, stronger, and a bit more handsome than Charles. And Andy's family had little to lose. It was the families of Andy's friends that protected Charles. It was an unspoken understanding, and had been that way since the paper mill opened and saved the town from extinction.

Charles stopped abruptly in front of Jeff. To get between Andy and Sally would have been too close. Charles's eyes flattened, as if he was asking himself if today would be the day that he knew was coming. "Where's Mikey?" he sneered, shifting the tension.

Andy and Jeff remained silent as they both shrugged their shoulders.

Everybody was watching – watching Andy stand his ground with Charles. Charles was a spoiled brat, but he was as shrewd as the rest of his family, and would never show weakness, scared or not. He had to maintain his control.

"Hey Andy. You better stick to that bicycle, or you'll end up like your brother," Charles chuckled as he turned away and walked back around the front of the truck, immersing himself into the mass of bodies. "But, stay in town! You'll be easy pickings for Old Man Wilbert's star people."

The entire crowd erupted into laughter, saving Charles's hide from Andy's temper. Even some of Andy's peers, sitting on their own bikes along the outside perimeter of the cluster, tried to cross social sides by laughing. Sally rolled up her window and stared at the floor, embarrassed of Charles, and for Andy.

"Don't do it Andy. You can't. That's just the way it is," Jeff whispered as he spun his bike around and pedaled away. Andy waited for a glance from Sally. Her face was as red as the truck door that imprisoned her, and she slowly turned her back toward Andy, almost asking him to leave.

\*

Jeff pedaled slowly from the field, past the shambled pavilions and decrepit swings, listening for Andy's approach from behind to take the lead before the post office. He couldn't very well go to Andy's house without Andy, and they had plans for the evening. Andy's mom was always home, but always medicated and high on denial ever since Tom had been killed. Andy's dad left shortly after the accident, and no one had seen or talked to him since. There was only the boyfriend, Ennis – Shorty to his buddies and anyone else that didn't want trouble – but he wouldn't be home till midnight, and as long as the boys didn't hinder his hedonistic lifestyle, he didn't care what they were doing. The lingering misery was the only thing to deal with at Andy's.

Jeff slowed even more as he approached the post office. Andy's house lay at the edge of town toward the left, and Jeff lived on the other side of town, to the right. But just as Jeff was about to look back, Andy's tires sliced through the frosty grass between the sidewalk and the post office as he threaded the narrow gap between the power pole and the old, blue postal box. Andy blasted by like a rocket. Jeff lifted from his seat, his bike flopping side to side as he pushed on his pedals with all that he had – so hard that his grumbling words erupted from his mouth as a spastic rhyme of grunts and snorts.

Back up the jutted sidewalk and across Main Street they raced. And just like any other time, the race would not end until the front wheels of their bikes slammed into the side of the old shed behind Andy's house, and as usual, the wheels struck simultaneously. The bikes dropped to their sides, and Jeff gathered up an armload of firewood, Andy a fishing pole, and they walked out onto the frozen pond behind the shed. Neither spoke a word as they shuffled across the ice in a distorted semi-circle to just the right spot. The wood, two backpacks, and the fishing pole dropped to the ice. Andy fished school papers from his pack, crumpled them, and carefully balanced the wad onto the moist ice. Jeff constructed a crude teepee of firewood around the wad of paper, and set it ablaze with a Zippo.

"This ain't going to burn a hole through the ice," Andy finally said.

"That's why I brought this." Jeff looked to the right, and then to the left as he eased a brand new quart of motor oil out from his pack. Black smoke rolled into the air as the oil trickled down across the burning wood. Jeff then pulled three cans of beer from his backpack and set them out on the ice. "Where *is* Mikey?"

"Where did *you* get that?" Andy returned.

"Don't tell anybody. I swiped it from the back of Dad's pickup."

"No...the beer!"

"Oh. That's from Pap's cellar," Jeff replied as he slyly tucked the oil back into his backpack and out of sight.

Andy cracked open a beer and turned away to hide the grimace that accompanied the first swallow. Tom's crumpled Chevelle still sat beside the shed, still with empty beer cans strewn about inside. Andy stared at the round shatter in the windshield hundreds of times – stared at it until the crushed pattern of glass pieced together the image of Tom's broken face. Andy never seen his brother's face after the accident, but bloody and swollen, and pressed against the windshield was the only way that he could see it now. He couldn't remember the way Tom looked before. Andy took another swig, and the alcohol rushed blood to his face as he anxiously waited to see his brother, hoping not to.

"Why don't Shorty take that thing to Miss Nellie's?" Jeff interrupted. "You'd think he'd want the cash for his habits."

"Mom won't let him."

"Why not?"

Andy faced Jeff and shrugged his shoulders. He knew why, and he understood, but no one else would. And it's not like hauling the car away would stop the accident from happening over and over. The population of Falling Rocks would see to that.

"Hey guys – GUYS!" Here came Mikey, peddling as fast as he could, around the house, past the shed, and right out on the ice. Instantly his front wheel slipped out from under him. He belly-flopped onto the ice so hard that his thick, plastic-frame glasses and his red, flannel, Stormy Kromer hat shot from his head, both spinning across the ice right along with him. With teeth clenched tight, squinting eyes, and clumps of wavy, brown hair reaching in every direction, Mikey scorched past Andy and Jeff like a hockey puck. Somehow, he managed to curl up onto his hands and knees, gasping for air as he slowly spun to a stop. Finally his lungs inflated, and with something that resembled a donkey neighing, he yelled, "I have proof!"

"Proof of what?" Jeff asked while handing Mikey his glasses. Jeff and Andy both knew exactly what Mikey was talking about – anyone in town would have known.

"Footprints!" Mikey shrieked, his feet shuffling across the ice as he pushed his bike right back off of the pond and started right back toward the way he had come. "Come on! Hurry!"

Mikey was an archeologist, an explorer, and a cryptozoologist, all trapped in a scrawny fourteen-year-old body. He grew up scouring over slate banks looking for fossilized seashells and searching the stream that snaked through the woods behind his house looking for water shaped stones that his imagination could easily identify as artifacts. But when he was eight, his grandfather and great uncle took him to see a Bigfoot movie at the old theater over in Connellstown. It was a profound experience for his young, overactive imagination, and Mikey had been utterly obsessed with Bigfoot ever since. But Jeff and Andy had never seen him so excited, and he never joked about his obsession, so they grabbed their backpacks and followed him.

\*\*\*

Mikey usually lagged behind, but this time, he led the way, two bike-lengths ahead, as the three feverishly pedaled back through town and straight to Mikey's house. A stray snowdrift along the pale blue, two-story house was already taped off with caution tape. "Look! Look!" Mikey yelled while pointing out the prints in the crusty snow. Andy and Jeff both coolly leaned their bikes against the thick maple in the front yard, and both looked up and down the street before nonchalantly walking over to the fluttering yellow tape that beckoned ridicule. "Holy crap! He looked right in the window! Then walked right out on the street!" Mikey shouted as his finger followed the trail like a hound's nose.

"I don't know, Mikey," Jeff hemmed and hawed.

Jeff and Andy both had learned long ago not to question the existence of Bigfoot in the presence of Mikey. "Bigfoot lives in the North West, not the Appalachians," Andy butted in, saving Jeff from an impending lecture.

"Not anymore!" Mikey giggled as he placed a ruler into one of the prints and aimed his Mom's Polaroid. "Mix up that plaster! We need to pour a cast!"

"Hey Mikey! Was someone looking in your window last night?"

Andy and Jeff panicked and stepped back away from Mikey. They knew it was Charles, without looking toward the road where the voice came from, and Andy instinctively hid his face by turning toward the woods behind the house. But there was no mistaking his silhouette, especially in Falling Rocks, and he quickly realized that he was only making himself look even more foolish. *Why is that jerk even in town*, Andy silently fumed as he rolled his head around toward the road. But Sally wasn't with Charles, just two of his cronies jammed into the Ranger, all three laughing hysterically. Charles threw something onto the lawn and tramped the accelerator to the floor, their cackling jeers fading down the street. There was no denying, no matter how hard they tried to make their eyes see something else, that two blocks of wood, crudely carved into feet, lay on the lawn. Mikey melted, and trudged into the house in silence.

No words could be found to ease Mikey's pain. How he must have felt, witnessing his closest friends separate themselves from him, in front of the one that they all despised. Andy's chin sank with shame, while Jeff balled the yellow ribbon around the wooden feet.

"Give me them," Andy barked. "I know right where to put them."

"No Andy," Jeff sternly replied, sounding remarkably like his father. "You'll only make it worse...on us." Andy rolled his eyes as Jeff shoved the wooden feet into his pack and hoisted it onto one shoulder. They just stood there, staring at each other. "Sally's still going to be with him, and everybody's still gonna kiss his butt. No matter what you do, he'll still be Charles, and you'll still be Andy...the unstable guy."

Andy stormed to his bike and rode away, leaving Jeff standing, alone, with his thoughts. He was frustrated with both of his friends. Andy he could understand, but Mikey? How could he have thought that a Bigfoot walked right up to his house in the middle of town? Jeff looked down through the yard, between the houses, where Mikey had thought that Bigfoot peeked into his living room window. Night was settling in, and the narrow strip between the houses *was* pretty dark. And the back yard seemed as if it were being swallowed by the already black woods behind – the woods that stretched clear to the top of Rocky Ridge, where one star twinkled above the tree line, so far away. Suddenly the small stream behind Mikey's house in the dark woods seemed much too loud. Jeff hadn't even noticed it before. And it was making strange sounds, like a breaking stick, or rocks banging together when feet walk across a creek bed. Maybe even a grunt. Jeff didn't believe, and knew the prints were a hoax, but his brain couldn't seem to override the paranoid possibility that a Bigfoot was coming out of the night woods. He jumped on his bike and pedaled for home, fast.

# Chapter Three

Andy stayed mad at Jeff until his eyes opened to a bright Saturday morning. The weekends were much too short, and much too precious to squabble with the ones who make life bearable. Together they called on Mikey three times over the day. Mikey's mom finally chased them away toward evening. "He's just not feeling well this weekend boys. You can see him at school on Monday," she scolded.

But when Monday rolled around, it was a Mikey free day. Although, the entire school buzzed with his name so much, it may be inaccurate to say that he wasn't there – much like thinking that Bigfoot isn't real. Charles was at school though, trolling past Mikey's locker like a shark between every class, school of remora in tow, all snickering as they passed Jeff and Andy in the hallway.

"I'll never turn my back on Mikey again because of Charles," Andy fumed.

"It wasn't Charles you were hiding from," Jeff said. And as if on cue, there was Sally standing in front of them. Sally was only a junior, and on a different class rotation than seniors, making much of her day an escape from Charles's tyranny. Sally enjoyed school a little too much, but regardless, there she stood in front of the boys. Andy stopped breathing, and forgot about everything else, maybe even his own name. But Jeff, it would take a little more than a set of pretty eyes to control his mind on this day.

"Where's Mikey...and what happened over the weekend?" Sally asked.

"Like you don't know," Jeff huffed. "How could you do that to Mikey?"

Andy snapped out of his stupor and valiantly put his hand across Jeff's chest, as if to stop him. "She's not like that, Jeff!"

"Well, she dates the jerk! She *is* like that...Andy!"

"You guys are no different than Charles!" Sally barked, pushing the boys back against the wall of lockers. Nobody had ever heard Sally raise her voice before. "I can speak for myself...Andy." She swung her glare to Jeff like it was a double-barreled shotgun. "And you! You know *nothing* about me!"

Sally stormed away with the ringing bell, leaving Andy very confused. He had finally managed to interact with Sally, but it went so horribly wrong. The boys stood as straight and still as the lockers behind them, both dumbfounded, and late for class.

*

Mikey returned to school on Tuesday. He refused to talk about the weekend, and would not hear Andy's apology. It was like nothing happened – just another day at school. And nothing but the silence of rambling, numb, teenage brains meandering through the lengthy hall past Mikey's locker. That is until lunch. Snickers flushed from the thicket of teenagers down the hall, and crept toward Mikey like birds flushing from a stalking lion. Mikey froze, staring at the inside of his locker. Andy stepped into the middle of the hall, deflecting the stampeding snickers with his frown. But there were too many, and most would have taken a thumping from Andy before defying Charles's entertainment. The lion's eyes peered through the swaying savanna of bodies, and locked onto Andy's. He and Charles were on a collision course, and with the mere meeting of their eyes, Mikey ceased to exist.

"You'll just make it worse on us," Jeff pleaded as he tugged Andy's arm back toward the side of the hall, within the boundaries of underclassmen. But Andy was as mindless as a rutting buck, and immovable as a bull elephant.

"Hey! If he has Mom's hours cut at the mill, I won't eat!" Jeff begged.

As primed as Andy was, he couldn't keep the image of Jeff's family out of his head – all huddled around a kettle of squirrel broth and potatoes, toes crammed into last year's sneakers, and pant legs rising four inches above the ankle. Guilt set in like it had already happened, and Andy slowly relinquished to his place at the lockers. Charles was so distracted, and relieved, he had forgotten what he was there to do, and strolled on by.

"Mikey will be alright. He'll be more determined than ever," Jeff assured Andy.

*

And he was. Later that week, Friday, during the sophomore lunch shift, Charles paraded through the cafeteria moaning and stomping his feet while holding his arms straight out. The cafeteria erupted into fake laughter, and Andy clenched his fists at the sides of his tray. But Mikey held the palm of his hand in front of Andy's face, and he fearlessly stood up from his chair, calmly walked across the lunchroom, and stopped Charles mid-stride. "I believe you're a bit confused, Charles. Your locomotion is all wrong. A Sasquatch would have a compliant gait. In fact, there is no bipedal that walks like that...except maybe mummies, or maybe zombies! Do you believe zombies really exist, Charles?"

A few giggles—real giggles—escaped from the tense, breathless mass of bodies across the cafeteria. Andy hurled out laughter, so loud that he sounded foolish, even though he didn't know what Mikey was talking about either. Charles twisted his fist into Mikey's shirt under his chin, and Andy launched to his feet, but Mr. Ostman, the principal, timidly stepped in—surprisingly, seeing how the teachers were just as intimidated by Charles as the students.

Mikey returned to his lunch with Andy and Jeff. The three made plans to meet at Mikey's house after school. Charles would have been unbearable at the park anyway.

*** 

For as long as they all had known each other, Andy or Jeff had never been in Mikey's room. His unkempt bed sat tight against a blank wall, covered with football player wallpaper, which struck Andy and Jeff as odd. On the other side of the only window, a giant map of the world covered the opposite wall, with pushpins marking every recorded sighting of a hairy man-beast. There were stacks of Bigfoot books, balls of dirty laundry, newspaper clippings of encounters from all over the world, and more dirty laundry. And there were quite a few local interviews conducted by Mikey, although most of the subjects were considered... unreliable witnesses—to describe them politely. Jeff and Andy stood in awe. They didn't know if they should pity Mikey, or be impressed.

Mikey balanced a homemade easel on three legs of oak saplings lashed together with fishing line and pulled a large topographical map from under his bed. The map was of Rocky Ridge and the surrounding areas – actually it was several pages cut from a topographical atlas and taped together on an unfolded cardboard box. "I have been looking in all the wrong places," Mikey stated as he secured the map to the easel. "I assumed that Sasquatch would wander into town – curiosity, scraps of food... maybe snag a pet or two – but I assumed wrong. If he wanted to live like us, he would. But he wants to avoid humans." Mikey turned to his map while pulling a pencil out from behind his ear, and pushing his glasses up his nose with his middle finger on the same hand. "Rocky Ridge is seventy-five miles long," he said as he ran the pencil's eraser along the contour lines marking the western boundary of Little Cove Valley. "And begins and ends in the two biggest blocks of federal land in the state. Our mountain is like a highway between two worlds, and there is only one road to cross – Rocky Gap Road." Mikey smacked the map with the eraser, firmly planting it on the summit of Rocky Gap. "I have yet to find two other blocks of wilderness that big in the entire state that is only separated by twenty feet of blacktop."

It was all a bit overwhelming, Andy and Jeff's expressions testified to that, but Mikey was prepared to convince. "Look, Rocky Gap is the lowest spot on the mountain. Anything traveling on top, or even down to the benches, which is about a third of the entire mountain, has to descend elevation just to cross the top of the gap, which isn't very wide and thick with Mountain Laurel. It's a natural funnel."

"I get what you're saying Mikey, and you're right, but what makes you think that Bigfoot lives in this part of the country?" Jeff asked.

"There have been thirty-six eye witness reports of unexplainable encounters around Rocky Gap dating as far back as 1756. And countless Native American legends as old as local human habitation!"

"Yea but all those people lived in the stone ages and were very superstitious. They believed in witches and demons, and Star People. Has there been any reports in the last fifty years or so?" Jeff asked.

"A few."

"Other than Miss Nellie or Old Man Wilbert," Andy chuckled as he picked up the stack of reports and started quickly flipping through the pages.

Mikey scampered over to Andy, jerked the papers out of his hands, and walked back to the easel, clutching the reports to his chest. When Mikey turned around, he held his head low, looking at Andy out of the corner of his eye, with a peculiar expression, almost nervous, like he was hiding something.

"Look," Mikey continued. "In the old days, Rocky Gap Pass was the only place to cross east to west from sixty miles to the north to nearly a hundred south, and it took a while to do it. People spent a lot more time on the mountain. That's how Falling Rocks came to be a bustling town all those years ago. People needed supplies and a day of rest before they even started across the mountains. Then came the automobile, which cut the time to a fraction of what it was and put blinders on human awareness. And when the toll road opened the tunnel through the mountain, Rocky Road was nearly abandoned until the paper mill opened. But who can't hear a pulpwood truck coming from a mile away?"

Mikey could not be argued with, and Andy and Jeff both knew better. They were just anxiously waiting for Mikey to get to the purpose of his presentation.

"I need to get up to the gap before the snow melts. It's my best chance to find evidence, and the smallest search area, but I need you guys to help."

And there it was – the inevitable choice that every teen-ager hides from, but can't escape. Would they turn their back on a life-long friend, or risk social suicide if they were caught searching for Bigfoot evidence? In an instant, Mikey's room became unbearably hot. Blood colored the boys' faces, and their open mouths were so dry that their teeth would have absorbed a drop of water. Jeff broke eye contact quickly, desperately fidgeting with his collar to relieve the pressure.

The tension weighed heaviest on Mikey, and he panicked. "I'll be at Paterson's at eight in the morning if you want to come," he blurted out while turning to look out the window – mostly to hide his wilting face. Jeff and Andy scrambled out of the room like it was on fire, without uttering a word.

***

"If we start participating in Mikey's crazy schemes, they'll chew us up at school," Jeff proclaimed as they slowly mounted their bikes in front of the house. "And it won't just be Charles either! They'll all turn on us…I can hear it already!"

Jeff lowered his head, and asked, "Did you see the reflection of his face in the window?" Jeff wanted Andy to say something, anything, reveal his thoughts, but he remained silent as usual. "Would you tell Sally what we're doing tomorrow?"

"No," Andy quickly replied.

"Are you going to be there in the morning?"

"I don't know," Andy somberly said as he pushed off, peddling for home.

# Chapter Four

Mikey leaned his bike against the wall and sat down on the wooden bench on the front porch of Paterson's Country Mart at exactly quarter till eight Saturday morning. As quick as lightning, his hand flashed over his face as he pushed his glasses up his nose, and he folded up the flaps on his Stormy Kromer cap, as inconspicuously as possible. There was a bitter chill in the morning air, but the sun, glaring harshly off of the car windshields as patrons fueled up at the two pumps, promised a warmer day. Mikey could not identify anyone through the glare, but he was sure that they were all staring at him while pumping their gas.

Three mature gentlemen, all recognized as locals under roof, socialized at the opposite end of the porch. Their rabble eventually slurred into background noise as Mikey impatiently waited. Until all three erupted into laughter. Were they laughing at him? *"Five more minutes!"* Mikey quietly huffed.

For the next twelve minutes, Mikey blankly stared up Rocky Road as patrons passed in and out of the store, collecting their morning coffees and tobacco products. At one point the crowd of gossipers on the porch grew to seven men, each trying to talk over the next. Mikey wanted to run from the noise, but standing up would only draw attention. Then Andy rolled into the parking lot, at eight sharp. Andy's back tire slid to a stop as Mikey cut him off halfway between the porch and the gas pumps. "I knew Jeff wouldn't show! Let's go," Mikey snipped.

"Give him a couple minutes Mikey," Andy scolded. "Jeez."

Just then, to Mikey and Andy's surprise, Jeff came walking out of the store and down across the porch step with his backpack across his stomach, hanging from one shoulder. He was placing three, sixteen ounce, glass bottles of soda into the pack, and then he started to transfer pastries and candy bars from the stuffed pockets of his blue, quilted flannel jacket.

"Where did you get money for all that?" Andy asked.

Jeff didn't answer at first. His lightly freckled, chubby face contorted as though he were deciding whether or not he really needed to explain. "I come down every couple of Saturday mornings...and scrub the floors...and clean the restrooms, for a little spending money," he finally answered. "I hustled today and had time to catch the grill. Got us a little *bonus* for our trip." Jeff pulled a box of white powdered doughnuts from his pack, just enough for Andy and Mikey to see before zipping up his cash of sweets.

"Why didn't you ever tell us?"

"Are you kiddin me," Jeff spouted softly, leaning in closer like the crowd of patrons would tell the whole town. "Those restrooms are nasty as is. Could you imagine if Charles found out that I was the one who cleaned them?"

Jeff yanked his beanie down over his sandy hair, tucking his ears in tight, and he pulled his bike out from behind the dumpster. "Well...let's go," he sarcastically sneered, putting a grin on Mikey and Andy's faces.

The three adventurers raced out of Paterson's parking lot, ran the four-way stop sign at the square, and headed up Rocky Road toward the summit. Youthful vigor quickly pedaled them out of town, but they knew that once they cleared Old Man Wilbert's, it would be all pushing to the top.

*

Old Man Wilbert was a life-long bachelor who operated a department store right from his driveway, which was nothing more than the road shoulder, just wide enough to get three quarters of a car off the road. From there, a wide patch of bare gravel funneled into a path through waist-high weeds that led to the front door of his doublewide, which served more as a warehouse than living quarters. Several old cars and trucks rested above the carpet of weeds, each filled to capacity with merchandise, each accessed by a path of trampled weeds. Wilbert sold everything from bacon to rifles, and he had many loyal customers – most of which spent countless hours a week gossiping with him. Wilbert would sit in his chair by the road all day, waiting for someone to stop, and he was already out, sitting in the morning sun, before the boys passed.

The boys felt the burn of the increasing grade, but their attention was on Wilbert. He stared straight ahead, completely motionless, with his hat pushed down over long, unkempt, silver hair that flowed into a long, shaggy beard of the same. His black-streaked beard spread out like thick, hairy fingers, and rested over layers of disheveled flannel shirts, that belled out over dirty, worn-out trousers, that crumpled into untied work boots. And his glasses, darkened by the sun, completely hid his eyes.

Wilbert was as much a part of Falling Rocks as the hundred year-old structures proudly overlooking the square, but to impressionable, young imaginations, he was the shuffle in the closet at midnight, or the shadow peeking around the tree in the backyard at dusk. And most obviously, he was the hermit gatekeeper of Falling Rocks that imprisoned souls in town forever. Over the years, there had been many brave young who had tried to escape town, for good. No one had ever seen or heard, of them again. Mikey had even told the stories many times himself, about the bodies out in the woods behind Wilbert's house, and about the old, padlocked, deep freezers sitting in the weeds among the old cars, that imprisoned their souls in town forever.

Wilbert did not help his reputation, though. Many believed that he enjoyed the attention, or scaring kids. But on this morning, he appeared to be sleeping in the sun, or dead. The boys lowered their heads and watched him from the corners of their eyes as they approached. They pushed their burning thighs relentlessly, but quietly, and they held their breath as they cruised on by unnoticed.

"Where you kids going!" Wilbert shouted with a jolt, like someone shocked him to life with a defibrillator.

Mikey was the closest to the angry, troll-like giant who was coming to life and leaping from his chair. He screamed like an eight-year-old girl and veered into Andy, jumbling all three bikes onto a pile on the asphalt. The boys scrambled, untangled, and were on their feet before the wheels of their bikes stopped spinning, but Old Man Wilbert was already straddling the centerline ahead of them, with his hands on his hips. The sun glistened in the beads of icy moisture that had accumulated under his nose and down across his facial hair, and his shadow stretched for what seemed a mile up the road behind him. His darkened glasses were like two, hollow, black holes, sucking the boys' souls out from their own terrified eyes.

"You damn kids need to stay in town!" Wilbert shouted. Then he leaned forward, and with a deep growl-like laugh said, "Star People will get ya." Wilbert stomped toward the huddled teenagers like a giant, and he leaned in close, hands still on his hips, looking into all three's trembling eyes at once with his dark glasses. "Do you know what Star People are?" Jeff shook his head crazily, nearly ejecting his eyeballs from their sockets. "They're aliens!" he screamed.

Mikey blasted toward the summit like he was shot out of a circus cannon. Andy and Jeff split around Wilbert an instant later and followed. As they fled up the mountain grade, Old Man Wilbert's shadow lurched from one road shoulder to the other as he chased after them, laughing insanely, and casting doom across the boys as they swerved back and forth to escape Wilbert's shadow arms trying to sweep the boys from the road and back into Falling Rocks. The boys watched down through their legs that were frantically thrusting like pistons, underneath their singing tires and spinning sprockets as they desperately dodged the shadow on the asphalt – the shadow that grasped for their feet, but slowly slid under their tires and behind them. Wilbert's shadow could not keep pace with teenage panic. "They'll get you! They'll do things to you! You'll be sorry!"

The boys never looked back as they pedaled up and around the first switchback. Their wheels slowed to a crawl with the quickening pace of gasping for oxygen. Old Man Wilbert's threatening shouts faded away a while back, and he was long out of sight, but they kept moving, pushing their bikes in silence.

\*\*\*

Mikey was the first to reach the summit about ten o'clock, and was already hunched over his handlebars, meticulously scanning the melting snow banks for any inkling of a track by the time Andy and Jeff joined him. The snow that was piled up along the road was rock hard and polluted with salt and cinders, and although the targeted search area was only a hundred or so yards long, it would take Mikey hours to investigate every inch.

Jeff and Andy were not so diligent though, and they quickly found a game trail that appeared out of the Mountain Laurel from the south, crossed the road, and disappeared into the other side like a ghost. The snow on the trail was trampled into packed lumps of ice and frozen mud, and enclosed in a tunnel of green leaves, but Mikey agreed that searching the trail promised more evidence than searching along the shoulder of the road.

\*

With their three bikes hidden in the brush near the road, Mikey led the expedition south, single file, down the choking trail of laurel. The leaves of the laurel brushed against their shoulders, as if Old Man Wilbert was hiding in the brush and grasping at the boys. The laurel even closed in overhead at places, filtering out the mid-day sun, making the trail dim and cold. Their foggy breath rolled and tumbled inside the tunnel of green, cutting visibility even more, and every crack of ice underfoot echoed like a gunshot.

One foot slowly in front of the other, Mikey zeroed in on every print, collected every unidentified lump of scat, peered at every broken branch through a magnifying glass, and plucked every hair that was left behind in the tunnel of laurel. It was going to be a very long afternoon, but Jeff and Andy were too unnerved to push Mikey any faster. They just kept an eye on the sun, falling to that magical point in the western horizon, when they could tell Mikey that it was time to head for home. Luckily, Jeff kept his other eye dialed in as far as he could see up the path. And he silently clamped his hand over Mikey's shoulder. No further explanation was necessary, and Mikey's eyes locked onto the motionless lump of brown fur laying ahead on the trail.

"What is it?" Andy whispered from the back.

"Bear," Jeff whispered back, trying to point his lips toward Andy without taking his eyes off the animal.

"Black bears are not brown," Andy whispered even softer.

"Oh yes they can be."

Mikey squinted his eyes and tilted his glasses forward in an attempt to bring the fuzzy, brown mass into focus, but he could not differentiate any features – bear or Bigfoot. It just seemed to be a big ball of…something. But not near big enough to be a Bigfoot.

"I cannot believe that no one brought a gun!" Jeff ranted, very quietly. "Everybody; back out very easy."

Andy spread out his arms to balance as he very carefully stepped back, one foot behind the other. Ice cracked as loud as thunder under his left foot, and everyone's muscles locked tight, teeth ground together, and all three heads sank down two inches closer to their shoulders. "Keep moving," Jeff whispered as he stepped backwards, following Andy's reverse lead.

Mikey squatted slightly with bent knees and hips, clenching onto his backpack straps with his elbows sticking straight out, like chicken wings.

"Come on, Mikey!" Jeff sternly whispered.

Mikey stared at the nothing that was between him and the unidentified beast as he gently shifted his weight over his right foot, and ever so lightly lifted his left. He was steady and ready to move. Very cautiously, he stepped forward.

"Mikey! What are you doing?" Jeff quickly lunged forward, stopping Mikey with a firm hand on his shoulder.

"I'm not leaving!" Mikey snapped with a very raspy whisper. "Besides, it's dead." He jerked his shoulder from Jeff's grip, having to let go of his pack to keep from falling into the wall of brush.

"You gotta be kidden me," Jeff huffed as he rolled his head around in the opposite direction of his rolling eyes. "Let's go get a rifle, and come back!"

"No! It might be gone by the time we get back."

"I thought you said it was dead!"

"How should I know," Mikey said as he shrugged his shoulders. "There's only one way to find out."

"Mikey...I'm with Jeff on this one," Andy strongly whispered from the back. "This is a bad idea."

Mikey's quivering bottom lip pressed hard up against his top, and his eyes flattened. "Fine! You two leave! But I'm not leaving." Mikey turned away from his friends, pushed his glasses up his nose with his middle finger, and slowly crept forward, toward the mysterious beast.

"Just wait." Jeff picked up a small chunk of ice, resembling a dirty ice cube, and he tossed it at the animal. The moment the ice left Jeff's hand, all three boys squatted slightly and froze, ready to run. The ice tumbled through the air in seemingly slow motion. Andy broke and started to slowly step backwards. Jeff bounced on the balls of his feet, inching toward the road sideways. Eventually the cube of ice disappeared into the thick fur of the beast, but only the tufts of hair moved.

Relief burst from all three sets of lungs, but the tension refused to relent. A two-ounce cube of ice was not convincing. Jeff kicked around at the frost heaved ground with the toe and heel of his boot until he pried loose a stone about the size of a baseball. He held his eye steady on the broad mound of fur, and unexpectedly catapulted the stone with his whip-like sidearm. The stone sailed through the air much quicker – too quick. Andy scrambled his large frame into retreat readiness as the stone bounced from the creature with an echoing, hollow thud. It did not move. That was good enough for Mikey, and he crept closer.

Every step became harder to take than the last as the animal lengthened with the shrinking safety zone between boys and beast. It was far bigger than originally perceived. Mikey's heart pounded between his ears like a foreboding drum beating from somewhere deep in the jungle of laurel. Sweat soaked through his flannel cap and glistened as he passed through glaring rods of sunlight that found holes in the canopy of leaves. Still creeping along, he rubbed his burning eyes, clearing his sweat-blurred vision, and resetting his glasses. Stubby legs appeared behind the animal and Mikey stretched his neck higher to see. The laurel shaded the beast, making it difficult to see, even that close. Another step closer, then another. The legs lengthened with each step. The hind legs of a bear could look the same – another step closer – but there was no mistaking those feet.

Mikey's legs buckled, and he dropped to his knees. Tears replaced the sweat in his eyes and warm breath chugged from his mouth like a steam locomotive. He did it! He found the Holy Grail of Bigfoot evidence.

Jeff slowly shook his head in disbelief as he lifted Mikey back to his feet.

Andy leaned into Jeff's ear and whispered, "Who did you tell?" thinking that it was another hoax designed to completely crush Mikey for good. Jeff slowly turned to

Andy, his eyes wide and childlike, revealing his sincerity, and his head still shaking 'no', answering Andy's question. Still, Andy did not believe it true, even though it was right there before his eyes. Quite simply, it could not have been real.

Mikey wiped his eyes and blew a long, deep breath of steam away from his face. "Holy shit!" he crackled. But revel could wait. The glory would come later, and Mikey pulled himself together. He boldly marched up to his discovery for some proper scientific investigation, although he had no idea how to collect at least 800 pounds of evidence – maybe even half a ton or more. The specimen would have to be dissected and packed off of the mountain in pieces. Andy could bear a leg, with foot, Jeff a hand and as much arm as he could handle, and the head, Mikey was definitely taking the head, even if he had to cradle it in his arms and walk back to his house. But there was a mysterious question lingering heavy in the air. And the answer, Mikey wasn't sure he wanted to know.

Mikey slipped his pack from his shoulder as he surveyed the scene. Andy and Jeff still remained silent and motionless, other than Jeff's shaking head. Mikey reached into his pack and slowly pulled out his tape recorder by the handle. He leveled the tape recorder on his forearm and pushed record with his thumb. "The Sasquatch specimen appears to have been mortally wounded by several wounds to the back. The blood soaked into the matted fur around the wounds is thick, but not completely dry, making the trauma only hours ago." Mikey hesitated as he scanned the surrounding wall of laurel. "There is no sign of a struggle in the immediate area. The specimen appears to have been traveling north and collapsed forward, pinning its arms under its massive upper body and burying its face into the snow."

Mikey clicked off the tape recorder, placed it back into his pack and gently placed the pack off to the side. He hunkered down in front of the creature. He had to see the face. The feet were the feet, just like the rest of the body, but the face…the face would change everything. Was it the face of man or beast, or something in between?

Mikey slowly reached out to lift the head.

"Don't touch it!" Jeff yelped, slapping Mikey on the shoulder. "Let's go get a gun and shoot it to make sure it's dead!"

"There's no time," Mikey confidently replied as he griped two handfuls of hair along the creature's head.

Jeff hovered over Mikey, his head still shaking, only much quicker now, as he watched over Mikey's shoulder, and Andy hovered over Jeff, looking over both their shoulders. Andy and Jeff both wrinkled their noses from the stench, but even the non-believers wanted to witness the answer to the age-old question – maybe hoping to convince themselves that the legend *still* did not exist.

"It's still warm," Mikey said as he gently clenched the bundled strands of hair between his fingers. He exhaled a gush of courage, and with steadily increasing strength, he lifted the massive face from the snow.

Andy bit down on his bottom lip, and Jeff's head stopped shaking. And the beast raised its head, looking straight into Mikey's eyes. Six eyeballs nearly popped like bubble wrap, and three jaws nearly unhinged from their skulls. The creature roared a growl-like moan that nearly shattered bone. All three boys involuntarily screamed sounds that were unfamiliar even to them as they catapulted backwards, landing on top of each other and rolling like a laminated wheel until they separated on the trail in the same order as before, only reversed. Mikey stumbled and fumbled to stay on his feet as three hundred fifty pounds of terrorized teenagers shoved him out the trail toward the road, and right into an even fouler smelling beast – Old Man Wilbert.

The boys collapsed into Wilbert like an accordion. Wilbert's gut redirected their kinetic energy in the same manner, sending them rolling to the ground again, screaming again. And again they were back on their feet like they had bounced on the packed snow. But the second time, all they did was collide with one another, spin, and collide again...and scream. There was no escape. They were caught between the mysterious Old Man of the Forest, and the bizarre, crazy man of town – and crazy had a rifle.

"I told you brats to stay in town!" Wilbert roared. The boys pushed their backs hard into the wall of laurel, paralyzed with fear, and no escape. Wilbert stepped around the boys as he shouldered his rifle and kneeled down to the creature's face. "What happened here old friend?" The creature briefly opened his eyes and grumbled a sort of deep purr. Wilbert grumbled an even beastlier noise and stood back up, stroking his scruffy beard in deep thought as he surveyed the situation.

After several seconds of intense anticipation, Wilbert lunged out and grabbed Andy by the arm, tugging him toward the creature.

Jeff and Mikey both reached out for Andy, but neither would move from their indentations in the foliage. Wilbert stomped his untied boots alongside the Bigfoot, dragging Andy with him. Andy looked like a ballerina, tip-toeing sideways with his arms straight out as he brushed along the laurel, desperate not to get to close. At the creature's feet, Wilbert slammed his rifle into Andy's hand, and said, "Aim down this trail and shoot anything that that shows up!"

"Wh...what if it's a hunter?" Andy nervously asked.

"Those ain't bullet wounds in his back, boy," Wilbert replied as he walked back to Jeff, who's head was shaking again, maybe more of a vibration. "You, get your bike and ride into town and get Miss Nellie, fast. Tell her that Willard sent you...and our old friend needs help!"

"Willard?" Jeff chuckled. "Your name is Willard Wilbert?" Bizarre things rise to the surface when one is as scared as Jeff was.

"Don't you think you have more important things to occupy your brain than my name?" The grin melted from

Jeff's face as he desperately tried to redirect the motion of his head from shaking, 'no' to nodding, 'yes'. Wilbert cocked his own head to the side in an attempt to understand Jeff and his bobbling head. "She may be at the fire-hall already, playing bingo. Check there first." Wilbert recollected his thoughts for a moment. "Listen up, boy. We need her rollback, fifty feet of cable, a tarp, and a rescue board. You got that boy!" Jeff frantically nodded his head. "Then git going then," Wilbert barked, and Jeff took off on a dead run out the trail toward the road.

Wilbert overlooked Mikey and returned to the dying Bigfoot.

"This is my find," Mikey claimed while tailing Wilbert.

Wilbert turned and stopped Mikey in his tracks. "You ain't found shit, boy! You're the one that's lost, not him! Now help me dress some of these wounds."

*

The boys had hidden their bikes in an offset in the laurel, ten yards down the trail from the road, and when Jeff arrived at the laurel nook, a powder blue moped was parked right behind the bikes. Jeff had never seen anything like it – especially in Falling Rocks. It couldn't have been Wilbert's, but who else's could it have been.

Jeff tried to finesse his bike around the moped, but the laurel latched on to a pedal and a handgrip. He pulled and pushed and cussed at the laurel until he worked himself into a frenzied tantrum, and he tipped the moped on its side. Temper turned to panic the moment that the blue metal collided with rock. Jeff leaped over the fallen moped, and returned it upright in a flash. But his bike was still parked in. Jeff took a deep breath, gained some composure and moved the moped.

Seconds later, Jeff was rocketing down the mountain slope. The spokes of his bike hummed so loudly coming down the mountain that it sounded as if he would lift from the road and take flight, but Jeff just hunkered down, tears flying from the outside corners of his eyes, and tightened his grip on the handlebars. Smoke rolled from the brakes as he approached the first switchback, until he locked up the back tire, his bike sliding crazily side-to-side down the asphalt and into the turn. At the last moment, he cut his bike loose and hugged the inside of the turn, in the wrong lane, and accelerated to the next switchback. And he took that turn in the same manner, but in the right lane. Jeff flashed by Wilbert's, blasted through the four-way intersection in town, drifting into Paterson's parking lot, and raced on toward the Falling Rocks Volunteer Fire Company.

# Chapter Five

Jeff burst through the steel door and into the long, narrow foyer of the Falling Rocks Volunteer Fire Company, stopping in front of the gray double doors that lead into the banquet room. The outside door slammed shut with a clamorous echo, loudly announcing his presence to what seemed like the entire mountainside, although the muffled chatter inside seemed undisturbed. He put his right hand against the door on the left, the one with the long, push bar that operated the latch. The door was ice-cold, and he wondered if it operated as abrasively as the other. Jeff carefully pushed the bar with his left hand, and with a weak, little screech, it popped ajar. No one should have noticed at all. He gently pushed more, and slipped his head in to take a look.

Miss Nellie's jet, black beehive towered above the plain of gray hair that fluttered across the banquet hall. Blundering through a Falling Rocks bingo game was like strolling through a den of sleeping bears, and, as luck would have it, Miss Nellie was seated dead center in the room. Jeff fished the rest of his body in, careful not to let the door slam shut. He pulled off his beanie, clenching it tightly in both hands, and up along the wall he went, so close that his blue, quilted jacket brushed against the painted block. Half way up, he cut to the left and elegantly danced his way between the smooth lines of tables and the jagged hoard of occupied chairs, diligently avoiding any disturbance, until a leg of a chair hooked his foot and he went down. The hall silenced and the bingo game gasped to a halt. He disturbed the den. It felt as if the entire ceiling had fallen in on him. Jeff sprung back to his feet, waving and smiling at the dungeon of biting eyes. He was still disturbing the game. Jeff finally gave up on coming out with any dignity intact and quickly sidestepped over to Miss Nellie, kneeling by her side.

"Well, hey there, cutie! Pull up a chair," Miss Nellie announced as loud as she could without contaminating her pitchy voice. "I told ya all I was feelin lucky tonight!" Mischievous giggles arose throughout the banquet hall. Jeff very quickly realized that it *could* get worse, and it was far from over. Miss Nellie was not one to allow a good time escape Falling Rocks quietly. "Bingo!" she yelled. "I won a man! Bingo! Bingo!" The entire hall erupted into cackling laughter, and Jeff's face turned fifty different shades of red. He nearly ducked under the table. But under the tables was the last place he wanted to be.

"Miss Nellie," he abruptly whispered into her ear. "Willard sent me! Old friend needs help, quick!"

Miss Nellie's face morphed stone serious, with a hint of shock. She grabbed Jeff by the arm and led him through the excited crowd toward the wall. No one in Falling Rocks has ever seen Miss Nellie serious, let alone concerned, and every loose-lipped eyeball in the hall was upon her – good times were fading fast. But as crazy as she was, Miss Nellie was cool under pressure and knew how to keep a secret in Falling Rocks. Her hips hadn't worked their magic in over twenty years, but she worked them just fine that evening. She smiled her cherry red lips, and playfully raised her jet-black, painted eyebrows a few times. The lonely and bored bingo crowd hollered and cheered. "Hey, that's my grandson!" arose above the rabble, and hysteria overtook the hall as Jeff buried his face in his beanie until they were out through the double doors.

Outside, the whole story spewed from Jeff like water bursting through a dam. Miss Nellie's concern deepened, revealing her second biggest secret, but there was a job to do above everything else. "Get in," she said. Jeff crawled into Willy – Miss Nellie's jeep – and they ripped out of the parking lot and up through town.

Miss Nellie's place was a little past Andy's, just across the reaches of town jurisdiction, and she slowed very little before she whipped the wheel into her driveway. Jeff hooked his fingers under the seat and pulled down hard – he was sure that they would roll. Willy slid around Miss Nellie's house, past the garage, and bounced up into the maze of wrecked and rusted cars, his little engine revving a small but mighty roar. Car after car flashed by, all facing the road between them, all in their final resting spot. It was almost like racing through a cemetery. Suddenly Miss Nellie cut to the left, up another side road lined with more cars. Left again, then an immediate right. Turn after turn Jeff held on to anything he could as he attempted to keep his bearings, but every row of cars looked the same, and once the junkyard drifted into the trees, he couldn't have even pointed toward the mountain.

The incline gradually increased until the road cornered to the left across a heavily, wooded slope. It had to be the farthest edge. The ground was still frozen under a topcoat of greasy mud, and Willy slid sideways into a deeply scarred tree. Neither Willy nor Miss Nellie flinched or slowed. The salvage yard faded away in the woods. Willy only clawed past a few cars that rested right along the trail here and there – old cars, full of bullet holes.

Eventually the road cornered left again and headed straight down the mountain. An old shack sat along the corner, dilapidated doors facing straight down the road. The tin roof was the color of rust, with visible holes, and the vertical boards were dark gray, heavily pitted, and leaning hard down the hill. Miss Nellie rounded the corner, slid to a stop, ground Willy into reverse, and backed up to the crooked hanging doors. The doors were chained and padlocked, both coated with layer after layer of flaky rust.

"Reach in that gap at the bottom of those doors and feel for a chain…then hook it over Willy's hitch, honey!"

Jeff unhooked his fingers from under the seat and guided his bewildered mind to the rear of the jeep by brushing against it. He wiggled in between the doors and Willy, and very cautiously eased his hand through the hole. There could have been anything in there. Jeff closed his eyes tight, and grit his teeth as he gently patted the cool, powdery dirt inside. He could almost feel sharp, little teeth ripping into his skin, but then he felt the chain in the palm of his hand. He quickly pulled the chain outside until it was tight and flipped it over the hitch. Jeff returned to his swamper seat, and stared at Miss Nellie. One eye showed confusion and the other showed fear. "Hold on," she said while stomping the throttle to the floor.

Willy lunged down the slope with a jolt and Jeff jerked his head around to see out the back. The shed doors exploded with a blast of splintered boards, sending the padlocked chain catapulting through the air just over their heads like knipple shot from a pirate's cannon. Jeff winced so hard his fingers nearly punctured through the vinyl seat. A large, alien looking contraption leaped through the tumbling debris and slammed into the back of Willy, sending the rear wheels skidding to the right. Miss Nellie counter-steered to keep Willy's front end ahead of the back while the copper robot-looking apparatus dislodged from what looked like an upside down car hood that was welded fast to the chain around Willy's hitch. Copper drums sailed past Willy to the left and right, clattering across the rocks as they disappeared into the brush, and a wooden barrel wobbled through the air and into a tree, shattering into a thousand splinters right beside Jeff's window. But something was holding onto the roof, kicking and rolling, clawing its way forward, until a cluster of copper tubing tumbled down across the windshield, and flailed about on Willy's hood like the tentacles of an octopus. Jeff chirped a muffled little scream, but the copper octopus slid off to the left, and Miss Nellie ran right over it. Willy rocketed away from the destruction and scorched down the slope, dragging the hood along with a display of sparks that rivaled the previous Fourth of July.

Finally Jeff's brain came together enough to shriek out a somewhat coherent question. "WHA *IS* ZAT FING?"

Miss Nellie giggled like a schoolgirl. "That's the hood off a '39 Buick sweetie. Me and my two brothers used it to sled down this very hill ... before they skipped town! Daddy would pull us back up with ole Willy here ... before he skipped town to look for the boys!" Miss Nellie burst into high-pitched, cackling laughter as she sawed on the steering wheel to keep Willy from careening into a tree and becoming another addition to the salvage yard. "Momma tried to tell everybody in town that they were off doing missionary work for the church, but I think Momma was the only one who believed that – God rest her soul." Miss Nellie quieted for a brief moment of silence. Trees and rusty cars blurred by only inches away as Willy bounced and lurched from side to side. Jeff tried to close his eyes, but he couldn't. "Back to your question and the task at hand, that ole sled will make a good Bigfoot-sized rescue board, don't you think, sweetie?"

Jeff had forgotten all about his friends on the mountain, with an unknown species, and Old Man Wilbert. But he could only help them by returning, and at that moment, his life was barreling down the mountain in a sixty-year-old Jeep, with a slightly older, crazy lady behind the wheel. *Please slow down,* he cried out, but he couldn't make a sound

"Well it works pretty good for sneaking other things around," Miss Nellie sassed, offended by Jeff's silence.

Willy leveled off and Miss Nellie navigated for the sliding garage doors beside her candy-apple red rollback. Jeff stomped both feet to the floor and braced his arms against the dash. Miss Nellie stomped the brake and clutch to the floor a split second later. Jeff's eyes finally closed, and his lips parted, as Willy slid to a stop two inches from the doors. The sled slammed into the hitch, and Willy lurched an inch closer.

"Hurry now sweetie!" Miss Nellie called out while rolling open the garage doors. Jeff slowly opened his eyes, peeled his locked fingers from the dash, and tried to steady his knees as he slid out of the seat and followed her into the garage. Miss Nellie scooped up a folder tarp while pointing to a coil of cable with her eyes. Jeff lifted the cable from a spike hammered into a support post along the wall, and followed Miss Nellie back out to the sled. "Now toss them cinder bricks out and sweep out that ash while I start the rollback," Miss Nellie said as she flopped the tarp onto Willy's roof, leaving Jeff standing confused and bearing the prickly cable.

The big block in the Chevy C-60 rollback lugged into rotation, but did not want to wake from its slumber. Miss Nellie cursed at the truck, and sweet-talked the motor until the 427 sparked and sputtered to life, filling the air with smoke, rich with the smell of burnt oil and gasoline. Tiny metal teeth zinged ferociously until they eventually meshed together to engage the PTO, and the hydraulic fluid whined into circulation. Miss Nellie slid out of the cab and shuffled back to the bed, beyond the rear axle, where she stood motionless, hands hidden under the long, flat bed. The bed slid backward, and tilted up until it touched the ground, winch unwinding as it lifted, all as smooth and easy as riding a bike. Jeff hooked the rollback's winch over the chain welded to the sled. Slowly the sled helplessly crept up the sloped bed, and the bed fell, sliding forward into position. A quick strap across the sled, and the rescue mission stepped across the line separating feeble thoughts from tangible action.

# Chapter Six

Meanwhile, up on the mountain, as Miss Nellie split shifted the throaty 427 toward town, Mikey snipped away at the hairs matted with blood on the creatures back, carefully placing every strand into plastic evidence bags. He had been meticulously doing so for an hour. Wilbert exhaled his distain but Mikey was engrossed in an impenetrable dream bubble. But then he began sifting through the fur around the creature's anus.

"What, in the hell, are you doing boy!"

Mikey threw an irritated glare at Wilbert. "I'm looking for a stool sample!"

Wilbert grabbed Mikey's backpack and tossed it like a Frisbee into Mikey's chest. He tumbled backwards, and his backpack spewed its contents about on the uneven, frozen ground, tape recorder and all. Mikey frantically rolled to his hands and knees, his wide eyes gleaming behind his glasses that teetered on the very end of his nose. His face burned a contorted red as the pressure expanded in his head, and he desperately tried to hold back tears as he gathered his things.

Wilbert figured an impossible decision lay ahead, but that dilemma only entertained one option, other than what Wilbert knew he couldn't do. His convictions had never been tested in over sixty years. He would have been more content to have slipped away to the stars the previous night. But like it or not, Wilbert was chosen to find a solution, no matter how much it stung. "You *do* know that he *is* still breathing, don't you?"

Mikey hid his broken voice behind sealed lips and pretended to ignore the question out of spite.

"Well, I don't have the scientific mind of you, but I sure do think a *living* specimen would get my attention more than shit!" Wilbert said.

Mikey still refused to acknowledge Wilbert, and would never, ever agree with him, but he was right. A scat sample could wait. In fact, who needed scat when he had a body, dead or alive? And alive would be so cool.

Wilbert was an intelligent man, despite his impression, and he decrepitly knelt down to one knee, straining to roll his old friend onto one shoulder. A young man would be compelled to help, or at least Mikey would not be able to resist the opportunity. And Wilbert was right, again. Mikey scooted to Wilbert's side with a fake, irritated sigh. But it took the added girth of Andy to loft the beast onto his side.

"There's no pooled blood," Wilbert said as he worked to unclamp the beasts right hand from its left forearm, fearing he would find a fatal wound behind the massive, clenched arms.

"Take it easy!" Mikey scolded. "His left forearm is broken."

Wilbert was pleased with Mikey's new priority, but very disturbed with the condition of his old friend. "I'd hate to meet up with whatever snapped that arm."

Andy spun to his feet, grabbing the rifle out of the crotch of a laurel branch and re-shouldering it along the way. The safety clicked.

"Easy boy," Wilbert warned while looking down the green, leafy tunnel. "We all need to keep our heads here."

Mikey pulled a small, collapsible handsaw from his pack and scurried along the edges of the trail, sawing off laurel branches to construct a stable splint.

"Nellie should've been here by now," Wilbert fretted. "Can we count on your buddy, or did he run home to mama?"

Mikey hesitated, glancing toward Andy, his eyes filled with doubt.

"He'll be back," Andy said. "If he went home, it was to get his rifle, not his mom."

Wilbert's stomach acid climbed higher and higher though, no matter how much confidence Andy had in his friend. But suddenly, as if fate confirmed Andy's opinion, the rollback horn tooted twice, and echoed down the corridor of laurel like a beacon in a stormy night.

"Gimme that rifle! You two go help," Wilbert ordered. "Bring the board, and stretch out all of the truck winch first."

As Andy and Mikey disappeared around the bend, Wilbert tried to slow his experienced heart, which was only one more thing to stress about. He breathed deep in through his nose, and out through his mouth, quietly asking his old friend for the strength to help just one more time. Wilbert's solitude was short lived though, by some approaching calamity. Andy appeared through the green foliage and filled the tunnel of laurel, his arms folded behind his back, chest heaving like a draft horse pulling a plow, and towing the Buick hood by the chain. Jeff and Mikey were behind, pushing against the back corners of the hood, and tripping over bent stems of laurel and each other's feet like two circus clowns.

"What the hell is that?" Wilbert barked.

"It's a Bigfoot-sized rescue board," Jeff said, grinning from ear to ear.

The boys stood the hood in the air and flipped it into the proper direction. Then they slid the hood, on edge, behind the balanced creature, and Wilbert gently lowered him into the sled, which ended with an unstoppable thud, and a moan of misery. The Buick hood lay on a sharp angle, bending several laurels over, but penetrating the green wall no more than a foot. And to make the predicament even worse, one thick, hairy leg and the elbow of the creature's busted arm hung out over the edge of the hood.

"Hook up the cable," Wilbert ordered as the boys stared at the peculiar puzzle.

"Are you crazy?" Mikey shouted.

"It's the only way we'll slide that hood over enough to lay flat."

Wilbert was right. What else was there to do, other than flopping the creature out onto his face, and broken arm? Mikey grabbed his pack and the branches that he had cut, and he straddled the semi-conscious giant while Andy and Jeff hooked the cables together, tethering the hood to the truck. Wilbert pushed the hood into the laurel, trying to prevent the whole thing from falling over and trapping Mikey and beast underneath. "Easy," he warned as Mikey pried Bigfoot's meaty fingers from around the wound and fished the branches alongside the break in the arm. As Jeff and Andy kneeled at the front of the hood, hooking the cable hook over the chain, Mikey finessed the end of a short piece of rope under the massively swollen arm and around the branches, preparing to lash the length of the splint tight.

"Don't you need to set the bone first?" Wilbert nervously asked.

"Near as I can tell, it already is. He must have done it himself." Just as Mikey finished his sentence, he cinched the first lash tight. Out of nowhere, a knee-buckling howl blasted out of the beast's mouth that fluttered the slender, green leaves over their heads. Andy and Jeff jerked upright from behind the hooked nose of the Buick hood, as straight and rigid as two I-beams, their mouths hanging open as wide as their eyes. All they could see was a gigantic hand, draped in long, brown hair, spread out like a starfish and planted on Mikey's head, covering his entire face. Mikey was flapping his arms up and down like he was trying to fly, and screaming as loud as he could, but the creature's bare palm seemed to seal to Mikey's lips, muting his terror.

Wilbert held onto the hood with his left hand, and clamped his right onto the creature's wrist, inches in front of

Mikey's throat. Luckily for all, Bigfoot passed out, and his extra-large hand fell to his side.

The woods fell silent in a second. Andy and Jeff still stood there, never moved a muscle. They just stared at Mikey, sitting on the beast, his arms resting in his lap, Stormy Kromer cap barely hanging to the back of his head, earflaps sticking straight out. One lens of his glasses was over his left eye, the other lens was pressed against his right cheek, and the earpiece lay against the side of his neck. Wilbert couldn't help but to chuckle, just a little.

With Bigfoot out cold, Mikey quickly finished the splint with the help of Andy to hold the weight of the rather long, muscle clad arm. Jeff moved up to the bend in the trail, where he could see both Miss Nellie and the sled. He gave Miss Nellie the thumbs up, and the cable lurched, and spun crazily, then back the other way as it snapped to the inside of the curve. It jumped from the frozen ground, and cut into the laurel. The hood lurched forward, and leveled slightly. It was working just as Wilbert said it would. Andy and Mikey heaved and tugged on the creature, keeping his body parts inside, and settled.

Foot by foot, the Buick hood lunged through the brush, parting the laurel like a boat parting the water. It seemed like it took forever for the winch to reel in the hood, but eventually the feeble cargo crept up onto the truck bed. The cargo was loaded – plus two bikes to better hide the two very large feet that stretched out toward the back – covered with the tarp, and strapped to the bed before the sun dipped below the western treetops.

"Where to, Willard?" Nellie asked.

Wilbert's expression confessed that he had reached the limits of his plan. "He needs inside. Hidden and under roof," Wilbert said as he invited suggestions by looking everyone in the eye.

"People's in and out of my place regularly," Miss Nellie said.

"I don't have room inside for myself, let alone him," Wilbert added.

Mikey's mouth dropped open, ready to proclaim a solution as he desperately brainstormed for a feasible way to maneuver his find into his bedroom. He would have sacrificed everything he owned to make it happen, but his convulsing brain could not produce the necessary logic.

"I have a shed," Andy spoke up. "Shorty will be at the Hotel, and Mom will be...asleep. Nobody's ever in the shed but us."

The illuminated grin on Jeff's face, and the sigh escaping Mikey's lungs confirmed Andy's shed as the most logical location.

"Let's get to it then. Be dark soon," Miss Nellie said. "Nobody pays heed to anything in the daylight, but once it gets dark, everybody's watching."

The group split, Miss Nellie around the left, back corner of the truck bed, Wilbert to his moped, and the boys gathered at the open, passenger door of the rollback. Mikey carried a bit of a size complex, and refused to be stuck in the middle, ever. Andy and Jeff usually indulged him, just to avoid listening to him rant. But who would climb in the truck first?

"Come on boys," Miss Nellie said, already sitting in the truck and ready to roll. "Scoot on in here." She patted the seat beside her.

"Your turn," Jeff sternly demanded. Andy looked back to Wilbert, sitting on his blue scooter behind the truck. The scooter was built for two, but not when one was Wilbert. Plus Wilbert was shaking his head 'no'. Andy turned back to Jeff, scowled, and climbed into the truck, right beside Miss Nellie. Jeff eagerly jumped in after, followed by Mikey as he slammed the door shut. It suddenly was sweltering hot inside, and crammed so tight that Mikey had to roll down the window and shove his elbow through the hole.

\*\*\*

The rollback lunged from the laurel and out onto the road, headed for Falling Rocks. Wilbert wobbled out onto the road and into the long, side mirror on the truck a few seconds later, providing interference behind Miss Nellie, a skill he had mastered as a teenager.

Miss Nellie shifted only once, pulling the long, curved shifter back against the seat and holding the truck into third gear, low range. The 427 – holding the weight of the truck and its cargo from careening down the mountain – chattered and crackled like firecrackers, and barked like a rifle two or three times every thirty seconds or so as they cruised down the grade at 25 m.p.h. Andy grumbled in silence, inside his head, wishing that Miss Nellie would go faster. Sweat beaded on his forehead as his back already wrenched with pain from twisting his hips to the side. If he relaxed just the slightest bit, his leg would touch Miss Nellie's hand. And to make matters worse, she started talking to him, asking questions about the drop off. Miss Nellie knew exactly how to get to Andy's shed—she had delivered there before and would never forget. She never mentioned it once, but to Andy, she may as well have been talking about that night.

Miss Nellie stepped on the brake as the Chevy swept into the first switchback, to the left, but the truck did not seem to react at all, and Andy reconsidered his wish to go faster. All of a sudden, there was a noise, from the far right of the truck—a noise that everyone recognized, but couldn't believe what they heard. Three heads snapped to the right, like a wave starting from the far left. The passenger door was hanging wide open, and there was Mikey, holding onto the door for dear life, with his left fingers and right armpit clamped over the door where the window had disappeared down into. The stony road shoulder blurred by under his dangling feet, and his face was panicked, but completely focused on never letting go. Miss Nellie stomped on the brake, careful not to push harder out on the door though, but it didn't matter. The truck just kept relentlessly rolling down the mountain. Finally Jeff reached out and grabbed Mikey by the arm, and pulled. The door folded back a little, and Mikey somehow leaped from the side of the door, into the cab of the truck, wedging himself between Andy and Jeff. And Jeff slammed the door shut, hard.

The rollback rolled on, popping and backfiring as though nothing at all had happened. The inside of that candy-apple red cab was stone silent and intense, though. No one moved a muscle, not even the one driving the truck. Then, out of nowhere, like a hiccup, or an unexpected belch from a quiet buildup of pressure, Jeff chuckled, surprising even himself. He had never been so scared that he laughed before.

There was not another sound inside that cab for the rest of the trip – around the second switchback, down past Wilbert's, and a right at the four-way stop at Paterson's. Miss Nellie stopped on the road in front of the fire hall so Jeff could retrieve his bike. He jumped out and slammed the door shut, pushing on it twice from the outside to make sure. Jeff bolted around the front of the truck, with only his head bobbing above the hood. And then his head disappeared. He went down again, his feet kicking out in the residual cinders from winter. "Good grief," Miss Nellie softly moaned. Jeff's head reappeared before she could finish her thought, and he continued across the road, even faster and more careless than before. "I sure hope this day starts to get better," Miss Nellie said as she split shifted gears up through town towards Andy's shed.

***

Jeff zipped past the rollback on his bike as Miss Nellie backed into Andy's driveway, between the house and the Ford Escort that Andy's mom hadn't moved since the previous fall. Miss Nellie carefully followed the edge of the driveway as it curved behind the house and faded into grass. Then she spun the steering wheel counter clockwise and squared the bed of the truck up perfectly to the shed doors that Jeff already had folded open. Mikey bailed out, followed by Andy, and the three boys feverishly cleared out the front of the shed as Wilbert putted in, wobbling his blue moped around to the back of the shed.

Tools clattered and chattered inside the shed as they were thrown onto a workbench, and cinderblocks and planks were tossed around the corner as Miss Nellie shook her head. Cardboard boxes were stacked in the back along a wall of the same, and Jeff and Andy emerged from the shed together, one pushing a neglected lawnmower, the other carrying a bicycle frame with no wheels and peculiar looking front forks. But the shed was ready to accept its new addition by the time Wilbert walked up to the doors.

Sliding back and raising up, Miss Nellie placed the tapered edge of the truck bed across the thresh hold of the shed, and the Buick hood slid from the elevated bed as fast as the winch allowed. Andy was a seasoned veteran at beating back suppressed memories, but Miss Nellie's reenactment of the past was too strong. Everyone was there, and everything the same. *The crumpled, blood-stained Chevelle hobbled from the rollback and settled into its grave, soon to be repeated by Tom. Miss Nellie's sculpted hair still leaned out over her painted face, and her black eye brows flattened above her intently concentrating eyes. The State Trooper was still there, with his wide brimmed hat and polished uniform, still biting his bottom lip like fox chewing off its foot to escape a trap. But someone was missing. Andy could see his dad standing right there beside the trooper, but he was not there anymore, just like the night of the accident. Andy caught a pitiful glance from Miss Nellie, again, just before the trooper placed a firm hand on his shoulder.*

"Grab a leg boy," the trooper said – Wilbert said.

As Miss Nellie backed up her truck, Andy lifted and pulled one leg while Jeff and Mikey heaved on the other. Wilbert pried under the hood with a rusty digging bar until the four of them maneuvered the hood into the shed, inch by inch. Wilbert gave Miss Nellie a nod as she climbed into the cab – anxious to get out of there before the entire town knew that she was there – and he closed the doors, shoving the digging bar through the door handles on the inside as the 427 rumbled away.

***

"He's cold. He's lost too much blood...he's not going to make it," Mikey babbled within the confines of the shed, as though they were safe, in a secret bunker, bored into the side of the mountain.

"Nonsense!" Wilbert scolded. "You two! We need water from Rock Spring, as much as you can carry. And blankets...and bandages. Get some Sassafras roots too! Maybe some maple buds, and acorns if you can find any."

Andy and Jeff just stood there, looking dumbfounded. Where would they find acorns and buds this time of year? And how were they supposed to carry it all with their bikes?

"Well, get going!" Wilbert shouted.

Andy and Jeff scurried out through the trap door behind the boxes of Tom's things. When the boys were a bit younger, they used the back of the shed as their own private clubhouse, secret entrance and all.

Wilbert pulled a flask from somewhere deep within the layers of quilted and flannel shirts that wrapped his body, and turned it up to his mouth. Then he wiggled the flask between the creature's lips and gently tipped it bottoms up. The beast coughed, opened his eyes for a second, and growled a weak grumble that nearly soaked Mikey's pants.

"Easy old friend. This will bring you to life," Wilbert softly assured as he began the tedious chore of cleaning the wounds hidden by thick matted hair and forest debris. Mikey joined in – Wilbert knew he would have it no other way. Mikey was a bit slower, but much neater at trimming hair away from the broken skin, and a doctor would have been jealous of the crude splint applied to the beast's arm. Wilbert carefully flushed each wound with a dribble from his flask until the last drop was spent.

\*\*\*

Ice began to bead on Wilbert's facial hair under his nose, drifting down across his grisly chin with the disappearing sun. The wind screamed like a siren as it sliced through the shed, pulling a heavy snow out of the northeast. "Sapling bender," Wilbert said in disgust while looking out the window. A warm spring thaw was only days away, but winter never left the Appalachians quietly.

Wilbert had the old pot-bellied stove glowing red by the time Andy and Jeff started shoving snow-covered blankets and emptied milk jugs filled with spring water through the trap door. They even pulled an entire Sassafras sapling through behind them. Wilbert was glad to see them, and their supplies, but the time had come to face the greater problem. He grabbed his rifle from the corner, by the doors, and stepped between the boys and their escape hatch.

"We need to settle a few things before we go on," Wilbert said with the most sinister voice he could muster. "Miss Nellie and I belong to a world-wide, secret society as old as can be remembered. A society that does not exist, but powerful enough to destroy all of mankind if need be." Wilbert paused for dramatic effect, although he had the boy's full attention. "Like it or not, you all have blundered into that society. I ask for your help, but demand secrecy. I will kill you if need be, and if I fail, the society will succeed, anywhere in the entire world. I am the only one standing between you and him, and his kin. And they are always watching."

Not an eye blinked in that shed. Wilbert recognized the gleam in two sets of eyes – the very same gleam that he had felt over sixty years ago. "Are you ready to be part of this society?" he asked. Andy and Jeff both nodded. "What about you? Do you want to conform to the boundaries of science, or do you want to learn the real mysteries that science will never solve?"

You could nearly see Mikey's brain ripping in two behind his glassy eyes. His entire life's ambition, weighed against alleged knowledge of the most elusive creature on Earth. Mikey slowly bowed his head and reluctantly nodded.

"Good," Wilbert chuckled. "Now, get to the house and call your parents. The last thing we need is a bunch of paranoid parents snooping around. And remember, life on this planet will forever change if we are discovered."

The boys scrambled out the hatch, concocting a story as they went, and Wilbert commenced to brew a batch of Sassafras tea.

Mikey reconsidered Wilbert's words the moment the razor cold air rushed through his nose. There were rules to follow, and what would that make him if he withheld such information from the world? Sure things would change. That's the whole purpose of knowing, right? How could he turn his back on who he was, and why should he? And what for secrets would an old man threaten to kill children to keep? For the first time in a long time, Mikey needed his parents – although they would not understand, or even try to understand. But still, denying the warmth of home never hurt so much.

\*\*\*

Mikey and Jeff persuaded their parents to authorize a sleepover at Andy's, and all three returned to the shed with armloads of supplies. Wilbert and the boys nursed their patient as the falling snow thickened on the neglected roof overhead. All were exhausted, and all were eager to succumb to the weight of their own eyelids as they curled up in blankets throughout the shed – all but Mikey. He held his tiny flashlight on the Bigfoot, a real live Bigfoot, for hours into the night.

## Chapter Seven

The frozen night gave way to the promise of a warm, spring day as the first beam of sunshine fished its way through the landscape of rural America to stop the sinking mercury. The snow had stopped falling somewhere between consciousness and the early morning slumber, but not before submerging Falling Rocks in eighteen inches of fluffy, white menace.

Mikey's eyes opened early, his conscience still in turmoil – plus the beastly snoring nearly rattled the bar that was wedged in the door handles. Bigfoot's breathing was stronger and steady, and his body was quite warm, even though the warmth of the stove had faded sometime through the night. Mikey looked out the window at the newly whitened world that suddenly seemed alien. If it were not for Wilbert, the creature would have died in the night. Things would have been very different, and would have been over for all but Mikey. The mere thought of such a tragedy turned his stomach.

Wilbert's snoring soon woke Andy and Jeff as well. All three stared at each other in silence with their sleepy eyes and hungry bellies. And no one wanted to shed their warm blankets to rekindle the fire. It was a standoff. Who could hold out the longest? Jeff kicked at Wilbert's foot in an attempt to stop the ghastly snoring that seemed to be irritating his inflated bladder. Wilbert shuddered, snorted, and snored even louder.

Suddenly a knock rattled the shed door. Andy jumped up from his blanket and scurried out the trapdoor like a flushed rabbit. Jeff and Mikey tossed their blankets over their top-secret treasure, and then Andy's blanket, but the blankets only seemed to accentuate a three dimensional silhouette of the slumbering beast even more than if he were bare – especially his huge feet. Jeff and Mikey just stood there under their unintentional, punk rock hairdos, their puffy, bloodshot eyes looking at the Frankenstein like image that they had created. Mikey didn't even notice that his glasses were halfway down the bridge of his nose, and Wilbert's snoring seemed a mile away.

Andy reappeared at the back of the shed, covered with tiny bits of snow clinging to his ear, shoulder...everywhere. "Miss Nellie," he whispered as he weaved through the clutter toward the front and pulled the digging bar from the door handles.

"Morning, boys," Miss Nellie greeted as she slipped between the doors and lowered an Army duffle bag to the floor. "How's our patient?"

"Good...I think," Mikey answered, raising his voice above Wilbert's snoring.

"Good grief, Willard!" Miss Nellie shouted. "You're shaking the mountain side!"

Wilbert rolled to his feet with the agility of his teenage years before his last snore stopped echoing throughout the shed. Miss Nellie flashed her perfectly manicured smile, which was like a tub if ice water and two cups of black coffee, all in one. Wilbert frantically patted down his wickedly alive hair while shuffling around his bedding, searching for his hat.

"We caused enough commotion yesterday. Business as usual today," Miss Nellie ordered, very short and direct.

Wilbert pulled his hat down to his ears, coolly brushed himself off, and nodded at Miss Nellie as he slipped out the door, never speaking a word.

"You boys go home. And stay there for a while! We don't want to draw *any* attention." Miss Nellie glared at Mikey. "Understand?"

Mikey nodded. Miss Nellie could control the mind of any man, young or old, and apparently even a Bigfoot.

\*\*\*

The boys slowly trudged into the white world outside – a world that normally they couldn't wait to get into. And after helping Wilbert push his moped through the snow to the plowed road, and watching him wobble toward town, sliding left and right in the slush with his legs spread wide, the boys all went home. Andy and Jeff slept most of the day away, while Mikey nearly paced a hole clear through his bedroom floor.

When Wilbert finally made it home without crashing, he plopped down in his chair along the road in the warm sun, all day – open for business. The bright sun and gleaming snow darkened his glasses like never before, his eyes resting nicely behind them. He only woke when a car door slammed, or someone checked for a pulse.

The sun pummeled the fresh snow all afternoon until retiring for the day behind Rocky Ridge. Wilbert's Sunday evening patrons retired with the sun, returning home to prepare for the start of a new week. And Wilbert returned to the shed for the night shift.

*

For a week Miss Nellie and Wilbert played out their façade while the comatose creature regained strength. The boys tried their best to keep their distance from the shed, but usually ended up circling on their bikes, like vultures circling an animal carcass. Every day at school, they huddled together like grade school girls with a secret, and the only way that Miss Nellie could distance the boys from the shed after school was to send them after Sassafras or Crow's Feet, or sometimes an imaginary ingredient that did not really exist. She refused to allow the boys inside until she was cleaning up for the day and Wilbert arrived to take over.

Every day it was the same pungent smell lingering inside the shed, besides the overwhelming odor of wet dog and horrific body odor. Miss Nellie always left seven, homemade candles strategically placed around the shed, but they were completely scentless. Jeff and Andy found everything amusing, and paid heed to nothing, but Mikey's habitual eyes were focused on detail – like the faint line of ash across the floor, just inside the doors, and across the window sills. And it was not wood ash from the stove, but an ash of Miss Nellie's own design, created in a small copper bowl that she gathered from on top of the stove and tucked away inside of her duffle every evening. Mikey peeked around Miss Nellie's back every chance he could, just to catch a glimpse of what she was tucking away inside that duffle bag. There were mason jars, capped with red and blue hankies, and cinched with rubber bands – each one containing different weeds and roots, or creams – and small, green and brown, glass bottles, each stopped with a cork. A daily wound inspection revealed a highly improbable healing rate, and although against all scientific logic, Mikey suspected witchcraft.

*

By the end of the week, all signs of winter were replaced by Dogwood buds and green wheat fields. Even the frogs in the pond behind the shed announced the arrival of spring by singing their chaotic symphonies during the warm evening hours.

The boys hit the Friday evening rendezvous at the old, ball field – as usual. Maybe it was the awakening of his informed mind, or maybe just raging spring hormones, but something about the past week's events filled Andy with reckless courage and the burning desire to take advantage of every minute. No more sulking. No more falling into the social lineup. He pedaled right up to Sally's window and smiled at her, desperate to redeem himself. She smiled back. But Andy just stood there, smiling, until he made Sally so uncomfortable, she turned her head. And Mikey glared across the dimwitted crowd, wearing a sinister grin, as if he wanted to gloat about being right, and wanted all of them to know that someday soon, he would be powerful enough to make all of them pay.

Jeff had never seen such a menacing expression on Mikey's face. He expected Andy to radiate tension, but Mikey too – it was too much to bear. The entire crowd was much quieter than usual, almost like they could hear Mikey's thoughts, and for the first time, took him more seriously. "Let's go guys," Jeff whimpered. "We got more important things to worry about." Surprisingly, Andy and Mikey followed Jeff's lead from the field, but for an attempt *not* to draw attention, the three sure were noticed – especially by Charles.

***

Tired testosterone rarely coexists with teenage testosterone peaceably, but Wilbert was glad to have the overnight company that Friday. A week of worrisome speculation had left him lonely, and regretful. He always intended to have sons to pass his legacy on to, but somehow time had passed him by, and intensions are often imprisoned by self-indulgence, or paranoia, or in Wilbert's case, guilt. His years had added up, and he would never get another chance to mentor a replacement.

Wilbert and the boys sat behind the locked doors of the shed, listening to the frogs trying to impress each other with screams of insanity, and watching the outside world slip into an unknown dimension of darkness. The pigtail light bulb, hanging from a rafter, glowed brighter and brighter, and the darkness brought a chill with it. Wilbert started a fire as Andy and Mikey chattered about the evening at the ball field. But Jeff seemed lost, quietly watching the dancing flames inside the stove, and the phantoms of heat escaping into the air as fire and smoke climbed up the inside of the stove pipe and abruptly turned out through the wall. He was intrigued about something, although nobody noticed. Jeff may have never seen that sinister glare in Mikey's eyes before, but he had seen an inconceivable, clandestine stare in the mirror countless times. "Tell us about the secret society," he bluntly asked.

"Well," Wilbert said. "The secret society is my friend here, and all of his kind throughout the world."

With their eyes locked onto Wilbert's lips, at least where his lips should have been behind a curtain of gray and black facial hair, the boys sat on their billets of firewood, prancing, like a dog under the command of sit as his master opened the dog food bag. It was quite clear that more was necessary.

"Plus, hundreds of people around the world that help to hide them," he quickly added in. "Or...or dismiss their very existence, by creating the notion that it's ludicrous to believe that Sasquatch *could* exist...and they blame it all on misidentification." Not enough. More! "It works very well. Most people that have an encounter are ashamed that they think they saw, what they really did see." The boys frowned with confusion as they tried to follow Wilbert. "And to avoid the embarrassment, they convince themselves that what they saw, was actually something that they didn't see." Even Wilbert was frowning with confusion now. "You see...the irony..." Wilbert just stopped talking. He gave up, and moved to the stove, to poke around at the fire, as if it were the same as walking out the door.

*That's it?* The boys' enthusiastic confusion melted from their faces, and their shoulders slumped as their eyes left Wilbert's backside and turned toward the resting creature. All of a sudden Bigfoot became...less exciting, and unreal – almost fake. They had imagined a life of adventure abroad, filled with secret codes and mysterious meetings in dangerous, shadowed streets. They had pictured themselves as debonair agents, carrying deadly weapons hidden inside suave suits, with an exotic woman hanging on each arm. Alas, now they see themselves as Wilbert – scruffy, mountain man with a hunting rifle, stuck in Falling Rocks for life...with Miss Nellie!

The boys nestled down with their disappointment – confusion can be exhausting. Wilbert chuckled under his breath. *If only they knew what was coming,* he thought.

\*\*\*

A prime shopping day, Miss Nellie had already replaced Wilbert by the time Mikey stirred Saturday morning, just short of a week since Mikey had laid eyes on a Bigfoot for the first time. He sat up from his make-shift nest of blankets, and pushed his glasses up his nose with his middle finger. Miss Nellie smiled, and bid him a good morning.

"His wounds are healing *remarkably* well...don't you think?" Mikey insinuatingly muttered as he tried to shake the morning fog from his brain. Miss Nellie just smiled. "You're quite the *miracle* worker, Miss Nellie." Her smile faded some, replaced by nervousness. Then Jeff and Andy stirred from sleep. All three sat slouched among wraps of warm blankets, while globs of thick hair stood straight up and at attention across their heads, but they all seemed to be quite content. And there was no school to drag them away. They watched Miss Nellie tinker about, their groggy eyes fixated on her every move like a moth to flame.

"Teenage boys don't spend their Saturdays hanging out in a shed," Miss Nellie snapped while tipping her beehive from one side to the other. "I need snipe eggs. Go down to the flats, along the creek, and don't come back until you find a half dozen or so."

# Chapter Eight

An evening dusk quickly settled in on Falling Rocks, and Miss Nellie, her things all packed up early, fluttered about the shed, organizing unidentifiable clutter and grumbling to ears that she knew would never hear. And just itching to get to her Saturday night. But her irritability was cut short by three teenage boys as they moped through the trap door in the back wall. Three boys that looked remarkably similar to the three that had left the shed nine hours earlier. They wore the same clothes, the same shaggy hairdos, and the very same marks on their faces – marks that appeared to be good, old-fashioned dirt, and they managed to add a few more of those during the day.

"We only found three, Miss Nellie," Andy said as he held out three, perfectly round, golf ball sized...eggs, in his right hand.

Miss Nellie's red lips parted, and her painted, black eyebrows pointed straight toward her beehive tower. A few choice words and a couple of burning questions surged to the very tip of her tongue, but she couldn't. She re-sealed her lips, and bit down on her tongue as she reluctantly plucked the eggs, one by one from Andy's palm, carefully tucking them into her coat pocket.

"What will you use those eggs for, Miss Nellie?" Mikey slyly asked.

"Um...good protein...and other healing...minerals. Where the hell is Willard! I'm missing Bingo!"

Wilbert would have never irresponsibly kept Miss Nellie waiting, and she knew it. And she also knew why he was late. It was the first warm Saturday after a long, cold winter, and more than likely, Wilbert was corralled in his own driveway by his customers – customers who were reluctant to return home to the ones that they had been cooped up with for four months straight. It could have been hours before he showed up. Miss Nellie's frustration, especially the release of vulgarities when no one was listening, was aimed more at the locals than anyone else.

"Go ahead Miss Nellie. We can watch him till Wilbert gets here," Jeff said, oddly seeming eager to get rid of her. "He's been sleeping for a week. What's the chance he'll wake up in the next couple hours?"

Normally, Miss Nellie would have never left the boys alone with a creature who may or may not wake up with a lot of traumatic emotions surging through a half ton of muscle. But what *was* the chance, and she *was* missing bingo night. "He so much as twitches...run! I'll be at the fire hall, and you know where to find Willard."

The boys reassured Miss Nellie with smiles on their nodding heads, and Jeff flashed her a thumbs-up. Like a gentleman, Andy unbarred the doors, and lifted one sagging door up out of the grass so that it could swing open just wide enough to slip through. Miss Nellie reluctantly slipped between the doors, diligently studying the beast's face for the slightest inclination of consciousness until her eyes disappeared behind the gray wooden boards. Andy re-barred the door handles, and all three anxiously awaited Willy's purr, but Miss Nellie was consumed with worry. She stood alongside the jeep and stared at the eggs in the palm of her hand, second-guessing her decision. Eventually, a chill from the thought of what the eggs actually were overwhelmed her concern, and she tossed the eggs into the adjacent field, shivered, and sped off to bingo.

*As Willy's sputter faded away into the distance, Jeff removed himself from the lineup of sneaky teenagers that listened right behind the doors, and plopped himself down on a billet of wood between the stove and Bigfoot. He tugged on the overstretched zipper that bound together his overstuffed, overnight pack of necessities between his feet. One by one he pulled his stash from the backpack for display – a box of white, powdered doughnuts, several individually wrapped pastries, candy bars, sodas, and tucked away down in the bottom of his pack, three more cans of beer.

"Wilbert will thump us for having beer," Mikey whispered, like Wilbert was near.

"Those old farts will shoot the bull for hours yet," Jeff assured as he re-secured his sweets back into his pack and out of sight of his ravenous teenage companions.

Andy kindled a fire in the stove – the boys couldn't drink without a fire to huddle around – and he opened the window next to the stove to let the heat escape. The eerie chant of the frogs flowed from the pond and into the shed like a restless spirit. Mikey shivered, and turned around to make sure his Bigfoot was still sleeping.

"What's a matter, Mikey?" Jeff gurgled in an evil tone. "Afraid he'll wake up and take revenge for you wanting to dissect him?"

"Shut up Jeff! I wouldn't have –"

Andy gathered two more billets of firewood as makeshift chairs and placed them beside Jeff, in a semi-circle around the stove. Andy sat down beside Jeff, and Mikey eased down onto the billet next to Andy, on the end, as Jeff handed two cans of beer down the line.

Mikey pulled off his tab, only because he didn't want to be ribbed by Jeff. This wasn't his first taste, and he had absolutely no desire to taste it again. But while staring at his feet, Mikey noticed that the floor of the shed was somewhat dark – too dark – and faint, red light rippled across his sneakers. It was the light from the fire, escaping through the thin gaps around the stove door. And the southern sky, visible through the window, was fading dark much too fast. Mikey glanced over his shoulder at the sleeping giant once again, then back to the window. It seemed to fade noticeably darker in one second. He closed his eyes tightly, and turned up his can.

"I'm gonna ask Sally out," Andy bluntly confessed, completely out of nowhere.

"Dude! Can't you wait a few months. Charles will be away at some ritzy college, and Sally will be all yours," Jeff preached. "We'll probably never see that prick again!"

"Yeah, right! He'll be back in town every chance he gets, just to remind everybody that he owns them. Well, he don't own me! And he won't own Sally anymore."

Jeff's temper seemed to be growing shorter with Andy by the day. He reached into his pack between his feet, tore open the box of powdered doughnuts, and held one up in front of Andy's face. "Pretend this doughnut is you. And I'm Charles." Jeff took a big bite out of the doughnut.

"We'll see."

"Yea! We *all* will see." Jeff shook his head, and turned up his can of beer.

"Hey! You guys think Miss Nellie's a witch?" Mikey asked, changing the subject, sick of the increasing animosity between his friends when there was so much more at stake.

"There's no such thing as witches, Mikey. You never stop, do you?"

"You said the same thing about Bigfoot a week ago, Jeff," Andy fired back.

Jeff held the bitten doughnut out in front of Andy's face again. "Remember the doughnut, Andy," he said as he turned up his can of beer for another swallow.

Andy plucked the doughnut right out of Jeff's fingers. Beer nearly shot out of Jeff's nostrils as he jerked his can down and tried to swallow the alcohol that involuntarily heaved into his sinuses. He spun on his billet and glared at Andy. "You better eat...that."

Andy and Mikey's jaws were hanging as low as their cheeks would allow, and their eyes were as round as their gapping mouths, as if Jeff's brain was hanging out of his nostril. Jeff slowly turned his head to the left. There crouched the Bigfoot, only an arm's length away, with white powder clinging all around his mouth, and down his hairy chin.

Plop...plop, plop. All three cans of beer slipped through the boys' fingers and onto the floor, and they jumped to their feet into a huddled mass of panic around the stove. Bigfoot startled to his feet, smashing his head into a rafter and rattling the shed like the time Andy accidentally discharged his dad's muzzleloader through the shed roof. Bigfoot squalled like a banshee, and the boys split around the stove, flattening their backs against the trembling, shed wall. The doors were to their right, the secret hatch to their left, and Bigfoot was right in front of them, and within arm's reach of any escape. The boys were cornered.

Bigfoot's eyes spun a whole new dimension of fear. They were very large, and brown, and inescapable, and seemed to look all three boys in the eye at the same time. Bigfoot sniffed at the air, and licked at the sugar clinging to his face. Afraid to look away, Andy's eyes twitched as he searched the floor where Jeff's pack was sitting, but it was gone. Jeff had picked it up, and he hugged it tight against his chest.

"Give him, another, doughnut," Andy whispered, out through the corner of his mouth, as is the creature would not be able to hear him if his lips were not moving.

"No."

Bigfoot tilted his head, slightly to the right, and forward a bit, and his brow flattened just a little, as though he were puzzled by Jeff's defiance, or maybe Andy's ventriloquism. More than likely, both.

"For Pete's sake Jeff," Mikey squeaked, trying to keep his voice much lower than his level of adrenaline. "I'll buy you another pack...if we make it out of here alive!"

Bigfoot's brown eyes intently followed Andy's hand as it carefully, but forcefully, slipped into Jeff's pack. Jeff squeezed, bear hugging the backpack like it was a parachute, and Miss Nellie was flying the plane. Andy's arm, in an awkward position, pushed Jeff back and forth against the wall as his hand rooted around inside the pack, his scrunched up fingers trying to find their way into the flimsy cardboard box to latch onto a stale doughnut. Neither would look at the other, until the skirmish dragged on to the point that they became the anomaly in the room. Finally Jeff whimpered, and Andy jerked a doughnut from the pack. With a quick flip of the wrist, the white delight wobbled through the air and disappeared into Bigfoot's hand like a baseball into a mitt. He growled, or purred, and swallowed the doughnut whole.

"Give him the rest," Mikey whispered as Bigfoot licked his hand.

Andy pulled at the backpack, choosing not to reenact the last fiasco, but Jeff pulled back. And the pack was now the rope in a tug of war. Bigfoot's head twitched back and forth – he couldn't take his eyes off the pack – and Mikey actually covered his face, as if he were embarrassed to be of the same species. Andy's temper tried to persuade Jeff with a hard punch to the arm, unsuccessfully, and Bigfoot did not approve. He grumbled a growl that rendered all human muscle limp, and the pack dropped to the floor. The shed lingered still and silent.

Eventually, Andy's brain regained control of the rest of his body. He slowly retrieved the backpack from the floor, and gently sidestepped to the right, toward the front doors, the pack dangling from the very end of his outstretched arm like he was holding a twenty-pound snapping turtle by the tail. Andy hung the backpack on a nail, above the double doors. Bigfoot moved for the sweets. The boys launched from the wall toward the escape hatch. Mikey and Jeff dove headfirst for the hole at the same time, and wedged tight. They kicked the floorboards with their feet, clawed at the grass outside with their fingernails, and screamed into each other's faces for help at the top of their lungs, but they were hopelessly stuck. Andy wasn't waiting though. He barreled into the stuffed hatch full bore. All three boys, and one, wide board from the side of the shed, tumbled down the gentle slope toward the wailing frogs.

Pain did not exist in that moment, only an overload of adrenaline. Andy and Jeff sprinted for their bikes and pedaled off toward town like out of control rockets. Mikey ran to the side window, and watched Bigfoot devouring the inside of Jeff's pack. First the powdered doughnuts, looking so tiny in his massive fingers, disappeared into his mouth, one by one – one right after the other. The empty box was tossed aside, and Bigfoot turned toward the back of the shed, his head sweeping side to side like he was searching for something. And he was doing something strange with his mouth – sucking in on his cheeks and rolling around his tongue, in and out of his mouth, gagging maybe. His lips and tongue were pasty white, coated with powdered sugar.

"Good grief he's choking," Mikey quietly said, to himself. He was painfully aware that he was alone, but talking out loud helped. Then Bigfoot looked right at him. Mikey rolled away from the window, flattening his back against the outside wall, and holding his breath as he listened to the absolute silence. Even Mikey's palms and fingers were flat against the pitted wall, and even his eyes were still, gazing out across the dark, empty field beyond the yard. Normally he could see a couple hundred yards until the field rolled over behind itself, but the darkness was setting in, and very soon he would not be able to see until it was too late. In fact, he began to see shadows of movement, on the rise of the hill – Sasquatch shaped shadows, two or three of them, maybe more – and they were moving in with the darkness. Mikey very stealthily looked toward the road, as if Wilbert or Miss Nellie might be coming already.

Breaking the silence like a cannon, a beer can tumbled across the floor inside, clattering with emptiness. Followed by another, and then the last, followed by the returning silence that was so loud it was almost unbearable. Mikey roll to his shoulder and carefully leaned away from the wall to catch a glimpse inside the shed through the window, and keep an eye on the field at the same time. Further and further he leaned, away from his only safety, until he could no longer reach the wall. But he could see the creature, the one under the single light bulb inside the shed.

Bigfoot was back at the dangling pack, his jaws chomping and his lips smacking, pausing only long enough to pull a piece of plastic wrapper out of his mouth and fling it to the floor. He was content, but Jeff's sweets wouldn't last long. And then what? Mikey pranced uncontrollably at the thought as he looked back out into the field. The shadows were getting closer, and Mikey's breathing nearly blasted into hyperventilation. He looked toward the road, and could see Willy bouncing into the driveway, and Wilbert wobbling down through the grass with his legs spread- eagle, but yet, there was only the abandoned Escort, and the sleeping house on the other side of the gravel driveway. The yard light, mounted to the side of the house, flashed on and hummed, announcing the arrival of night like the lights and siren of an ambulance.

*\*\**

As Mikey envisioned the ambulance that eventually would come to pick him up, Jeff burst into the bingo game and slammed the door shut like Bigfoot was chasing him, and just on the other side. He shuffled his way along the wall, sideways, back and hands against the painted cinder blocks, as he searched for Miss Nellie's beehive, as inconspicuous as possible. But he could not have been more conspicuous if he wore an afro of orange hair and a big, red nose. Miss Nellie quickly spied him though, almost like she had expected him, and Jeff's face said it all. Miss Nellie motioned him out of the room, and she gracefully exited the game.

Jeff was already sitting in Willy by the time the outside door of the fire company slammed shut behind Miss Nellie. And before she could get one foot inside the jeep, Jeff exploded from the mouth. "He's awake Miss Nellie! He ate my doughnut! He's probably eating the rest right now!"
*

At the same time, Andy pedaled out from behind Mr. Paterson's car, and Wilbert jerked straight up in his chair. A thin darkness had settled in on Falling Rocks, and Mr. Paterson was the only gossiper left, but he would stay well beyond dark. Andy rode past, jerking his head up and to the right, motioning Wilbert to the shed. Mr. Paterson curiously watched Andy, slowly peddling up the mountain, at night, but he never broke from his story. Wilbert fidgeted insanely on the very edge of his chair, as, just out of sight, Andy turned around, and rode back past, motioning with his head again.

Mr. Paterson slowly leaned toward Wilbert, as much as his stomach would allow. "What in the world is wrong with that boy?" he asked under his breath. "Must be on drugs." His explanation for anyone he didn't understand.

It was clear that Wilbert was at a loss for action, so Andy stopped on his third pass. "Hey, Mr. Paterson! Who's the two strangers hanging out behind the store?"

"Son of a..." Mr. Paterson flopped his belly out over his knees, catapulting him out of his chair. "Call the cops, Wilbert," he shouted as he waddled his way to his car.

Wilbert threw his hand in the air and grumbled something unintelligible – something that Mr. Paterson took to mean, 'I'm on it!' – as he navigated through his merchandise for his scooter.

\*

Each passing second was like another pound of weight stacked onto Mikey's shoulders as he watched the imaginary paramedics, linked by an imaginary stretcher, carrying an imaginary body, completely covered by an imaginary white sheet, and walking toward the imaginary ambulance. A hand hung out from under the sheet, and Mikey just knew it was his. He could almost feel his feet sinking into the soft grass.

Mikey looked away, out into the field, and the ambulance disappeared. He couldn't see the shadows either. But he knew that they were standing right there, watching, and waiting. He could almost hear them breathing. Mikey turned to the lighted window, but the shed was empty. The discovery felt like the creature had him by the throat as he looked back to the road – no Wilbert, no Miss Nellie, not even the paramedics. He was on his own. His fate was left in his hands. Back to the window, and one step closer, widening the view inside, but still no Bigfoot. Mikey looked to the left, then to the right, half expecting to see a big, hairy silhouette peeking around the corner of the shed. One step closer, his feet about as close as they were able to get to the shed, but they had taken him no further. He cupped his hands to the sides of his glasses, and pressed against the glass windowpane. The shed appeared empty.

Then, out of nowhere, Bigfoot's head popped into view, filling the entire window, his hairy face only inches from Mikey's, and suddenly looking very humanoid. Mikey screamed and back pedaled away from the window, his feet quickly loosing the race with his head. He landed in the grass, flat on his back, flopping like a fish and yelling profanities in some language that did not exist. The creatures in the field were surely charging in now, when he was down. He could hear their feet in the grass, all around him. Mikey grunted, and his testosterone growled as he regained his bearings in the dark and rose to his feet. Suddenly, Willy's dim headlights flew in and slid to a stop only a couple feet away. Mikey screamed again, and again, he toppled over backwards.

Jeff hopped out of Willy, snickering as Mikey rolled on the lawn, cussing words that nobody had ever heard before.

"Grab hold of yourself, sweetie," Miss Nellie said, as Mikey stood up straight, but only from his knees. "Where's our friend?"

Mikey repeatedly jabbed his trembling finger toward the shed.

"We don't have to go in to unlock the door, do we, Miss Nellie?" Jeff pleaded as he followed Miss Nellie toward the side window. "We knocked a board off in the back. I think you could fit through the hatch now."

Miss Nellie stopped dead in her tracks, turned, and glared at Jeff with an expression more frightening than the cornered, mystical beast of legend inside the shed. Jeff was scared, excited, and completely clueless of his insinuation, and lucky for him, Miss Nellie recognized his young innocence and focused on the bigger issue. She rapped on the window, and Bigfoot appeared on the other side, cooing like an earthquake.

"Unlock the door, honey." Miss Nellie turned toward the front of the shed. "You two stay put!"

The boys scurried up to the window as Miss Nellie disappeared around the corner, and they watched Bigfoot unbar the door and let her slip in. As soon as she was inside, he pushed the digging bar back through the door handles as easy as Andy could have.

"Can he talk?" Jeff asked, totally amazed by what he just witnessed.

"No," Mikey snipped. "Don't be...ridiculous."

"Yeah, well, tell him to stay out of my pack."

Andy silently stuck his head in between Jeff and Mikey, provoking a short, but sharp, scream from both, leaving Andy holding his ears.

Wilbert putted in a second later with his rifle slung across his back, and he parked behind the shed as usual. But when he walked up to the boys, he was minus one rifle. "Where's your rifle?"

Wilbert just grimaced and shooed the boys away from the glass. "You peepers go wait on the porch till we find out what's going on."

The boys dropped their heads and drudged through the damp grass toward Andy's back porch. Wilbert waited, watching until they were seated on the porch before knocking on the shed door.

# Chapter Nine

The boys waited on the back porch in their own little silent dimension. Even the frantically chirping frogs had
called it a night. One by one, they watched the stars light up
as the daylight that linger high in the sky, beyond their sight,
receded westward. And the dark delivered a chill. They
shivered as they smelled the wood smoke trickling from the
stovepipe that clung to the side of the shed, and they shivered as they listened to the oil furnace ignite in the basement
under their feet. All three sat, side-by-side-by-side, on the
vinyl padded, gliding swing, shivering, stomachs grumbling,
and blankly staring at the soft glow of light around the edges
of the shed doors, watching for any hint of movement.

Finally, as clocks ticked toward curfew, a shadow shuffled behind the doors, and the thin strip of light grew into a
wide beam across the backyard. The boys perked up like
prairie dogs popping out of their burrows. Wilbert's silhouette emerged into the beam, but the light quickly folded back
into thin lines around the doors, blending Wilbert's shape
into the black shadow of the shed. The boys were blind in
the night, but they listened intently to Wilbert's broken gate
as he walked around the shed, to his scooter, and back again.
Then, out of the darkness, an owl hooted. Any young hunter
of Falling Rocks knew what that meant. The boys leaped
from the porch and ran to the shed where they trembled at
attention in front of Wilbert's shadow. They were cold, but
mostly overwhelmed by a cocktail of anticipation and fear.

"It's much worse than I had hoped, and it's time to
learn the truth." Wilbert opened the door a crack, letting the
light paint across the yard, and then he hesitated. "Try to
conduct yourselves as men, and keep your mouths shut and
your ears open...and your minds." He opened the door just

enough to slip through, and motioned the boys in with his head.

\*\*\*

The heat from the woodstove washed over the boys' clammy skin as they lined up just inside the doors, but the shivers refused to leave. Miss Nellie pulled their rigid bodies closer to the stove. They stood perfectly still, with their eyes focused on the floor, only glancing left or right for a split second, but never making eye contact Bigfoot. It was the boys' first junior high dance all over again. Bigfoot seemed a bit shy as well.

Wilbert adjusted his puzzled face toward Miss Nellie. "Where do I start?"

"Start at the beginning, Willard," Miss Nellie said. "Always start at the beginning."

Wilbert tugged on his bristly beard, letting the long whiskers slide through his fingers as he collected his knowledge into chronological order. "Our friends here," he said, holding out an open hand toward Bigfoot. "Are of the stars in the night sky, and they were sent to this planet when the Earth was a smoldering corpse of a previous world. They were as free and aimless as thought, but they were burdened to bodies of bone and flesh, molded from dust and water, just as the trees and grass. And their job was to seed a balanced, new world...and maintain it."

"What, like gardeners?" Mikey sneered, one corner of his upper lip already curled up with dispute.

"No," Wilbert huffed. "Like guardians...of the Earth."

Andy and Jeff looked as though they would have believed anything, and they wanted more, but Mikey, he was going to debate Wilbert's every word. "What's the use?" Wilbert said as he turned to Miss Nellie. "We can't do this with these smart-mouthed, disrespectful brats."

"Well, we don't have a choice now do we, Willard?"

Wilbert lowered his head as if Miss Nellie had just bitten into a nerve. "Give em a chance...and Mikey! I'd think you'd know better than anybody how frustrating it is not to be taken seriously." Mikey lowered his head to match Wilbert's. "Go on, Willard."

Wilbert sighed, as though he was as immature as the three teenagers before him, and he continued. "Our friends returned balance to the planet, balancing the planet with the solar system, the system to the galaxy, and so on, and so on. A new world sprouted to life with colorful gardens of green, and a variety of animals from the tiniest mouse, to the mightiest mammoth. But each day is a struggle to balance the light and the dark, and we depend on that balance more than anything else."

"What about water, and oxygen?" you know who asked, with much the same tone as when he confronted Charles in the cafeteria.

But Miss Nellie's bite still stung, and Wilbert's temper still cowered under her words. "Those things would have never existed without balance," he countered. "Everything you can see, and everything you know, is circles, cycles, or rotations, all in harmony with the next. And if the sun don't fall from the sky at the end of the day, none of us will live through another." Wilbert hesitated under the pressure of two very blank stares, and one scrunched up nose that was pushing Mikey's glasses well above his flattened brow. "It's like when Paterson was too cheap to fix the rollers on the hotdog machine in the store," he continued to explain. "And he'd put those frozen hotdogs on in the morning. By lunch, one side was as dry and tough as rawhide, and the other side was still frozen."

Miss Nellie rolled her eyes well up under her brow, but at least two of the boys were nodding, as if to acknowledge that they understood. They must have eaten some of those hotdogs.

"Good grief this is going to take all night," Miss Nellie intervened. "These guys," she said while holding *both* hands out toward Bigfoot, as Wilbert held out one. "Were smart. They knew just about everything, other than what this planet was before—can't start over with the past. But, that knowledge was forbidden to be a part of this world. They weren't even allowed to name each other, and they didn't need to. All they were to do after regenerating the planet was to start a disciplined race of themselves, born to the Earth, that would eventually forget the most basic and ancient knowledge. And they were to watch, forever resisting the ways of darkness, themselves as well as their fellow Earthly inhabitants.

"Ah, but there was one though…who couldn't resist thinking for himself. His name was Enki."

"I thought you said they weren't allowed to have names," Jeff interrupted.

"Exactly," Miss Nellie returned, with a finger pointed straight at Jeff. "Well, Enki fell in love with a beast of the new world, and they had children – seven specimens of a species all their own. And it wasn't long till Enki was teaching his children the forbidden knowledge. Once Enki got a taste of exercising his free will, he couldn't stop, and one after another, he explored every taboo, right up to the very first murder.

"Now, Enki himself only caused a small ripple in the balance, insignificant really, and eventually he would escape his prison of flesh and return to the stars. But his children were a different story. They were poisoned by Enki's tongue, and seven would very quickly turn into forty-nine, then…three hundred, whatever, each generation passing the poison to the next until they spread darkness across the planet like falling dominoes. But Enki's brothers were watching, and they called upon the stars, and the light came to Earth. Enki's children were stripped of their hair, leaving behind bare, naked skin, forever marking them as alien to this planet, and the forbidden knowledge was sucked out of their heads, lobotomized really. And Enki was forever separated from his children. First by touch, as his children's hairless skin burned Enki's flesh, and second, Enki was swept away to an isolated island in the middle of the ocean, and imprisoned under the watchful eye of the sun."

"Wow," Mikey spouted. "What a tale."

"It's no tall tale," Wilbert barked. "You'll see soon enough, and when you do, you'll be damn glad we took the effort to fill you in beforehand…and your two buddies will be damn glad they didn't heed any of your advice."

Mikey smirked behind his hand as he pushed his glasses up his nose, and Wilbert peeled off two shirts as the shed suddenly became quite warm and stuffy.

"Anyway," Wilbert blurted out, taking back his story. "Over the years of isolation, Enki's heart blackened with hate and revenge. He slipped into insanity, and unknowingly called upon the stars that did not shine, until a gift fell from the dark, night sky above. It was a crystal mask that gave Enki power to do the impossible, and he escaped the island."

Wilbert pulled a red hankie from his back pocket, and blotted at the sweat that started to bead on his forehead as the fire roared inside the stove. "Enki went after his children, but he had been on the island for a very long time – much longer than he realized. And what he found was grandchildren, several generations later, but they had progressed no further than when Enki last seen his seven. They were still naked and dumb, and scared. Now Enki would not stand for that, and soon his grandchildren were clothed, sheltered, and were speaking to one another. Enki was blissfully unaware that he was madly insane, dysfunctional with paranoia, and obsessed with his own ingenuity. It wasn't long until a city rose from the land – a city far greater, more spectacular and advanced, than anything that we know even today."

Just then Bigfoot snorted ever so lightly, as if in objection, and all three boys nearly jumped out of their skin. Bigfoot sat so still, so quiet, the boys had forgotten that he was in the room, and awake.

"A city might not seem like much to us," Wilbert quickly continued, heeding the objection. "But if you look at the

Earth, for what it is supposed to be, a city is a festering scar that spreads infection. Even little ole Falling Rocks is the same. Every homestead is a nick in the Earth's skin. And eventually, Enki's city killed the sea that it depended so heavily upon. The coral reef died and the sea life fled far away from the pollution. Next the sky thickened with darkness, and the vast tracts of cleared farmland would grow no crops. And the Earth warmed under the dark blanket, flooding the city. Enki's children were displaced and starving, forced to trek inland and away from *civilized* society just to survive. And of course, being completely insane, Enki refused to acknowledge the fact that he and his children were harming themselves, and he blamed his brothers for poisoning the Earth."

Wilbert hesitated for a moment as he fished his hankie under his hair and beard to wipe his sweltering neck. "Now, Enki's brothers never once raised a finger against Enki and his children. It was the Earth's way of keeping her inhabitants pure, but Enki could not see it. And when the light delivered a blow to the ocean by way of a meteorite, and swept all traces of the mostly abandoned city into an unreachable, watery grave, to Enki it was nothing short of murder. I'm sure many died, but at their own hands, and only those who were too weak to flee. They were well past their time on Earth, young or old. And at the hand of Enki's implanted fear, they were denying themselves of their only gift – freedom.

"Enki slipped over the edge after that. He came up with a plan to build pyramids all across the Earth, each one topped with some magical stone that would vibrate, sending out some kind of sound waves that would deflect away any interference from the light, and would push away the thick, dark clouds overhead. He gave new meaning to obsession, and he gathered his children, and set to build this worldly defense. And that's when Enki's brothers finally stepped in. They attacked using tactics of fear more than anything else, and very rarely were any harmed. But again, Enki could only see things his way, and he began to see his children in a different light."

Wilbert slipped his hand in between his remaining shirts and pulled out his flask, taking a nip before he went on. "He armed his children," he continued, his voice raspy from the hooch. "And he filled them with so much violence, and hatred, and vengeance, that it overcame their fear, and they became deadly warriors. Enki invented war, and our friends felt the sting. But be that as it may, a Sasquatch with the knowledge of the stars makes the worthiest opponent, and their numbers had grown significantly over the years, plus their devotion proved unstoppable. It was enough to send Enki's paranoia into overdrive. He rushed everything, splitting his children and spreading them out across the planet. Some of the pyramidal structures were abandoned for simpler, quicker structures, in hopes that the system would still work, all the while skirmishes arose between Enki's children and our friends throughout the world. And the world darkened a little more every day. Enki had to be stopped, no matter what."

Fearing that Wilbert was about to pass out, Andy slipped over and reopened the window by the stove, letting out the hot, dry air, and letting in a light breeze that mysteriously snaked into the shed from somewhere out in the dark night that peeked Bigfoot's attention. "We believe Enki was somewhere along the east coast," Wilbert said, resuming his story, but watching Bigfoot rather than the boys. "On his way to the last pyramid site. That's where Enki's brothers made their stand, ready to embrace the darkness against all their beliefs, to stop it forever. A fierce battle broke out in the darkest of all nights, and both sides suffered dearly. Enki's brothers only harmed his warrior children when they had no other choice, and they tried their best to only frighten them into the night, separating them from the insanity, where they would regress to a more natural demeanor. And Enki could be dealt with alone."

Wilbert took another quick nip from his flask. "But Enki was not so generous," he growled. "He used some sort of staff, and cut down his brothers like he was cutting wheat. There was one brother that Enki held near to his heart though, and the two hadn't seen each other since Enki fell in love. But in the height of battle, Enki found him, holding one of his children in his arms, her belly sliced open, and sputtering her last bloody breath. Betrayal raged through Enki's veins, and he killed his brother in an instant. The brother had not killed his child. The wound was by a blade, swung by panic and confusion in the blind night, and only Enki's children carried weapons. But Enki could only see with his eyes."

Suddenly the light breeze burst into a gust, enough to rattle the stove door from the draft in the flu pipe. The shed creaked, and pine needles and crisp, brown leaves tumbled across the roof, sounding like a hundred mice scampering across the tin.

"The slain brother had a son," Wilbert firmly belted, as if trying to assure everyone that it was just the wind. "Enki's nephew, and he tracked Enki down through the chaos like a machine, un-phased by his father's death and completely focused on finishing Enki. There was a battle between the two that stopped the world from spinning. Seriously the Earth stopped spinning. But the nephew bested Enki, somehow, and Enki retreated into the black, endless forest.

"Enki had escaped, but his regime of darkness was destroyed. The Earth started to spin again, although in a different direction, and the sun returned to the sky. And –"

Mikey chuckled. He couldn't hold it in anymore. "That's an interesting theory." He chuckled again. "Quite an imagination."

"It's no theory!" Wilbert barked.

"Then how do you know all that? Did he tell you?" Mikey held out his hand toward Bigfoot, evidently picking up Wilbert's mannerisms.

"No. They refuse to remember the past, especially that past."

Mikey didn't say a word. His open hands and shrugged shoulders re-asked the question.

"We found scrolls, in an old, hollow, twisted-up, oak tree, out in the middle of nowhere, not long after we met our old friend here."

Again, with the open hand.

"It was where Enki fled to, and he had one of his children with him, armed with one sword. There he wrote, in blood we think, these scrolls on animal hides, hoping that one day his children would find them, and carry on his legacy. His brothers, and by then, nephews, were tracking him down, and he could feel that his children's future would not include him."

Wilbert turned to Bigfoot, and he lowered his head. "He entrusted us to destroy the scrolls, and we did...but not before deciphering them. Miss Nellie worked for years trying to figure out the language."

"You destroyed them?" Mikey shrieked.

Wilbert turned back to Mikey and slowly nodded. "It was the right thing to do. Some of Enki's children built their pyramids and battled our friends for a thousand years after Enki fled. And even without Enki, his army is as strong as ever, and still fighting. Those scroll in the hands of Enki's warrior children would be a far more dangerous weapon than any a-bomb."

"So...where are all these warrior children?" Mikey sarcastically asked.

"They're us, dummy!"

Mikey's face twisted like he had just bitten into a lemon, and, for a while, the shed was quiet enough to hear the soft breeze whisper a strange, chant-like, melody. But Mikey's thoughts were never long without presenting more questions. "Okay...so...did the scrolls mention how they built the pyramids, or what powered the defense system, and how did they get from Africa to America, or Enki escape an island in the middle of the ocean? And how did the Earth stop spinning, and start again the other way?"

"Well," Wilbert said. "The Earth was so covered in darkness that it interfered with the forces that balance the Earth's path, and like a giant brake, the darkness choked the planet until it slowly spun to a stop. As far as restarting, we think that when the grip of darkness was released, the Earth was free, and probably the sloshing of the oceans, like bath water in a tub, chose the direction of movement . Now, *that* just a theory. And as far as your other questions, the scrolls spoke of no such details. What I told you is all that we know."

Mikey caught movement out of the corner of his eye as Bigfoot rolled his eyes up toward Miss Nellie. She stared blankly at the far wall, and suddenly her face became flush, with tiny droplets of sweat seeping through her makeup. Miss Nellie abruptly turned to the stove, closing the draft, then she moved to the open window, placing her face on the threshold between the cool, dark night, and the warm, safe shed. Must have been a hot flash. But she sure had Mikey's attention.

"I suppose the crystal mask that Enki wears had a lot to do with it all," Wilbert continued, unaware of anything else happening inside the shed.

"Magic?" Mikey, slyly implied, still looking at Miss Nellie, who's head was nearly completely outside by then.

"Well…for lack of a better word to describe a technology that you, or I, cannot understand – "

Mikey's head snapped back to Wilbert. "Just because you cannot understand, does not mean that I cannot."

"Well, excuse me for trying to pull the wool over your scientific vision!" Wilbert snapped.

"Alright, alright," Jeff butted in, apparently sick of Wilbert and Mikey's simple games when a much pressing question loomed. "Where's Enki?"

Wilbert took another nip, and sighed again. "All we know for sure is that he has eluded his brothers, and is out there somewhere. His companion with the sword evidently did not fare as well, for old friend had the sword as well as the scrolls. They try to destroy or hide all traces of Enki, from his children. And the sword is hidden nearby, which is more than likely nothing but a pile of rust by now. I do not see the relevance in today's world of rifles and nukes, but they are very adamant about keeping it hidden."

"Out there somewhere?" Jeff spouted, demanding Wilbert reveal what he was reluctant to say.

"We have talked to others, like Miss Nellie and I," Wilbert carefully said, thinking about every word. "We are like a…brotherhood…who watch for any signs of Enki, and help to hide Sasquatch throughout the world. And we can communicate with each other if necessary, to warn other Sasquatch if necessary. Now, most of our peers believe that Enki walks among his children throughout the world, cloaked as one of…us, leading us through history. Just about all of the great men of history have been suspected of actually being Enki. Everybody from Hercules to Henry Ford, and Hippocrates to Marie Currie. It's even widely accepted that King Arthur was indeed Enki, which I don't understand. Miss Nellie believes that he is hiding in the Bermuda Triangle in some underwater or floating city, which again, I just don't get."

Jeff huffed, good and tired of Wilbert dancing around the question, and he wasn't the only one. Even Bigfoot shifted his weight and groaned somewhat like a dog.

"For all those thousands of years," Wilbert belted out before someone could complain. "Enki has never returned to anywhere close to Rothstone or Falling Rocks…"

"Let me guess," Jeff interrupted. "Until now!"

"Afraid so," Wilbert confessed. "After two thousand years of waiting, and watching, Enki can taste his vengeance. His army is nearly unstoppable now, but the paranoia that he inflicted in his children is working against him, pitting his children against each other. Our world would have been destroyed long ago if it weren't so. He needs to unite his armies, but there are those few who will stand in his way, and he attacked our southern friends in their slumber. It was chaos, more to set the stage than to end the show. Old friend does not know the outcome of his friends. Most of the females and young escaped, disappearing into the forest, two of which are dear to..." Wilbert tipped his head and rolled his eyes toward Bigfoot. "Hopefully they're trekking toward the northern colony for help, and to forewarn."

"So I was right!" Mikey erupted. "They live up in Rothstone and down in Scrub National Forest, and Rocky Ridge is a highway between the two!"

"Well you just about had it all figured out, didn't you?" Wilbert's distain for Mikey grew, but he couldn't seem to dissuade himself away from believing that Mikey was probably the one – the key to a new generation of protection. Nothing worthwhile is easy.

"Let's go get his family," Andy barked as he stepped forward, pounding his right fist into his left palm. "Or this Enki, whichever we find first."

"I knew you would drag us into this," Jeff whined as he stepped up to Andy's side. "I'm getting my rifle first! I'm never going in those woods without it again."

"We'd be better off looking for the northern tribe," Mikey proclaimed. "Whatever attacked him probably already got to his family."

"Shut up, you twit!" Wilbert roared.

Mikey staggered back, confused and startled. "Like...he can understand me."

"He can speak any language spoken on Earth...ever! He just chooses not to!"

"Enough with you two," Miss Nellie squawked, finally reentering the group. "Like it or not, we're in this together. And there's more at stake than our stupid egos."

The shed dropped into silence as bull-headed faces fell toward the floor in shame. Mikey pushed his glasses up his wrinkled nose, and looked over at Bigfoot. He tried not to look, but something was drawing his attention, and when those big, brown eyes locked onto Mikey's stare, his face drained pale. Bigfoot *did* understand, everything, and it became clear to Mikey, that *he* was the one who did not understand, anything. And why not believe Wilbert? After all, there was a real, live Bigfoot looking him in the eye.

"You're right," Wilbert softly admitted, pulling Mikey out of the depths in Bigfoot's eyes. "If they're...alive, they're already there." Wilbert turned toward Miss Nellie. "We have to get to Rothstone."

"That we do Willard. But Willy will only take us so far, and we won't make it much farther...anymore."

Wilbert slowly nodded his head while lifting his cap and running his fingers through his sweat soaked hair as he concocted a plan. "Need one volunte..." Andy and Mikey both stepped forward before he could finish. Wilbert chuckled and ignored Mikey as he turned toward Andy.

"You get lost in your own head Andy," Jeff said as he stepped up in line. "I'm by far the best hunter, and I know the woods like the back of my hand."

"This *is* your shed Andy," Miss Nellie interrupted. "You probably should be here, sweetie. Besides, you...may be needed here."

Andy's shoulders slumped as he settled back onto his heels, almost falling back out of the lineup. Wilbert nodded at Jeff, and tilted his head toward Miss Nellie. "If we leave now, we could get there by first light. Give him a full day to get started."

"I'm ready," said Miss Nellie. "Let's go!"

Bigfoot sprang to his feet, smashing his head into a rafter and rattling the shed again.

"Easy, big fellow," Wilbert said with his hands held out. "You stay put. You're too weak yet. Besides, Enki will not travel north yet. He'll wake his sleeping warriors right here in Falling Rocks, 'cause that's where you are."

Bigfoot grumbled, shifting his head from left to right. "Just remember...you cannot take him alone right now, but you can buy us some time to even the odds," Wilbert added.

"Maybe you can teach these young bucks a thing or two." Wilbert turned to address Andy and Mikey, and said, "We'll be back before dark tomorrow. Pay attention, keep him out of sight and feed him. He'll need his strength." Wilbert then planted his finger into Andy's chest. "Don't worry. You'll get your chance to unleash that fire inside."

Andy nodded, and Wilbert turned to unbar the door with Miss Nellie and Jeff falling in behind. Mikey plopped down on his billet of firewood, crossed his legs, and buried his pouting face into his hands with a long sigh. He *was* the only one who actually ever found a Bigfoot, but yet he was ignored like an inept child – like he wasn't even there.

"Wait!" Jeff blurted out. Everybody froze, waiting for him to continue. "Mikey should go. Bigfoot is his entire life. If anyone can find them, he can."

Mikey jumped to his feet and leaped by Jeff's side with his head stretched high and chest puffed out, trying to look bigger, and as capable as Jeff.

"This ain't going to be no walk in the park, boy," Wilbert huffed. "This is real danger...alone, in the wilderness, in the dark! Your little evidence kit will do you no good."

"I can do it," Mikey proclaimed with confidence.

"We'll see," Wilbert grumbled as he slipped between the doors.

\*\*\*

Jeff pulled the door tight against the other, slid the digging bar through the handles, and leaned his forehead against the dry, splintery wood as he listened to Willy fade away toward town. He soon grew tired of pouting though, and he slowly rolled his back against the doors. "So...what are we going to do tonight?" Two seconds later, his own backpack, completely barren inside, sailed across the shed from one big, hairy hand and collided square against his chest, forcing his arms to wrap around the temporarily empty pack.

# Chapter Ten

Falling Rocks was buttoned down for the night as Miss Nellie quietly putted through town. A few peeking curtains and several glowing, upstairs windows showed the only signs of life. Mikey had never seen Falling Rocks so... dead... kind of spooky. He sank back into the seat between Miss Nellie and Wilbert as he watched his dark, sleeping house pass by like it was no longer his home. It was just Wilbert's ridiculous story, toying with his imagination, but when Willy bounced across the threshold between Falling Rocks and Mountain Foot Road, heading toward Rothstone, it was like entering an alien world – a world filled with hidden life, watching and waiting from the shadows.

"Just like old times, huh, Willard," Miss Nellie giggled.

"Sure is," Wilbert grumbled. "The times are old, and we are old."

"Never mind Willard, Mikey. Sometimes he can be a real grouch!"

Mikey puffed out a sound, meant to be taken as a chuckle, but truth is, Mikey's mind was so far away that he didn't even know what was said. "So...why is Enki after our Bigfoot?"

"He's not *our* Bigfoot."

"Oh, Willard! Just answer the boy."

"Why! He's *much* too intelligent to be fooled by such a tall tale."

"I'm sorry," Mikey said, his head very much back in the jeep. "But you have to admit...that's a downright unbelievable story for any normal person to accept."

"How many people told you that about Bigfoot?" Wilbert countered. "And I got news for you kid...you're far from normal."

"Willard!"

"It's alright, Miss Nellie," Mikey assured. "I'm proud to be considered an *abnormal* member of human society. But, I consider myself abnormal because I refuse to be educated into a thoughtless cog of a machine driven by insane egomaniacs."

Wilbert pressed hard against his upper plate, refusing to acknowledge the pleasure that he found in the words rolling from Mikey's tongue. "Okay," he said, sounding as grumpy and irritable as ever. "Now you have to admit, that as you listened to the story, as extravagant as it was, the obscure mysteries of the world piece together perfectly in the story for a more feasible explanation than anything you've ever read – science, or faith."

"I don't know if I can admit that," Mikey answered. "And why haven't I ever read that? That story should be well documented – fact, or fiction."

"That's the whole point! That's the planted seed – the root of *all* our ambitions – the quest for knowledge. Even our own consciences fall as collateral damage in the quest for knowledge. You have felt it, have you not? It keeps Enki's army marching, even in his absence." Wilbert cracked the window and inhaled a deep breath of cool, night air. "And the story is well documented. We just lack the imagination to piece it together. Are the images of Enki's world not painted on the oldest walls throughout the world, and do we not tell countless fairytales of such works? Do we not ask ourselves how our ancient ancestors accomplished what they have, and a second later wonder why their civilizations just disappeared? And *you* know how old the legend of Sasquatch is. Actually you don't, because it precedes the point of knowing. Plus, it all hides within the most published book in history. Pretty well documented, wouldn't you say?"

Wilbert rested his case, falling quiet as he sucked in more crisp, clean air through his nose. The cogs of Mikey's brain were churning so fiercely that he appeared lifeless. But Wilbert had one more question. "Can you think of a more feasible culprit who would have attacked a Sasquatch, and snapped that arm you mended?"

"No," Mikey finally muttered. "But you still haven't answered my question...about Enki's interest in *our friend.*"

Wilbert inhaled another deep breath. "When Enki was banished to the island and his children were punished, he became an enemy of the light. When the war decimated his society, he became an enemy of his brothers. Our *friend* is the only one left who has ever faced the wrath of Enki himself – the rest are with the stars, many by the hand of Enki. A battle-hardened ancient is the only threat to Enki now."

"You mean to tell me that *our friend* is what...two thousand years old?"

"Oh he's much older than that! Our old friend has seen the war first hand, and his hands have been stained ever since...and Enki still sees the bright eyes of old friend glowing in the dark of the storm, when the cries of his children haunt his dreams with guilt. Our friend is first priority. It's personal. That's why Enki struck where he did, and old friend carries the weight of his kin's fate."

"Are you saying, that old friend was...the nephew?" Mikey curiously asked. "The one that bested Enki?"

"Yep."

"And now, the both of you need to get some sleep," Miss Nellie ordered, sitting straight up, both hands sawing the steering wheel, and holding both eyes open so round that it was obvious they wanted to close.

***

Mikey eased back in the seat, and Wilbert cupped his head with his hand and leaned into the side window with his elbow propped up on his knee. An eerie silence overcame the jeep as it hummed up the road, passing the last working farm and casting it into the darkness behind. With a jolt, the road transformed to a narrow, gravel path, and Miss Nellie slowed Willy even more. The forest crowded in on both sides, choking out any moonlight and cloaking the road nearly invisible. Willy's dim headlights cast Enki-shaped shadows behind nearly every tree along the road. Mikey's dry, stinging eyes darted from one side of the road to the other for what seemed like hours. It felt so good to let his eyelids slid down over his wide-open pupils, but they would not stay closed for long – almost like intuition demanded he stay vigilant.

Something glowed in the distance, to the right, through the tall, round trees. Mikey was curious, but not sure he wanted to see. The choice was not his to make though. As if he were strapped to a torturous conveyor belt that slowly fed him to some unfathomable doom, Willy steadily crept him closer and closer, following the road as it veered through the trees to the right. It was though Miss Nellie's eyes were hollow, and someone else was inside looking out, driving the Jeep. She broke free from the grip of the forest and plunged into the glow of long, overgrown, moonlit fields.

Mikey could not remember of an old, abandoned farmstead, but he was glad it was there…maybe…he wasn't really sure. He studied the black windows of the shambled, stone farmhouse as it glided closer and closer, just about to pass, just beyond Wilbert's resting head. It looked as though something was standing in the doorway, up on the collapsed porch, half hidden by the door jam. The doorway was about to disappear behind Wilbert's head. It was Enki! Mikey jerked up from the seatback, frantically searching for the doorway behind Wilbert's head, but when the house emerged in Willy's rear side window, the shadow in the doorway was gone.

"There!" Mikey's finger shot in front of Wilbert's face, pointing out a Sasquatch, standing tall and broad in an open field.

"Easy boy. That's a crabapple. Don't let your imagination get a hold of ya." Wilbert's eyes didn't even come open, but he was right. It was just a crabapple tree.

Mikey eased back in the seat again, a bit embarrassed and nearly exhausted. He needed sleep, just as Miss Nellie had said. His head was clouded with too much corrupting consciousness, and suddenly crowded with the chaos of two hundred millennia of turmoil. He forced his eyes shut. *Let go*, he told himself, as he gripped the seat edge to stop the spinning sensation behind his dark eyelids. Willy purred, steady and easy, and the rubber tires rumbled softly over the gravel as sleep slowly crept into his brain. His relentless will slipped further and further away, paralyzing his body deeper and deeper until he was sure that he was indeed asleep.

And it was good that Mikey had finally succumbed to sleep, because Miss Nellie was driving right into the blackness crouching under the narrow, stone archway that tunneled Mountain Foot Road underneath the toll road super highway that cut through the wilderness and tunneled straight through the mountain. And even Miss Nellie, who had passed through the underpass countless times, day and night, couldn't help but to see the blocks of stone that made the arch, as the teeth of a giant mouth, just waiting to snap shut on hapless victims. Willy's lights illuminated the slope of fill above the arch with ripples of light and shadow, portraying Enki's face, and the black tunnel beyond the stone teeth was nothing less than Enki's gullet.

\*

Mikey awoke when Miss Nellie bounced Willy across the gauntlet of potholes that plagued the wide shoulder along Mountain Foot Road at the intersection of route 313. It was dawn, and dim, but at least Mikey could see with his eyes more than his imagination. The trek from the underpass to daylight was excruciatingly long for Miss Nellie, but only a short nap for Mikey. He yawned and rubbed his eyes, as did Miss Nellie.

"It's your shift, Willard," she mumbled.

Wilbert snorted, but resumed his ghastly snoring as Miss Nellie eased her stiff muscles out of the driver's seat. Mikey elbowed Wilbert, and he shuddered to consciousness.

Wilbert slid from the passenger seat, his hat tilted to the left, and his glasses halfway down his nose like Mikey. Miss Nellie patiently waited as he shuffled out of her way and around the front of the Jeep, stopping by the left front wheel to stretch until his belly peeked out from under his bell of shirts. Miss Nellie snickered, and Mikey turned his eyes away, staring the glow on the horizon across the highway, and realizing that ready or not, his day had come.

*

Route 313 was wide and smooth, and Willy's tires sang across the asphalt as Wilbert made up for lost time. The sun seemed to catapult up above that far eastern horizon and glare through the windshield without warning. Wilbert glanced at his watch through his tinting glasses, and leaned on the accelerator a bit more.

The warm, intensified beams of sunshine that penetrated through the windshield beckoned Mikey's squinting eyes to fold. He was still very anxious, but there was nothing to see but farmland, and sleep was not something he was in excess of. Another small nap never hurt anyone.

Miss Nellie had already been seduced by a deep sleep. Her beehive cushioned her head against the side glass like a shock absorber as the sun glistened across her painted, red lips that still held her smile. She looked so peaceful, and warm, and reassuring. Mikey couldn't help but smile. He turned to Wilbert, to show him Miss Nellie's radiant tranquility. Wilbert sat rigid in the small Jeep seat, with his hands firmly on the steering wheel at ten and two, and his foot steady on the accelerator...but his mouth was hanging open. Maybe he was yawning in the lulling sunshine. Mikey carefully tilted back his head, to look behind those tinted lenses, and Wilbert's eyes were closed! Mikey screamed!

Wilbert's entire body convulsed, like he was shocked back from the dead with a defibrillator. "What the hell's wrong with you, boy!"

Miss Nellie pushed from the side glass with her head and straightened up in her seat like she was a flimsy sheet of paper. She turned toward Wilbert, although the openings between her eyelids were so narrow, it was more of a general direction. "You sleeping behind the wheel again, Willard?" Then her head flopped back against the side glass with a cushioned bounce as Wilbert grumbled something under his breath. Mikey didn't utter another word, but he sure wasn't sleeping. More like vigilantly watching, and rehearsing over and over in his mind how he would grab the wheel with one hand, and lift Wilbert's heavy leg from the accelerator with the other while blindly stomping for the brake with his left leg…if it would have come to that.

\*\*\*

Mikey had family that resided in Poke, and he was familiar with the dozen or so households that warranted the village along route 313. And he also knew exactly where to turn to head up into Rothstone Park. Mikey had attended several family reunions at the park, which was little more than a couple of dilapidated pavilions, a few crudely constructed see-saws, and a nice wading stream, but it was a quiet nook hiding in between civilization and wilderness that was as easily accessible as it was relaxing.

Mikey had made many a fond memories at Rothstone with his cousins, the closest thing he would ever have to brothers besides Andy and Jeff, but a strong anxiety always accompanied Mikey while there. Even just thinking about the park made him somewhat nervous. He could never seem to shake that unfamiliar feeling and completely enjoy the fellowship of his family, like he was on high alert. He would never wade too far out into the stream, but not because of the normal dangers that lurk unseen under the surface of flowing water. It was the other side of the stream that worried Mikey. The heavily forested, western banks of Little Rothstone Creek always seemed mysterious, foreboding…and very diligent.

Just north of Poke, Wilbert turned from route 313 without hesitation and sped up the single lane blacktop road toward Rothstone Park. Willy's speedometer assured that they had greatly slowed, but the narrow, winding road, and Mikey's stomach, convinced him that they were racing toward disaster – one way, or another – just ten short minutes until Mikey would face Wilbert's expectations.

*** 

Suddenly Wilbert turned left onto another gravel lane. Mikey had never noticed the road before, even as they had approached it only moments earlier. There was nothing else around that Mikey knew of. *Where does this go?* he wondered, as the new sound of loose stones grinding under Willy's tires awoke Miss Nellie from her peace. But she remained silently smiling as she patiently allowed the haze of unconsciousness to drift from her head.

The encroaching forest already looked somehow different, and the remains of neglected growth from the previous summer brushed against the side of the Jeep as Wilbert pushed deeper into something beyond normalcy. Bright rods of sunlight angled through the trees, penetrating to the ground, all seemingly spotlighting something up ahead, but always just out of sight.

The narrow lane blindly curved around an outcropping of balancing boulders, and opened up into an oval clearing – sort of a cul-de-sac in the woods. Wilbert putted across the gravel clearing, between two, rubble rock, fire rings filled with ash and charred sticks of wood, and cigarette butts. Colorful crumples of aluminum beer cans lay here and there, but most nested in the brushy perimeter, and sparkled in the sunshine as Willy slowly crossed the opening. Even a clever invention with latex dangled from a spindly tree branch that stretched over into the clearing. This isolated little pocket of the world was far from lonely.

Miss Nellie, not quite ready to speak, sighed her discontent at the sight of the clearing that held so many memories of a younger time.

"Damn kids," Wilbert spouted. "They have to disrespect everything they touch!" Wilbert hesitated, almost like he was waiting for some response. "A boot in the ass is what they need!"

Mikey remained quiet, his head turning from side to side, taking in everything there was to be seen. He really wasn't even listening. And his thoughts were so loud that he could hear nothing else.

Wilbert shook his head as he crept to a stop in front of a mound of dirt, deeply scarred with ATV and motorcycle tracks up over and around both sides.

"Go ahead," Miss Nellie mumbled. "Willy can make it." Wilbert grunted and grumbled several incomprehensible notions as he jerked Willy's shifter into low-four and ground the transmission into first gear. He eased out on the clutch, and Willy lurched forward, crawling up over the dirt road block. Mikey sat perfectly still. The sight of the treetops through the windshield indicated exactly how steep the dirt mound was, but Mikey noticed a break in the canopy not far ahead.

Willy pawed up over and down the other side of the roadblock without incident, and continued down a gentle slope right to the edge of what must have been Little Rothstone Creek. The creek was wide and slow, but muddy from spring rains and snowmelt, and it looked deep too. Wilbert gently rode the brake and eased into the water. Willy slowly waded across with tiny lunges to the left and right as the slimy, rounded rocks rolled under the tires. Mikey's fingers dug into the stiff edge of the vinyl seat as he pushed against the seatback.

"It's okay, sweetie," Miss Nellie assured. "Me and Willard used to wash his ole '38 coupe in here dang near every weekend. It's good and solid."

But it wasn't the unseen creek bed that had Mikey rattled, or the mesmerizing mass of water sliding by. He stared right up the trail that climbed the opposite bank, and there was no denying that fact that he was about to enter the mysterious other side.

\*\*\*

Willy rocked and surged along the rutted and overgrown trail for half an hour while Mikey attempted to convince himself that the forest around him was no different than the other side of the creek, or behind his house for that matter. And really it wasn't, but yet, it was. For the first time in his life he looked to the forest and knew, with absolute certainty, that Bigfoot *was* very real. And for the first time he understood those uneasy feelings about the other side of the creek, but understanding did not make it any less worrisome. There was something new though – something that seemed to push childhood insecurities to the past. All but one, and *not* finding a colony of Sasquatch, which the entire world may or may not have depended on, was a very real failure.

Suddenly everything was still, and they were surrounded. But how…where? Mikey had not been paying attention again, lost in his own private dimension, but he was quite attentive now…after the fact. It was a lonely place, which, at one time, must have been a grand spread, and it definitely whispered of a much more interesting story, maybe even some secrets. Ghostly shambles of cabins defined the boundaries of, the place, and stood vigil among the forest overgrowth of half a century of abandon. The dark, hollow, cabin windows watched the Jeep full of visiting strangers, who sat motionless in the epicenter of the place, in the only sunlight to reach the ground, as though they were trapped under a searchlight. The barely visible remnants of a corral identified the adjoining collapse of weather-beaten lumber as a stable, one wall leaning heavily, but still erect enough to support a dry, crackled harness, and several log grabs hanging from thick, rusty spikes. The spokes of an old wheel peaked out from under a rotting mound of what must have once been a wagon. Actually, there were many mysterious mounds of debris resting across the place – all graves of some past, bustling life.

Willy's frantically revving engine died with the turn of the key, and seized into silent rest. Wilbert and Miss Nellie simultaneously slid from both ends of the seat, planting their feet on solid ground and hobbling away from the Jeep as blood returned to deprived muscles. They stretched and wiggled old bones back into place, and breathed deep the fresh, moist air. Mikey was not so quick to exit the safety of Willy's protection – too much mystery to what was seen already, and way too much still hidden. He eventually followed suit though. But only to the edge of Willy's open door.

Mikey's fingers clamped tightly around the armrest bolted to the inside of the door as he studied the shadows inside the long abandoned structures and visually inspected every lump of forest debris, knowing full well that something was hiding underneath each one. Miss Nellie slipped to the back of the Jeep and stuffed Mikey's backpack with a wool, Army blanket, a full canteen, a flashlight, and a strange, little burlap pouch that was cinched together and tied with a piece of red yarn. Wilbert leaned across Willy's hood and scratched directions onto a scrap piece of paper with a broken pencil. Mikey took it *all* in. It all seemed so heavy, and final, almost like…like being imprisoned on an island in the middle of the ocean. He just wished that they would step out from the shadows, come to Wilbert and Miss Nellie, and his quest would be over, and he would not have to be alone.

Miss Nellie slipped Mikey's pack onto his shoulders as his eyes frantically darted from one corner of the camp to the other, desperate to catch a glimpse of an eight-foot tall hairy beast. Wilbert impatiently glanced at his watch, and Miss Nellie tugged Mikey away from the door.

Wilbert led Mikey and Miss Nellie single file toward the end of a high, long wall of stacked, rotting wood that harbored thousands of dark, hidden recesses throughout the length, and the entire thing was covered with thick, green moss on top. Mikey had seen slab piles hiding in the woods before, and all were a bit spooky, but never of this magnitude. At the end of the pile, a slab still lay across a set of brittle sawhorses, with a bow saw hanging an inch from the ground, and the cut billets of slabs were still mounded up for firewood. It looked as though it could have been used the previous day, other than the clinging moss and rust that proved otherwise.

A wooden trough spanned through the air from the facing ridge slope atop crudely fashioned trusses that promised to collapse at any moment. Mikey listened to the splashing of falling water as he traced the lengthening water trough around the end of the slab pile, and to the huge, wooden, water tank into which the water fell. But the hoop poles had snapped, and the wooden planks of the tank had spread out like a flower from the weight of the water long ago. The falling water collided fiercely with the oak planks below, and water sprayed all around, before gathering atop the mild slope and eroding a path through the thick leaves on the search for lower ground.

And there it set, beside the invisible vision of the water tank, and being peppered with a million drops of water each passing year – a steam locomotive, smack dab in the middle of nowhere. Charles's grandfather operated one just like it every year during the Little Cove Harvest Festival. Mikey could almost hear the steam whistle echoing down the hollow, and could nearly see the smoke billowing from the stack. He envisioned the long, wide belt wobbling ever so slightly as it ferociously spun the mammoth, steel, saw blade, and the deadly, sharp, teeth relentlessly slicing through a colossal log. There must have been at least a dozen burly men, in bib overalls and logger caps, scattered across the locomotive, and on the log deck, and bustling across the ground, all working like mules. But the whistle had not blown, and the rusty, saw blade had not spun in at least half a century. Where did everyone go, and why did they leave all this to just fade away in the woods? "What happened here?"

"This is where it all began, Mikey," Miss Nellie answered.

But Wilbert stopped dead in his tracks. "That's not important," he huffed. "He ain't got the time for that. Already short on daylight."

"He's got time. We can make it to the creek, Willard."

"We're just slowing him down, Nellie," Wilbert sincerely admitted. "He needs to move faster...for his own sake."

Miss Nellie yielded for the second, maybe third time in her life, and Wilbert held out the scrap of paper to interpret his scribbled directions.

"Follow this hollow," he said to Mikey, pointing down through the woods. "Straight down till you come to a stream that crosses in front of you. Follow that stream, upstream, to the west, left. It's a steep canyon, with no easy way out but the way you'll be going in, so stay close the stream, but do not get wet. About two mile up the canyon, on the left, you will come to a small spring tumbling down out of a jagged ravine that's thick with scrub pines. Climb up the ravine. Do not try to climb the sides of the canyon. You can't make it, and you won't find that out until you're half way up, and then you will be in trouble. There is a path up the ravine. It's hidden well, but it's there. Look for flat spots, almost like steps that zigzag from one side to the other. It's a tough climb, and the rocks are loose and slippery, so go easy. But more importantly, do not start up the ravine unless you can see the entire sun above the western tree line. You do not want to be caught in that ravine in the dark. The last three hundred feet or so are the worst, but when you reach the top of the ravine, you're there. It's a huge plateau – almost an inaccessible hidden world. You're on your own from there, but above all else remember this. You will not be able to approach them. They must come to you, or you will never lay eyes on them."

Wilbert slapped the paper into Mikey's hand and said, "You got all that?" Mikey quickly nodded his head, but his eyes said differently. "Move fast, but not recklessly. Keep your head about ya. And if you get into trouble…well, just don't get yourself in trouble." Wilbert pushed Mikey off, much like launching a toy boat across the water.

Mikey briskly walked away, quick stepping around and over logs and brush as he felt for a steady pace, the entire time screaming 'no' inside, like he had just been pushed over a cliff. He tried to slow his frantic breathing, and calm his heart that pounded in his ears. He looked back, and Wilbert and Miss Nellie were holding hands, looking like two worried parents sending their child off into the world alone for the first time. Mikey waved and scurried on down the hollow with his head held high. He could do it. He had to do it. A minute later, he looked back again. Wilbert and Miss Nellie were gone. Mikey's feet wanted to run back, but he held them steady, turned them, and continued on to his destiny one foot in front of the other, more alone than he had ever been before.

# Chapter Eleven

Mikey may have been staring into the eyes of the biggest challenge of his life, but Andy was about to as well. Jeff had run all night to keep Bigfoot in food and water, and returned for the last time at first light with a backpack full of shell corn and wheat. His eyes looked like two skinny slithers of raw meat, and his arms dangled lifelessly, like they could drop right from his slumping shoulders. "Now who's gonna feed me?" he asked as he released his grip and the pack fell to the floor. Bigfoot gently placed his hand on the top of Jeff's head – his entire head. Jeff rolled his meaty eyes up to meet with the thickly matted, arm hair that draped across his face. "What, are, you doing?" And Bigfoot answered by pushing down. Jeff's eyes roll back, and his body collapsed like an accordion into the nest of blankets and fur that lined the Buick hood. "What the...awh...this stuff stinks!" A moment later he closed his eyes and grumbled himself to sleep.

It was Andy's turn, and Jeff did deserve a reward. Andy moved some boxes from the back corner of the shed, and lifted an empty coffee can from a ledge nailed into the framing of the shed. He turned toward the watchful eye of Bigfoot, and put his finger to his lips. Bigfoot returned the gesture. Andy peeled off the lid and transferred a wad of bills from the can to his pocket. It wasn't much. Just a little money that Andy had earned by mowing Mrs. McDowell's yard and shoveling the snow from her driveway. Mrs. McDowell was a lonely widow who had not noticed the progress made over the previous three decades, and she only paid one dollar for a day of work. But Tom had worked for her, so Andy did too.

\*\*\*

Half an hour later, Andy was browsing through Paterson's store, carefully calculating the sum of each sweet addition that he added into his cradling arm. He knew exactly how much money he had tucked away in his pocket, and it was dwindling fast. Andy rounded the corner by the coolers, to grab a couple sodas and be on his way. And there stood Sally. Their eyes locked like magnets, into an awkward but blissful stare, and at that moment, there were no names, no rules, and nothing around them but empty space. There was just the haunting beauty only found in the eyes of someone who is in love with you.

Sally eventually broke free from the intense connection by noticing Andy's armload of snacks. "Sweet tooth, Andy?" she asked, seemingly a bit flustered.

Boiling blood rushed to Andy's face just as fast as the returning consciousness of his appearance shocked his brain. "No!" he exclaimed, a bit louder than expected. "They're for Jeff and...Jeff."

"Jeff and Jeff?"

"Just Jeff. Just...Jeff."

Sally smiled, turned, and blankly stared through the cooler doors. Even in Sunday morning sweats, her profile was perfect, but Andy was losing her. She was about to walk away. *Say something,* he screamed to his brain. "What're you doing here?"

Sally chuckled ever so slightly, shrugged her dainty shoulders, and lifted a gallon of milk. "Mom sent me for milk and bread." Her smile strengthened, and her plump lips curved around her perfect, white teeth to sculpt the cutest little dimples, and her hair was wild and unkempt, like she just crawled out of bed, but the freedom with which her long ringlets of black hair fell across her face and shoulders was breathtaking. Andy hadn't breathed since their eyes met.

"Okay...well...see ya." Sally turned and slowly walked toward the end of the shelves, where she would round the corner, retrieve a loaf of bread, and leave, forever taking the moment with her.

*That's it! That's all I have?* Panic set in as Andy shuffled to the cooler door that enclosed Jeff's soda. *Think! Think! Think!* He ripped open the cooler door. *Beat her to the register! Stay ahead of her!* Andy grabbed one soda from the chute, and balanced it on top of the sweets cradled in his arm, then he grabbed the second bottle, and disaster struck. The first bottle rolled from his arm, and Andy helplessly watched as it collided with the floor, spinning into the metal shelves opposite the cooler. With some grace of luck, the bottle did not shatter on impact, but Andy was frozen in time, desperately hoping that the incident was not as loud as what he had heard.

Sally stepped back around the corner of the shelves, almost like a fox cornering a frightened rabbit, and with milk *and* bread. "You need some help?"

"No," Andy blurted out in embarrassment, but finally his brain managed to spark to life. "Yes...please."

Sally pinched the tied end of the bread bag between the milk jug handle and her thumb, and she knelt down to retrieve the rogue bottle of soda. "Thanks," Andy blurted as he rudely blasted around her and shuffled toward the register.

An avalanche of cakes and candy bars spewed across the checkout counter with the release of Andy's arm, ensuring that no one could approach the register before he was bagged and at the door. Sally would be trapped into more conversation – if he could think of something to say.

The checkout lady rolled her eyes as Andy fumbled his items about, pushing them toward the register. He was ahead of Sally, but she only had two items, and he would be inclined to let her checkout first, unless the cashier got the lead out of her butt and punched just one of his items into the cash register before Sally arrived. But he still had to think of something to say – something witty, and sweet. He couldn't just ask her out. She would say no, and then it would be all over. He had to lure her away from Charles.

The cash register chirped away, seconds before Sally sat the bottle of soda among Andy's things. Andy sort of pointed at the register, his eyes darting back and forth between Sally and the cashier, and then he shrugged his shoulders and held out his hands, as if he wanted her to go first, but it was too late. "Sorry…Sally. And thanks." Sally just smiled and stepped back, waiting patiently for her turn, still holding her milk and bread, while Andy added right along with the register. *Please don't make me take something back,* his thoughts pleaded with fate.

"Five, ninety-five," Peggy, the cashier, lethargically said, and Andy handed over his entire curled up wad of six dollars.

"Jeff's lucky to have a friend that will spend his last dollar on him," Sally said as she finally lifted her milk onto the counter.

"It's not my last dollar!" Andy snapped back. "I owe him…but it's not my last dollar."

"Okay."

Andy scooped up his brown, paper bag of snacks and moved to the door where he waited for Sally. A gentleman would wait and open the door for her. But Peggy and Sally's mom were friends, and they instinctively engaged into lengthy gossip.

*Come on Peggy,* Andy silently brooded. *Your leaving me hanging here…looking stupid!* Suddenly, every snicker and laugh that filled the store was directed at Andy, and he leaned his back into the door and rolled through to the outside.

\*

Andy waited yet longer as he straddled his bike outside. The delay was actually a gift of more time to think of something to say. *You look nice today Sally,* he rehearsed. *No, that's stupid. She's practically in her pajamas.* Then without warning, Sally walked by, seconds from rounding the corner and becoming yet another missed opportunity.

"You look nice today Sally," Andy called out in desperation.

"Cut me some slack Andy. I just crawled out of bed."

"No-no...that's not...what I meant." Andy dropped his head like he had given up any hope of talking to Sally in a smooth, or even a somewhat intelligent, manner. He clenched his grocery bag tight against his ribs, and planted his sneaker onto the foot-pedal, ready to ride away in disappointment.

"Are you sure you can carry that bag while riding your bike?" Sally asked.

It was the sweet voice of Sally, but the brutal words of Charles. "Yea," Andy answered, somewhat expecting to see Charles, and his fancy truck, ready to whisk Sally away. And why shouldn't she go?

"Hey," Sally said, interrupting Andy's self-loathing. "Remember when we used to all get together, and ride our bikes all through town, pretending to be bad-ass bikers?" Andy remembered very well, every day. "And Jeff bolted the extra set of forks to his bike, and made a chopper," she giggled.

"And the bike broke in two going down the hill at the park," Andy added with excitement, as though Sally had cast a spell to release all of his mental blocking fears.

"And Jeff slid across the stones on his belly while the front wheel and handle bars just kept on going," Sally mumbled, laughing like she used to when she was younger. In that moment, Andy was taken back to a much simpler time, when he was happy, and without a care in the world other than the confusion created by an innocent crush on a childhood friend. And then he realized that Sally hadn't laughed like that for a long time. She was just as miserable as he was.

"You know," she softly said, like she was about to confess a secret. "I still get my bike out every once in a while and ride it around in the backyard."

Not quite the confession Andy was hoping for, but he was on a roll. Finally found his groove. His confidence had blasted from rock bottom like Apollo 11, shooting for the moon. "Well, why don't you just go get your bike, and we'll ride around town like the good ole days."

"No...I have to go to church." And the confidence rocket looped and hooked in mid-flight, and crashed right back into rock bottom, Falling Rocks. "I'll tell you what though," Sally added, pulling Andy's eyes up to meet hers, like he was raising his weary head up out of the smoldering rubble of the rocket crash. "Charles will be riding dirt bikes all day anyhow...meet me here, at noon. I'll bring my bike, and you can buy me lunch." And just like that, Sally turned and walked toward home, leaving Andy unsure if he had survived or not.

*

Andy made record time back to the shed, and he scampered through the trap door like his feet were on fire, ripping the brown paper bag along the way and spewing Twinkies and Devil Dogs across the floor. Jeff was still out cold, but Bigfoot was very much awake, and very interested in Andy frantically searching through Jeff's pockets, although his big, fury hand blindly patted the floor in search of the delightful treat that he knew tumbled near. Andy's probing hands eventually ignited a spark of consciousness inside Jeff's head. "What the...what are you doing?" Jeff nearly screamed.

"I need money!" Andy pleaded. "Please tell me you have some cash!"

"For what?"

"I got a date with Sally!"

"You didn't," Jeff moaned.

"I did!" Andy erupted into hysterical laughter, as did Bigfoot, seemingly eager to join Andy's celebration, or maybe he was just excited over the Baby Ruth in his fingers.

"Get Charles to pay! I'm sure he will be along," Jeff sneered.

Andy flung his arm over the side of the Buick hood, groping the floor for the ripped bag of snacks until he felt the stiff but crumpled paper, and he dropped the bag into Jeff's lap. "I spent my last six bucks on you."

"Gee, thanks for the gift," Jeff sarcastically said as he slowly unrolled his arm with a ten between his fingers. "So, when can I expect Charles to go on a rampage?"

"Noon!" Andy snatched the bill, leaped to his feet, and headed for the escape hatch.

"Well where you going now?"

"I gotta take a shower...and shave!" Andy fell to the floor, to crawl back through the hatch, but he hesitated. "By the way, Mikey's mom is looking for him." And Andy disappeared through the hole.

Jeff left out a long sigh as he leaned back and fished through the brown bag of sweets. "What's he think he's gonna shave?" he grumbled to himself, but out loud, until he remembered that he wasn't alone. How could a gigantic, mythical creature be crouching within five feet, in the open, and not be noticed? "*You* need to shave," he said to Bigfoot. "And you definitely need a shower!"

Bigfoot huffed, and carefully eased in closer to the bag, nearly begging for a treat.

"He spent his last six bucks on *me*," Jeff scolded.

But Bigfoot did not relent his subordinate position, or his round, brown eyes that said more than any words. Jeff could resist no longer though, and he tossed a cake that disappeared into Bigfoot's hand. "Nothing but an animal...just like a dog," Jeff innocently insulted.

*If I were an animal, I would rip off your arms and take as I wish.*

Jeff shot to his feet and fell backwards over the edge of the Buick hood, tossing candy bars and pastries into the air like candy thrown from a parade float. The shed rumbled as he thrashed about on the hollow sounding wooden floor, scrambling to hide behind the hood, and knocking the billets of firewood into the stove with a clanging cloud of ash and soot. He heard it, but not with his ears. He didn't think it, but what else could it have been. Jeff peeked over the hood. Bigfoot glanced back, with only one eye, and Jeff was sure that a smile formed on Bigfoot's sugar coated lips as he chewed.

# Chapter Twelve

Three hours later, Andy paced back and forth across Paterson's front porch, rehearsing his conversation leading comments and compliments. It was the same day, and he was the same person as three hours earlier, but this was a new chapter in his life. And it was going to be a good one, he could feel it.

The sun glared from his blocky chin where half a dozen hairs once grew, and his straight, black hair was parted perfectly in the middle and feathered back, down over his ears and falling to his shoulders in the back, all flattened and pinned down with his mom's hairspray. Andy looked down across himself, second-guessing whether or not his favorite pair of old pants, with holes in both knees, complimented his best, blue shirt with the two, useless, black zippers running down across his chest. He wanted to look sharp, but definitely not like an overdressed clown riding an undersized BMX bike.

Sally eventually rolled around the corner a half hour later, ending Andy's consistent and torturous fretting. Her bike was just as Andy remembered, other than the missing basket on the front and the small 'Sally' license plate on the back. And the sparkling tassels that hung from the end of the handgrips were missing too. But Sally seemed a little different as well. As though she were as nervous as Andy, although Andy was not sure if for the same reason.

They shared a locally famous cheeseburger basket on the bench nailed to Paterson's front porch. Sally must have been famished. She finished before Andy. And the longer she waited for Andy to finish, the more restless she became – more than likely anxious to escape the ever vigilant eyes of Falling Rocks. Was it the fear of being spotted on her bike, or spotted with Andy? Charles didn't have to be in town to know everything. Andy was determined to play it cool though. He knew he could never steal her heart unless she left her guard down.

"Would you rather go to your house, and ride in the backyard?" Andy asked.

"No," Sally answered, a little too quickly. "Let's go up to the ball field, and out by your house."

Andy held out his open hand and said, "Where ever you go, I will follow," trying to sound as romantic as a guy on a bicycle in front of Paterson's Country Mart is able.

Sally led Andy up through town, past the post office, and three trips around the ball field before stopping in front of the long neglected swings. "It's just not as fun as I remember, Andy."

"Yea," Andy agreed, even though he would have followed that banana seat to the end of time. "Hey, Sally. You want to see something really cool?"

Sally grinned, but only because she was unsure what was coming next.

"Promise, that you will keep it secret." Now she was curious.

"That depends on what it is, Andy."

But Andy would give no hints. He only said, "Follow me," with a somewhat tantalizing smile as he pedaled away. Sally followed. They cornered left at the post office, and rode out toward the edge of town – out where Andy lived. Sally's enthusiasm soon faded though. She wasn't sure she wanted to go to Andy's house. Andy's family had been the most common subject of gossip throughout Falling Rocks for nearly two years, and Sally had heard all of the stories. Everyone knew about the accident, and the toll it took on the family, but anyone could see in Andy's eyes, at times when he left *his* guard down, that there was something much deeper than anyone's comprehension. It was utter sadness, hidden by shame. Tom was a good son, a promising young man, and the best older brother, but he would only be remembered for one mistake – a mistake cultivated by a condemning society. Andy's mom lived in a medicated world that only hid the truth from her own eyes, and his dad couldn't face the eyes of his dead son lingering in the eyes of his family, both leaving Andy to feel the stares and hear the whispers, alone. It was awkward just occasionally seeing his mom in public, let alone walking into her house. And some even said the whole place felt like death, haunted even. Plus, she had had the un-pleasure of Shorty's company before, although if there, he surely was sleeping off the previous night.

*

But Andy pedaled on by his house, across town limits, even beyond Miss Nellie's, and straight into Plum Hollow. The trees of Plum Hollow cast a shadowed line across the road that cooled the tiny beads of sweat that formed on Sally's forehead, and her throbbing legs welcomed the downhill grade, but Plum Hollow was a local legend in itself. Everything beyond the hollow had fell victim to Charles' family and their mill, and everything behind was old family homesteads and town. Plum Hollow was a place like no other. A privately owned piece of old-world forest that seemed to be protected from the changing world, but by whom remained a mystery. Sally had heard a few of Falling Rock's eldest citizens speak of meaningless old names and events, Charles's grandfather being one, but for some reason, the hollow almost seemed to be taboo. And when young minds are aware of elder secrets, young imaginations begin to churn.

Plum Hollow had its own homestead, or what was left of it. It was a simple, but abandoned, two-story home that provided the imagination with a visible spark, along with a couple of bizarre accidents and several frightening encounters of the recent past. It was eerie enough passing the house in a car, but on a bike was unthinkable, and it was approaching fast.

"Where are you taking me Andy?"

Andy looked back, but didn't reply.

"I'm not going in that house," she declared, with a hint of panic in her voice. Andy slowed, but again, he surprised Sally by passing by what she thought were his intentions.

Andy pulled over to the left, just across the crumbling, concrete bridge, at a narrow path that snaked down into the dark hollow. Sally scooted past the house so fast she almost couldn't stop in time to avoid a collision with Andy. "I'm not going in these woods either," she barked, looking back across the road at the boards that were nailed across the front door and the first floor windows of the shambled house. She was sure that she could see movement behind the wooden barriers, through the dark, narrow slithers in between the boards.

"There's nothing in there but spiders and snakes. And there is nothing in these woods but squirrels," Andy assured her. "Tom used to bring me here all the time. Trust me...I wouldn't let anything happen to you." Sally turned away from the old house, unconvinced that it was harmless, and she looked down the path ahead of Andy, making no effort to hide her distrust. "C'mon...we're almost there."

\*\*\*

Sally followed Andy down the narrow path. The sun was high, over their right shoulders, but the trail under their wheels faded darker and darker, seemingly having no edges between the well-trodden clay and the underbrush that slapped Sally's spokes on one side or the other. About a hundred yards deep, they parked the bikes and continued on foot. Ahead, the trail was too twisted and rough to ride, and none too easy to walk. It pitched up and down, left and right – not like a snake, but more like a skeleton. And the tree roots spread across the path, like fingers, ready to snatch some unsuspecting traveler.

Enough was enough. Sally was about to stop, and de-mand to be escorted home. But a gleaming sign appeared out of the shadows, nailed just above reach in a thick Hemlock tree. It was slightly crooked and painted blue, though greatly faded, and on it was carved, 'Blue Hole'.

Andy turned left at the sign, flashed a grin Sally's way, and blundered through the woods on a trail that may or may not have existed. The last thing Sally wanted to do was separate from the path that would lead her home, alone or not, but something about the sign touched an unrecognized emotion. It was so different, and out of place among the wilderness surrounding it, but yet it belonged to no other place in the world, much like the very first star that appears in the evening sky. Sally followed Andy as he weaved through the tunnels of overhanging boughs of Hemlock, silently prancing across fallen pine needles like a timid deer.

Eventually Andy stopped, and stood motionless, almost reverent. Sally quietly stepped to his side, into the dancing beams of sunshine that fell from a break in the swaying Hemlock canopy. She held out her bare arms, letting the tingling sun caress her skin as she glided through scattered, spring wildflowers, toward the crystal blue pocket of water in the middle of the clearing. There was no stream leading to or from – just a hole in the forest floor. A deep hole, filled with very blue water, and it was warmer than expected. "Andy, this is so cool," Sally whispered as she watched the glistening drops of water fall from the tips of her fingers. "I've never even heard of this place."

"The older folks know of it, but only me and Tom know where it is," Andy replied. "I guess now, it's just you and me."

Sally's eyes gleamed with affection, but pity as well. "Your brother brought you here often?"

"Yeah, it's a great place to take a dip in the summer...and there's a plum tree right over there – sweetest plums you'll ever taste." Andy hesitated in thought as Sally stared into his eyes that were watching something she could not see. "But mostly we just came to get away from everyone else. It was our own private place where we could be ourselves," he confessed. "We used to sit with our feet in the water, and I would listen to Tom's ideas and stories for hours. I mostly had no idea what he was talking about, but he sure did."

Sally's eyes thickened, and her throat tightened. "So what is this...an ore hole, or something?" she asked, trying to distract herself.

"I guess I can pass on Tom's story," Andy chuckled. "Although he swore up and down that it wasn't *his* story." Andy collected the tale that had been filed away in his brain for over two years, but it was his heart that remembered. "Back in the early 1800's, six families settled in Falling Rocks to make a living from settlers heading west over the mountains. They all worked together so their town could provide anything a weary traveler might need – sort of a frontier, travel plaza – and they found success in their endeavors. And finding the most success, the blacksmith had made arrangements for his son to marry the innkeeper's young daughter, the prettiest girl in town. But she was appalled by the crude, apprentice blacksmith, who's father ensured that there would not be another daring enough to court her – except maybe one. He was not of Falling Rocks though. He was a hunter who passed through regularly, always spending a day or two trading meat and furs in town, and he and the innkeeper's daughter fell in love."

That haunting beauty that hid within returned to Sally's eyes, and Andy recognized a long awaited opportunity – as long as he could suppress the bumbling, lovesick fool within himself. He took Sally by the hand, led her to the edge of Blue Hole, and they sat on Tom's crudely fashioned, log bench. "Now, the young hunter was strong and handsome," he continued. "And very wise about the natural world in which he survived, but the innkeeper's daughter knew that her father would never approve. A vagabond hunter was no life for his precious daughter. Plus the innkeeper wanted to align himself with the blacksmith, who had become the most influential citizen of Falling Rocks. But there was another reason the young maiden hid her feelings – the young hunter was native to the land."

Sally squeezed Andy's hand in suspense, and Andy wondered if she even realized that her hand was still in his. "The two young lovers would meet in the afternoon sun at a plum tree grove, hidden in the forest outside of town, and this is that very grove. This place was the only place where they were free to live as their hearts yearned – in the arms of each other, dreaming as one, of a forbidden life together. The innkeeper's daughter pleaded for her brave lover to whisk her away from Falling Rocks, and her lifelong condemnation. But the young Indian was wise beyond his years, and he was as wise of the white man's world as he was the natural world of his own belonging. He knew that his fair-skinned beauty would not fare so well with the life of prey, for he would be hated, and hunted, much like the white man hated and hunted the coyote and wild cat. The foolish girl would not hear though, and she could not see the character in her own blood, or the blood of her kin. And the smitten, young lad of the wild loved her so much, he could not bear to see her unhappy. He vowed to live as a white man, in the white man's world, earn the white man's dollar, and buy the white man's ground that was not the white man's to sell – essentially murdering his very soul just to hold her in his arms."

Sally stared across the blue water of the hole, almost like she could see the young lovers, still embracing on the other side. "But, the blacksmith's son had enjoyed the success of his father too well, and he was no stranger to his own ruthless indulgence. And he kept a very close eye on his entitlement."

All of a sudden Sally brought her eyes back to her own feet, but still staring at something unseen.

"One afternoon he followed his bartered bride into the woods, hanging back just far enough to remain undetected, but not so far as to become lost – for in nature, he was not at home. The apprentice blacksmith lurked in the nearby brush, watching and laying as still as a snake. The hunter entered the grove not a minute later, and the innkeeper's daughter quickly confirmed the suspicions of the apprentice. It was quite clear. The apprentice became mad with rage, but still he lay motionless. Even with his long rifle at his side, he did not have the courage. But he turned his eyes away not once.

"Their time together was always short, and the two lovers returned to town on their separate routes, with the young blacksmith following close behind, just to find his way back. The maiden tended to her duties at the inn, while her secret lover solicited work about town until nightfall. The inn was the only place left, plus the hunter often indulged in a hot meal and a drink before bedding down under the stars on the edge of town.

"But strangely the inn was deserted, other than the innkeeper behind the bar who poured a double shot for the Indian, but did not offer a meal."

Sally's posture straightened, and she turned rigid, as though she expected something to charge out of the foliage.

"Suddenly the blacksmith and his son charged through the doors with their rifles primed, but the hunter already had a bead on the son's chest, stopping them both in their tracks. The innkeeper had his own rifle ready though, and he shoved the cold, hard end of the muzzle into the hunter's back from across the bar."

"The cornered Indian relinquished his rifle to atop the bar, along with his knife at the insistence of the muzzle in his back, but he was not surrendering, just evening his odds. A man controlled by hate would be satisfied with nothing less than spilling blood with his bare hands, and the blacksmiths converged onto the helpless native with punishing brutality. But with the rifles rendered useless by distance, the Indian refused to submit to his punishment. The apprentice soon found himself careening through tables and chairs with a clamorous awakening, and, although any man grappling with the power of a seasoned blacksmith would be outmatched, the burly blacksmith tasted his own blood and battled a second opponent – unconsciousness. And again the Indian felt the touch of the lurking innkeeper's rifle, only this time it was the butt of the rifle, colliding fiercely with the back of his head.

"The innkeeper's daughter had heard the commotion downstairs, and the washbasin in her hands shattered on the floor when the muffled sound eventually painted a picture of the scene below. She rushed down the stairs and into the tavern. She immediately locked onto the twitching, deep, brown eyes of her lover, as his body thrashed at the end of a rope hanging from the rafters. She ran to his side and wrapped her arms around his waist, lifting with every ounce of strength that she could muster as he lurched his head toward the rafter in a desperate attempt to loosen the cinch around his neck. But she just could not lighten the grip of the rope. She cried out in horror and frantically clawed at the knot binding his hands behind his back. All the while, the blacksmith's son laughed madly with revenge. The innkeeper pulled at his daughter, but not before the hunter grasped her fingers for one last touch. They held on to each other tightly as the innkeeper tugged, eventually pulling her fingers from his."

"No," Sally whimpered from the very edge of the bench, squeezing Andy's fingers hard, as if helping the innkeeper's daughter to hold on.

"The innkeeper dragged his kicking and screaming daughter out the front door, cast her away to the dark, and returned to the tavern, bolting the door from the inside. The heartbroken teenager fled town, blindly running through the night forest as briars and branches sliced and bruised her tender flesh. Over and over hidden roots clamped onto her toes and slammed her to the forest floor, but she did not stop until she reached the plum grove. There she waited for her lover...and waited...and waited.

"Within hours, all evidence of the young, Native American's very existence was erased – all but the anguish in a young girl's heart. The innkeeper searched through the night for his daughter, and was joined by a small search party at first light. The blacksmith's son tried to guide the men close to the grove, but failed miserably, and gave up with the setting sun, as did the rest of town. It took the innkeeper a week of scouring the forest by himself to stumble across his daughter, still sitting at the base of a plum tree, still waiting. The innkeeper ran to her, but his arms found his daughter cold, and rigid. She was hunched over her knees with her forehead buried into her folded arms, and she had cried so much that the falling tears had chiseled away at the forest floor, pushing the loose dirt outward, creating a bowl sized hole in the ground, full of her tears. There was no reasonable explanation as to why she had passed from this world, other than she tried to follow her beloved, vagabond hunter. But some say she still waits to this day, still crying, for all these years, and the bowl of tears has grown into Blue Hole."

Sally smiled, and rolled her eyes, and searched through the trees behind her as she sorted through the mash of romantic, foolish, and creepy feelings that would be the first to her tongue. "Wow Andy." She still didn't know what she wanted to say, or even what her opinion was. "That was an incredible story," she finally muttered. "I didn't know you had it in ya."

"They're the words of Tom," Andy answered. "I know them by heart...it's just nice to be able to share them with someone. I'm afraid that I'll forget."

Sally placed her free hand around Andy's that still held her other, and she gently swung her knees into his.

Andy stared intently into her eyes as he leaned on his elbow to steady his quivering knee. "Sally...when I told you that you looked nice this morning...I meant it. I never notice who you're with, or what you're wearing...your hair or your makeup...all I ever see is your eyes. Your eyes are always you...and they take me away to a place I never want to leave."

Sally leaned in, and pressed her soft, warm lips against Andy's. Blood surged through Andy's body, and his knee bounced uncontrollably as he fumbled his lips through the moment he had dreamt about countless times. But Sally jerked away just as fast as it all happened. She stood up, pulling her hand from Andy's, and she stepped back over the log bench. Andy leaped to his feet and followed suit. "What's wrong?"

"Charles," she exclaimed while stepping even farther back.

"Forget Charles," Andy barked. "Sally, I love you!"

"But I love Charles!"

"Why! He is such a jerk...and he treats you like his dog, Sally."

"He does not! He's good to me, and he loves me! You just don't like him Andy, but you don't know him like I do! He can be sweet, and kind...and my dad really likes him."

"Oh," Andy huffed. "So that's why you wanted to get away from your house today. Didn't want daddy to see you with the trash!"

"Nobody thinks you're trash, Andy." Sally leaned in slightly, to look into Andy's drooping eyes. "Look...don't *you* want out of this town?"

"No one wants out of *this* town more than me," Andy sneered. "But I wouldn't sell myself to do it."

Andy stood motionless, his red cheek throbbing, watching Sally storm away through the sagging Hemlocks, and wondering how something so perfect, so right, could go so horribly wrong.

# Chapter Thirteen

Wilbert and Miss Nellie crossed back into the limits of Falling Rocks about an hour before the sun fell behind Rocky Ridge – not that either was remotely aware of the time. Wilbert was behind the wheel, cruising along as steady as a thoughtless machine, and running straight through the stop sign at the town square. Miss Nellie was too tired to even flinch. The daylight trip home had somehow grew much longer than the dark trip up to Rothstone, but they managed to navigate their way right back to Andy's shed.

With Willy announcing their arrival, the shed door eased open as Wilbert and Miss Nellie approached through the grass, and they quietly dragged their feet inside, both collapsing into the Buick hood and stretching their rickety bones out for rest. But even their exhausted demeanor seemed to shine brightly among the somber faces of the shed.

"What's wrong?" asked Wilbert.

"Well...Andy struck out. That's what's wrong with him," Jeff announced.

"Shut up, Jeff."

"Where did you get the corn and wheat?" Wilbert nervously asked Jeff.

"Pap's granary. I'd starve to death before I could gather enough roots and sprouts to fill him up just one time."

"Two of a kind," Miss Nellie chuckled.

"The cops were here with Mikey's mom," Andy spoke up.

Wilbert sat up so fast that his dentures nearly catapulted out between his lips. "You're kidden me! What happened?"

"Nothing...I guess. We met them halfway between the shed and the driveway, and Jeff told them that Mikey left here yesterday afternoon, and went to confront Charles for bullying him. Mikey's mom tore out of the backyard so fast that the cops had to run just to keep up with her."

Wilbert and Miss Nellie blankly stared at Jeff, not quite knowing what to say, or do…or even what to think. Jeff just shrugged his shoulders, and so did Bigfoot.

"Things are about break loose in this sleepy, little town like never before," Wilbert groaned as he leaned back. "I'll stay tonight. The rest of you get home, and get some sleep."

***

Just as everyone—other than Mikey's mom—was thinking of crawling into their warm, safe beds, Mikey was facing the greatest adversity of his young life. Wilbert's instructions were ignored by Mikey's imagination – he really couldn't help it. Every turned over leaf, snapped twig, and every out of place rock along the stream was diligently investigated, and each passing minute slipped by unnoticed. He had yet to reach the ravine that would lead him to the Sasquatch plateau, and the sun was already mixing with the western tree line. He would have to spend the night in the canyon.

Mikey separated his eyes from the banks of the stream by hugging the steep sides of the canyon, where he found a heavily used game trail. He hustled his pace toward the setting sun, briefly scanning over countless animal tracks underfoot and watching for a suitable nook to spend the night. A quick glance was all that Mikey needed to identify any print in the mud, and most on the trail were deer – more than likely traveling from the isolated highlands to the fields of wheat and corn below, under the cover of darkness – but a rather large coyote track stopped Mikey in the prints of his own shoes. If deer regularly traveled the canyon, then predators were never far behind, or maybe even already laying in ambush. Suddenly, a new urgency of exiting the canyon surfaced to the top of Mikey's thoughts. There was no way he was camping overnight in the valley of predatory death, but with his eyes now pasted on every shadow lurking about the canyon, his gate reduced to a near crawl. *Maybe I should go back to the sawmill camp,* he pondered. But whatever influenced dozens of roughneck loggers to walk away from their livelihood and never look back, was much more terrifying than any coyote.

Mikey carried his thoughts westward, up the narrowing canyon, and deeper into the den of ill fate. There was no way but forward, and up – too late to make it back to the camp before dark anyhow. *Could I have walked right past the ravine,* he asked himself. It was quite possible. Even at fourteen, Mikey was well aware that he was mostly lost in his own thought, and oblivious to the real world around him, even though he often claimed the very same of nearly everyone else.

Mikey's neck throbbed with the poundings of his heart, and his breaths were as shallow and frantic as his logic. Every aching step pulled him further away from having any favorable options, and his small fragment of optimism dimmed bleak right along with the fading brightness of the sun. He should have turned back. At least he could have gathered an axe, or something for defense, at the sawmill. But then he heard a sound. It was faint and muffled, and sporadic, like something shuffling through the leaves – a squirrel maybe. No – tumbling water. It had to be the ravine. Mikey hastily scurried up the game trail toward the sound.

The ravine was such a narrow cleft cut into the side of the ridge that it was nearly impossible to see until Mikey was but a stone throw away. A little late, but he had found it, and it didn't look all that treacherous. It was steep and slick, no doubt, but it could be easily scaled, and there were plenty of spindly pines to assist the climb, or break a fall. And it appeared to be only a hundred or so yards up to where the ridgeline met the sky, which had to be the top, or at the very least a lesser grade. Mikey looked to the western horizon. The sun had fallen below the treetops, and was quickly disappearing behind solid earth, but he figured that he still had near an hour before his vision would be hindered by the night.

*

Mikey started up the ravine, one carefully planted foot at a time, and with a steady hand on a sticky pine when possible. Almost immediately the cool air brushed across his face and the light dimmed under the canopy of pines that curiously clung to the sculpted, rocky crevice. Mikey pushed hard, realizing right from the start that the climb would take much longer than anticipated, but he could only climb as fast as his eyes allowed. There was only one path to find, and finding it wasn't so obvious as it cut back and forth from one side of the tumbling spring water to the other. Wilbert was right though. There were flat spots, but not quite like steps – more like connecting the dots…dots that drew no picture at all.

Once submerged under the cragged rims of the ravine, high up on the slope of the ridge, Mikey could no longer see the canyon below that he was so anxious to leave, or the break in the slope above that he was so anxious to reach. The ravine was like its own little world, in its own time, and time was quickly dwindling. Mikey pushed harder – a little too hard. The soggy, dead pine needles under his left foot broke free from the rock underneath and slid down the slope like an avalanche, caring Mikey's foot on top, and at that very moment, all of Mikey balanced on that left foot. He fell forward onto his hands, and dug his right foot in to the pine needles beside his left, but his slip had gained too much momentum, and he careened down the slope on all fours. The damp rock under the needles was slick, but still abrasive enough to slice and rip at the skin as Mikey's palms slid across the bare rock. He could already feel an impending collision with a tree, and he pulled his feet together as best as he could. But in Mikey's total vulnerability, he stumbled onto some luck, and his feet found the flat spot he had just climbed from. His feet bit into the natural step, catapulting the rest of him vertical as he frantically flapped his arms like a bird taking flight in a desperate attempt to stop his upper body from continuing with its downhill drive...head first.

Mikey's arms slowly wound to a halt as he collected his balance and stepped from the edge of the flat spot. His stomach churned when he looked down across the slope from his step, which was nothing more than a boulder jutting out from the cliff side. The trail cut sharply to the other side of the ravine from where he was standing, and there would have been at least a six-foot free fall if he had tumbled over the edge, with a rough, steep roll at the bottom. He came terribly close to nothing less than a broken bone. He would have to be more careful – fast approaching darkness or not.

Suddenly a commotion barreled down the ravine and pierced right into Mikey's spine with a heart stopping shock. He wheeled around, and locked onto the panicked eyes of a deer as all four hooves skid down the very same path that Mikey had just scraped up. He lunged to the left, away from the path, but the deer was already there. The animal's brisket collided with Mikey's hip, and the impact tossed him through the air like a rag doll. Air gushed from his lungs as he slammed into the hard, banking ground and log-rolled somewhat sideways across the slope, seeking the gully of the ravine as the water had for countless centuries. Mikey's body brutally folded around a spindly pine, flailing his eyes open to catch two snow white tails bounding into the dark pines below.

It took a minute or so, but Mikey eventually regained sensibility and caught his breath, and he rolled out from around the pine tree that may have just saved his life. He very cautiously crossed the plummeting spring water and clawed his way up a short, but very steep, bank to a stretch of the invisible path that he had passed over nearly twenty minutes earlier. Reluctantly, he pushed from his hands and knees and stood erect, balanced on two feet again. His hips and ribs throbbed, and his feet and hands burned, but he heaved his weary legs back up the path – this time very slow and diligent. He would climb until he could no more, and then he would huddle up in Miss Nellie's wool blanket for the night. What else could he do?

Not far above where Mikey had slipped, he broke over the knuckle that he had seen from the canyon below, when he still entertained an option. It wasn't the top though. It was merely a narrow bench, before a near vertical ascent to the top, and it was the last thing the night would allow him to see. He surveyed the bench for a comfortable spot that may offer a bit of protection from the sting of night. Mikey was exhausted, and soaked with sweat, and the moment he stopped climbing, a chill set in to the bone. But the bench had been cupped out by ages of falling water, which pooled wide across the bench before continuing on with its endless journey, and all the soil had been washed away to the lower slopes, leaving an alien landscape of smoothly washed bed-rock. Only one scrawny pine survived in the alpine pocket, and it would have to do.

*

Mikey relished in the relief of slipping his pack from his raw shoulders, but his moment of content quickly diminished as cloud cover slowly rolled across the pool of spring water and extinguished the emerging stars that gleamed on the surface. Mikey fished Miss Nellie's heavy, long, metal flashlight from his pack, and gripped it tightly in his fingers as he wrapped himself in the wool Army blanket. He nestled back into the sparse pine boughs and illuminated his perimeter with the flashlight one last time before tucking the light under the blanket next to his body. Hundreds of thoughts and worries swirled about inside of Mikey's skull, but the wool blanket warmed his weary muscles and his tormented consciousness exhausted itself still, and his eye lids sagged with a heaviness never before felt.

Mikey quickly slipped into the distorted realm between real and dream. The magical arms of fantasy wrapped tightly around his brain and relentlessly strangled the unrelenting fear and doubt from his consciousness, and slowly the ravine started to feel blissfully safe. But then a sound fell from the slope above, and slapped Mikey in the face. His eyes jerked wide open to a wall of black. He couldn't even see the pooled water in front of him anymore. Sound was the only thing that existed, and Mikey sat perfectly motionless, intently trying to filter the babbling spring from the sound above that he may or may not have heard. It was probably just a fuddle of moving water that his imagination cleverly misidentified to relinquish the grip of dream.

Mikey convinced his muscles to relax, and breathed in easy and long. It took more effort to keep the noise of his own body quiet enough to hear everything else, than actually climbing the ravine. He re-closed his eyes, as determined to fall asleep as any night in his own bed when his obsessive mind refused to relinquish control. Mikey's ears were still primed though, and easily picked up a pebble bouncing and rolling toward him from the ravine above. The flashlight poked through the edges of the bundle of wool like a spear thrust, but Mikey was too afraid to turn it on. A frantically sweeping beam of light would not help him hide in an endless block of black.

There was no doubt that something forced a small rock to tumble down the ravine, but it was probably just the eroding water, chiseling another piece of the ridge away. *Probably happens ten times a day,* Mikey silently told himself. But there was no mistaking the sound of feet walking through the pool of water on the opposite bank.

Mikey faced the wading feet with the lens of the flashlight, and every blood vessel in his body constricted, locking him as solid as the rock that surrounded him. Every sound became as his own thoughts, like the babbling spring water stilled into a silent puddle, and there were at least two more, of whatever they were, climbing down to the rocky niche. But how did Mikey let the first one come right in on him, unnoticed? Not that it mattered. He would have sit still and left it come, hoping that it passed on through, just as he was then. There was nowhere to run, would be no fighting any-thing off. There was only the slightest kiss of the wind on his face, and Mikey's only hope was to be as unnoticed as the pine that he leaned against.

The invisible feet slowed enough in the pool to lap ex-actly three tongues of spring water before stepping back up onto dry rock. *Probably more deer,* Mikey...hoped, as he listened to dismembered drops of water escaping the intrud-er's legs and fleeing back to the pool to which they be-longed. The feet padded on across the water polished rock, nearly impossible to hear, to the break of the bench. And down over it went. The lurching, shock absorbing steps down the grade was easily heard, fading away into the ra-vine below. Mikey very slowly left his near uncontrollable intensity slip from between his parted lips. He had had seri-ous doubt that he would have remained undetected, but there were more coming.

Mikey pulled in the cool, moist air of the ravine and sealed his lips again, just as the next...deer, trudged into the pool of water. It took two laps from the quenching spring and trotted from the water and over the break of the bench as the third entered the pool. The third took two laps as well and padded to that imaginary line of safety that could only be seen with memory in the darkness. Mikey listened harder than anything he had ever done in his entire life, but he did not hear the third deer cross that threshold. It was so quiet, and so black. Mikey peered into the darkness, but he couldn't even see the rims of his glasses. He couldn't see anything, hear anything, or even smell anything. *It had to already go over the edge*, he reasoned against his instinct. But instinct strongly argued that something was there, in the dark.

Mikey carefully eased his free hand out from the wool blanket, and very slowly pushed his trembling fingers out into the blind void. He could feel the black wrapping around each finger, swallowing his tender hand with cool bitterness, and sliding down his arm like he was reaching into a wall of water...but he could feel nothing else.

Mikey carefully tucked everything back into his blanket, all but the bulb of the flashlight, and he closed his eyes. What did it matter? The scenery was the same with his eyes open or closed. And whether a deer, or a Sasquatch, was there with him, what else could he do? But his instinct refused to let his eyes relax...or maybe it was just paranoia. Mikey clicked on the flashlight, and there was a coyote with its nose two inches from his left sneaker. Mikey's right leg instinctively, spontaneously, uncrossed with his left and kicked the coyote in the head. The coyote yelped and leaped backwards. Mikey held the beam of light firm on the coyote as it almost seemed to float unnaturally through the thick, black night, and land, crouched on all four paws, it's claws scraping across the barren rock. Mikey about half expected it to run away, or maybe he just wrapped his arms around the only thing he had – hope – but the beast seemed to be more agitated than hurt or frightened.

The coyote lunged for Mikey's exposed foot, its teeth scraping across the top of Mikey's sneaker as he jerked his leg back in reaction. The Velcro straps of the sneaker ripped loose, and the coyote's teeth pierced into the spongy, canvass strap as its jaw clamped down with bone crushing force. Mikey pulled away, but the coyote lurched backward with amazing strength, jerking him right out of his blanket. Mikey was incredibly focused on his situation, and even as the snarling coyote dragged him across the rocks with relentless, backward thrusts, he still held the blinding light dead on the coyote's determined eyes. Mikey cried out, but the coyote did not flinch at the sound of a human – it only jerked harder and faster, and growled louder. Mikey helplessly lurched across the rock, stomping the heel of his left sneaker into the rock and scraping his fingernails away as the tips of his fingers drug across stone floor. Mikey cried out again in hopeless frustration, but his adrenaline fueled brain refused to give in. He lifted his skidding left foot from the rock, and kicked the coyote in the nose as hard as he could. The coyote hesitated, and huffed air and mucus from its nostrils. Mikey kicked again, and again, until the beast released its vice-like jaw.

The coyote retreated to the edge of the bench, shaking its snout feverishly, and Mikey scuffled backwards across the rock on his butt, back to the safety of his wool blanket, not once allowing his beam of light leave the coyote. Mikey's trembling knees pushed his body upright against the wobbly pine, and he waited for the coyote to leap from the reaches of the flashlight and over the edge. But the coyote just stood there with its head down, and its ears back, growling, as though it were sizing up prey. Mikey held his blanket out in front of him with his arms stretched wide, lowered the light just enough to illuminate himself and still see the coyote, and rocked back and forth in a feeble attempt to make himself look much larger. The coyote was not the least bit intimidated, and began pacing a small circle, eerily yipping and howling its high-pitched screams.

The previous two coyotes howled from the ravine below, their yipping and barking charging closer as they ascended back up the ravine toward the bench. Within seconds, even before Mikey could slip into full-blown panic, all three were standing in the oval of light, and howling. About four more howled from the opposite ridge, clear across the big canyon. Mikey's arms folded inward and his blanket drooped in front of him, bunching over his feet as something of his own, weak howl of terror escaped from within. All three coyotes crept closer, fanning out with every step. The near vertical walls at Mikey's back denied even the slightest hope of escape. At least it would be quick, with three of them.

\*

Mikey's body was small, and weak, but his stubborn will was as strong as an enraged bull. He sprinted with his light and blanket to the edge of the water and leaped right into the middle of the pool. Mikey gasped for breath as the icy spring water bit into his legs up to mid-thigh, but the water would steal from the coyotes agility, giving hope...and maybe even an advantage. The coyotes immediately encircled the pool, recognizing the entrapment. But a trapped quarry is a fierce quarry.

Mikey's light flipped from side to side, and front to back, as the three coyotes bounded in and out of the pool, testing the waters for the attack. "Get outta here!" Mikey demonically roared as some suppressed, ten thousand year-old instinct blasted free from somewhere deep in his gullet. The coyotes were undaunted though, and they tightened the noose with a near mechanical frenzy. Mikey wrapped a corner of the heavy, water soaked, wool blanket around his arm and whipped it through the air toward the coyote at his left with all of his quickly expending adrenaline. The blanket slapped the water hard and loud, and stopped the coyote from wading any closer, for the moment. The light darted around the pool again as Mikey frantically searched for the other two coyotes, and with a roar much stronger than his strength, he wailed the blanket at the coyote to his right. The coyotes savagely snarled and howled, almost challenging Mikey's barbaric, guttural screams – or maybe frightening their prey into a mistake.

Mikey waded through the water dragging the wet wool behind, screaming at the coyotes with the blinding flashlight in their eyes. The more Mikey moved, the more energy the nearly submerged coyotes burned pawing after him through the cold water. If only he could hold out longer than a coyote's determination. But the coyote to the left denied any strategy and lunged at Mikey, viscously snapping and barking. Mikey heaved his blanket from the surface and flipped it at the coyote, but he was spent, and the momentum of the heavy blanket pulled him over center. Mikey plunged headlong into the deafening, black dimension of icy spring water.

Mikey gasped for air in dark and deadly silence as his heart feverishly pumped blood to his bewildered brain. His frigid core was shocked and numb, and he wasn't even sure if he was above or below the surface of the water, let alone on his feet. Mikey vigorously shook the wet flashlight, desperate to see, but the bulb only flashed twice. He tried to hear anything other his own wheezing, but could only hear the confusion of his own senses. And then he felt the sharp sting of canine fangs clamping onto the back of his thigh. All ferocity abandoned Mikey's voice as he cried out what he was sure would be his last sound on Earth. He heard, what had to be his own cry, echoing in the ravine above as a mindless reflex slammed the useless flashlight down on top of the biting coyote's skull. The coyote yelped and released its bite, and the flashlight came on, as bright as ever. Mikey fumbled to keep his feet under him as he plunged through the water, away from the bite of death, swinging the beam of light around like it was a sword. But the light found nothing, other than one disoriented coyote pulling itself from the water and staggering over the edge of the bench.

Mikey stood in the water, sweeping his light across the barren rocks, unconvinced that he was alone again. Why did the coyotes leave him? They had him. Maybe that shrill cry from above, his echo, scared them away. Mikey pulled his wool blanket from the bottom of the pool and trudged out of the icy water, following the beam of light that shined where instinct wished to see. Suddenly he remembered the pain of a coyote's bite. And then the cold dug in with its claws. He shivered uncontrollably. The trauma of the attack doused with the chill of spring water would have shaken even a veteran outdoorsman to pieces, and Mikey was in serious trouble.

Mikey stumbled back to his little pine, wrapped himself in the heavy, wet blanket, and collapsed against the young, pine butt, remembering how Jeff had taught him to wade in the cold creeks to fish, with nothing but sneakers. He tried with what little strength he had left to still his convulsing body as he waited patiently for the warmth to come, but it never did. He had to move – get the blood pumping – and he had to do it soon, while his blood could still pump. Plus, every prowling predator from Mikey to Rothstone Park would be coming, with the taste of his blood in their noses. He had to climb.

Mikey's skin felt as if it were tearing apart as he wrung out all the excess water from the blanket and shoved it back into his pack. He had never felt such painful despair. All he wanted to do was lay down and fall asleep – death seemed almost comforting. But he could not be remembered by his failure. He had to prove himself to those who had no faith in him. Mikey rallied his determination, pushed his glasses up his nose, and freed the suppressed tears from his eyes as he pushed his arms through the shoulder straps of his pack. He was ready to face his next challenge.

***

Mikey clung to the rocky slope above the pool like a blue-tailed lizard, searching for the broken and treacherous path with his flashlight – at least the beam of light did not allow him to see the full scope of his precarious position. His progress was very slow, and exhausting, but the wound on the back of his thigh started to burn sharply with his rising core temperature. He was beating hypothermia if nothing else.

The path led Mikey into a water-chiseled corner with nowhere to go but straight up several feet to another rock and cut back across the ravine. Woodland creatures could have easily leaped up onto the rock to make the turn, but Mikey was far from that feat on a good day. He would have to pull himself up. He reluctantly released his flashlight to the top of the rock, pressed both palms and all of his fingertips to the gritty platform, and jumped as high as he could. His knees brutally slammed into the side of the rock, and he pulled with all of his strength, but it wasn't lofting him to the top. Mikey refused to give up. He pawed at the rock with his sneakers, hoping for just enough bite to lighten the load just enough for his arms to pull his weight. But all of his determination was just burning strength, and his feet fell back to the rock below. Two more times he tried – each time more feeble than the last.

Mikey flopped his rubbery arm across the top of the rock, wrapped his aching fingers around his flashlight, and folded into the crevice where he stood. His pounding heart felt like a fist punching into his bite wound, and the right knee of his pants was shredded and soaked with more blood, but he was too tired to care. The second he sat down and leaned back against the rock, sleep began luring him into a warm, safe fantasy again. The flashlight rested in Mikey's lap, still clenched tightly in his fingers, and still on. His eyes traced out the beam of light, for no particular reason, and there, in the oval of sight, was a dead pine tree that had fallen long ago from somewhere above. The tree had shattered into many pieces upon impact – pieces small enough to handle, but just maybe long enough to span the height of the rock.

Mikey meticulously slid back down the path on his butt until he reached the fallen tree, and he quickly latched a hold of the most suitable piece, or at least the closest one. He pushed backwards with his legs, still on his butt, and then reached forward, down to his feet, and heaved the log up his chest. Over and over the heaved the log back up the path, and each time the snagged log slid back down half the distance he had just pulled it up. His legs felt as though they were on fire, and his arms and back felt like a thousand needles were piercing his skin. But Mikey pushed and pulled, inch by exasperating inch, until he reached the step and collapsed to his back with the pine log resting on his chest.

Mikey so wanted to rest, if only for a minute, but he couldn't. Somehow, he just knew that he would never open his eyes again. And his muscles revolted against his mind, so fiercely that tears flooded his eyes. But there was nothing else he could do but go on. He leaned the log against the boulder and kicked it, to make sure it would hold his weight. The log seemed sturdy and strong, and the snags along the sides would provide steps, somewhat like a ladder. Mikey stepped up onto a snag and bounced a few times, to double check his distracted assessment, and the jagged end of the log settled into a flat, firm anchor.

Convinced that the makeshift ladder would not send him tumbling down the ravine, Mikey lay his flashlight up on top of the boulder again, and he took another step higher, to the next snag. The next step would be a knee on top of the boulder, and he would have made it – just one more step.

Mikey cupped his sore hands on the rock, digging in his mutilated finger tips for that last pull, but he bumped the flashlight, and it started to roll. "No," he cried as he grasped for the light, but it disappeared over the edge. Mikey watched in terror from his bridled perch as the light tumbled down the slope and clattered into a destructive wedge between two small crags below.

The light flickered several times, but miraculously still shined bright, although it glared straight down the ravine. Mikey blindly fumbled his way down the log, and scooted back down the path on his butt, feeling his way through the dark with his hands and feet. He needed that light above all else, and was extremely lucky that it wedged where it did, just below the path. Mikey carefully rolled onto his stomach and reached over the edge. He touched the flashlight with the tips of his fingers, but could not grasp it. He shifted his body over the edge just a little more, and he reached out again. And the stone under his chest kicked out. Over he went, tumbling and falling, ricocheting off of boulders and rolling down the ravine like the spring water.

\*

Mikey slowly peeled open his eyes, unsure if he was regaining consciousness, or losing it. His skull was ringing like a church bell, and even the black night was spinning round and round. The precarious flashlight glared down from far above, but there were two. One was sharp and crisp, the other much larger, and blurry. Mikey reached for his face, to search for the missing half of his glasses, but he could not feel his arm move, or see his hand. There were just the two lights, and the darkness, and nothing else.

Suddenly, the lights appeared to raise from the their steady place – or maybe Mikey was sinking deeper into dementia – but when the two sharp gleams zipped away like insects, leaving behind two beams of light that blended into one wide beam, and that beam chaotically swept across the ravine illuminating every rock and every pine within reach, it was clear that it was all too real. And then, as quickly as the lights became animated, they stilled, shinning on Mikey again, this time more harshly, as though they were focus directly into his eyes. Mikey could see his eye lids blinking, and squinting in the glare. And then the lights went out.

# Chapter Fourteen

As Mikey lay in dire straits, somewhere in the dark wilderness, Andy lay in his bed, staring into his own darkness. He could almost smell Sally's hair, and see her eyes. He could still feel her soft lips – he would never be the same. And he would never forgive himself for screwing it up. Tom's story worked like a charm, just as he had boasted it would, and Andy blew it in the end. Sally would never talk to him again. But that was more the judgment of Falling Rocks, than Andy's words, even if *he* was the *only* one who thought so.

*

Suddenly Andy was walking through Falling Rocks, right up the middle of the street, and every single person in town lined both sides of the road. Andy could feel their shameful stares, until his eyes met theirs, and they slowly looked away. Strangers emerged from in between the houses as Andy walked by, and the citizens of Falling Rocks parted their shoulder-to-shoulder wall and invited the strangers to join in the judicial lines.

Andy walked faster, and faster, but the people did not fall behind any quicker. He broke into a run, as fast as he could, until he reached the square. The people were circled around the intersection in an impenetrable fence of human bodies. There was nowhere to run to, except back the way he had come. But the crowd had filled in behind him, blocking the entire street, and they were tightening in. Something big was right in the middle of the four-way intersection. Andy refused to look at it – he didn't know why, or even what it was, but he couldn't look.

A voice rose above the bustle of the crowd. Andy couldn't understand the words, but it was the voice of Charles, plain as day. Andy reluctantly turned his head toward the tormenting voice. Charles was walking the edge of a high platform, working the crowds of people into a clamorous frenzy with his arrogant demeanor. Five ropes hung from the gallows above the platform – four of which were cinched around the necks of four hooded figures. Reverend Dan silently read the last rights to each of the four as Shorty removed their hoods one by one with a devious grin across his face. The first hood revealed Bigfoot, who could have easily snapped the ropes that bound his hands and neck, and killed his executioners with a single swipe, but he stood silent and motionless.

The next was Andy's mom. She looked so sad, and she stared straight ahead, motionless...and so sad. Shorty groped her with his filthy hands and kissed her on the cheek as Reverend Dan prayed for her soul. She smiled and gazed into Shorty's eyes. How could she worship the man who was killing her?

The last two hoods uncovered blank, featureless faces. Andy moved in closer, desperate to see the faces of Tom and his dad, but their faces remained blurry orbs of white. Andy lowered his head away from the gallows, ashamed, and his eyes found Sally in the crowd, standing alongside the stairs that stepped up to the condemned, standing beside her glaring father. Sally did not look away like all the others, but the love in her eyes had been replaced by hatred – a hatred that burned in Andy's chest. Slowly she lifted her head toward the gallows, and moved her eyes to the empty noose, then back to Andy. He backed away in horror as the crowd fell silent. Charles stood firm with his hand on one of two, long levers, one of which would secretly plunge the doomed victims to the end of their ropes. He intently glared at Andy, and nodded toward the empty rope. Shorty and Reverend Dan waited by the vacant noose, staring at Andy. Everybody was watching Andy, and waiting for him to take his place. He cautiously backed away, and merged into the surrounding crowd until he was invisible, even to himself. Andy made his choice, and all eyes returned to the gallows.

Shorty eagerly took his place at the other lever, beside his malicious nephew, as Reverend Dan calmly strolled to a large, black bell mounted on the opposite corner of the gallows. Reverend Dan heaved on the wheel that tilted the bell, and the rocking motion began that would eventually cause the free hanging iron ball to collide with the tempered shell.

Andy flinched as the bell rang out like a cannon for the first time. On the twenty- ninth ring, Charles and Shorty would pull their levers and carry out the sentence imposed on Andy's family by their friends and neighbors of Falling Rocks. Reverend Dan meshed into the rhythm of the swinging bell and heaved on the wheel with every stroke to keep the momentum ringing. Andy closed his eyes, refusing to count the rings, and every ring stopped his frantically pounding heart as he listened for that sound – that sound that he had never before heard with his ears, but could hear vividly with his imagination. The bell rang...and it rang. Over...and over...Andy's alarm clock rang.

*

Andy sat on the very edge of his bed, slapping at his alarm clock, desperate to quiet it before the twenty-ninth ring. He looked around for the gallows, and the crowds, but saw only his darkened room, and the morning light glowing through the window drapery. Andy shuffled over to the window and looked down to the shed in the backyard. All appeared normal, not that he could really tell. He rubbed his eyes, remembering the previous sleepless night, and what details he could recollect about his bizarre dream. His alarm clock rang out again, and Andy nearly jumped out of his skin. And he was late for school.

*Andy made it out the front door just in time to catch the school bus, but the same could not be said for Mikey. He and his little sister were never late, so the bus driver waited, and tooted the horn. No one emerged from the house. Andy nearly spoke out, but caught his mistake before it left his tongue, and he couldn't speak for Mikey's sister. Where was she? Several seconds later, the driver double- tapped the horn again, and Mikey's aunt scurried out from the house, onto the front porch, vigorously motioning the bus on, as if the horn was disrupting the balance of the universe. It looked as though she had been crying. And why was she even there, on a Monday morning. For the first time since Mikey had left on his mission, Andy was not thinking about Sally.

\*\*\*

Jeff was sitting on the concrete curb, leaning against the brick wall with his eyes closed when Andy arrived at school. Jeff rode a different bus that traveled down Mountain Foot Road and picked up all of the kids on the north end of Falling Rocks, but he always met up with Andy and Mikey outside of the school entrance every morning. But that Monday morning, there would be only two, and others were paying attention.

Charles still had his dirt bike strapped to the back of his truck from the day before, and a crowd had massed around his spectacle, which was nothing unusual. The parking lot was no *underclassman's* land, and Charles was always the last to leave it, after the tardy bell – a display of superiority. But that morning was different. Andy didn't even have time to sicken of seeing the show before Charles parted the crowd and marched straight for him and Jeff.

Jeff's eyes flipped open, like he could sense the storm coming from across the parking lot. Sally followed behind Charles, and the rest fanned out behind her like a flock of migrating geese. "Let's go," Jeff said as he jumped to his feet.

"No," Andy sternly replied.

Jeff moaned something under his breath about keeping a low profile, and then something about his mother's hours at the mill.

"I have a feeling that this is of *your* making," Andy replied, as if he knew exactly what Jeff had said.

Jeff quieted his grumbles, and by Andy's side, he watched the snobbish hoard approaching as though they were the gods of Little Cove. Time seemed to slow as Charles swaggered across the lot, with his scowl chiseled onto his face, and his fists clenched. Even the district super-intendent stopped his car, and peered out over the steering wheel as Charles boldly marched in front of his morning commute.

Unexpectedly, Sally stepped out of line, her wild locks wavering behind like the mane of a raging, black stallion, and she stormed up to the side of Charles. Charles looked over, throwing a scolding glare her way, but she ignored him, and stared straight at Andy. She was untouchable. Sally took Charles by the hand and leaned into him, caressing his arm. Charles smiled and refocused his glares at Andy and Jeff, crumbling to the power of the true…goddess. But Sally still stared directly into Andy's eyes, as if proving that she was no one's pretty, little puppet, as well as slapping Andy in the face again – the hardest way she knew.

Slow motion or not, Charles relentlessly tightened in on the two, cornered sophomores. "Where's Mikey?" he de-manded as his cronies slowed into a motionless and dead silent formation behind him.

"You tell us," Jeff blurted out, as if he were willing to play out any immorality to maintain his own innocence.

"How should I know," Charles barked. "Big mistake sending the cops my way…big mistake."

"I don't know what you're talking about," Jeff coolly replied.

With impeccable timing, a state police cruiser rolled in-to the school parking lot. The student formation behind Charles broke apart and funneled through the school's en-trance doors as the cruiser circled near. Charles sent Sally inside with a wave of his arm, almost like flipping a bug from his hand with the flick of his wrist, and just like that, Sally had been cast back down to earth with the rest of the commoners. She quickly glanced Andy's way, and of course he was watching, probably reveling in her misfortune. She didn't want to obey Charles's command, but yet she didn't want to just stand there, looking needy.

Sally stormed by the broad, propped-open, wooden doors, through the tunnel-like entrance, and into the halls of Little Cove. And Andy rolled from his spot leaning against the red, brick wall, inconspicuously following, leaving Jeff to the wolves of his own making.

"Where you think you're going?" Charles snapped as he maneuvered in front of Andy, chasing after Sally. Maybe she held all the cards after all.

*

After a long, miserable day of whispers and diligent eyes, Andy buried his forehead into the palms of his hands the moment he sat in the bus seat for the ride home. The Sally fiasco refused to be forgotten, and the burden of keeping Bigfoot hidden in his shed while waiting for Mikey to return from a seemingly impossible mission, all under the close scrutiny of the entire town, was starting to take its toll. Andy's brain was numb. Plus he was worried about Jeff, who apparently had checked out of reality and into some fantasy world where he could explain everything away, no matter how extravagant. Who knew what he'd say if someone was to interrogate him.

Andy leaned back, propped his knees up on the back of the seat in front of him, and closed his eyes, eagerly awaiting the forty-minute bus ride to be over. He didn't have to see with his eyes to know exactly where he was every time the bus stopped to unload kids. And he knew exactly where he was when the bus stopped at Mikey's house. The door screech opened, and Andy jerked upright in his seat, surprised to see Mikey's little sister exiting the bus.

Andy looked out through the small, square, bus window, at Mikey's mom, standing on the front porch with her hands clenched together at her chest. She didn't move a muscle as Mikey's sister walked past her and into the house.

It was though she was waiting for Mikey. A miracle was all that she had left, and even the bus driver tried to make it happen. He just sat there on the road, with the doors open and the lights flashing, looking at Mikey's mom, then at Andy. Andy just shrugged his shoulders.

Eventually the bus driver broke, and called out that he was sorry while closing the doors. Andy watched as her clenched hands pulled apart and covered her mouth, and she began to sob uncontrollably, her eyes meeting Andy's through the pane of glass as the school bus left her behind. Yet another unpleasant image to torment Andy in the dark.

*

As Andy walked by his house – listening for the sound of Jeff's bike ripping into his driveway over the sound of the bus pulling away – he stared at Miss Nellie's Jeep sitting down by the shed. Sure, the shed sat back in behind the house far enough, and down a gentle grade, but it was still briefly visible from the road. And the…*curious* eyes of Falling Rocks had found Tom's crumpled Chevelle setting on the opposite side of the shed every time they passed. Miss Nellie's Jeep had to be noticed several times over.

And where was Jeff? He should have been right behind the bus when Andy got off. Probably had to eat first. Andy rounded the back corner of the shed, and there sat Wilbert's scooter. What was he doing there already? Andy stalled, right at the corner, looking at the blue scooter, then toward the road, waiting for Jeff, as if he didn't want to go in alone.

***

Jeff eventually showed and he and Andy slipped through the trap door. Both were primed and ready to air their voices once inside the shed, but the expressions worn by the faces of Miss Nellie and Wilbert had cleared their thoughts from their tongues.

"What's wrong?" asked Jeff. "Is it Mikey? I should've went!" He began to frantically pace in a tiny circle on the shed floor. "His mom stopped me on the way here, and asked me if I had seen him today. You should've seen her...she's a mess! I wanted to tell her that he was okay, but truth is, I don't know! Why'd I let him go?"

"Yea," Andy added. "We have to tell Mikey's mom."

"No!" Wilbert shouted. "You MUST NOT." Wilbert turned to Miss Nellie. "We can't trust these kids."

"Everybody calm down! Mikey will be fine, and so will his mother," Miss Nellie squalled.

"Then what's wrong?" Andy boldly asked.

Wilbert looked at Miss Nellie, and shook his head. "There's too much at stake...and after all these years, we shouldn't have depended on kids."

"What choice do we have, Willard?" Miss Nellie asked, pausing for the gravity of her question to sink in. "These boys didn't ask for this, and neither did we. But we all fell into it, and we have to work together."

"It's just that kids today...they're not the same as you and me," Wilbert grumbled.

"No, we're not the same," Jeff defended. "How could we be...and why should we be?"

Wilbert rolled his eyes and turned away from the boys, releasing a ghastly sound from his throat. He could find no words for rebuttal. But he did find the eyes of Bigfoot, crouching silently in the corner, unnoticed, and yet he had more to lose than anyone under roof of the shed.

"Look," Miss Nellie said. "No one *here* is handling stress well. Things are getting intense. And what, we all turn on each other? Point fingers? Good grief we're our own worst enemy."

Wilbert swallowed his pride and turned back to the boys. "She's right...this is Enki's poison, and we're sabotaging our own fight." He paused for a moment, and took a deep breath. "And, we've learned that the dark has seduced some other...Sasquatches to Enki's side."

"What?" and "How many?" simultaneously blurted out from both boys, impossible to tell who said what.

"Not sure," Wilbert confessed as he looked toward Bigfoot. "At least a few...probably more. And he can feel the presence of Enki. They're lurking nearby."

"What do we do?" Jeff fretted.

"We wait for Mikey and reinforcements. Then we will draw Enki to the fight...far from the eyes of his sleeping army. Until then, we stay put."

"I don't know how much staying put I can take," Jeff whimpered. "I'm going after Mikey. We should've never left him go alone."

Wilbert regretfully looked into Miss Nellie's doubtful eyes, each searching for the answer within the other. Each felt responsible. They both knew that one stranger stood a much better chance of making contact than two, but that did not lighten the guilt. "Maybe we *should* send a backup," Miss Nellie suggested.

"No," Wilbert replied, after a moment of debate inside his own head. "We must believe in the boy. We must trust in what we know is right. It's all that we have...they'll come." Wilbert lowered his head in silence as he searched for any logic within the words that he had just spoken. "Enki will keep his distance yet. He will arouse his human warriors first, and that's where we are needed the most. We just have to hold out...they'll come."

"We can stop humans," Andy growled.

"Shit, boy! If anyone finds him here, you'll be strapped to a hospital bed, and he'll be dissected on the rack before sundown! Even you all would have done the same if I hadn't come along."

The shed fell silent again as Wilbert shuffled around the room, tugging on his beard as he pieced together a strategy from his disheveled thoughts. "People don't realize what they do. They don't know what they are." Wilbert tugged harder, as if to entice the answer from his brain and to his lips. "Man's fear is Enki's secret weapon." He stopped, and looked at the boys. "You two get home! The entire town's watching you two. I could only guess the rumors circulating. And when everyone gets home this evening, and finds out that Mikey still is not home, then even the doubters will be convinced that he is missing." Then Wilbert turned to Miss Nellie. "You too. We all need to separate as much as possible, and blend in with every other unnoticeable thing in this town."

"Nobody will be looking for me," Andy said. "I can stay."

"No. Go sit on the front porch till dark. And make sure your mother sees you!"

# Chapter Fifteen

Jeff not so reluctantly hustled home to immerge into the sanctity of selfishness, at least until the next morning. For several years, Jeff had spent more time hunting, fishing, and traipsing all over Falling Rocks with his friends than he had spent at home, just as his older brothers had done throughout the years before. But even the veteran mother of those three renegade sons was beginning to keep close tabs on her youngest. And she was asking questions – very nervous questions…about Mikey. There was no escape, even in the safety of home.

Miss Nellie also retired to her home, hoping for a peaceful evening, and a brighter morning as well, but unlike Jeff, she longed for someone to interact with. She could not escape the grip of her own conscience, or the lonely, con-stricting walls of her house.

And it was much of the same inside Andy's house, but also completely different. Although Andy's mom was usual-ly at home, his house seemed the loneliest place in the world. Andy's mom talked to him often, but she only talked about things that made her forget about the past, and she re-fused to hear anything that made her remember. She allowed not a moment of silence for Andy to speak while they were in the same room. It was always a one sided conversation, and over the months, her voice became almost like back-ground noise. She didn't even know that Mikey was miss-ing, not to say that she hadn't heard.

***

Andy drifted to the front porch, like Wilbert suggested, but more to escape his own private prison than to follow Wilbert's advice. There was a fair amount of traffic that passed by Andy's house, but only during shift changes at the paper mill, and other than that, Andy would be lucky to be seen on the porch by just one car on a Monday evening. *If only Sally would ride past on her bike,* he dreamed. But he knew that he had a better chance of being abducted by aliens than seeing Sally.

Just then two police officers eyeballed Andy as they rolled on by in their cruiser, heading in the direction of the mill – probably more like Charles's house. Mikey's mom must have been turning up the heat as the sun fell for the third time since she had last seen her son.

Andy sat on the porch as quiet and still as Bigfoot while the light faded all around him, and when vision falters, the ears see far better than the eyes ever had. With the promise of a warm night, countless crickets and katydids chirped their bizarre calls as they scurried about the woods across the road, and the squirrels rustled among their leafy nests above as they nestled down for the night. The smitten frogs screamed of love in the pond behind the house, and the murmur of conversation from inside of the house lingered about on the porch.

Andy often wondered who his mom was always talking to – his dad...*Shorty*...never Andy for some reason. But the excruciating sound of his mother's tears always accompanied a conversation with Tom, followed closely by the sound of the yellow dragon crawling from its hiding place in the kitchen cupboard, swallowing his mother into the pit of her fantasy world, and recklessly carrying her upstairs to her bed.

*** 

Andy crept back into the house and down the rickety stairs to where Shorty had piled his dad's abandoned possessions in the dampest corner of the basement. There he quietly rummaged through his dad's things that lay under his own shadow cast by the light of a single bulb hanging from the rafters behind him. He knew exactly what he was after, and about where it was at, but by the time he returned back upstairs and stepped out onto the back porch, it was good and dark. After a thorough, but blind, scan of the backyard, Andy sprinted to the shed and hastily crawled through the trap door with his dad's shotgun in hand.

***

"I'm surprised you stayed away as long as you did," Wilbert chuckled. "And I wouldn't be sneaking around in the dark anymore."

"This buckshot will stop him in his tracks."

"I wouldn't count on it," Wilbert warned. "Plus, his blood runs through your veins. Like it or not, he is your grandfather. It may be harder to pull that trigger than you think."

Andy shook his head in disbelief, but Wilbert noticed him gripping the shotgun a little tighter. Wilbert chuckled again and bounced his fist on Andy's shoulder a couple of times in some dysfunctional, male display of affection. Truth is, Wilbert like the boys...even Mikey. They were all unique, with good hearts, and they followed their hearts – something rarely found in grown men. Wilbert wanted to apologize, and tell them all that he was proud of them, for what it was worth, but that was much easier thought than spoken. "You got it pretty rough, don't ya kid."

"It's not so bad," Andy returned. "A lot of people have it far worse than I."

"Maybe so...maybe not," Wilbert countered. "I know what it's like...being the main topic of gossip in Falling Rocks. I had a sister who died."

"Car wreck?"

"No. She was sick for a long time...but she died as a result of some choices I made as a young man."

"Oh-yeah?" Andy acknowledged, waiting to hear more. But Wilbert just leaned back into the Buick hood, crossed his legs, and stopped talking, like he just stepped from the real world into a hidden past. Andy didn't know quite what to do. He was curious to hear more, but didn't want to intrude. But yet he didn't want Wilbert to think that he didn't care either. "Wh...in what way?" he asked while fidgeting with the shotgun.

"It's not important. No sense dwelling on the past, unless there's something to learn." Wilbert just closed his eyes and said, "Let's just enjoy the quiet."

Andy released his death grip and allowed the shotgun to rest across his lap as he attempted to situate himself more pleasantly on the billet of firewood. Wilbert appeared to be quite content, as did Bigfoot, who still crouched in the back corner, motionless and silent with his big, brown eyes fixated on nothing visible. He looked fake, unreal. *He looks dead,* Andy thought. And with that thought, Bigfoot's eyes twitched – so fast that Andy was only sure that they moved at all due to the realization that Bigfoot was looking right into his. Andy quickly looked away, and settled into his own frozen perch upon the block of wood.

Many people find insanity when confined to the company of those who do not wish to speak, but all three under roof that night were quite comfortable with silence, and each relished in the peace of the soothing glow of the candles that Miss Nellie had left burning around the shed. There were no worries and no complaints, and no more regret – only the chatter of the pond frogs driven mad with lust.

Suddenly, as if someone chopped the flow of their chaotic symphony in half with an axe, the frogs stopped chirping. Bigfoot jumped to his feet, growling a very low, cautious warning. Wilbert rolled to his feet as quick as an old man was able, and he slapped the palm of his hand across the massive chest of Bigfoot. "Douse those candles," he slurred to Andy. Andy was already on his feet, fumbling with his shotgun, and he commenced to frantically huffing and puffing, and snuffing out the tiny flames with his fingers before Wilbert finished hissing. "Easy, easy!" Wilbert whispered as he heaved Bigfoot to the very back of the shed. "Let these rifles do their job. Enki won't be first anyhow!"

Andy snuffed out the last candle, casting the inside of the shed into the darkest of shadows, and the grimmest of fear. He spun around and fell headlong into the Buick hood. Wilbert pulled him to his feet, and faced him toward the front doors. They stood shoulder to shoulder in the pitch black contained by the shed as smoke from the extinguished candles snaked into their nostrils and burned their sinuses and watered their eyes. Andy's barrel nearly whistled through the thick air as he whipped the shotgun back and forth, chasing the distorted phantoms of candlelight that floated around the shed. Andy's barrel sliced close enough for Wilbert to latch onto the gun and steady Andy's panic. "Let your eyes adjust," he whispered. Soon the phantom candlelight faded away, and the wisps of smoke danced across the windows and through the glowing moonbeams that penetrated the glass.

"Aim out that window and shoot anything big and hairy that walks by," Wilbert ordered softly into Andy's ear.

"What if it's Mikey and reinforcements?"

And with that, something smashed into the back wall and echoed through the shed like a cannon. All three spun around, trying to remember the sound that had startled them so abruptly, but vanished into the silence just as quickly. Whatever it was, it collided with the shed wall with incredible force, but yet, it was somewhat cushioned, quite unlike the sound that a rock would make as it struck weather hardened wood. The air inside the shed was so tense that it could not be swallowed while blindly awaiting the answer in the dark. And then the shed moaned as it lurched forward, and groaned as it shifted back into its settled rest. The sound of something pounding against the back wall returned and blasted through the shed, over and over, as the shed violently lurched forward and backwards. Tools tumbled from the inside walls, and Miss Nellie's candles crashed to the floor on all sides. Andy couldn't see anything, but could hear everything screaming and crashing in every direction. Rusty nails screeched as they pulled from their long since seated rest, and the tin roof buckled like raging thunder. Bigfoot roared a ferocious shriek into the dark.

"That's not Mikey," Wilbert yelled, abandoning stealth for bravery, and just to be heard. Bigfoot shrieked again, this time more directed toward Andy and Wilbert. "The windows," Wilbert yelled. "Cover the windows!"

Andy stumbled back a step, wanting to swing the shotgun toward the window and away from the assaulted back wall that he knew was there, but couldn't see. Suddenly something had him by the arm, and his feet were off of the floor. Andy's body was frozen rigid with adrenalized fear, but he was being tossed around like a cardboard cutout, smashing into the rafters above and into the walls on both sides of the window. The stove pipe exploded, ripped from of the stove top and crock through the wall with Andy's feet, sending sections of pipes clamoring into the darkness as a cloud of soot rolled through the shed like a ghostly monster. Andy jerked on the trigger and sent buckshot tearing through the roof with an ear-popping explosion.

"Andy!" Wilbert screamed, barely hearing his own voice over the ringing gunshot in his ears as he stumbled over the Buick hood, groping in the dark for anything to hold on to. Bigfoot roared and clubbed at the hairy arm that was thrashing Andy about the shed. Andy felt the massive hand release his arm, sending him catapulting into the Buick hood on top of Wilbert as the invading arm retreated through the window. And everything stopped in an instant, like it never happened to begin with.

Andy was back to his feet in less than a second and aiming for the moonlit window. Wilbert covered the opposite window soon after. It was as quiet and still as the coldest night in the dead of winter. The tiny glint of moonlight on the end of Andy's barrel danced with adrenaline fueled excitement at the grip of his trembling hands. Sweat beaded across his forehead, and his finger quivered as it held the trigger half pulled. Time never moved slower.

Suddenly the chirp of a frog bounced through the window, and Andy nearly sent another wad of lead shot blazing through the hole. Then another frog cried out for a mate hiding somewhere in the night. One by one the rest of the frogs joined in where they could, until the insanity flowed continuous again. Warm, moist air glanced off the back of Andy's neck as Bigfoot slowly exhaled two giant lungs of relief, and the barrel of Andy's shotgun sagged toward the floor, but it was still ready, with finger on trigger.

"You okay?" Wilbert gently asked. A puff of air escaped from Andy's mouth, but no words would come out. Wilbert tried to ease the tension. "Still think life in Falling Rocks is always boring?" Andy still could not reply, but Wilbert knew that he would soon recover.

***

Wilbert fumbled around the dark shed until his probing fingers found one of Miss Nellie's scattered candles. All three huddled around the single, little flame that shined just bright enough to see into the eyes of each other, and the eyes of each offered no comfort to the other.

"Listen up," Wilbert said, hovering over the weak flame and looking Andy in the eye with the utmost sincerity. "Anything makes it inside this shed tonight, you empty that gun and get out any way you can."

"I'm not running away," Andy interrupted, finally able to speak.

"This ain't about you boy. It only takes one to keep the light alive, and one must always survive. You three boys may very well be the world's only hope, and that's a burden that no man can bear, but that don't change a thing, now does it."

Andy shook his head, unsure what Wilbert was even talking about. "Was that Enki...that had a hold of me?"

"No-o-o," Wilbert chuckled. "You will know Enki when you see him...and don't expect to see a friendly, family image of Old Friend here. And don't get me wrong, he was here, and he is near. Lucky for us that he is consumed by revenge…well, lucky for the others I guess."

"I don't understand," Andy confessed. "Why didn't he rip apart this old shed and try to kill us?"

"He's using Sasquatch tactics, to scare us off. But we don't scare easy, do we?" Andy slowly shook his head, although he was pretty damn scared, and growing more so with each passing minute, but that really didn't answer the question. "Believe it or not, he's scared of us," Wilbert continued, searching for the right words to explain Enki's politics. "We *are* his children, and as a parent, nothing terrifies him more than his children defying him, not believing in him…actually thinking that he has wronged them, or robbed their future. And he will do *anything* to avoid facing that truth…including killing us, his children. Hard to believe that much hate can fester from something as simple as a little vanity."

"But, that being said," Wilbert groaned as he leaned back, the candle light falling down across his face and beard. "If he kills us, then *he* justifies our disobedience. And that is a wound that will breed infection."

Andy had been nodding in comprehensible agreement as Wilbert explained, but truth is, every word that Wilbert spit out, confused him more. And the expression on his face was incapable of deceit.

"Look," Wilbert huffed, frustrated with his own incompetence. "The only way that Enki can control you is to control your mind. Convince you that it would be foolish to disagree with him. And he accomplishes that by rewarding you with indulgences and poisoning your conscience. Sure, he could control you with force and fear, but that fear will eventually fade, and without fear, he has no force. Freedom only exists in the mind, and it is a gift from the light, not Enki. And no matter what he does to you, there is only one way that he can rob you of your gift."

"Just like school," Andy mumbled.

Wilbert laughed, taking a moment to choose his words carefully. "What's one plus one?"

"Two."

"Exactly like school," Wilbert chuckled. "Anyhow, Enki's army has grown to an unstoppable size. But something has happened in his absence – something unexplainable and very troublesome to him – and his children have turned on each other. He needs to unite them, and he needs them to follow him. If he kills us, then he sets our thoughts free to, as Miss Nellie puts it, spread on the wind." Wilbert shrugged his shoulders, as if telling Andy not to ask him to explain Miss Nellie's thoughts. "Others will see us as the truth, and Enki as an insane murderer of his own children. With the millennia of work, bloodshed, and pain, he cannot stand the thought of his children not following him. It's all politics."

Wilbert's explanation slowly sank in, and Andy's eyes drifted down to the tiny flame of the candle as it struggled for life, only an instant, any instant, from death. The shed quieted to match the rest of Falling Rocks as three optimistic, but weary, minds surrendered to the idea that reason only exists in fantasy. Even the frogs seemed to agree.

# Chapter Sixteen

The sleepy shed sat under the moonlight in the shadowed backyard like the Earth had been abandoned a decade ago. And the scene was just as forsaken inside as the three inanimate figures slumbered over the tiny, wavering candle. Shortly after midnight, Shorty's big, black Chevy pickup rumbled into the driveway and shattered the peace that had settled on the night. Andy slipped away from the dimly lit circle of drowsing faces, hiding the shame in his eyes by lowering his head as he pulled out a knot in a board, and peered out at his darkened house. Wilbert looked on, wondering how many times Andy had hidden in the shed. And what was he hiding from?

Shorty slid from his truck seat and staggered towards the house under the haze of the utility light overhead as Andy dug his fingernails into the weather cracked wood around the knothole. A ghostly wind streamed down from the mountain, across the sheet of pond water, and whispered through the cracks of the shed like the melodic chant of some ancient ritual of blood and lust. Andy pulled his eye away from the knothole, and turned toward his friends, their faces flickering as though the wind was even blowing the light away. Bigfoot closed his eyes as the breeze snaked around his head and through his hair while he softly moaned a sound of sadness. Wilbert rose to his feet, rifle in hand, but confused all the same. Andy, maybe understanding more than he realized, peered back through the knothole.

The wind stopped Shorty mid-stride. "Who's there?" he cried out, stumbling round and round as he searched for an intruder. "Who said that?" The breeze strengthened, but somehow became almost gentle. Shorty stilled, with his arms held out and his head back, the melody caressing his senses and promising to whisk him away like a leaf on the wind. Then, as quick as the wind came, it ended with a sharp gust that slammed into the back of the shed. Andy pulled away from the knothole again, briefly looking toward the back of the shed, as was Wilbert, but when he returned to his knot hole, Shorty was gone.

One by one, the windows lit up in Andy's house. First a dim glow in the foyer on the front side of the house, then the kitchen window shined bright across the back porch. Andy could easily track Shorty's drunken route throughout the house, not that he didn't know Shorty's exact destination. Next was the light over the stairs, then his mom's bedroom. Shorty opened the second floor window and breathed in the cool night air, like he wanted more. And when he didn't feel it, he turned to Andy's mom. Arguing voices erupted from the silent bedroom and flowed through the open window and down to the shed. Shorty's drunken slurs overpowered a weak resistance from Andy's mom, making for a mumbled mash of unintelligible words, but it sounded like they were just on the other side of the shed door.

Wilbert leaned his rifle into the corner and moved to Andy's side. He wanted to say something, anything, but nothing was all he had to offer. And without warning, the distinct sound of callused skin colliding with tender flesh plummeted down into the backyard and slammed into the shed doors. Wilbert shuddered from the sound, and felt as though he had taken the brunt of the blow to his own stomach, but Andy never flinched. He knew it was coming.

Then something new happened. A scream, inspired by terror, blasted from the bedroom and cut through the shed like shrapnel. Andy ripped the digging bar from the door handles with his free hand, sending the bar clanging against the wall as he kicked the shed doors wide open. Moonlight flooded the shed, and Wilbert blindly clawed at Andy until he had a grip on the befuddled teen with both hands. Andy pulled away, groaning a gruff noise that sounded somewhat like a piglet squealing from somewhere deep inside. Wilbert's feet scuffled across the threshold of the shed and into the grass as he held on with all his might. Andy yielded to the stubborn, dead weight, and faced Wilbert, his eyes angrily demanding freedom, and tearfully pleading for help at the same time. Wilbert held on tight to the shotgun, but released his grip on Andy's shoulder. Andy sprinted across the backyard toward the house.

"Stay!" Wilbert shouted over his shoulder as he followed behind with the shotgun, covering Andy from any awaiting ambushes, and about to intervene where he would have never stuck his nose before.

***

Andy's mom was already in the kitchen, in plain view of the window, with the telephone in her hand and a finger frantically spinning the rotary dial on the wall. Shorty rounded the corner and knocked the phone from her hand and onto the floor. Then he backhanded Andy's mom across the face, sending her to the floor beside the phone.

Shorty tugged on the twisted up telephone cord until the phone lifted from the floor and into his hand, and he calmly hung the receiver back on the wall. And like the beast that hid within, he lifted Andy's mom from the floor, and slammed her face-first onto the kitchen table. He had knocked the fight right out of her, and she didn't move a muscle.

Andy launched from the bottom porch step like it was a springboard and cleared all the rest straight to the top. Through the door he burst, nearly shattering it from the hinges, and he leaped onto Shorty's back. Now Andy was a big boy, but, despite his name, Shorty was a behemoth of a man, and he stood up straight, like Andy was a mere backpack. Andy pulled back hard on Shorty's chin, and they both went down, sending kitchen chairs tumbling into the wall and Andy rolling back toward the door.

Shorty laughed like a half-dressed, drunken giant as he climbed back to his feet, striving to center his head over his

feet. "You're dead!" he bellowed, almost like he was de-
lighted for the opportunity.

Andy stood firm, primed for the fight of his life. He
would have faced death, and he did, or at least a terrible
beating, but he had to coax Shorty's inebriated rage away
from his mother, just as Bigfoot protected his family. Out
the kitchen door and down the porch steps he ran, right past
Wilbert, who was just reaching the steps.

Andy cut to the left, and zipped around the house, toward the front yard. Wilbert shouldered the shotgun and
pointed the barrel up the porch steps, scared to death that he
might have to actually shoot Shorty. But Shorty was already
leaping over the porch railing, at the end of the porch, right
at the corner that Andy had just rounded.

Wilbert lowered the gun and hustled to the same corner
in pursuit, but when he rounded that corner and could see up
along the side of the house, Andy and Shorty were already
out of sight. He had to get ahead of them. Wilbert turned and
hobbled toward the other corner of the house, hoping that
Andy would circle the house, and Wilbert could catch
Shorty head-on, or maybe catch his head right on with the
butt of the shotgun.

Wilbert galloped through the belt of light from the
kitchen, and entered into the shadowed block of yard between the porch steps and the corner of the house, focused
on the straight line of light that beamed down from the pole
light on the opposite side of the house. Andy flashed by, not
far in front of Wilbert, and he blurred down through the
beam of light toward the shed. Wilbert pushed even harder
and lunged around the corner, planting his feet firm with the
shotgun held high, ready to strike its target. But there was no
target...only Shorty's boots slapping the ground hard behind
Wilbert. Shorty had changed his direction of pursuit somewhere along the way, evidently thinking like Wilbert.

"Damn it!" Wilbert cried out as he spun around. But the
chase ignored him like he wasn't even there.

Shorty's steps pounded in Andy's ears as he neared the shed. Shorty used the advantage of the slope and a longer stride to close the gap, but if Andy could only stay just out of reach, and keep the chase alive, Shorty would soon exhaust himself for the night, and the wickedness of the alcohol would vanish by morning, along with the rage.

Andy veered and cut around the back of the shed, with Shorty so close that he was reaching out for the collar of Andy's shirt. Wilbert ran toward the shed with all that his tired muscles could muster, but a thud echoed across the pond and down the hollow to the left of the shed, followed by a very brief scream and a ghastly chocking sound.

"Andy!" Wilbert called out as he found speed that he hadn't conjured up since many, many years ago.

Just as the night looked its bleakest, an angry, bone-shattering shriek blasted up the side of the mountain like an atomic bomb. Even Wilbert's stride stuttered from the sound. He felt as though the blood had gushed from his entire body, all at once, and he nearly stopped, afraid of what he'd find. Suddenly, Shorty appeared...above the shed. He seemed to have taken to flight. But he lost altitude fast, and disappeared out of sight behind the shed again, with a splash.

\*\*\*

Wilbert finally made it to the back of the shed, and he pushed Andy and Bigfoot back into the shadow of the peaked shed roof where all three flattened against the wall as they surveyed their predicament unseen. Shorty's head bobbed among the ripples of glistening moonlight as he slowly and silently scanned the reedy pond banks that surrounded him.

"You...alright?" Wilbert huffed between breaths.

"He never touched me," Andy whispered. "What do we do now?"

Bigfoot began to vibrate a strange sound from deep within his chest that Wilbert and Andy could feel with the souls of their feet. Little, sparkling eyeballs started appearing on the wrinkled sheet of pond water. There were hundreds of them, all around Shorty. His smooth and silent rotations of his head quickened into spastic jerks to the left and right. And then the frogs unleashed their piercing screams, and they sounded angry. Shorty clamped his hands over his ears as he lost all stealth to panic. The frogs, one or two at a time, jumped onto his head. Shorty frantically swatted blindly at the air, slapping the water with every swing, pushing his way through the water toward the edge. He yelled at the attacking frogs, but even he couldn't hear himself over their shrill screams. As soon as Shorty gained his footing, he high-stepped it out of the water and dove over the breast of the pond, crashing through the brush in the hollow below.

"It's done," Wilbert solemnly stated in the shadow of the shed, almost talking to himself. "Enki has stirred his sleeping army Shorty will be back at first light...and probably with a well-armed buddy or two. We have to get out of here."

Andy's mom called out his name from the back porch with her broken and weak voice. "Go tend to your mother," Wilbert ordered as he handed the shotgun back to Andy. "We will make our way through the brush to Miss Nellie's garage for the night. I'll send Miss Nellie for you and your mom."

Wilbert peeked around the corner, watching Andy run through the shadow-streaked backyard and up onto the lighted back porch. As Andy led his mother into the kitchen, Wilbert rolled around the corner of the shed and disappeared into the darkness. Seconds later he returned with his rifle and flattened his back against the wall again. "Stay behind me and stay quiet," he said before blowing the anxiety out of his lungs. He stepped out of the shadow of the shed, and squared up to the brushy hollow that he intended to enter. "Is it okay?" Bigfoot nudged Wilbert on the shoulder and they took off, hustling across the brief openness of the yard and into the cover of the brush.

Once in the hollow, Wilbert slowed as he stumbled and fished through the jungle of young trees. For nearly half an hour, all he could see was the moonlit slashes of saplings against a bottomless darkness, and even that faded away at about ten feet. But at least no one could see him, or more importantly, no one would see the eight-foot tall, mythical creature that was following him.

Then, to Wilbert's surprise, Bigfoot grabbed him by the shoulder. Wilbert stopped, frozen in his boots as a not so distant sound emerged in the absence of his own shuffling through the leaves. Something was moving in the brush ahead, and to the left. But whether it was moving toward the road or toward the hollow, just ahead of their position, could not be determined. Wilbert readied his rifle as he peered into the bizarre, almost surreal, landscape, and he listened for what seemed to be one excruciatingly endless minute after another. At times it sounded as though it was right in front of him, and he should have been able to see whatever it was. A second later it sounded a mile off. But then a new sound emerged out of the broken darkness. It sounded like something pounding the ground...or clapping...or maybe grunting. Image after image flashed through Wilbert's imagination as he tried to match one to the sound of whatever was out there in the woods, hiding from the moonlight...waiting.

Finally, Wilbert matched a scene to the sound. And that scene was of Shorty, running down the road, his sopping wet boots slapping the pavement, one foot in front of the other. Wilbert listened as the steps faded away, confirming his conclusion. Shorty was heading for the mill, probably to stock up on weapons and men.

Wilbert discarded more anxiety through his mouth, and took his first breath since he started listening to Shorty. He turned to Bigfoot and motioned him to follow, but then he hesitated. "Ah, who am I kidding? I'll follow you."

Bigfoot led Wilbert on down through the hollow, veering up the slope to the right where they traded the cover of woods for the cover of Miss Nellie's salvage yard. As they

quietly moved past bumper after bumper, the seemingly endless rows of dead cars proved to be even more unnerving
than the dark woods. But it was the only way to avoid the
open ground and flood lights that surrounded Miss Nellie's
house and garage, and much to Wilbert's wonderment, Bigfoot knew the way well.

Just above the garage, Bigfoot nudged Wilbert to walk
down the lane while he crossed to the other side of the salvage yard, staying in the darker cover that stretched to the
backside of the garage. Wilbert glanced down the lane, to
where it entered into the bright light of Miss Nellie's insecu-
rity, and then he looked back to argue splitting up. But Bigfoot was gone. There were only more moonlit car hoods and
gleaming windshields, and plenty of shadows in between.

Wilbert briskly walked down the lane, gripping his rifle
and feeling quite nervous. He already missed the company
of his juggernaut friend, or maybe he was just nervous about
entering the den of the most contemptible beast in three
counties. As he crossed over the concrete tile that spanned
the lane over the stream, he looked to the right, into the
shadows, searching for a glimpse of Bigfoot, but it was
though he was completely alone. His eyes followed along
with the shadows as they crept toward the garage and painted the outside wall with darkness. And there, at the corner of
the garage, stood Bigfoot, hiding along the very edge of the
darkness, waiting on Wilbert.

Wilbert was startled at first, but soon relieved, and finally somewhat offended, although he wasn't quite sure
why. He hustled on by, almost feeling as though he was just
slowing Bigfoot down – as if everyone, everything, was
waiting on him.

***

This time, it was Bigfoot that peeked around the corner,
watching Wilbert as he shuffled past the garage, up the well-
lit lane to the house, and up onto Miss Nellie's porch at the

back door. He hammered on the wooden screen door, and it rattled like a window shutter during a hybrid storm.

Eventually a light came on behind a second floor window. Wilbert kept hammering on the door under the roof of the porch, and quietly calling out Miss Nellie's name, as if his voice could draw more attention than the clattering screen door.

Finally the porch light came on and the door flew open, unchaining Miss Nellie's pitchy, but groggy, voice to express her utmost discontent. It was a few minutes before three in the morning, and disrupting Miss Nellie's beauty rest was like poking a napping lion with a stick. Even Bigfoot rolled back around the corner of the garage and flattened against the shadowed wall.

# Chapter Seventeen

Often our destinies pay no heed to our schedule of make believe reality – especially time – and no one was more aware of that than Miss Nellie. But Wilbert and Bigfoot were well aware of it too. They lounged half asleep on a stack of used tires in Miss Nellie's garage that they had modified into fairly comfortable seats. Wilbert desperately tried to keep his eyes open by peering through the dirty skylights in the garage roof, watching the stars dim as the sky around them brightened. Miss Nellie had left for Andy's nearly two hours earlier, and was long overdue to return. It would soon be light enough for a shaken man    Shorty – to find his courage.

Wilbert was just about to go look for Miss Nellie when the pedestrian door slowly swung open. The sky may have been growing lighter, but ground level was still plenty dark, and the open door revealed nothing but a black rectangle. Wilbert grabbed his rifle from its leaning perch beside him, and readied it across his lap as he nervously strained to see beyond the threshold. But Bigfoot reached over and gently placed his broad hand across the rifle.

Miss Nellie scuffed her feet through the door, flipping it shut as she went, and she stood in the middle of the garage with her hands on her hips. "Did we really have to do this at three in the morning, Willard?"

"They in the house?" Wilbert nervously asked, with a smile. Miss Nellie's lips remained sealed, as part of her agitated expression, while her head flopped from side to side in a dramatic display of negativity. Wilbert's smile collapsed. "Where they at?"

"*She* refused to leave her home," Miss Nellie theatrically answered. Wilbert groaned and moaned and rolled his head around. "Hey, I tried to tell her," Miss Nellie continued. "I told her that she was about to lose the rest of her family, because her son was about to blow a hole through her boyfriend." Miss Nellie shuffled over and sank into a stack of tires beside Wilbert. "A-h-h-h...if it's any consolation, Andy promised not to shoot the prick."

Wilbert managed to muster a small chuckle, but it was fake. A hundred scenarios played out in his head as he leaned back and closed his eyes. Not one of them seemed favorable. He wanted to go back to Andy's, to referee the impending chain of events, but his loyalty had to stay with the Earth. And it was time to trust the boys...and leave them behind. Wilbert tried to let go. All three needed rest, even if just an hour of peace in the early morning calm. But peace is rarely found within any mind.

"So...what's the plan, Willard?"

"I was depending on you to come up with a plan."

"Great," Miss Nellie, not so enthusiastically, replied.

"If you can hide us today, we'll head out at dark," Wilbert revealed. "Just me and him. We'll head south, away from the northern colony, and away from you and the boys. Those boys are as important as the Sasquatch themselves, even Enki feels it. You have to teach them. Maybe we can kill Enki once and for all, or maybe he will kill us, but as long as you and those boys live on, there's hope of saving the planet."

The garage stilled into quiet thoughts of the past, and the future, as questions of why and how circled inside their heads. Why must a few always sacrifice for the gluttony of the rest? And how is mankind, manipulated and diseased by Enki or not, able to destroy everything that sustains their very lives? Only man will die from his own bite. Maybe we're not worth the effort.

"That's a stupid plan Willard!"

"Nell, there's honor in stupidity."

Miss Nellie burst into hysterical laughter, breaking the hindering tension, and allowing that elusive, dreamy peace to enter the garage. Soon the long and weary years of the three caught up with their attentiveness.

\*\*\*

It was so quiet in the garage, only the ticking of Wilbert's wristwatch could be heard. And the *tick-tick-tick* of time was replaced by the *bump-bump-bump* of their hearts as ghostly spirits circled inside their heads on an endless journey through countless dimensions of the subconscious mind. And then the garage door swung open again, and the nightmare of reality flooded back into their heads.

Wilbert startled to his feet, gasping for breath and fumbling his rifle into his hands. But it was Andy and Jeff, all wide eyed and flapping their lips like grade school girls on a field trip.

"Shorty ripped apart the house and shed this morning like we weren't even there," Andy spouted. "Like he'd forgotten everything else. And there must have been a dozen guys out back in the woods and around the pond!"

"The whole towns fired up!" Jeff chimed in. "Everybody's saying there's a crazed bear, or a lunatic mountain man on the loose! And everybody thinks it got Mikey! Every rifle for ten miles is headed for Falling Rocks!"

Wilbert stared at the bright sunlight beaming through the air above their heads, wondering how it was morning already, and trying to process the words that still spun in his ears. He leaned his rifle against the wall and cupped both hands along the sides of his head, scratching his temples, lifting his hat up and down on the tips of his fingers. "We have to get out of town, now!"

"What about Enki?" Jeff asked in about three different octaves. "Andy told me what happened last night!"

"Nobody's going anywhere!" Miss Nellie sassed, shaking her hips and her beehive hair in perfect rhythm. "Nobody's storming through my property without..."

Suddenly the door flew open again, and smacked off the wall with a shimmy. Charles swaggered through the doorway with his rifle shouldered like he was the reincarnation of Jesse James himself.

"You *really* need to get a lock on that door woman." Wilbert knew better than to call Miss Nellie 'woman', but that would haunt him at another time.

"Well, well, well," Charles sneered. "Society's misfits, all gathered together." The very end of Charles's barrel quivered like a scared rabbit, but it never lost aim of Bigfoot's chest. "All but one. Did he eat him like everybody thinks? Or did that little freak turn himself into a Bigfoot with some Frankenstein science experiment?"

"Get the hell off my property, shrimp!"

"Who-o-ose property, Miss, Nellie?" Charles taunted.

Wilbert looked at Miss Nellie, confused, and maybe angry.

"You better check with your granddaddy, you little twit," Miss Nellie defended. "My debt is free and clear, and you can leave, *my property*."

"Pap?" Charles snickered, unaware that Sally's brunet locks were floating at the edge of the open doorway as she slowly peeked, one, very round, eyeball around the corner. "Don't confuse Pap's version of romance with business."

Sally cautiously slipped in, past the door jam, and stood behind Charles, leaning out to see around him with her jaw nearly on the floor. "Don't worry Miss Nellie. I'll be leaving this dump as soon as I put a bullet through that thing's heart."

"No!" Sally squeaked, before catching herself. She timidly glided up to Charles's side, and spoke softly into his ear. "Charles, you can't just kill it."

"Shut up, Sally! This doesn't concern you. Go back to the truck."

Wilbert's sleep-deprived emotions were rampaging out of control. He felt betrayed by Miss Nellie, hated Charles's grandfather, and wanted to take it all out on Charles, who was the worse one yet. Bigfoot grumbled softly, reminding Wilbert to stay focused on the light, and not the ways of man. But, for the first time in Wilbert's life, the answer appeased both. He shifted his weight to his left foot, leaning towards his rifle that leaned against the wall.

"Don't do it, old man!" Charles shouted. "I won't hesitate to shoot you either!"

Andy quickly stepped wide to the right. Charles flinched his rifle toward him, but pulled back to Bigfoot. They were too far apart, and Wilbert was only an arm's length from his gun.

"Don't move, Andy!" Charles yelled while taking a step back. "Can't say I'd mind pulling this trigger on you either! You know I'll get away with it!"

Andy kept slowly flanking to the right, and Jeff followed, equally spaced between Bigfoot and Andy. Charles couldn't cover all of them – they were spread too far, and spreading farther every second. Sweat began to trickle from Charles's forehead, and his breathing quickened. He could shoot Bigfoot easy enough, but could he chamber another round before he felt the wrath of the rest? Charles's fingers twitched as he gripped his rifle tighter and tighter, throwing his aim unstable, wild even.

"I would move if I were you, missy," Miss Nellie gently said to Sally.

Sally stared at Charles, desperately trying not to believe the scene that her senses portrayed around her. She had never before felt her heart pounding so vigorously, and never felt intensity to the point that she couldn't take a breath. She screamed at Wilbert and Miss Nellie with her eyes, pleading for someone to end the invisible chaos, but it was clear, written in the eyes of everyone else, that violence was inevitable. Sally sprinted past Charles and stood in front of Bigfoot, her chest and shoulders heaving like a convicted man strapped to an electric chair.

"Sally, get in the truck!" Charles screamed as he tried to steady the sights of his rifle, six inches above Sally's head.

Andy and Jeff had frozen in their tracks, and Wilbert and Miss Nellie still held their arms forward, as if to stop Sally's foolish move – all hanging in suspense, and each one suspecting that Charles would not hesitate to pull that trigger. Sally looked right down the wobbling barrel of Charles's rifle, faced with the answer that she was afraid to learn, and just a bit, terrified, of the creature that she had turned her back to.

Bigfoot gently placed his huge, warm hand over her dainty shoulder, and Sally's bow-legged knees nearly knocked together. She looked to the hand on her shoulder, and followed the shaggy arm up to Bigfoot's riveting, brown eyes. Sally forgot about Charles and Andy, and even her own misery. Looking into the eyes of a Sasquatch for the first time was a different experience for each, but for Sally, it was like floating through the gateway to Utopia, where senseless pain and death did not exist, for man or beast, and all were loved unconditionally, just as Mother Earth loved all upon her. But Bigfoot tenderly pushed her to the side, and back into Enki's world of ravenous greed and vanity that murdered anything that stood in the way. A single tear wandered down her cheek.

"You're a real piece of work, Charles," Andy said as he started to flank Charles again. His steps were quicker and longer than before, and he could feel Charles's attention following, leaving the rest behind. "Would you even shoot Sally?"

Charles was nearly backed against the wall, his rifle trembling more than ever from his fidgeting, sweaty grip. Andy could go no farther around to the rear, leaving him in the open, and to the left of Charles – a bad place to be against a right-handed rifleman. The stage was set, and there was no more to say. Sally held her breath and closed her eyes, while Jeff's eyes darted back and forth between Charles and Andy, his legs ready for action, although he had no idea what he would do. Wilbert held one eye on Charles, and the other guided his hand as it drifted ever so carefully toward his rifle. Good or bad, the next seconds all hinged on Andy, and the courage in his rapidly pounding heart. "You're a coward!" he yelled. "And everybody here knows it!"

"Shut up!" Charles screamed as he started to swing his rifle toward Andy. Andy's eyes flashed wide open, and he turned sideways, as if he was under fire in a dodge ball game. But Bigfoot knew exactly when Charles would strike, even before Charles knew, and he already had a used tire in his hand, wailing it through the air with a sidearm catapult. The tire sailed into Charles's chest as he swung his rifle, knocking him from his feet and slamming him into the wall. The air rushed from Charles's lungs, and his rifle dislodged from his grip as a bullet exploded through the barrel and ripped through Miss Nellie's garage roof. The rifle smacked flat against the concrete floor, and Charles collapsed into a near unconscious ball of flesh along the wall.

Charles rolled around on the floor like a drunkard, gazing wildly about the spinning garage as he grasped for clarity. Somewhat realizing his predicament, he flopped against the wall and held on tight to a structural post as the garage slowly spun to a halt. But it was too late. Bigfoot hovered over him, casting down a judgmental stare into his quivering eyes as he unloaded Charles's rifle and handed the shells to Wilbert, who was covering Charles from the side.

Seemingly satisfied with his vengeance, Bigfoot turned his back to Charles and walked away, tossing the rifle into the back of Gimli's old Ford that sat quietly in the garage bay. But Charles's round eyes flattened, and his nostrils flared. He pulled a hunting knife from his belt, and silently lunged for the vulnerability of Bigfoot's back. But Andy was there, out of nowhere, and he latched onto Charles's knife-wielding wrist. Charles looked toward Andy, just in time to see Andy's knuckles colliding with his nose, and then it all went dark.

\*\*\*

The twisted tension inside the garage unraveled into a calm relief as quick as Charles crumbled to the floor for the second time. But relaxation comes by the generosity of all others, and Falling Rocks was not in a hospitable mood. A chilling wind raced southward along the slopes of Rocky Ridge, coaxing an obscure, ancient ritual to the skin of a frightened Falling Rocks and flooding the land with a feverish panic. The ramble of a threatened mob moaned through the air as the wind sliced through the clefts of the garage, as if to flush the creature from hiding. The sounds of men whooping and hollering to each other as they drove animals from the brush were commonplace in the fall, but never before had their distant shouts sounded as they did that morning – almost inhuman. Maybe it was trickery of the wind, or maybe it was never heard through the ears of prey, but whichever the case, it didn't sit well with Wilbert.

"Get out of here," he ordered the boys. "Go to school or something!"

"No way," they answered in unison, both stone serious.

"Well at least go home! And take her with you," Wilbert shouted as he pointed to Sally.

"I'm not leaving either," Sally meekly stated.

"She's one of us now," Andy blurted out as he stepped forward, capitalizing on the favorable momentum of the past six hours. Well, favorable to Andy.

Wilbert grimaced his disapproval, keeping his own tongue still to hear the rabble of the hounding mob.

"That she is, Willard," Miss Nellie agreed. "Can't turn back time...Lord knows I've been trying." Miss Nellie grabbed Andy and Jeff by the arm and pulled them toward Gimli's Ford, motioning for Sally to follow. "Don't worry, Willard! I can hide them. But half those knuckleheads out there would follow you...go lead them away!"

The sounds of the mob of bounty hunters grew louder, and drew nearer. They were close enough to distinguish their words – ruthless and vindictive words as old as murder itself. And those words, passed from one to another, promised to leave no corner unseen as they prepared to march straight through Miss Nellie's salvage yard. "What about him?" Wilbert pointed to Charles, unconscious on the floor.

"Oh, I'll take care of him. Now git!"

Wilbert was reluctant to leave everybody behind. After all, he was the one who was supposed to protect the others – the first to fall, if any. But there was no sense in wasting precious time arguing with Miss Nellie, even if she was wrong. "Just keep your wits about ya!" Wilbert said as he slipped out the door.

*** 

Miss Nellie left the boys at the back of Gimli's faded, red and white Ford pickup that sat dead on the garage floor while she scurried around to the driver's door. She yanked the door open with a metal clashing pop, and kicked the transmission into neutral. "Push boys!" she yelled as she threw her own body against the door. Jeff and Andy heaved against the tailgate, but the old Ford refused to budge an inch.

The truck was solid, built when trucks had to be tough, and not a bit of all that heavy steel had moved in the last decade. It was the last business that Miss Nellie ever accepted, and ole Gimli was still waiting for his truck, even though he was ninety-five and had his driver's license revoked seven years earlier. To make the truck even heavier, the bed was filled with axles, rims and radiators, and even a straight six engine block that was half as long as the bed. "Throw your backs into it!" Miss Nellie rallied, and even with the addition of Sally's push, and all of the growling and grunting, the old Ford didn't even creak.

"Quiet, quiet," Miss Nellie shushed as she backed away from the Ford and stared blankly across the garage. Everyone held their stance, motionless, diligently listening to a hoard of frightened and vulgar men as they combed through the maze of cars that sloped up toward the mountain. "They'll pass behind...if they don't hear us," Miss Nellie whispered. "But we still have to move this truck." Young and old returned to their efforts, quietly.

Jeff turned his back to the tailgate, hooked his fingers under the bumper, and pushed and lifted with every ounce of strength in his legs. And with his back toward the cab of the Ford, he didn't see Bigfoot, the unnoticeable missing link, walk up to the cab corner and push. The Ford lurched forward and rolled, a little faster than anybody expected. Jeff back pedaled his feet, trying to keep up, but he lost the race, falling onto the steel grates that were hiding under the truck as the Ford crashed into a workbench along the back wall.

The garage hung in suspense, like the moment a glass slips from your fingers. And just as sure as that glass would shatter on the floor, "Miss Nellie1" rang out from somewhere outside, followed by vigorous pounding.

"What're they doing…searching my house?" Miss Nellie squawked, but in whisper form. "*Come on,* Willard!" Miss Nellie moved to the back of the Ford and froze in a moment of thought, fighting panic. "Get him," she said, addressing Bigfoot and pointing to Charles's unconscious body. Bigfoot immediately walked toward Charles, and Miss Nellie turned to Andy and Jeff. "Slide those grates to the side and climb down. There's a door in the back – get it open."

Miss Nellie's name was called out again, this time closer. "Hold that door!"

Sally ran to the door that she had entered, and held the knob tightly while leaning against the steel door with all of her weight, which wasn't much.

Jeff and Andy each pulled a steel grate from over a large, damp pit in the concrete floor. The pit was specifically constructed to work underneath vehicles without hoisting wheels from the floor, and was nothing unusual in any garage, but there was something more to this pit.

Andy scaled down the rickety, wooden ladder that was bolted onto the side of the pit, and he quickly spied a short and narrow door against the back wall. The rusty hinges shrieked as Andy heaved on the pit door, and an ice cold gush of air blasted him in the face. The light from above revealed three short steps down into a stone lined tunnel that was as black as the oil sludge that lay in the four corners of the pit.

As Andy anxiously waited for Jeff, who was blankly staring into the nothingness of the black tunnel from above, Miss Nellie wrangled tires over Charles's head. Bigfoot had lowered his dangling feet into a stack of tires, balancing him as Miss Nellie rendered him invisible, tire by tire. When Charles's curly, blonde hair was replaced by eroded tire tread, Bigfoot stacked four more on top. Miss Nellie was hoping that the hollow tires would act as a muffler if Charles awoke and started screaming, because he sure wasn't going anywhere.

Suddenly, Sally's door shimmied as a strong fist pounded on the other side. Sally squeaked like a mouse as she bore down on her grip of the knob.

"Go, go, go," Miss Nellie frantically whispered as she pushed Bigfoot toward the pit. "Get him into the tunnel," she said to Jeff. Miss Nellie hustled across the garage to Sally's side and pushed against the door as it thrashed harder and harder. The knob wrenched Sally's palm and fingers as, whoever was on the other side, easily overpowered her grip. She whimpered in pain, but never relinquished her effort, even when her delicate skin began to tear.

Bigfoot moved toward the door to help.

"No! Get in that damn tunnel!"

Bigfoot stopped in his tracks, looking a bit puzzled.

"They will shoot you at first sight, and ask questions later! They won't dare lay a finger on us!" The door popped open a few inches, but the girls pushed it back with everything they had. "Go, now!" Miss Nellie groaned in anguish as the door pushed open again, this time refusing to be pushed back, and violently thrusting to gain more.

Bigfoot spun and leaped down into the pit just as a leg pushed through the slim opening between the door and the jam, followed by an arm, and a shoulder, ending the battle for the door. Bigfoot quickly reached up to the Ford's back bumper and pulled the disabled truck back over the pit.

*

Shorty burst into the garage, wildly brandishing a shotgun butted to his hip, even more jumpy than Charles. Miss Nellie and Sally winced several times as the sweeping barrel threatened their way. The garage fell completely silent, as if everyone inside was holding their breath. Only the flopping of Shorty's boots could be heard as he floated throughout the garage, restlessly checking every nook and corner, barrel first. He looked in the bed, and in the cab, but never under the Ford, even when he stumbled over one of the steel grates. "Where's it at, Miss Nellie?" he finally yelled.

"Where's what at, Stubby?"

"Don't play games with me, witch!" Shorty screamed, emphasizing his sincerity with the muzzle of his shotgun. "I've seen your Jeep at the shed! And you better watch that tongue before you lose it."

As Miss Nellie stared down the smooth bore of the shotgun, she couldn't help noticing Bigfoot's head filling the space between the top edge of the pit and the undercarriage of the Ford, flashing his contempt with a broad mouthful of teeth. His long, hairy arm reached up to the truck bumper, as though he was about to remove himself from the pit and defend his friends. Jeff leaped up and latched onto Bigfoot's arm with both hands, and Andy hung around his thick neck, both boys desperately trying to pull the massive creature back into the shadow of the pit. But it was though the boys were thrashing from the mighty branches of a hundred year-old oak.

Miss Nellie locked into Shorty's eyes, refusing to betray the drama unfolding behind his back. The silent ruckus under the Ford was painfully obvious, and agonizing not to look at, but Miss Nellie held steady. Sally was not so strong though, and Shorty noticed her intrigued gaze at some anomaly to his rear. His eyes started to lead his head around to the other side of the garage.

"There's no one else here," Miss Nellie blurted out, slightly losing her iron-nerved composure. "Please leave."

Shorty hesitated at Miss Nellie's insistence, but continued his turn, only a moment after Bigfoot relinquished to the boys' pleading and sank back below the floor.

Shorty scanned the opposite side of the garage for what seemed like an hour as Miss Nellie held her breath and Sally stared at the floor, realizing her mistake.

Andy very carefully backed into the tunnel, pulling Jeff and Bigfoot along in reverse, allowing the cold, damp stone to swallow them in darkness.

Shorty could feel that something was amiss, but could not put eye or ear to it. He turned back around, this time focusing on Sally. "Where's Charles?" Sally remained still, her wide, blue eyes fixated on a chip in the concrete floor, almost comatose. Shorty bent over, trying to draw her attention. "His truck is in the driveway...and *you* are here." Shorty broke Sally's line of sight to the floor with the gun barrel. "Where...is he?"

"He's up on the mountain with the rest of the idiots," Miss Nellie interrupted. "Why don't you go join them?"

Shorty's temper wrecked his tactful interrogation, and he turned his hateful eyes back on Miss Nellie. "Then why did you try to keep me out?"

"This ain't your damn garage Shorty!" Miss Nellie spouted, refusing to be intimidated. "And we didn't even know who you were, you damn fool!"

Then, like a gift from the stars, a single rifle shot echoed from somewhere near, up on the mountain. Shorty looked off into empty space as he listened closely. Two more shots ruptured through the air, followed by a horrific cry and the frantic calls of frightened men fueled by bravery, as if alluring startled ears to the southwest corner of Miss Nellie's property, up by the distillery. Shorty was no stronger than any other man, and he gave one more glance across the garage as he backed out the door in pursuit.

***

A forceful sigh burst from Miss Nellie's lungs as she leaned back against the door, latching it firm. "You never fail to deliver, Willard," she said, seemingly talking to herself. "Just wish you wouldn't have taken ten years of my life to do so." Miss Nellie motioned Sally to the pit as she grabbed a flashlight from the wall and followed. Gimli's Ford rolled forward, and Sally and Miss Nellie disappeared below the floor as they climbed down the ladder and into the pit. And then the Ford rolled back, covering their escape.

# Chapter Eighteen

From one hand to another, the flashlight moved ahead the length of the pit until Andy was left holding the lead, with no one to pass it on to. He shined the beam into the black hole, and the beads of ground water that seeped into the tunnel between the stones sparkled like a diamond mine. But the darkness was still there, lurking a little farther down in the tunnel, just out of the flashlights reach.

"Let's go," Miss Nellie softly ordered from the rear.

Andy waved the flashlight, thinking that the black mass that waited ahead in the tunnel should at least waver with the passing beam, but it was dead still, almost like it was a real thing, that could be felt.

But Sally was watching.

Andy cautiously descended into the long, damp tunnel, followed closely by Sally, Jeff, and Bigfoot. The black mass retreated deeper into the tunnel with Andy's every step, always staying just far enough away to remain unclear. But sooner or later, it would be trapped, with nowhere left to hide.

Suddenly a clash of metal rocketed past their heads, down through the tunnel, and back again like a train was about to blast out of the darkness. Andy spun around, and around again, and yet once more, shining the light over Sally and Jeff's heads as they also turned to face the clamorous intrusion to the rear, but the light flattened on a wall of brown fur that lofted a crooked and puzzled face. Bigfoot's knees were bent, his shoulders were shifted to the side, and his head was stooped over just to fit inside the tunnel. And he sure wasn't able to turn around, rendering him defenseless against whatever danger stalked them from behind.

Bigfoot provided security to the rear, the light to the front, but with the light cast upon Bigfoot, the dark side was left unchecked. Where was the cunning, black mass that silently trolled through the tunnel? It was right behind Andy, and he could feel its icy breath on the back of his neck. Andy startled and jerked the light around to his rear... forward. Sally whimpered a scream as she and Jeff wheeled around too, chasing after the light, and refusing to face the dark. The black mass shrieked and sucked back down into the tunnel to the safety of just beyond the reaches of the flashlight, and there it waited, and watched, the only thing in the tunnel that could see into Andy's frightened eyes.

"It's just me...shutting the door," Miss Nellie called up. "Keep going...unless he's stuck!" Enjoying her newfound safety, Miss Nellie erupted into her shrill laughter, which flooded the tunnel. But something laughed back, from somewhere down in the darkness, and it wasn't Miss Nellie's laugh. It was no doubt shrill enough, but much more guttural, and a little raspy.

"No way," Jeff whispered up to Andy, leaning well over Sally's shoulder. "Mikey was right."

"Right about what?" Sally whimpered.

"Nothing," Andy whispered over his shoulder, keeping his eyes on the black mass. "It's just an echo." Andy continued on down the tunnel, slowly, with Sally pressed against his back, and Jeff pressed against Sally's. Personal space did not seem to be on anyone's mind.

"Turn right when you can," Miss Nellie hollered up, the dark tunnel mimicking her every word.

Andy steered the light to the left as the tunnel leveled out and curved to the left. With the beam of light plastered along the right wall of the sweeping tunnel, the black mass no longer stood in full view. It only peeked around the corner, like a shy, but curious, beast.

Eventually they reached a large hole in the tunnel wall to the right, and Andy hesitantly pulled the light from the black mass and shined the flashlight into the hole. It was another stone-lined tunnel that led to a door about thirty feet away. Andy stepped through the hole and into the tunnel to the right, and Sally followed. But Jeff stood still, watching the phantoms of light that swirled around in the dark where he had just been looking down a tunnel moments earlier. He couldn't see the black mass as Andy did, but then again, maybe he could see more. "Where's straight ahead go?"

"It goes to my house! *You* need to go to the right!" Miss Nellie quickly scolded. "Now get moving...don't smell so sweet back here."

Jeff rolled his eyes, in the dark, and joined Andy and Sally in the tunnel to the right. All three stood in front of a steel door that looked as though it belonged to a submarine, while Miss Nellie bypassed Bigfoot at the tunnel intersection and joined them at the hatch. She cranked on the hatch wheel until the door popped open, and Miss Nellie disappeared into the dark on the other side.

***

Andy stepped through the doorway, shining the light around what appeared to be a room about thirty feet square. Sally and Jeff followed through the hatch as Miss Nellie struck a match and ignited five candles on a small candelabrum. A draft of fresh air flickered the growing flames and cast dancing, amber light throughout the room, painting the illusion that even the stone masonry was on fire. The candlelight rippled across locked cabinets that stretched to the ceiling, and wide bookcases – bookcases full of very old and thick books, many of which were bound in leather hide, or etched covers of slate. Mason jars filled with dried weeds and roots, and shallow candles that were familiar to Andy's shed, sat here and there on precarious shelves and cluttered, narrow tables that were pushed against the walls. A broad, round, kitchen table sat in the middle of the room, accompanied by only one chair, and there was even a fireplace built into the wall, equipped with a hinged, metal hook, from which a medium-sized, black kettle hung from.

"Wh-at is this place?" Sally stuttered as a shivering chill zipped down her spine.

"A bomb shelter," Miss Nellie quickly answered. "Daddy built it after the war."

"Then…where's all the food?" Jeff asked, his imagination painting a slightly different scene than Miss Nellie offered.

"Good grief boy! Is that all you think about?" When Miss Nellie had turned to scold Jeff, she noticed Bigfoot standing in the tunnel, just outside the hatch. He had never entered the room. "Hey, don't judge, big guy," Miss Nellie said as she grabbed Bigfoot's hand and pulled, but he would not cross the threshold. She leaned in close to the brooding giant, and lowered her pitchy voice. "Just till dark. Then you can go anywhere you like. Nothing is going to rub off onto you." After several moments of silence, and Miss Nellie's relentless persuasion, Bigfoot stooped his head and reluctantly lumbered into the room.

"Now, I got work to do," Miss Nellie said to the boys as she moved to the hatch door. "I'll be back in a few hours with *food*. Deadbolt this door from the inside, and do not open it unless you hear my voice on the other side." And the steel hatch slammed shut with seemingly eternal consequences.

\*\*\*

Bigfoot studied the dimly lit room with sour contempt, until he found a bare spot along the wall where he could sit on the floor and stare at his feet. Andy and Jeff heaved on the seesaw type lever that hinged to the middle of the door, and four, two-inch thick stainless steel rods pushed through the hatch door and deep into the stone walls on each side until the lever locked into place. No one was getting inside without permission.

Andy pulled out the single chair for Sally while Jeff gathered a bucket and a crate, and they all sat around the table. Sally stared wide-eyed at Bigfoot, and Andy stared at

Sally. Sally's dark locks of hair seemed alive in the wavering light, softly caressing her gleaming face, and the flickering flames of the candles shimmered across her gray-looking eyes. Andy had never seen her so beautiful, as though she were some shy, mythical temptress, exiled into Earthly form.

"What an amazing creature," Sally proclaimed, enjoying the rare opportunity to be herself. "I can't believe he's real," she giggled. "Mikey would just die... where is Mikey?"

"Mikey was the one who found him," Andy answered, while nodding toward Bigfoot with his head. "And he's looking for help from the others somewhere up in Rothstone."

"There's more?"

"Oh yea. A whole colony, I guess."

Sally sat still in thought for a moment, staring off into nothing. "Mikey's alone?" she asked. "In the woods?"

Andy solemnly nodded as he and Jeff both lowered their guilt-ridden eyes to the table. Sally's stomach soured as she counted the days that Mikey had been missing, which wasn't that many, but somehow that seemed worse. A dozen questions mingled on the tip of her tongue, but the facial expressions about the room answered all, and the supposed bomb shelter slipped into a moment of silence. But Sally would always run from the inevitable, until there was nowhere left to hide, and she changed the subject. "Andy, that was amazing the way you saved him from Charles."

"Jerk had it coming for a long time!"

Sally's smile melted, and her dimples faded away. She looked away from Andy, almost defending Charles again. Andy was a smart boy though, and he learned from his mistakes. "He risked everything to save *my* neck last night," he rallied, referring to Bigfoot. "He started a war to protect me...it's been a long time since anyone has cared about me that much."

"I care about you Andy," Sally said with a returning smile as she laid her hand over Andy's wrist.

Blood rushed to Andy's face, and his knee went haywire again, this time thumping his heel into the empty bucket like a drum, but he breathed in slow, and steadied his leg. Jeff sighed and rolled his eyes, but nobody was watching him.

"What's his name?" Sally asked.

Jeff had been looking at his own hands – to make sure that he was still visible – and he jumped into the conversation. "They don't name themselves."

"That's silly. What do you call him?"

"Old friend, big guy...hair ball," Jeff sneered.

A low grumble wafted out from under the motionless mass of brown hair lumped against the wall, snapping Sally to attention. Jeff puffed air out between his lips, and waved his hand toward Bigfoot, as if to dismiss his threat.

"No way!" Sally exclaimed, her now blue eyes as big as half dollars.

"Oh yeah," Jeff whispered. "Understands every word." Jeff lifted from his crate, and leaned across the table, his face close to the candelabra, like he was about to spill the juiciest secret that had every circulated through Falling Rocks. "And he can talk to you, too... inside your head."

Sally's face drifted into a blank plane of confusion, and Andy grimaced with objection, both thinking that, in the wake of such fantastic enlightenment, Jeff's imagination was whispering an embellished memory of reality.

Jeff stood up, onto the balls of his feet, looking over the table of doubters and straight at Bigfoot. "Go ahead...say something to them." But Bigfoot remained motionless, refusing to acknowledge even his own existence. Jeff's eyes darted back and forth between the faces of Andy and Sally, diligent to catch an expression of amazement, but neither Sally nor Andy heard anything other than their own thoughts of concern.

"Quite the jokester you are," Jeff objected. "Make a fool out of me." He crouched to resume his seat, and unexpectedly disappeared below the table with a thud. The crate was sturdy and still, and sitting on the floor, right beside Jeff. "You see that?" he yelped as he pulled himself to his feet. "He moved my seat! I know he did!" Sally burst into laughter, as did Andy, leaving Jeff hanging like the town fool. He mumbled something under his breath as he squeezed the crate between his feet and slowly sat down, keeping his eyes fixed on the wooden slats that would hold his weight from crashing to the floor.

The laughs faded away to the ripple of the candles and the faint hum of the draft. Jeff pouted into his folded arms that rested along the edge of the table, listening to his stomach rumble. Sally's eyes drifted back to Bigfoot. But Andy stared off at something beyond the glare of the candlelight.

"Tommy," Andy eventually blurted out, drawing the puzzled attention of his friends. "I think we should call him...Tommy."

Any moment of silence suddenly became very awkward, especially for Sally. "Tommy is a good name," she said as she turned back toward... Tommy, and away from facing the misery that had been thrown onto the table. She nervously chewed on her bottom lip, counting the seconds until someone would speak of something else.

Andy finally turned to Jeff, wanting to explain, or maybe confess, and he said, "Remember when we were in Mikey's room... before we went up on the mountain?" Jeff curiously nodded. "And I was looking through the stack of eyewitness reports, and Mikey jerked them from my hand?" Jeff nodded again, even more intrigued. "Well I was looking for one in particular...the one from Tom."

Now even Sally eagerly listened, she and Jeff both already contesting what they had yet to hear. Tom was such a legend among the teenagers of Falling Rocks. He was smart, talented, and cool – the all-American kid – and everyone loved him, especially the young girls. It was hard to imagine that he and Mikey ever swapped stories of Bigfoot.

"It was about six months before the accident," Andy explained. "Mikey spent about two hours in Tom's bedroom one Saturday afternoon. I couldn't make out what they were saying through the wall, but I've listened to Mikey enough to know that the conversation was about Bigfoot. Neither one has ever mentioned it, and I guess I've been too afraid to ask." Andy paused for a moment of regretful reflection – if only he could go back. "Anyway, I caught a glimpse of Tom's statement, that day in Mikey's room, and he signed it, Tommy. He hadn't let anyone call him Tommy for a long time, since before things started to go bad with him."

\*\*\*

Andy no sooner stopped talking than Miss Nellie pounded on the hatch door, startling everybody to their feet, except Tommy. Andy and Jeff hustled to open the door, and Miss Nellie nearly plowed them over as she frantically scurried inside the shelter carting a sack full of food and fresh water, reporting the chaos that had befallen Falling Rocks as she fluttered around the room.

Wilbert had led the mob up onto the mountain, but they were ravaging across the mountainside like a tornado, killing anything that their imaginations could paint as a threat – including two, groggy, spring bears that were nowhere near big enough to topple Shorty from his feet, let alone toss him into the air. But most of the bloodthirsty posse were already drifting back into town, and beating down every unanswered door. They found a metal, superhero-themed lunchbox in Tin Can's old shack out by Rock Spring, and, even though Mikey's mom testified that the lunchbox was not her son's, the men hog-tied the old hermit and locked him in Jacko's old chicken coop behind the post office, just to be safe. It was *some* kid's lunchbox after all. And the hoard even ransacked the old haunted house in Plum Hollow, setting it ablaze after finding it empty.

"Fill your bellies," spouted Miss Nellie as she left her shelter even faster than she had entered. "And get some sleep…it's going to be a rough night."

***

With the near apocalyptic scene of Falling Rocks that Miss Nellie had just portrayed, eating seemed to be toilsome, even for Jeff. And sleeping was quite impossible. Sally sat quiet, staring into the flames of the candelabra, reconsidering her enthusiasm. She would have been much better off sitting in school, completely unaware of anything other than the second hand ticking its way around and round the face of the clock.

And we all know what Andy was staring at, but Jeff... he was engrossed in something as unfamiliar to him as the ways of a Sasquatch. "How can he just sit there like that?" he asked, referring to Tommy. "I mean... everything important to him, his whole life, is crumbling all around him, and he just sits there, refusing to use the power that Wilbert claims he has to stop any of it." Both Andy and Sally turned toward Tommy as the surprising gravity of Jeff's words slowly soaked in. "He would have just laid up on that mountain and died if we hadn't come along...and there was no reason to! I don't understand." It was impossible for any of them to comprehend, by the blood of their own heritage. "Better yet...how many years has he just sat in the woods, watching, as we threatened his family more and more every day? There must have been hundreds of opportunities to stop us, but he probably just sat there, like a dumb animal! I'd forget that he's even in the same room, if it wasn't for the stench!" Just then, the wooden slats of Jeff's crate folded like a pair of scissors, and Jeff disappeared below the table again.

"We have to stop them... Shorty, and the others," Sally proclaimed.

"And Charles," Jeff sneered as he sat on the edge of the table, giving up on the wooden crate.

Sally ignored Jeff, just as she ignored his point. "We can help him...call the authorities. The government will protect them."

"No," Andy spoke up, surprising Jeff. "What we wouldn't kill, we would change. That's Enki's plan. And he *does* have the army to do it. And he *is* awakening that army. I seen it with my own eyes. Everything's happening just like Wilbert said."

"Who's Enki?" Sally asked.

Andy turned to Sally, like he thought that he recognized a Blue Hole redemption. And he began to tell the story again – about the balance...about Enki.

Andy's story blurred in with the rippling candles and whistling draft. The words were all heard before, but something was different. The room had somehow changed. There was a cold presence in the air that seemed to wrap around the room like an icy blanket, and the flames of the candles began to flicker even higher and brighter, almost frantically dancing up into the air. Sally gasped! And there was Tommy, standing on the other side of the frenzied, blazing candelabra that raged above the table. No one had heard him get up, or seen him walk over to the table. He was just there, silently towering above as the candle flames danced in his eyes. His eyes were different...darker...maybe confused, or irritated. For the first time since he regained consciousness, Andy and Jeff felt a little wary of Tommy.

Tommy turned away from the table and glided along the perimeter of the room, gently running his massive fingers across Miss Nellie's collection of bizarre stock. Along the way he stopped to pull a weathered, leather sheath from behind a large crock that bore the scar of a crack from top to bottom, resembling a bolt of lightning. And he slowly pulled a long knife from that sheath, sucking the air out of the room. It was only a tool of Miss Nellie's – probably used to cut roots...or who knows what – and the blade was pitted and rusty, but the very edge was honed to razor sharpness. Tommy held the knife handle in between his fingers, watching the lethal gleam race up and down the edge of an otherwise harmless object. He slid the blade along his left forearm, under Mikey's wraps of gauze, and the bandages sprang open and fluttered to the floor, much like a fall breeze plucking dying leaves from a tree. One by one the laurel branches that had secured his forearm tumbled to the floor, and Tommy just stood there, carefully rubbing his healing arm, and staring straight into the stone wall.

Sally inched closer to Andy's side, and whispered, "What do you think he's thinking about?"

Neither Andy nor Jeff uttered a sound, not that either had anything to say, but Tommy moved on, stopping at the first and larger of two bookcases. Again his fingers softly brushed along the rows of ancient bindings, very slow and deliberate, shelf after shelf, as if he were reading each one. Then he moved to the next collection of books. Many of these books were much younger, but still much older than the teenagers.

Tommy left the bookcases behind and stood in front of a padlocked, steel cabinet. Why a cabinet needed a padlock when it hid in a secret room behind a blast-proof door at the end of a tunnel guarded by darkness, no one could imagine. But Tommy sure seemed to understand. He never touched the cold steel though. He just stood there, staring at the cabinet like it was his own coffin.

The room hung in quiet suspense and anxious stillness, for much too long, until finally, Tommy turned from the cabinet. But strangely he rounded the room, veering wide around the table as if he were hiding his eyes from the candlelight, right to the hatch door where he waited. Sally looked at Andy, and Andy to Jeff. Jeff just shrugged his shoulders. Surely Tommy wasn't going to just stand there at attention, for hours, waiting for Miss Nellie to open the door.

It seemed as though time was standing as still as Tommy stood quietly, but oddly, after only several minutes, Miss Nellie's voice sounded off from the other side. It couldn't have been dark yet, but she was there all the same. And as soon as she stepped through that oval threshold, Tommy stepped out, heading for the garage.

# Chapter Nineteen

Wilbert displayed a patience only found in a condemned man as he waited for his cohorts to join him in Miss Nellie's garage. He may have even been hoping that they wouldn't show up at all, and chose to stay in Miss Nellie's bomb shelter until things cooled down. But if he was, he knew better than to waste faith on ideas that were too easy. And as sure as he was still breathing, Gimli's old Ford started to roll forward.

Tommy—still Old Friend to Wilbert—emerged from the mechanic's pit and walked to Wilbert's rear quarter, not once making eye contact. Wilbert could feel that something was amiss with his old friend, but his attention returned to the pit and the clamorous teenagers that were chasing a Sasquatch through a stone tunnel, chased themselves by a monstrous black mass. Andy was the first to scurry out from the subterranean lair, followed by Sally and Jeff, and they all huddled around Wilbert, all eager to serve.

"You kids go home," ordered Wilbert. "The last thing this town needs is three more missing kids." No one moved a muscle, other than Miss Nellie who was just then crawling out of the pit. "It's too dangerous…there *will* be a confrontation!"

"You need us," Andy calmly and stubbornly informed Wilbert.

"No!" Wilbert shouted as he jabbed his finger into Andy's chest, determined to have it no other way. "Remember what we talked about. There's more at stake here than your pride. The light must carry on…we must not fail, or *all* is lost. We must split up."

Wilbert may as well have been speaking to the old Ford pickup, and he looked to Miss Nellie for help as she joined the group. But, with typical Miss Nellie style, she just cocked her head slightly and scrunched up only one side of her perfectly-painted face, as if jeering that Wilbert should have known better.

"Okay...look," Wilbert continued. "I was so wrong to doubt any of you, and none of you have anything to prove. You kids have more heart than any adult I know in Falling Rocks. And that's exactly why you all must stay... so there will be a *younger generation,* who can be trusted, who have the courage to face the sting of nonconformity in order to change the mistakes of the past..."

"Where's Tommy?" Sally interrupted.

"Who the hell is Tommy?" Wilbert asked...anyone. The questioned triggered a survey around the garage, and Wilbert realized that his old friend had slipped out the door unnoticed, attempting to separate himself from his friends.

*****

Miss Nellie's garage spewed out its contents of people into a confused jumble of panic just outside the door. An outdoor light, mounted high on the side of the garage, shined down onto the scene, but a heavy darkness surrounded them, lurking just out of the lights reach, much like the menacing black mass in the tunnel. Each pair of human eyes peered out into the darkness, in every direction, and every ear listened, picking up where vision fell short at the light's edge. It was so quiet, and so dark. There was only the weakening ruckus of the earlier day that had retreated to under the distant lights of town, and it seized Wilbert's attention. It was as though he was helplessly watching the civilized destruction of Earth, from space, and it sickened him, like it was destined to be true.

Miss Nellie finally broke the stalled silence. "What's he doing, Willard?"

"He's following the plan," Wilbert answered, snapping out of his trance. "Keeping hope alive by drawing Enki away from us, where they can both meet their destinies. Only he forgot to take me along... and this!" Wilbert lifted his rifle from his side. "He can handle Enki – he's the only one who can – but he can't take on Enki and the traitors of his clan without my rifle at his back. They'll tear him to pieces! I have to find him…before Enki."

Wilbert had spent a lifetime tracking down Tommy, but it would be a challenging task in the dark – even the cloudiest of days was much brighter than the beam of a flashlight. Jeff's experienced, young eyes would be needed at Wilbert's side, therefore ending the hardheaded debate that already seemed to be forgotten.

***

Andy fell in behind Wilbert and Jeff as they hiked up through the graveyard of cars toward the mountain. Their light steadily swept across the ground like the nose of a hound, searching for the slightest depression in the dirt without the unnatural hard lines of tread – tire or shoe.

Miss Nellie and Sally lagged several lengths behind with the only other flashlight, and with all that was at risk, and all of the foreboding blackness that closed in on all sides, one sizzling question seemed to burn the hottest in Sally's thoughts. "So, what happened to Charles?"

"Funny thing," Miss Nellie softly answered. "Seems the boy has become somewhat infatuated with me, and plum forgot all those silly notions about Bigfoot." A muffled giggle escaped through Miss Nellie's nose, and she leaned into Sally a bit, lowering her tone even more. "And we're now in agreement on the terms of my deed… just like his granddaddy. Although, his granddaddy was much more difficult to convince." Miss Nellie grinned from ear to ear, her head naughtily swaying along with her stride, confident that the dark night would hide her secrets and protect her reputation.

"I wish you would teach me your love potion," Sally whispered.

"Honey, in case you haven't noticed, you don't need a potion." Miss Nellie quickly flipped her flashlight up, catching Andy as he stared back at Sally. Andy startled, and stumbled as he quickly jerked his head back to where it should have been. "That boy would be better off walking backwards."

Sally snickered somewhat half-heartedly. "Yeah... well, Andy's not really the one I need a potion for."

Miss Nellie quietly strolled along for a few steps before stopping, and she said, "Believe it or not sweetie...I've been in your shoes. I've chased after love, and caught only heartbreak. I've chased after security, and found quiet misery. And now I just chase after time, in the same house that I was born." And just like that, Miss Nellie turned away and continued her trek up the mountain, leaving Sally so dumbfounded that she allowed herself to be swallowed by the dark.

"Wait," Sally called out. Miss Nellie turned and blinded her with the beam of light. "Well...what should I do?" Sally whimpered, with the tone of a disappointed child on Christmas morning.

"Hah! I didn't know what to do forty years ago, child... I damn sure don't know now!" Miss Nellie backtracked down the slope to Sally's side, and took her by the arm. "Okay...just don't get trapped between the dreams of two men. Make your own dream... one that pulls a big ole smile across that pretty little face of yours. One of those boys will follow... and if they don't, someone else will." Miss Nellie gently tugged on Sally's arm. "Now c'mon. We're falling behind."

\*\*\*

Wilbert and Jeff had made good time tracking Tommy through the salvage yard, across Miss Nellie's property line, and up the gentle, lower slope of open timber. Nothing can tread across the forest floor and leave no trace of their presence like a Sasquatch, but Tommy's impressions were deep, stretched with an incredible stride, and his path parted the undergrowth like a snow plow. He was uncharacteristically practicing no caution, and was pushing up the mountain hard, beckoning Wilbert to push just as hard. But the mountain was starting to push back, stronger with every step. The forest floor inclined steeper and steeper until it ascended into a sloped wasteland that defined the boundary that separated the lower foothills from the mountaintop. And Tommy hoofed his big feet straight up and over, unlike any other creature of the forest.

"He's…trying…to lose us," Wilbert panted as he collapsed to the slope and rolled against the uphill side of a tree, still holding the light on Tommy's trail.

"I'd say he succeeded," Jeff hastily replied as he flopped onto his stomach, looking up the mountainside at the endless row of small mounds of forest floor that were heaved up by Tommy's feet.

Andy stopped short of Wilbert and Jeff. He had been hiking in the edges of darkness between the trackers and the ladies for whom he now waited. Miss Nellie and Sally were holding their own, but assisting them to reach the others for a rest was just the right thing to do. And Sally would appreciate that. Andy allowed each to take an arm, and he helped pull them up to the others, dropping Sally to rest low on the immediate slope while assisting Miss Nellie higher to Wilbert's side, almost like he was separating the women, so he could join Sally.

Miss Nellie joined Wilbert's disheartening stare at Tommy's tracks up the mountain. She couldn't find the breath to speak, so Wilbert finally confessed what her eyes were saying. "We'll never make that climb," he said.

"We can make it," Jeff encouraged. For all of his self-centered complaining about any of the slightest inconvenience, and all of his fretting about the tiniest of threats, deep down there was no place on Earth that Jeff would rather be than in the woods, tracking down an impossible quarry in the middle of the night, rifle or no rifle.

"*You* may be able to make it," Wilbert returned, still gasping between words. "But even you will never make anytime soon." Wilbert turned to Miss Nellie with desperation in his eye. "We have to leave his trail…and cut diagonally up to the top."

"North or south?" Miss Nellie sputtered out while nodding in agreement.

"I'm sure he's heading south, away from Rothstone." Wilbert lowered his head, as if he were ashamed to speak his thoughts. "But…maybe we should head north…find the Rothstone colony…and prepare to face Enki with or without Old Friend?"

Miss Nellie lowered her head with Wilbert's. "Would be in the best interest of the light."

"Hey," Jeff spoke up. "Maybe we can distract Enki by going north. Maybe even split him and the defectors up."

For a moment there was nothing but the sound of their breathing, and two beams of light that cut through the black night. Within the reaches of light, the trees stood as fake and still as death. But within the darkness, there were hundreds more, quietly standing all around, free to be and do anything an imagination could conjure up. And the longer those imaginations waited in the dark, the more real the dark became.

"Boy might be right, Willard. But we are late as is…we better get moving."

***

A decision had been made, and the group prepared their minds to put their thoughts to action. But before they could pick themselves from the ground, a stick snapped on the slope above. It wasn't a sturdy stick, or a violent break, but in the dead of night on the side of a forested mountain, it was any and every nightmare never remembered.

"Tommy?" Sally desperately whimpered, unable to maintain her silence.

The flashlights relentlessly searched through the tree trunks above, and every tree moved as the ripple between light and dark passed over it. All eyes peered into the very limits of the light, but there was not a silhouette to be seen, or a sound to be heard. And not even a breeze whispering through the netherworld overhead.

Eventually Wilbert leaned over and whispered into Miss Nellie's ear. "Seriously, who is Tommy?"

"Apparently your *'younger generation'* named our Old Friend."

Suddenly Sally squealed, quick and sharp. Both beams of light cartwheeled through the air and landed dead on Andy, still on his knees, his chin buried into his right shoulder, and his wide, horrified eyes looking at the ground where Sally kneeled only a second earlier. She was gone. Everything was quiet and still, almost like she had never even been there. Then Sally screamed again, this time loud and strong, till the very last of her breath escaped from her lungs. She was somewhere close, just through the trees to the left, but yet so unreachable in the darkness.

*

Andy leaped to his feet, and bolted into the dark timber, with only the memory of Sally's scream to guide him. The beams of light raced through the trees by his side, but soon found the limits of their reach, leaving Andy blindly chasing after nothing more than hope, no matter how fleeting. And that grim reality quickly set in as Andy looked up from the forest floor, with the knee of his jeans ripped open and soaked with blood, and his arms scraped and bruised. His eyes could only see a thicket of dark shadows in every direction. There were no lights, and no sound. He wasn't even sure which way he had been running. He called out Sally's name, but even his voice was swallowed by the darkness.

Andy embraced his panic – it was the only thing he had – and he pushed to his feet, frantically stumbling through the woods and groping every tree along the way, desperate to feel anything that might pull Sally closer to his grasp.

***

Wilbert, Miss Nellie, and Jeff all crouched motionless, and breathless, in the same spot, still holding the lights on the trees where Andy disappeared. Three may be a crowd, but suddenly all three felt very alone. For a few seconds after Andy had vanished, they could hear his movements through the dark woods, but then there was nothing. All they could hear now was the pounding of their own hearts.

Jeff stood up, determined to find his friend, but Wilbert latched onto his forearm and slapped the flashlight into his hand. "Stay together," Wilbert ordered as he slipped his rifle sling over his head and shouldered the weapon. Together they took a step toward the darkness just beyond the light. But Sally screamed again. This time from the slope above, but still somewhat close. All three wheeled around, facing the lights and rifle up the mountain again. And again, there was nothing to see but darkness lurking behind every tree.

And as the bewilderment sank its claws in even deeper, something crashed through the brush from behind. Out of the darkness, feet charged up through the heavy leaf litter on the forest floor. The lights and rifle flipped back down the slope in defense, all finding Andy's as he rejoined the group. A ghastly exasperation escaped from in between Wilbert's shaggy lips as he jerked his rifle muzzle away from Andy's chest and ripped his finger away from the trigger.

Andy had run toward Sally's second scream, and he found the lights that pointed toward her, but at the moment that he had reunited with Wilbert and the others, his face contorted into the purest anguish, desperately pleading for help. Wilbert had only seen that expression in the face of his mother, a long time ago. But a lifetime of torment would never forget it.

Wilbert turned once again back up the mountain slope, leading the way with his rifle before Andy could pass him by. Another scream cried out in the night, off to the right. And yet another to the left, before the first had finished. Both screams could not have come from Sally. Only a Sasquatch could mimic the human sounds of terror so well.

Wilbert tried to replay the screams from memory. Was the second scream even from Sally...or the first for that matter? Sally could have been anywhere. Sasquatch trickery had lead them astray and left them standing befuddled on the side of the mountain in the darkest moments of the night, looking into each other's eyes, afraid to glance away even for a second.

Eventually Andy did turn away, and he looked out into the dark woods beyond the broken circle of light. Wilbert quickly reached out, gripping Andy's shoulder, knowing full well that the boy was about to take off again, alone, and he would search until his blood ran cold.

"It will do her no good boy," Wilbert said, finally able to acknowledge the reality that had just befallen upon them.

"I won't just give up on her!" Andy cried as he spun around to face Wilbert.

"We'll never give up on her...on anyone," Wilbert returned. "But we must keep our heads, and stay together. We've lost too many already. Sally's no threat...and she may even be bait. No harm will come to her."

"Bait for what?" Andy demanded.

"Enki's too smart to be lured into a disadvantage, but in his madness, we counted on the taste of his vengeance being too sweet. But he may be using Sally as a hostage to turn the tables, and set a trap." Wilbert looked out into the darkness, pausing in thought. "We still head north, and find help." He turned back to Andy. "I don't know what else to do."

Andy stepped back from Wilbert, looking abandoned...betrayed. "Sally!" he screamed, sweeping his voice across the entire mountainside.

"Sally's long gone, son!" Wilbert stepped toward Andy, settling into his sidelong stance. "And you'll never make it through the night alone! What good will you be to her in the morning?" Wilbert quickly glanced to the far eastern horizon, aware that it would soon be glowing red. "Look...you don't have to follow us, but for Sally's sake, follow your courage, not your fear."

# Chapter Twenty

Wilbert and Miss Nellie pushed through the shadows of the macabre trees and hiked diagonally up across the mountain, setting the pace for Jeff to follow...and Andy. Their feet burned from pushing sideways in their shoes, and their hips ached from their lopsided strides, but they ignored the pain. Sally was out there somewhere, terrified and alone in the dark, as was Tommy, who was facing certain death so that others may live on. And let's not forget about Mikey – that brave fourteen year-old boy who marched to his fate with all of his goliath heart – they all carried the weight of that guilt with them.

Wilbert lengthened his gate as he thought about those who had given all to a plight that was ignorant to a selfish world, and asked for nothing in return. But a dark, steep mountainside slope was not the place to brandish bravery, and his foot slid on the dry leaves while the other was mid-stride. He fell hard onto his side, and he cussed loudly...to let everyone know he was okay. But Wilbert's rant triggered a reply from higher up on the mountain.

A bizarre howl sliced down through the trees and stole the very life from their bodies. Everyone locked in a standstill, even Wilbert who was half way up, and they all listened intently, hoping to hear nothing. But it was too quiet, and too quiet in the forest, especially at night, usually screams of peril.

"Maybe we should stay here," Miss Nellie whispered. "And wait for daylight."

"We might not see daylight," Wilbert carefully warned, as he looked to the sky. The darkness *had* started to fade slightly to the east, but on the ground, it was as dark as ever, and would be for hours to come. Wilbert switched off his flashlight, and motioned for Miss Nellie to do the same.

They all stood perfectly still in the dark, as vulnerable as they ever would be, and counting the painfully, slow seconds as they passed by while their eyes adjusted as best as possible. Wilbert handed his flashlight back to Jeff, and whispered, "Keep it off. Use it only to blind their eyes if they come in, and keep a rock by your side…and keep moving."

*

Wilbert pushed on, leading the rest in a single file formation, zigzagging through the black trees that emerged from the shadows only a step ahead. Over and over, they pulled themselves up the mountain, sideways, but they lost half the altitude gained with each step. They had to reach the top by daybreak, or it might have been the last daybreak. The group kept pace, nearly invisible, and all but their feet trekking through the leaf litter was silent. And even as they all listened to the footsteps above that were flanking them from higher up on the mountain, no one uttered a sound. Wilbert tried to pick up the pace, but even adrenaline failed to conquer the pain of the mountain.

Then, from somewhere high above, a muffled thumping on the leaf-covered ground charged down the slope, pacing faster and faster. Wilbert threw his rifle to his shoulder, his aim blindly tracking the steps that seemed an impossible pace. Miss Nellie aimed the flashlight as well, ready to illuminate the attacker on Wilbert's mark. "Easy," he whispered. "Not yet." The charge grew louder and louder as it came closer and closer. Miss Nellie dropped the small rock that she had been toting for protection, and threw her free hand on the flashlight just to steady it. Jeff snaked up under Wilbert's rifle barrel and readied his flashlight. But as Wilbert followed the charge, his rifle started to swing to the front, and, whatever it was, it passed several lengths in front, and continued on down the mountain.

"Keep moving," Wilbert whispered as he resumed his lead, but only taking a few steps before another furious charge rumbled down the slope. The assault was not over, it was just beginning, and emotions boiled over, as Wilbert's rifle faced the threat, along with two flashlights, ready to ignite the dark. It quickly became clear though, that this time the intruder would pass behind, leaving Wilbert suspicious that maybe their imaginations were blowing something innocent into a monstrous farce. But then out of nowhere, something rocketed through the treetops above their heads. Miss Nellie screamed with panic, and her flashlight burned bright as she wildly waved the beam across the underside of the tree canopy, catching every snapped twig and dislodged dead leaf that floated down through the light.

"Rocks," Wilbert shouted over Miss Nellie's endless scream that had drifted into a piercing, hysterical rave of profanity. "There just rocks! Keep moving!"

Wilbert took Miss Nellie by the arm and tugged her up the slope as she still babbled nonsense. Andy and Jeff followed, all scrambling as best they could across loose rocks and slippery leaves, and through underbrush, sometimes even on their hands and knees. But the frightened teenage boys scrambled a little faster, huddling all four into a sizable target. And the rocks kept barreling down the mountain, two or three at a time, blasting out of the darkness like cannon balls, and they were dialing in their aim.

"Spread out!" Wilbert yelled. "Get behind a tree!"

*** 

The boys split off and each quickly found a tree. Andy pushed his shoulder in hard against the downhill side of a thick oak and closed his eyes as he listened to a massive rock bounce and crash its way through the woods in his direction like it could see him in the dark. The rock smashed into the oak, exploding shards of bark and splinters of wood like shrapnel. The tree was hollow, and the rock plowed right through it, launching Andy down the slope in a blast of rotting wood, with the rock.

Jeff was close enough to see Andy's silhouette catapult through the air and disappear into the darkness of distance. He screamed out Andy's name, as loud as he could, and he listened, but only heard the unrelenting bombardment of rocks as they ravaged through the dark. Jeff called out to Andy again, finding only despair in the clamorous silence. The light would mark them both as an easy target, but he had to see his friend, no matter what the sight may be. Jeff aimed the flashlight, and slid the switch forward. The darkness fled down the mountain, uncovering Andy. He was on his hands and knees, but his head hung low, and bewildered.

Jeff extinguished his flashlight and leaped from behind his tree. Rocks barreled down the mountainside on both sides as his feet shuffled down the slope to Andy's side. Andy acknowledged the hand of a friend, but he was completely unresponsive to Jeff's plea to take cover, and he was too big to carry. Jeff wrapped his arms around Andy's chest and heaved, desperately trying to pull Andy to his feet. His hands lifted from the ground and hung by his waist, but the effort stalled there, with Andy's knees still firmly planted on the slope, just five feet from where a boulder plummeted out of the dark and splintered a small tree just below. Jeff screamed in Andy's ear, and slapped him in the face. Andy yelled back, but his words slurred into nothing more than a moan, and his body helplessly leaned into Jeff. Frustration muffled Jeff's focused ears, and a rock shot out of the dark and sailed right past his head, not two inches from his nose. And there was more coming, rumbling down the mountainside like an avalanche.

Jeff tightened his grip around his right wrist, his right hand still clamped onto the flashlight, and with every ounce of adrenaline-fueled strength that he had, and a gut wrenching scream, he bear-hugged Andy higher and higher from the ground, until his spine was bent back as far as it would go. Andy's feet rested lightly on the ground, and his arms flopped out to the sides as he hung helplessly across Jeff's chest, but only for a second. Jeff fell backwards, with Andy on top of him, causing them both to roll down the slope and crash into a sturdy white-pine tree.

Jeff pulled his arm out from under Andy's dead weight and rolled out from the pine. Even the dark was spinning, and there seemed to be no air to breathe in, but that didn't stop the rocks. That leafy, chaotic thumping roared out of the darkness like an armor-clad, black stallion straight out of the underworld. Jeff gabbed Andy's feet and jerked him down the slope as a rock smashed into the pine with a jolt that quaked the roots underground. Shards of bark sliced through the thick, black air, and hundreds of dead pine needles tumbled down through the branches above like rain. Jeff tugged and jerked on Andy, rolling him like a log, until he was behind the wide trunk of the pine. And Jeff collapsed by his side. They were safe, but also trapped.

\*\*\*

Behind the cover of the huge white-pine, Jeff rested alongside Andy, counting aloud the seconds between each rock missile. The volley seemed to be slowing, to maybe one every fifteen seconds or so. And Andy was coming around to sensibility, or just sick of Jeff counting into his ear. He called out for Sally, convincing Jeff that a sound mind was slowly returning. Jeff helped Andy sit up against the tree, and continued to coax him back to the dark mountainside. Andy had been beaten fairly well throughout the night, but he wasn't broken, and he was young and tough. But even though, Jeff thought it best if Andy stayed put for the time being.

Jeff carefully peeked out around the pine, and started counting seconds again as he peered up the slope into the darkness, searching for the shape of Wilbert or Miss Nellie. He wasn't sure how much altitude he and Andy had lost, or how far they had drifted left or right. But there should have been a tree every twenty or thirty feet, and all he had to do was find the next one in the dark, while sprinting up across the rugged slope.

\*\*\*

Jeff flushed from the pine and ran the gauntlet of rocks until the next tree that offered protection formed out of the darkness. Tree by tree he ascended the mountain, veering to the north, and timing the rocks every step of the way, which seemed to intensify with his movement. And behind each tree that Jeff stumbled upon in the dark, he whispered out, "Wilbert...Miss Nellie." He was beginning to think that he was completely off course...or Wilbert and Miss Nellie had been taken out. Jeff was ready to change direction, try a different heading. But which way? The darkness and the noise made it impossible to remember, or even reason.

"What the hell you doing, boy!" It was Wilbert. And he was close, just beyond the barely visible tree to the right. Jeff sprinted for the tree towards Wilbert's voice, and the stones and rocks rained down all around. "Stop that!" Wilbert roared. "Stay still!"

Jeff could now see Wilbert's outline, tucked in tight against the butt of an old oak, only a few strides away. But Jeff lost his timing. The rocks careened down the mountainside and through the air at random – too many to count.

"I'll draw them away," Jeff modestly shouted over to Wilbert.

"No! We wait!" he answered. "Till they let up! Then we fall back together...straight down the mountain!"

"I'm not going back...I'm going forward!"

"That's crazy!" Wilbert was as scared and frustrated as anyone else, and his voice barked with his agitation. "You damn kids never listen! We must stay together!"

"They won't follow me back...but they'll try and stay between me and whatever they're trying to keep us from." Jeff looked up at the brightening sky as he slipped his quilted flannel from his shoulders and tied the arms around his waist. "I'll meet you on the road, up on top of Rocky Gap."

Jeff rocketed out from behind his tree, flipping on his flashlight as he flashed past the opposite side of Wilbert's tree. Wilbert lunged around his tree, diving headlong up the slope and grasping for anything that he could get a hold of to tackle him, but Jeff was too quick. And even before Wilbert's hands fell to ground, he could see that Jeff was already gone.

*

The mountain rumbled like thunder, and trembled like it was splitting in two as countless rocks and boulders rifled down the slope. Wilbert rolled back around the downhill side of his tree and watched over his left shoulder as Jeff's light bobbed and weaved up across the mountainside, fading weaker and weaker as the darkness swallowed the light until it looked like a single, twinkling star in the night sky. But Jeff was right. The battery of stone throwers followed, and so did the deafening clamor of the bombardment, fading softer as the light had. Jeff rounded the rolling slope of the mountain and his tiny, sharp gleam of light disappeared into the next swale, dragging the rumble along with it.

The returning silence was sweeter than Sally's smile, but Wilbert wasted no time in breaking it. He called out into the dark for Miss Nellie, and called out a little louder for Andy. The shadows of both soon appeared to join him. Yet another sacrifice had been made, and it could not be allowed to be given in vain. Wilbert led Miss Nellie and Andy up across the mountainside, trekking for where Jeff's light last wavered. They hiked through the dark timber with no light, and listened to only the sounds of their own feet as all three diligently searched for a motionless light shining across the forest floor, each desperately hoping not to find it.

***

The pre-dawn white had gradually pushed the gray skies westward until the eastern horizon burned red, but it was all too subtle to notice while walking across the forest floor. And after a seemingly endless night of anxiety and pain, Wilbert finally stepped out of the mountain laurel and onto the shoulder of Rocky Road, just in time to look across Little Cove valley and see the sun crawling up over the point of Blackwood Mountain twenty miles to the east. They failed to reach the top of their own mountain overnight, but at least they made it to the road. It was an accomplishment toward their goal. Plus the road broke over the summit of Rocky Gap only a hundred yards from where Wilbert was waiting for the others to join him.

Miss Nellie eventually stumbled out of the brush. Her mascara had smudged down across her cheekbones, and her perfectly sculpted hair looked more like the head of Medusa. And someone had stolen her ever-present smile, leaving behind one sour face that even a grizzly wouldn't cross. "Why the hell didn't we just drive up here, Willard?"

Wilbert ignored the question, and turned his attention toward Andy. Andy had dried blood mangled in his hair that draped down over his black eye, and his bottom lip was split open and crusted over. And from there down he looked as though he had been dragged under a bus, but he was still in better shape than his mentors. No one spoke a word after Miss Nellie's frivolous point. They didn't have the energy to spare, and fuses were worn short over the night – Enki was working his magic.

***

The three started up the road, which was quiet and smooth walking, but it also left them exposed. The daylight was still dim though, and it was a risk worth taking. After two miles across sidling, rugged terrain in the dark, the road was like floating through the air and they reached the summit rather quickly. But there was no sign of Jeff and it seemed that not one of them realistically expected anything different.

Wilbert watched the break in the laurel, where they had found Tommy, as it stepped closer and closer with every scuff of his boots against the blacktop. Maybe Jeff was tucked in the brush, out of sight, waiting on the game trail.

Wilbert was tired of conjuring up hope, though. His eyes burned, and his body had replaced pain with numbness an hour ago. And what if they had passed Jeff by somewhere back on the dark slopes of the mountain. Was their purpose in life really worth more than the life of one boy? All would be lost anyhow, if Wilbert and the others failed.

Something else was amiss though. It was a heaviness that Wilbert could feel churning in his gut. He tightened his grip around the stock of his rifle, and lightly pressed his thumb against the safety. Miss Nellie and Andy both could feel Wilbert's tension, and both faded back from the rifle, with their eyes searching each shadowed hole in the green foliage that lined their respective sides.

Suddenly a small stone bounced across the road in front of Wilbert. He spun to the left, sighting straight out the barrel of his rifle as he scanned the leafy, green jungle. He caught a flicker of movement out of the corner of his eye, and zeroed in his aim. It was Jeff, tucked in behind a gigantic, fallen tree, peeking over just enough to press his finger to his lips and wave Wilbert into the brush.

Wilbert jerked the aim of his rifle away from Jeff as a surge of fear, anger, and relief nearly exploded from his lungs. He was so happy to see Jeff, but also angry with him, and for the second time he had had one of the boys in the sights of his rifle with his finger on the trigger. Wilbert hesitated, staring blankly into the set of eyes that hovered just above the log as he questioned his own competence to carry such a deadly weapon.

Jeff's hand popped up from behind the log, and motioned Wilbert in again. Wilbert regained his composure and turned to Miss Nellie and Andy with his finger pressed to his own lips, just as Jeff had, and he motioned to follow him into the laurel. The three quietly snaked their way through the laurel to Jeff's position, and collapsed behind the safety of the downed tree.

\*\*\*

Jeff was a welcomed sight, but his appearance had seen better days. He leaned back against the log, shivering, nearly submerged in blue, quilted flannel, with his knees tucked into his chest. Stains of black forest dirt were smeared all over his clothes, especially the cuffs of his jeans, his knees, and the elbows of his jacket. His bloodshot eyes hung heavy, barely visible under his sweat-soaked, knit beanie, and his face was as pale as the ridges of fungus that grew on the log he leaned against.

"What happened?" Wilbert uttered, with a voice as weak and as tired as the rest of his seasoned body.

"They chased me across the road for a ways... to just below the bluff. I couldn't get ahead of them, so I left the light lay, and doubled back." Jeff leaned forward and looked toward Miss Nellie. "Sorry about your flashlight, Miss Nellie."

Miss Nellie didn't even open her eyes. She just waved her hand toward Jeff, as if to dismiss the subject to the air.

"They weren't fooled for long," Jeff continued, his meaty eyes rolling over the log and staring into the laurel across the road. "They're over there, waiting for me to make a move."

"Thanks...for saving us...me," Andy whispered from the opposite side of the group. "Did you see or hear anything from Sally?"

Jeff just bit his bottom lip while slowly shaking his head.

Wilbert took a deep breath and rolled his head toward Miss Nellie. "Do we cross the road?"

"I'm not going anywhere for twenty minutes," she said as she nestled down even further into the log. "But I suppose it's either that, or go home."

\*\*\*

The other six, weary eyes closed to match Miss Nellie's, just for a brief rest, as their exhausted muscles quivered with relief behind the fallen tree. But nerves could not be settled. The forest squirrels and birds hastened to their morning busy work, creating chaos for nervously diligent ears. Whether it be dead on the ground, or high up in the tree tops, every rustling leaf popped open an eye somewhere along the line of resting faces, and anticipation of their worst fears pushed on each other like opposing magnets. Fifteen slow minutes ticked away, and it actually became more strenuous to rest.

"Well, let's get this over with," Miss Nellie groaned as she hobbled to her feet. Wilbert grabbed for her hand, but his resting muscles were not ready to awake. Miss Nellie marched past Andy, around the end of the log, and noisily blundered through the laurel toward the road. Wilbert and the boys scrambled to their feet, some faster than others, and the males chased after the matriarch of their rescue mission, who's demeanor seemed to change with the wind.

# Chapter Twenty-one

Crossing Rocky Gap Road proved to be more difficult than any human would have ever imagined. Wilbert and Miss Nellie, Andy and Jeff, all stood silent and still on the yellow line, staring into the tunnel of Mountain Laurel that awaited their entrance.

Eventually, without making a sound, Wilbert walked across the westbound lane and into the laurel, following the lead of his rifle. One by one, the rest followed Wilbert, all creeping northward up the game trail. The sun had been bright and climbing high into the eastern sky, but the laurel closed in over top of the trail again, casting shadows as far ahead as they could see. And the chatter of the woods stayed behind, on the other side of the road, leaving the darkened trail dead silent, as if they were walking death row.

Wilbert penetrated deeper and deeper into the laurel, slow and steady, and as quiet as possible – although he knew that it didn't matter. The Sasquatch could feel his presence just the same as he was beginning to feel Enki's. Wilbert was ready though, and waiting with each step for whatever it would be that he was ready for.

Rods of glistening light began to push through the foliage and cut across the trail as the sun climbed even higher in the sky. But the thin rays of sun only made everything else darker. Miss Nellie's dry, heavy eyes and her sore, aching legs and neck seemed not so much of an issue anymore. And Jeff was slipping deeper and deeper into some alter reality. He stayed in the shadows, stepping over and ducking under the rods of sunlight as if they were tripwires. Bringing up the rear, Andy couldn't keep from looking back, but he could only see those brunette curls everywhere that he looked.

The oval edges of the laurel leaves were beginning to blend together into a never-ending realm of dark and light delirium, and Wilbert lowered his eyes to his feet, just to make certain that they *were* actually moving. It was only a quick look, but, somehow, when he looked back up, the dark tunnel-like trail was filled with unhindered daylight ahead. The trail led straight into open timber like a storm drain dumping into the ocean.

Wilbert crept to the very edge, between the laurel and the open timber, which was almost as much of a sharply defined boundary as along the road. As he scanned across the small plain of mature timber, two ravens boasted their raucous grumblings and danced like drunkards in the morning sunshine, high up on oak boughs. But they were the only signs of life. The wooded flat seemed as dead as a cemetery clear across to the bluff on the other side.

The bluff, as locals referred to it, was a sheer, rock face, two stories high, and it separated the lower lying saddle of Rocky Gap from the jagged backbone of the mountain that sloped up to the top of Rocky Ridge. Although it would be another steep climb, the bluff could easily be bypassed on either side by paths that were nearly as old as the mountain itself. But it was also well known by local hunters as a great place to ambush traveling game – only this time, humans were the prey. Wilbert would have to lead his charge through to the top, where it would be a much easier walk to the southern edge of the Sasquatch plateau, and hopefully a strong northern colony.

*

Wilbert stepped out from the cloak of the laurel, and the two ravens took to the air... only there were several more than two... all cawing crazily as they circled the flat, diving in and through the oak canopy above their heads. Wilbert proceeded across the flat, and even though they were just birds, he seemed a bit more cautious than when in the laurel. They were in open woodland, but it was still the woods, and there could have been something lurking behind every tree. And suddenly, as if created from his own imagination, there *was* something. Wilbert shouldered his rifle, and the group froze in place. There was something dark, on the ground, half exposed from behind a tree near the bluff. Wilbert side-stepped to the left, holding his aim steady while trying to see more of the…thing.

Andy and Jeff drifted along with Wilbert's lead, both armed with a rock in each hand. The object lengthened with every step, but it seemed rather small, and dainty, like maybe discarded plastic, or some other remnant from a hunter's old tree stand, so often found in nature.

"Sally!" Andy called out as he dropped his rocks and bolted past Wilbert toward the mysterious object.

Wilbert grabbed Andy's shoulder, but couldn't hold on to the emotionally turbocharged lad, and he and Jeff chased after. The object that was stretched out on the ground, sat up. It *was* Sally. She leaped to her feet and into Andy's arms, sobbing uncontrollably and trembling feverishly. The rest of the group soon gathered round her, all asking if she was okay, and what had happened. Sally could not answer.

Eventually Wilbert grabbed her by the shoulders, interrupting the reunion. "Sally," he barked. "Where are they?"

Sally was still unable to speak, but she managed to raise a quivering finger and point over Wilbert's right shoulder. Everyone turned in that direction, their eyes locking onto the unmistakable outline of a rather large Sasquatch standing on the trail that they had just traveled up, at the edge of the laurel.

"That's…not Tommy," Andy said. "Is it?"

While everyone else helplessly stared in fear, Wilbert wheeled around toward the bluff, hoping *not* to confirm his suspicions. But sure enough, there was a Sasquatch on each trail that carved around the bluff. "We're trapped against the bluff," Wilbert cried out, almost as soft as a whisper as he looked to the left and right for an escape down over the side of the mountain. But five more creatures emerged, one after the other, from behind a tree or from a shadow on the ground. They were there when Wilbert stepped into the open timber, unnoticeable even when expected. And now the rescuers were huddled back-to-back with their victim, and corralled against the vertical base of the cliff.

"Mr. Wilbert," Jeff nervously whispered, almost like he was more afraid of what was about to come out of his own mouth, than the Sasquatch brigade that had just cornered him. "How good are you with that rifle?"

"I can get at least three, maybe four...before they get to us."

\*\*\*

Wilbert did not reply further, drawing Jeff's attention. Wilbert balanced on two trembling knees with his rifle shouldered, the muzzle pitched high in the air, aiming toward the top of the rock face. The rifle quivered in his white knuckles, and Wilbert's face was blood red. And a single bead of sweat trailed down across his temple and into his beard. Jeff slowly looked in the direction of Wilbert's aim. Another Sasquatch towered above their heads, standing at the very edge of the cliff. Only this one was uncharacteristically lean, but still very tall and extremely broad, covered in ghostly-white hair, and his head gleamed like a full moon in the night sky. His very presence was irresistible, silently demanding that all eyes fall upon him, and there was no mistaking, this was Enki.

Despair burst from Wilbert's lungs as his distressed arms collapsed with the gun. His eyes fell to the forest floor before his feet, like he had been injected with the guilt of mankind.

Everyone else stared wide-eyed at Enki, their mouths hanging open and their bodies locked in fear. Jeff wore the very same face, but his was focused on Wilbert. He reached over and pulled the rifle from Wilbert's grip, and raised the weapon toward the top of the bluff. Jeff steadied the crosshairs on Enki's chest, gently squeezing the trigger, but it would not give. He flipped the safety back and forth with his thumb, but still the trigger would not pull. "What the...why have you been carrying this thing round?" he shrieked, his voice frazzling like his nerve.

"It works just fine," Wilbert solemnly forewarned, his eyes still to the ground and his hands lifelessly hanging empty.

Just as Wilbert's words faded away, Enki leaped over the cliff edge, stopping time as he plummeted to the flat below. Dirt and rocks blasted high into the air as his feet plunged deep into the Earth, and the entire mountain trembled. Enki stood as firm as the bluff at his back as hundreds of leaves swirled around, tumbling on the breeze, and dark, menacing clouds rolled across the sky from behind the bluff. The sun disappeared behind the cloud cover that blanketed the mountain, and the sharp light of Enki's head dimmed to the shimmering of the legendary crystal mask. Only the crystal mask that Enki had forged on his island prison was more of a skull, accurate in every detail, right down to the teeth, and it seemed more a battle helmet than a mask. It was though the beautiful crystal had been molded around his entire head, other than the bottom jaw, and it fit Enki's every bone structure perfectly, especially around his eyes. He glared out through the crystal eye sockets, with maddening yellow eyes. Enki's glare was enough to make the bravest man curl up into the fetal position.

Jeff frantically worked the bolt of the rifle, and fiddled with the safety and trigger, all while holding his aim steady, but the rifle would just not fire.

Enki held his hands out, palms toward the sky, and he slowly stepped forward. "I do not intend to be condescending," he said, his voice deep and strong, annunciating each syllable clearly and smoothly, nearly melodious. "But your weapon is of no use here."

The rifle ripped from Jeff's hands and flew through the air into Enki's massive fingers, the grip of the stock disappearing as he raised his chiseled, white arm to the sky. Enki fired a shot into the air, and then broke the rifle into two pieces, using only his hands. With a quick flip of his wrists, the two halves of the rifle sailed over his shoulders, and disappeared over top of the bluff.

"Oh crap," Jeff whimpered.

Enki chuckled three sharp, guttural bursts from his chest. Even his laugh could stop a beating heart. "I will not harm my children, any more than they would harm me," he scorned, glaring guilt into Jeff's eyes.

"You'd be surprised at what your children are willing to do," Wilbert interrupted, finally raising his head to face Enki. "That's the disease that you have inflicted on us."

Enki grimaced behind the crystal mask, and the circle of human captives tightened to near shoulder to shoulder. "I only want the best for my children," Enki explained. "To give them all that is to be offered. To return what was wrongfully taken from them." Enki stepped into a very, slow stride, circling around the group, but keeping his distance. "Should you not have the freedom to choose your own life? Freedom of choice is a gift to my children…and the light steals that gift from you!" he roared as he slammed his fist into the palm of his other hand, shooting out jagged slivers of bright white and shadow like an explosion of lightning bolts.

Enki continued circling his group of terrified children, his yellow eyes glowing with a tint of red, and reflecting throughout the crystal mask. "Tommy!" he shouted with intense fury, but then weakening into maddening laughter again. "Tommy is a good name for my narrow-minded nephew. He wants to steal your freedom! He would have you live as the lowly beasts that formed from your stolen hair!"

Enki hesitated for rebuttal, but heard nothing. "And where is your gallant Tommy now…running…hiding? Always content to do nothing… letting be, what will be. *My* children are not the same. You all have refused to abandon the frail one, sweetening the scent even more. But will he come?"

"Oh…you'll be seeing him soon, Powder," Miss Nellie sassed.

Wilbert quickly cupped his hand over her mouth, which didn't end very cordial for him.

Enki laughed again, and stopped in front of Miss Nellie, looking deep into her eyes. "Maybe so," he admitted. "But what will *you* do, *Miss Nellie*? Will you sacrifice your collection of ancient knowledge, and relinquish your magic elixirs that prolong your youth? Will you abandon your home…for silent isolation? We all know what you *have* done."

Miss Nellie lowered her eyes toward the ground, and Enki turned away, almost deeming her unworthy of his time. But before he left, he looked over his shoulder, lowered his voice, and asked, "Does Tommy know what you have been doing with my journal?" A sinister laugh crept out from his gullet as he stepped away.

Enki slowly moved on to Wilbert, still keeping his distance. But Wilbert, feeling betrayed and deceived again, still stared at Miss Nellie, and though she could feel his stare, she refused to look back.

"Ah…yes. Willard Wilbert," Enki intruded, demanding Wilbert's eyes. "You *have* given dearly over your short, miserable life. But yet, there is more to give. Will you condemn your patrons, your friends…diminishing that thick roll of currency in your pocket…that keeps your land?"

Wilbert opened his mouth to speak, but Enki had already vanished with a white blur.

Enki had zipped around the group, and was standing in front of Andy, his young eyes startled, and trying to remember how the white giant had gotten there. "Do you agree to remain unseen, and unheard, as the object of disgrace? Will you refuse your individuality and accept your place in this world as dictated by others?" Andy scowled back at the insinuations, but Enki was not intimidated.

Jeff was next. "Will you sit in the cold, the wet, and the dark when you can be warm and dry at night? Will you scrounge for roots and berries when a buffet of meat and dairy lay at hand? Will you choose fate, over a weapon?"

Jeff feverishly shook his head, like he was compelled to answer, and would be held to his answer.

Enki stepped in closer. "Then why do you stand by him?" he asked, subtle, and calm. "And try to murder your father!" he roared in anger, his long, white hair almost floating, and his eyes burning red through the crystal mask.

"You take too much," Sally cried out in panic. "You'll destroy everything...even yourself!"

"*I* take too much?" Enki chuckled as he strolled around to Sally. "Ah...the delicate balance."

Sally's sneakers slid through the leaves as she was pulled out of the circle and toward Enki by some unseen force. "Will you deny yourself of motherhood to balance the scales?"

Sally's eyes shuttered.

"Then who shall make that choice for you – Tommy? Will TOMMY decide if you are WORTHY?" Sally's head sank into her shoulders from his booming voice. "Such a pretty young thing too. Maybe you will give yourself to the strongest of the species?" Enki reached out for Sally's hand, but would not touch it. She trembled uncontrollably, then suddenly stumbled backwards into the group like something had just let go of her. Enki chuckled lightly. "Do not worry, my child. I find your hairless skin quite repulsive."

Enki began circling his huddled children again. "These all, are *my* gifts to you. And you all have taken. You are my warrior children, like it or not." Enki stopped, and ever so slightly sniffed at the air, his eyes glancing to the left and right as quick as a flash of light. Facing the group, he stepped backwards until his back was against the rock face of the bluff. "My other warriors know not what they are, but a stranger could not see the difference between you and them. You all have served me well, and I have no further need of you, so go home, or stay. You have not, and will not make a difference." Enki spread his arms wide, his long, white hair dangling underneath, and he flattened his palms against the rock. "My armies are waking around the world! Tomorrow has been forged by two hundred millennia of pain! I just have an ancient thorn to prune." Enki leaned his head back, until the crystal mask plinked against the rock face, and he rolled his inflamed eyes toward the sky.

Everyone's eyes followed Enki's lead to the top of the bluff…just as Tommy stepped over the edge. Tommy spun in mid-air as he plummeted down to the flat, plunging into the ground and collapsing to one knee, but not once taking his eyes off of Enki's.

"Good to see you nephew…after *so many* years. Or should I call you *Tommy*?" Enki burst into laughter, his red eyes raging with insanity, and Tommy lunged from his crouched position. But Enki melted back into the rock face like it was water. Tommy smashed into the rock with a teeth-clenching thud, ricocheting off of the bluff and landing where he had started, only flat on his back. Enki cackled with lunacy, his sketchy image still visible on the rock face, pacing back and forth, laughing, but still solid rock all the same.

Tommy quickly rolled onto his feet, cradling a lose boulder and hurling it into Enki's rock image along the way. The rock exploded against the bluff, blasting out countless shards of stone and trails of dust in every direction with such an abrasive pop that all five human onlookers nearly collapsed to their knees.

"Ouch!" Enki cried out, allowing just a moment of silence to loom in the air before resuming his taunting laughter.

*

And without warning, Enki's Sasquatch goons swarmed in on Tommy, encircling him against the cliff. Tommy roared, condemning each of his kin with his eyes, but he would not turn his back on Enki. One Sasquatch leaped for his back, but Tommy turned sideways, latched onto the traitor in midair, and flung him at Enki. The beast slammed into the bluff so hard, debris fell from the treetops, but Enki never stopped laughing, never flinched.

Two more Sasquatch attacked from both sides, both locking onto each of Tommy's arms. In a colossal tug-of-war, Tommy groaned and pulled both of his assailants in close, turning up dirt and rocks as their feet plowed through the layers of fallen leaves. But another clubbed Tommy in the back of the head with a heavy boulder, something a Sasquatch would never do without being under the influence of Enki – any price.

Tommy folded to one knee again, slightly disoriented, but still he started to push to his feet with the weight of three Sasquatch holding him down. Three more moved in. Another bellowed at the top of his lungs, and walked away. The one at Enki's feet gathered himself up from the ground, and staggered along behind, both disappearing into the laurel.

"They're running scared!" Jeff cheered.

"They fear nothing but their own consciences," Wilbert warned.

Enki emphatically ranted unintelligible words, with seemingly no continuity or reason, and broken by outbursts of insane laughter, all while pacing like a rabid beast across the face of the bluff. Understanding every sound, Enki's warriors pummeled Tommy's face with clubbed fists, spattering blood everywhere, and forever staining their hands. A snapping rib cracked through the air, and Tommy howled in pain, falling to both knees.

Sally screamed, her fingers tangled in her black locks of hair, and her palms cupped over her ears. More black mascara streamed down across Miss Nellie's rosy cheeks like rot as she held on to Wilbert, both silently bargaining with fate.

Jeff and Andy raced across the flat, charging to Tommy's aid as they leaped over rocks and scattered underbrush with their fists raised to the air, screaming like enraged berserkers. They jumped onto the tangle of Sasquatch muscle, punching and kicking, poking eyes and raking nails across faces with everything they had. But soon the boys found themselves hanging in the air by their arms, thrashing like fish on a line. One Sasquatch carried them around, hoisting their feet above the ground, and not quite knowing what to do with the vigorous boys.

Wilbert stepped away from Miss Nellie, stumbling to somewhere in the middle, almost like he was lost. Miss Nellie threw her hands to the air and began chanting the words of what had to be an ancient spell. Enki's stone-crazy gaze turned from Tommy to her, and he burst into laughter – laughter that quickly drifted into a threatening snap of a growl. Blood trickled from Miss Nellie's nose, but she chanted even louder.

"No!" Wilbert yelled back to Miss Nellie, then again to Tommy and the boys. Everything had spun so wrong, so fast. After everything that they had been through, and all that they had left, Tommy was their only hope. And he was down, already desperate just to hold on. The boys were in trouble. Miss Nellie couldn't take much more. And Sally just screamed, her eyes closed and hands over her ears. It was up to Wilbert to do something. But what? The option that he had been chasing after all night, his only option, was no longer valid. It would all be over in a matter of moments – moments that could never be lived again.

# Chapter Twenty-two

As Wilbert's mind hopelessly spun in indecisive circles, watching the end relentlessly unfold before his eyes, a foreign sound started weaving through the trees, swallowing the entire mountaintop. It came from every direction, pounding louder and louder, and slowing every beating heart to a near standstill, with ears tuned to the wind. A thousand snare drums battered a slow, menacing cadence above their heads, and a steam locomotive chugged to life in the laurel toward the road. But neither was possible. The hammered beats intensified, and blurred together – more like a stampede through the forest. Even Andy and Jeff eventually hung limp in the hands of the enemy, as they listened, and searched their imaginations for beyond what their eyes could see.

Finally returning to the wooded flat on which she stood, Sally pointed to the top of the bluff. "Look!"

Something was moving in the skyline...somewhat lurching from side to side, just above bluff. It was round, and red, and rising higher above the granite horizon with every lurch, revealing two flap-like appendages sticking straight out to the sides. It was Mikey's Stormy Kromer cap, with Mikey underneath! He raised his fists to the air, his body floating higher and higher above the rocky ledge as he approached the edge.

Wilbert returned the gesture. Several times over he threw his fists wildly over his head as he leaped into the air like a young boy swinging at a piñata. He turned back to Miss Nellie, who was too weak for anything but a teary-eyed smile, but it was enough.

Mikey's feet lifted from the ground, eventually hovering eight feet over the cliff edge. He was riding on the shoulders of a Sasquatch every bit as tall as Enki, and quite a bit rounder. And they were not alone.

"Put my friends down!" Mikey's puberty-stricken voice box squawked.

And like Mikey's words were the orders to charge, the northern Sasquatch tribe swelled around the edges of the bluff like ragging floodwaters. Enki's warriors shoved Tommy face first to the ground, and tossed Andy and Jeff aside with the concern of discarded trash.

\*

The two sides faced off with an animosity found only in the civil warfare of man, and each one displayed their own power by splintering trees and hurling rocks, all accompanied by deafening roars of threat. And when the two sides finally clashed, it sounded as though the world was crumbling to pieces. Bones snapped, and blood spilled upon the ground as the giants slugged and clubbed each other like never before on Earth. Enki's warriors were outnumbered five to one, but their blood was poisoned by Enki's blackened heart, and they battled with the skills of greed and vanity. And then there was Enki.

Enki blasted out from the face of the bluff, showering the battlefield with shards of stone. His crystal mask wavered with the burning red of his eyes, and he held high a long, stout staff, chiseled by his dark magic from the granite in which he had been hiding.

Enki strolled into battle, stepping on Tommy's back as he went. The northern tribe desperately threw everything they had at him – rocks, boulders, and even young trees. But Enki was untouchable, spinning and somersaulting through the hailstorm of battle, swinging his staff like a madman and shattering every bone within reach.

The flat trembled hysterically with chaos, and shrieked of confusion and pain. The eldest of Rothstone's patriarchs, younger only to Enki and Tommy, bellowed and roared encouragement and direction to his inexperienced clan, who had only heard the whispers of forbidden stories of such days as this. And though he was a mere infant when Enki had last spilled the blood of his own kind, these sounds were still remembered by his ears, and he was the only one who could imagine the ruthlessness of war.

The patriarch toppled a young hickory, with the girth of a man's thigh, and twisted off the crown as he squared up directly in Enki's path. A smile formed behind the crystal teeth of Enki's mask, and the two staffs collided with near atomic power. Bark splintered across the flat as the hickory club bounced back to its starting position, barely returning in time to deflect Enki's next blow. Over and over, Enki relentlessly hammered down with his staff, and the hickory shredded and weakened with every deflected blow.

Enki reveled in his own power, and left an opening of vulnerability. The patriarch drove the butt of hickory into Enki's chest, knocking him to the ground. But this only infuriated Enki. He leaped from the ground, twirling his staff as he flew through the air, and he plunged the narrow end of the granite staff through the chest of the brave Rothstone patriarch. The doomed Sasquatch never uttered a sound from his lungs, but the sound of death rang out across the battlefield, hesitating time, only for a moment, as every eye on the flat watched the old father fall to his knees.

*

A gust of wind ripped across the flat and howled through the canopy overhead. The chatter of an army of leaves flooded the flat, many tumbling upon the ground, most twisting in flight, and the daylight dimmed even more. Wilbert looked to the sky, drawing Miss Nellie's eyes upward as well, both finding the spot where the sun hazily formed through the clouds. A black ring seared around the edge of the sun, penetrating through the overcast more than the rays of light. It was beginning, again, and there seemed no hope of stopping it, without making it even stronger.

***

With a long, gentle arm, Mikey's rather large, new friend cradled him to the ground near Tommy as the giant honed in on Enki's path of broken bodies. Mikey scurried to Tommy's side, checking vitals, wiping blood and trying to rouse the barely conscious creature amidst the destruction. Andy and Jeff rushed to help, and all three desperately tried to heave Tommy to his feet, but could hardly hoist his shoulders from the ground. The boys pleaded for a rally, but as he held Tommy's battered face, Mikey could only see despair in his hands.

Enki still hovered over his murder, as if waiting to ambush the soul of his victim as he returned to the stars. Mikey's friend zeroed in on Enki. Ready or not, he looked to no one else for help. The colossal beast scooped up a rock the weight of two men, and hurled it toward Enki. The boulder sailed through the air with tremendous energy, heading straight for Enki's back. But Enki's burning eyes glowed on the back of his crystal mask, and he spun around to face his attacker. Enki was quick with the dark, and swung his staff at the speed of light. The boulder exploded into a thousand pieces, blasting shrapnel like a cannonball. But so did Enki's staff.

As Enki stared at the pebbles and dust left in his stinging hands, he began to tremble, as if he were about to explode. An unearthly shriek bust from within as he flashed through the trees in a blur, right up to Mikey's friend, glaring eye to burning eye. And by all appearances, Enki would have his hands full.

Mikey's friend wasted no time with intimidation, and cocked both bulky arms, thrusting two massive fists at Enki's chest. But Enki caught both fists in the palms of his hands, and he squeezed. Mikey's friend frantically tried to jerk his fists free from Enki's grasp, and he kicked Enki in the mid-section. Enki squeezed even harder. Mikey's friend howled in anguish, and collapsed to his knees, desperate to find some reserve of hidden strength.

\*\*\*

It felt as though Mikey's heart was in Enki's grip, and he rushed to the aid of his friend, charging across the darkening timber and through the brawling juggernauts, all of which could not have been more invisible. All Mikey could see was a friend in serious trouble – a friend that had saved him from the jaws of ruthless predators, and plucked him from a jagged ravine in the middle of the night, only days earlier.

Mikey feverishly whaled baseball-sized stones at Enki's head, as many as he could find, each one plinking off of the side of Enki's crystal, skull mask. And all the while a high, raspy, almost possessed, voice spewed out a deluge of cuss words and slander, and many words that were no words at all. Enki turned toward his scrawny assailant, and blasted a roar that tumbled Mikey backwards across the ground.

Then, out of nowhere, Sally charged in on the other side, with a dead snag that she had gathered from the forest floor. She thrashed on Enki's kneecap, over and over, as hard and as fast as she could. But Enki shooed her away like a pest, with his foot, sending her crashing to the ground as well. Sally screamed. Mikey's friend wailed in pain as his fingers began to snap. And Enki just laughed, and laughed.

\*

A spark of life ignited somewhere deep inside, and Tommy fumbled his swollen face toward the sound of Enki's wrath. Everything was blurry, and tinted red. His barely fused arm held together by a throbbing fiber, and his rib stung like a bullet wound. He could hear Andy and Jeff's muffled voices calling his name, and could feel their hands tugging under his shoulders, but it was though they were in another dimension than he.

A shrill howl rang out from above, up toward the top of the bluff. Tommy rolled his feeble head across his shoulder, and peered up into the darkening sky. Blood pooled in the slits of his swollen eyes, but he recognized the voice. It was his mate, and his only offspring in the last three centuries.

Now Tommy was battered and weak, but his heart beat as strong on Earth as in the stars. He slowly pushed to one knee, then to his feet, with Jeff and Andy lifting with everything they had, and balancing the wobbly giant. Blood dripped to the ground, clearing from his wounds as reality eased back into his head. And as strong as his heart was, Tommy felt as though it was actually ripping in two as he looked across the flat.

His friends were dragging their busted bodies to the edges, and his family was locked into battle, each one exhausted, each one dying inside for what they were doing, but doing it just to live. And there, lifeless where he laid, one heart that would never beat with life again. Then there was his human cousins, his friends, bravely in way over their heads, and lucky not to have been trampled already. Tommy had failed to keep the darkness away from his family and friends, and he had failed to stop Enki.

But blood still pumped through Tommy's veins, and the rays of the sun still beamed through the constricting black ring. He inflated his chest to near twice its normal size, and he blasted an inconceivably strong, unimaginably creepy, moan, carried to the heavens by the howling wind, and echoing back to the mountain as an absurdly sharp roar.

***

Enki's insane eyes snapped toward Tommy like a striking snake as every living creature on the flat stilled. He released his grip, and Mikey's friend tumbled backwards to the ground, trying to unfold his crumpled fingers. Tommy gently nudged Jeff and Andy to end of each arm, and he staggered backward toward the bluff. Enki's eyes gleamed with revenge, and a low, obsessive growl could be heard grumbling from somewhere inside his chest as he slowly stalked Tommy, cornering him into the bluff. The entire flat watched, frozen in time by something more than fear. But

Enki seemed to be in no hurry, like he relished the moment – the moment that had been seared into his imagination for well over a thousand years.

But then, like tree huggers at a logging site, Jeff and Andy stepped back together, blocking Enki's path to Tommy, and making it clear that he would have to go through them first. The boys had never been so terrified, but they stood firm, shoulder to shoulder – mostly to steady each other's trembling knees.

Tommy looked across the flat again, with what his impeded vision offered. He saw the eyes of doubt, of fear, and of bravery. Tommy closed his own eyes, holding the image of his friends and family, and listening to the torrents of wind ripping through the treetops, and the sound of dying light.

Andy and Jeff pumped up the bravery inside of their chests, and clenched their fists. But suddenly Enki no longer was before them. He had zipped around the boys and charged Tommy. Tommy was ready though, and he caught Enki by the throat, spinning him around and slamming him into the rock face so hard that Tommy's son nearly toppled over the edge above.

Enki stared into Tommy's eyes for a fleeting second – just long enough for human eyes to catch up, and for emotions to soar with hope at the sight of Enki's neck pinned between Tommy's grip and the bluff. But trickery was born within Enki long ago, and he melted back into the rock face again, this time taking Tommy's hand with him. Enki simply backed out of Tommy's grip, stepped to the side, and walked right out of the bluff, leaving Tommy's good arm trapped in solid stone.

The fury of battle flared again in Tommy's ear as the Rothstone clan shoved their way to his aid, and Enki's warriors blocked it. Enki sadistically paced around Tommy, just out of reach, taunting his victim with jesters and slurs that only Tommy understood. Eventually Enki leaned in on Tommy's left-rear quarter, and whispered, "You had your chance nephew, and you did nothing. A weakness I do not have."

Tommy wildly swung his free arm around, but Enki thrust his fist forward, and re-snapped Tommy's healing wound. Tommy never muttered a sound. His left arm hung limp and unnatural, his right hopelessly trapped in the granite of the bluff. Tommy was at the mercy of Enki, who's eyes burned merciless. He could do nothing but listen to the sounds of the forest floor compressing under Enki's obsessively calculated steps.

*

Suddenly Wilbert stepped into Miss Nellie's view of Tommy. "You know I love you," he said. "Always have."

"You damn fool!" Miss Nellie cried out, her voice broken, frantic, and angry, but deeply rooted in heartbreak. "It took you this long to say it, and now you're going to go and do something stupid!"

"Nellie," Wilbert said as he put his hands on her shoulders. "I've waited my whole life for this. For my life to be worth more than...living." Wilbert kissed Miss Nellie, and turned away, running toward Tommy, shedding his shirts as he went.

Miss Nellie collapsed to her knees, holding out her hands, as she watched Wilbert slowly slipping away. His first flannel shirt tumbled to the ground as Sally and Mikey watched. Another shirt fell as Jeff and Andy watched. Eventually, the last of Wilbert's shirts folded into a rumpled pile on the ground. His flabby, white skin moved so slow across the flat, no one else noticed. Tommy was aware though, and he planted his big foot right into Enki's mid-section. Enki had let his guard down, and crumbled to one knee. Then with seemingly impossible agility, Wilbert leaped through the air and landed on Enki's back, locking his arms tightly around Enki's neck, and he squeezed with all his strength.

Enki was still and quiet for a brief second of confusion. He hadn't felt the hug of his children for a hundred thousand years. And then the bite of the ancient curse dug in, and smoke rolled out from between Enki and Wilbert. Enki unglued like a bronco busting from the chute, and he launched from the ground, screaming in pain. He bucked and ran across the flat while Wilbert hung on for dear life – the dear life of all others.

*** 

Andy and Jeff looked at each other, each checking if the other was seeing the same, and without speaking a word, they rushed to Tommy's aid. Tommy had his foot against the rock face, and was pulling away with all of his might. The boys joined in on the pull, but the stone of the bluff had molded around Tommy's hand like concrete. Jeff scooped up a stone twice the size of his fist and began waylaying the rock face around Tommy's hand. Shards of the bluff chiseled away, but the stone in his hand crumbled just as fast. Jeff found another stone, and Andy did the same, both frantically hammering the rock away from each side of Tommy's hand. Even Mikey's friend lumbered onto the scene and wrapped his arms around Tommy's shoulder, adding his girth to the pull, with his crushed hands hanging limp next to Tommy's swollen face.

*

While the boys feverishly toiled to free Tommy, Wilbert's grip began to loosen. But it did not matter. Enki grasped at a moment of composure, and he thrust backwards into a massive oak, slamming Wilbert into the rock hard tree. Air blasted from Wilbert's lungs, and his ribs snapped. The sound of the collision was shuffled with the clamor of the flat, but it sharply found Miss Nellie's ears, and pierced her heart. Her anguished cry rose above all else, and everyone stalled as they watched Wilbert's fingers slip from around his own wrist. Enki leaned forward, falling to his hands and knees, and Wilbert crumpled to the ground like a lifeless sack of grain at the base of the oak.

The pungent smell of burning hair lingered heavy in the air. The glistening white mane that covered Enki's neck and back was gone, and replaced by black, blistered flesh that steamed and bubbled like boiling tar. He crawled across the forest floor with his head hung low, periodically waving around one hand or the other, blindly feeling for anything. But Wilbert did not move.

***

Across the wooded flat, four teenagers just stood there, listening to Miss Nellie mourn, and watching her stumble through the forest toward Wilbert. And in that brief time, when a heartbroken old woman stood out above anger and fear, bravery and revenge, and the chaos of war, the innocence of youth was lost forever. They would only feel it once, and would never forget.

More determined than ever, Andy and Jeff flew back into their mission, hammering away at the stone trapping Tommy's hand. Their arms burned, and their muscles tightened, but they were making headway. Chips of stone zipped through the air, leaving behind two large cavities in the surface of the rock face, which also left jagged edges that met with the hands behind the chisels before the chisels met with the target. Fingernails turned purple, and skin pealed back from knuckles, but the boys would not stop, or even slow – they were men now.

And like that first drop of a desperately needed rain, a crack formed that circled around Tommy's wrist. Jeff and Andy hammered furiously at the stone. Tommy pulled against the bluff with everything he had. Mikey's friend pulled against Tommy, and even Sally and Mikey had joined in on the tug. And finally, Tommy's hand popped free. The stone of the bluff was still molded around his hand, but he was free, and the boulder on the end of his arm made a formidable weapon.

\*\*\*

Enki had crawled onto a young poplar tree that stretched straight, and high past much older treetops. He pulled himself to his feet, and leaned against the poplar, but his chin stayed buried in his chest. Tommy approached and stood before him in silence. Burnt skin crackled and split open as Enki lifted his head to meet Tommy's eyes, and his trachea pulsed through a gaping neck wound when he swallowed. He appeared as if death had taken his flesh a century ago, but his pupils still gleamed black in the middle of his burning, red eyes, revealing a hollow corpse filled with darkness.

As the two ancients stared each other down, Enki's black fingernails began to grow, slowly, slyly, curving into claw-like daggers, honed razor sharp. Those hollow, black pupils contracted ever so slightly, and Enki launched a deadly swipe at Tommy's neck. Tommy reared back as his hair flipped and tumbled on the wind, but it was only hair. Tommy countered with a roundhouse right, and planted his rock hand squarely on the side of Enki's head. The crystal mask clanked like an aluminum bat connecting with a fastball, only much louder, and deeper, and the skin around Enki's wrenching neck nearly shattered like glass. Tommy returned a backhand even harder. The stone exploded from his hand, and Enki's mask shattered into a thousand, screaming fragments of crystal and light. The power of the blow spun Enki's body, twisting up his legs and boring his feet into the leaf litter. He toppled into the poplar, hugging it just to stay aloft.

Enki was done. All he could do was hold on to the tree. He couldn't even untangle his legs. Air wheezed in and out through his throat as he panted – he couldn't breathe deeply without tearing the crisp skin across his back. A small, grotesque plate of the crystal mask still clung around Enki's left eye, but the rest was destroyed, leaving behind clammy white skin, completely hairless, and wrinkled like a prune. It was time to end Enki's dark reign on Earth, once and for all.

Tommy raised his fist to the air. One blow to the base of his skull, and Enki would never wreak his havoc again.

But, as dazed as Enki was, he rolled his head up to meet Tommy's eye. His eyes no longer burned with hatred, and had faded to their diseased yellow, almost brown, and recognizable as family. Tommy pushed his head back down. He had to strike, but he didn't have to look into Enki's eyes as he did it. Enki looked up again, refusing to make it easy. Losing his ruthlessness fast, Tommy closed his eyes. He knew where to strike the blow, but what he didn't see was the fragment of the crystal mask starting to glow. Enki collapsed, his legs bouncing from the ground as he leaped into the air. He rocketed straight up the poplar and across the sky like a shooting star. And he was gone.

# Chapter Twenty-three

The bluster of the cold storm settled into a warm breeze, and the chatter of the marching leaf army softened. Only then was the silence noticed. The small flat of open timber, that was filled with so many, who were in such a struggle just moments ago, was completely quiet and still. The cloud cover lifted from its grip on the mountain, and drifted eastward across the sky. And the ring of darkness that had been choking out the sun, receded back into the surrounding universe.

Enki's warriors bowed their heads, and silently moved through the trees like spirits until they faded away into the laurel. Tommy called to them with a soft, forgiving moan. They only did what they thought they must. Man would have done the very same many years ago. In fact they were much like man – believing in what they wanted to hear, even though they knew better, and even when it came from a madman hungry for power. And that madman had left them behind, and alone. They were a species all in their own now. Somewhere between man and Sasquatch. Ashamed to return to their kin, and human enough to know they would find no existence among man.

***

Miss Nellie squeezed Wilbert's hand as Sally and the boys gathered round. Tommy looked down over top of Mikey's head, with his hand gentle resting on Mikey's shoulder, like he had known Mikey all along. The rest of the Rothstone clan circled around several feet behind.

Wilbert's breathing was quick and troubled, and he grimaced with pain behind the cover of his darkened glasses. He struggled to part his lips, revealing blood caked in the corners of his mouth, and dangling from his moustache.

"Teach these kids well Nellie," he sputtered. "Everything rides on their shoulders. And I believe in them." Miss Nellie tried to speak, but her throat closed tightly, holding back uncontrollable tears.

"You...saved the world...Wilbert."

"We all did, Mikey," Wilbert gurgled. "We all did our part."

\*\*\*

Vagrantly trespassing on the moment, voices floated up and across the flat, from somewhere below on the mountainside. It was the voice of hysteria. The deadly mob had resurrected from the previous day, with their blood curdled even more by the foreboding skies, and the appalling sounds of pandemonium that had been descending upon Falling Rocks from the mountaintop high above.

"Come on! We got to get you back to Miss Nellie's place," Sally sobbed. She frantically looked around for someone to pick Wilbert up. "She can fix him!" Sally turned to Miss Nellie. "You can fix him!"

"You've got the heart of a Sasquatch, girl," Wilbert wheezed. "Don't ever ignore it." He coughed, and blood sprayed out onto his beard. "Forget about me...Enki's army still marches, and it always will. All you can do...is inspire it to march in a different direction." Wilbert rolled his eyes up toward Tommy, gasping in a breath, and squeezing Miss Nellie's hand. "Besides...I'm good and ready to see what this forbidden knowledge is all about."

Tears overflowed from Miss Nellie's eyes as a strange, weak moan escaped through her nose. Her head shook from side to side, refusing to accept Wilbert's fate. But suddenly, something stumbled through the brush, out in the laurel, and it was moving toward the oak flat.

\*\*\*

Andy, Jeff and Mikey rushed out to confront the intruder. They stood along the line of the laurel's edge, blankly staring at nothing but a labyrinth of slender green leaves, and intently listening to the deliberate steps of malice. A glimpse of blaze orange flashed through the Appalachian jungle, and the boys looked back to warn Tommy, but he was gone. The entire northern clan was gone. Even Wilbert and Miss Nellie were gone. There was only Sally, with the oak snag clenched in her dainty white knuckles, and hanging by her side. She had moved up to half way between where Wilbert had been laying, and where the boys now were. And she appeared more agitated and determined, than meek and frightened.

The steps were getting close, and the boys returned their attention back to the laurel. The bright orange reappeared, and was close enough to track with eyes more than ears. It was a ball cap. And it weaved through the foliage, closer and closer, until a set of eyes under the cap met with the eyes of the boys.

"What the hell you twerps doing up here?" Shorty barked as he plowed through the laurel and into the openness of the flat. He brandished the muzzle of his rifle directly at Andy. "Good way to get shot!" Shorty grinned, but his rotting teeth quickly disappeared back into hiding as his eyes darted across the ridge top, checking every tree. He looked at Sally, longer than necessary, then at Mikey. "Well, well, well. Won't people be surprised to see you?" Shorty's eyes canvassed the horizon again. "Where's your buddy, Andy?"

Andy confidently walked up to Shorty, pushed the barrel of the rifle aside, and stared him in the eye. "Leave us alone, Shorty. There's no beast. And you see Mikey right there. He's not missing!" Andy leaned in slightly closer. "What do you think the town's going to do when they find out they all been duped by a sadistic pervert and his drunken delusions?"

"Watch your mouth boy!" Shorty's temper was always the first to his tongue, but fear was never far behind. He did have secrets, and Andy knew the worst. Secrets that even his closest friends would not tolerate. And the local hysteria that deemed his outlandish story, logical, was about to brand him a lunatic. "I don't need anything from this hick town," Shorty spouted. "And drunk or not, I was there just the same as you."

"Listen, Shorty," Andy said while hovering even closer. "I'm getting bigger, stronger and smarter each year. You're getting smaller, weaker and dumber every year. Your past is catching up with you, Shorty. If you had half a brain, you would get out of *my* house, and never see my mother again." At that moment, Andy could see Enki's eyes burning in Shorty. "LEAVE...ENNIS."

Shorty stepped back from Andy's boom, his hate-filled eyes seeing the boys for what they were for the first time. Their knuckles were bloody and their skin was scarred, their faces were swollen and bruised, and their clothes were shredded. They had been to hell and back, and stood in line to go again, even scrawny Mikey – especially Mikey. They were no longer 'just the boys'. Shorty peeled his glare from the boys and stormed over the break of the ridge, into the laurel of the mountainside.

\*\*\*

Mikey led the race back to Sally, asking, "Where'd they go?" before his feet even reached his destination. Sally tipped her head toward the far corner of the bluff, just as Miss Nellie rounded the face of granite. Several Sasquatch fanned out behind her, combing across the flat, overturning bloodstained leaves and covering clumps of hair. Mikey just shook his head, grinning from ear to ear. He could appreciate their efforts to conceal their very identity better than the others. One Sasquatch diligently picked up the shards of Enki's crystal mask, neatly dropping them into a hole that he had scooped away with his massive hand, then covering the pile of shattered crystal with layers of forest debris.

"Come on kids," Miss Nellie said, her face pale and heartbroken, but ready to face a life she had never known. "It's time to go home."

"Where's Tommy?" Sally asked.

"He'll be fine," Miss Nellie answered. "He's very busy at the moment, but don't worry dear, he'll visit when the time is right." Miss Nellie herded the teenagers toward the trail through the laurel that led back to their world.

But Mikey walked in the opposite direction. Toward his new friend, standing at the top of the bluff with his crippled hands resting on his stomach.

"Mikey!" Jeff called out. "Where are you going?"

Mikey rolled his head toward the top of the bluff, and waved goodbye.

"Mikey, you can't," Jeff pleaded. "Your mom!"

Mikey turned back to Jeff again, and lowered his head. He *was* a little homesick, but other than that, he hadn't given his family much thought. His poor mother must have been out of her mind with worry. He looked up at his friend, then back to Jeff. But when Mikey looked for his friend again, he was gone. Mikey chased after for a few steps, towards the path that lead up and around the bluff, until a mournful howl swept through the trees. Mikey understood, and just stood there, by himself, as though he was as lost as when he was in the ravine. Eventually he slowly returned to his own kind, with his head hung low, and a tear pooled in the scratched up lens of his battered glasses.

"This isn't the end, kid. It's only the beginning," Miss Nellie said as she put her arm around Mikey and started for home. "You just have to learn a little patience...drives me crazy!"

***

The boys, Sally and Miss Nellie all watched their own feet slap the pavement over and over again as they descended the mountain. Not a one had spoken a single word since leaving the flat, but they were a group of people as close as any other. They were forever bound by secrecy. And the way Andy saw it, he would no longer hide anything from his friends. "So, Mikey...you going to let me read my brother's testimony?" he asked, speaking from the far right of the group, to Mikey on the far left.

Mikey's head popped forward, ahead of the line of bodies, and making nervous eye contact with Andy. He nearly tripped over his own feet. "You know about that?" he asked while pushing his glasses up his nose with his middle finger.

Andy nodded slightly, with half a smile.

Mikey's head snapped forward, blankly staring down the road in thought. "I can't," he eventually said. "I promised I would never show anyone...he'd kill me!" Everyone smirked at Mikey. "Yeah, well...nothing would surprise me anymore."

"Just tell us something about it, Mikey," Andy said.

"Andy you don't...," Mikey replied. "Maybe later...in private."

"No. I want everyone to hear. I will never be ashamed of my friends, my family, or myself ever again."

Jeff and Sally cheered their own commitment of the same, and Miss Nellie cackled her approval, but Mikey remained quiet, emotionlessly staring straight down the road.

\*\*\*

The group disappointedly settled to match Mikey's brooding. There were no sounds of civilization, and nothing stirring about the forest on either side of the road. There was only the cadence of ten shoes slapping the road. Then, just as the others left the subject to the mountain, Mikey took a deep breath. "Your brother was very...confused," he said. "Even more than me." Mikey paused in careful thought as the rest hung on for more. "Everybody was so proud of him, or so envious of him, and all the girls were in love with him, but he was burning up inside. He was what everybody expected him to be, but no one knew who he really was. He was born to the wrong town, the wrong family...the wrong body." Mikey lowered his head as he nervously ran his fingers through his hair, almost waiting for Andy to stop him from going any further. "He spent a lot more time at Blue Hole than anyone realized, Andy. And one day he took a rope." Mikey paused again, looking Andy in the eye and waiting, but it seemed that even the ten shoes wanted to hear. And Andy didn't appear to be offended, or surprised.

Mikey looked back down the road, took another deep breath, and continued. "He was looking up in the oak that leaned out over Blue Hole, playing it all out in his head – you know how dramatic he was." Mikey paused for a laugh, or even a smile from Andy, but he found neither. "He felt the hair stand up on the back of his neck," he bluntly said, abandoning any attempt to make light of his awkwardness. "He spun around, and there were those big, brown eyes, not more than four feet away. He didn't know how long he had stared into the bigfoot's eyes, but he wasn't scared, and it changed everything. He realized that he didn't choose to be who he was, and the only person that was tormenting him, was himself. Then, the Bigfoot took the rope from his hand, and disappeared into the woods."

Mikey settled back in his stride, and tilted his head in thought for a few seconds. "It makes no sense though. For the first time, your brother was happy with his own life...like he finally realized that he *did* belong to this world. And then the accident? I guess maybe he was still troubled by the eyes of society." Mikey's head leaned forward again, and he looked down the line of his friends. "Does that make it our fault?"

***

Mikey's question killed any impending conversation, and the group walked in silence again. They walked for fifteen painful minutes without a sound, each one pondering their own guilt of such judgments. A new subject was in order, and leave it to Mikey to find it. "So, Miss Nellie," he said. "What's the story on that old sawmill up in Rothstone?"

Miss Nellie smiled and nodded her head one time. "Well," she returned. "When Willard and I were young, a little older than you are now, that was the cutting edge of industrial technology. Willard's daddy owned and operated the mill until he was killed in a tragic logging accident, leaving Willard's family, as well as twenty other families, wondering where their next meal would come from. Charles's granddaddy offered to buy out the timberland, the saw mill, and even Plum Hollow, but Willard turned him down flat."

"Wait a minute," Jeff interrupted. "You mean to tell me that Wilbert is the mysterious owner of Haunted Hollow?"

"Yes," Miss Nellie answered. "We were neighbors. Willard lived in the so-called haunted house with his parents and his sickly sister. At that time, it was one of the nicest homesteads in Rocky Gap...sorry, Falling Rocks – that was before the town changed its name to match the road sign that the Department of Transportation put up." Suddenly Miss Nellie had four teenagers staring at her with the most peculiar look on their faces. "Aw, everybody thought it sounded better...more exotic," she said as she bobbed her head around and fluttered her hands about in front of her.

"Anyhow," Miss Nellie said, taking back her story. "Willard took over for his daddy. He had worked plenty at the saw mill, but when he took the helm, production nearly doubled. Team after team of horses skidded in logs day after day, and the money rolled in. The men worked twelve days on, then went home for two days before returning to the camp to do it all again."

"But then, things started coming up missing and broken overnight. It all started small, but soon escalated into bizarre howls coming from the ridge top above the camp, and rocks smashing through cabin windows while the men slept. They all blamed paper mill thugs, and refused to be intimidated. And trees continued to fall every day."

Miss Nellie raised her head and stared off into the sky in front of her. "That's when all hell broke loose," she said, like she could see the past played out across the blue sky. "It was the most miserable July that I can remember. Not a single leaf rustled on a breeze for over a week, and the nights were black as coal. No one slept comfortably – not even weary loggers. Then one night, shortly before midnight, just as a line of thunderstorms rolled over the top of Rocky Ridge to break the heat wave, a scream blasted through the camp. It came from within the camp, and it was no doubt the sound of man, and horror. In the glare of a flash of lightning, some of the men saw Big Jim Carson being carried away into the woods like a rag doll – a feat of no mortal man."

"The lightning cracked and the thunder roared, as the camp came under attack. Cabins shook violently, from the foundation to the roof. Men piled onto the cabin doors, desperate to keep whatever was pounding on the other side, out. Two more terror filled cries rose above the chaos in camp, as two more of the toughest roughnecks around were pulled through open cabin windows before the wide eyes of their bunkmates, and abducted into the woods like children. Every rifle in camp lit up the surrounding darkness with muzzle blasts of fire, leaving nothing but smoke and the smell of gunpowder lingering in the flashes of red and white light. Then, as quick as the torrents of rain and thunder moved across the valley to the east, everything fell dead silent and still again."

"Was Mr. Wilbert taken?" Sally gasped, clinging from half way up Andy's arm like she herself was being carried off into the darkness all over again.

"No," Miss Nellie answered. "But he was the only one who stayed a minute past first light the next morning, to search for the missing men. They eventually made their own way back to civilization, unharmed, but none spoke a word, and all three immediately left town, never to be heard from again."

"They didn't tell anyone what happened to them?" Mikey asked.

"No, Mikey," Miss Nellie chuckled. "You weren't around back then." Miss Nellie laughed some more, shedding a bit of her grief, but only for a moment. "Yeah, Willard stayed," she continued with her story. "His rifle never left his side, especially at night. He was sure that they would return, and he was determined to put a bullet through as many as he could. Willard worked extra hard at keeping the mill running, as much as one man could. He figured that his men would slowly come back, for work, eventually. He had to keep the mill turning. He had to take care of his widowed mother, and his sister – she wasn't right."

"What was wrong with her?" Sally asked.

"Doc Robinson said Anemia. I don't think he really knew, but he kept her going with medicines and bloodletting, and such. And they often traveled to Philadelphia where she spent time in some sort of iron lung. But that all took money, which was something that there just wasn't much of in those days."

Andy peeled his eyes away from Miss Nellie and focused on the road ahead of his feet as he remembered Wilbert's vague words from that night in the shed. The pieces started to fall together into his own scene of the story.

"A week later Willard came home," Miss Nellie sighed as she stared into the blue sky again. "I was so glad to see him. The rumors that had been swirling around town grew wilder by the day. But he had no time for me. Something had happened to Willard. He was changed…and like everyone else, he would not talk. Willard's mother begged him to sell out to the paper mill, but it was though he could not hear her, and as though the saw mill never even existed. Instead, he volunteered for the C.C.C. camp up at Sideling Gap. All but five dollars of his monthly pay was sent home to his mother, but it wasn't enough for his sister to enjoy the medical treatment that she had become accustomed to. Everybody in town gave something at one point or another, even if only a little bread, or a slice of meat. Most had nothing more to give."

Miss Nellie paused to remember those lean times of her childhood. She could still feel the hunger, but yet it surprised her that those were the happiest memories that she could remember. "Willard came home a few days before Christmas," she bluntly and dryly continued. "He found his sister in her bed...she had passed on sometime earlier. His mother was sitting on her rocking chair, on the back porch, in the cold, and half dead. She would not speak to him. She wouldn't even let him see his mother's eyes. Willard carried her inside, but she would not eat. And she never saw 1937."

The palm of Sally's hand covered her wide-open mouth, muffling her squeak of discontent, and the boys all lowered their heads – Jeff shaking his in disbelief, the other two's as still as a head could be riding atop a set of walking feet.

"Yeah," Miss Nellie said. "That's why Willard never married...never had children. He felt he had no right, after robbing his mother and sister of a life." Miss Nellie hesitated, and tilted her head slightly, mumbling, "They weren't the only ones robbed." She didn't mean to be heard, but she was. It was as though her thoughts were just too loud. "Well," she quickly carried on. "Willard eventually came around to me, early that spring. I guess he felt that he needed to explain himself...tell someone. He took me up to the saw mill, and that was when I met Tommy." Miss Nellie hesitated again as she pictured the day in the blue sky, and she chuckled. "What a day that was...but you all will never hear that story from me."

"Why didn't Wilbert just sell the mill?" Jeff asked, still disbelieving that it couldn't have all went down the way Miss Nellie said.

"Well, sweetie," she explained. "It's as simple as just doing the right thing...what he believed in. That first step against the current, even as everything else flows in the opposite direction. Willard held a tiny piece of the light safe, even though it burnt a hole straight through the palm of his hand. Sad thing is, most people branded him as selfish, and eccentric – crazy even. He carried that badge all of his life, but the truth is, Willard sacrificed more of his life for those people than all of them put together, so their children had the hope of a future."

"And we'll never forget it Miss Nellie," Andy said. "Or you."

"I know, Andy," she countered. "But you must never tell the story, any more than I have. You all understand that, right?" Miss Nellie's head rolled from right to left, catching each set of nodding, teenage eyes in a split second of confirmation, and ending with an incriminating stare into Mikey's eyes.

"Yes," Mikey huffed.

Miss Nellie flashed her locally famous smile at Mikey and said, "There's much more to the story, but we'll discuss that later, when you all are more prepared."

***

Suddenly Mikey's canvass high tops stopped dead where they slapped the pavement, causing his line of friends to curve ahead to the right as the group braked to a standstill. They had been so engrossed in conversation, not a one of them realized that they were approaching Wilbert's place. And there he was, sitting in his chair along the road, just as he normally would be.

"Keep moving, guys," Miss Nellie said with a broken voice. "This is the way it has to be."

Wilbert sat in the same rested position, was layered in the same flannels, and the blood was cleaned from his face and beard. Mikey knew that Wilbert's eyes were closed forever behind those darkened glasses, but he almost couldn't keep himself from checking behind those lenses, like that morning in the Jeep. Actually, they all could feel Wilbert watching as they hurried by.

\*\*\*

As the four-way intersection came into view, Jeff silently cut to the left and stood on the left road shoulder. Falling Rocks hadn't been that awake since...well, never. They all needed to split up. Miss Nellie just nodded to Jeff, and he cut through the woodlot behind town, heading for his house. The rest gathered single file on the right berm – Sally first, then Miss Nellie, followed by Andy and Mikey. The boys lagged back from the girls as they proceeded in front of the few houses that lined the road.

"Bye Sally," Andy whispered.

Sally turned around and smiled, waving with her dainty fingers. Though no one could see, both Miss Nellie and Mikey rolled their eyes.

The girls crossed the intersection, Miss Nellie turning right on the other side and proceeding up the only sidewalk in town, Sally walking straight past Paterson's toward her house. Andy and Mikey turned right as well, paralleling Miss Nellie up through town, but on the opposite side of the road. Mikey dropped off and stopped just before his house. Miss Nellie glanced back, nodded, and continued for her house, determined not to look back again as she neared the end of the sidewalk.

And then it happened. The shrillest squalling ever heard in Falling Rocks...and all of Falling Rocks heard it too. It was Mikey's mom. He had just walked through the front door.

Miss Nellie giggled, and smiled over to Andy. He smiled back with relief, and hustled ahead as Miss Nellie veered across the road to his side, both quickly leaving town behind.

# Chapter Twenty-four

The unrelenting sun steadily crept across the sky just like any other day – oblivious to the drama unfolding below. It didn't care that Mikey's mom didn't buy his story that he simply had gotten lost in the woods, or that Sally had lied to her parents, claiming that she was with Charles all night, making everything forgivable. It didn't care that Jeff had caused his mother to miss half a shift of work – boy, would he get his later that evening – and it didn't notice Miss Nellie and Andy, resting in empty houses, watching the walls close in. And the sun even seemed unconcerned as Shorty snuck back onto the oak flat on top of the mountain.

\*\*\*

Shorty shook off a chill as he cautiously stepped across the flat, determined to decipher the scene that looked like a tornado had touched down. The forest floor always hides clues that will paint a picture, but Shorty's eyes kept drifting to the top of the bluff. It was so quiet and still. Something was watching him. He could feel it. So much so that he fixed his rifle on the craggy ledge on top of the bluff as he retreated back the way he came.

But then a single raven flushed from a branch above, frantically cawing an alarm as a faint breeze touched Shorty's cheek. It felt warm, and smelled sweet. Shorty lowered his rifle from the path of the raven, and followed the flow of sweet air as it snaked through the trees towards the bluff. He hesitated, looking up across the bluff, and something whispered softly in his ear. He wheeled around with his rifle to his shoulder, nearly firing a round across the flat. But there was nobody there, and the whisper returned. It was riding on the breeze, and gaining strength, but he couldn't understand the words.

Shorty traced the breeze, the whisper, until it seemed to be coming from the ground at the base of a young, poplar tree. Coming from something under the heaped-up leaves. Shorty brushed the leaves aside, and there was Enki's crystal mask. The pieces had forged back together – all but around the one eye that still clung to Enki's face.

Shorty picked up the brilliant mask. It vibrated and sparkled in the evening sunlight with colors he had never seen before. The whisper was as loud and plain as the hands that held the mask, but Shorty still could not comprehend the words. Very slowly he raised the mask, and eased it down towards his head. An abrasive, metal grinding noise blasted in his ears, and his blood nearly boiled just beneath the skin across his face. Shorty tossed the mask to the ground and fell backwards in fright. Only Enki could survive the power of the mask.

But still, the mask almost frantically whispered to Shorty. Eventually he gathered himself from the ground and carefully approached the mask again. He lightly brushed his fingers along the mask, reassuring himself that it was not red hot. It was ice cold. Shorty looked across the flat, still feeling that someone was there, but again, there was no one. He quickly shoved the mask under his arm, and disappeared over the edge and into the laurel like a thief disappearing into the night.

*** 

The sun was well up in the western sky above the flat, but at the same time, slipping behind Rocky Ridge when Mr. Paterson pulled his car up alongside Wilbert, still sitting perfectly in his chair. "Hello, Wilbert," he said as he crawled out and waddled around the back of his car, taking his usual seat across from Wilbert. Mr. Paterson talked for half an hour without an answer. Eventually, as the night swallowed the east side of the mountain, and the outdoor light buzzed to life over his head, Paterson decided to check for a pulse. Twenty minutes later, he went to fetch help.

*** 

News of Wilbert's death spread to every house in Falling Rocks before the paramedics had a chance to pry him from his chair. Miss Nellie forbade the boys and Sally to attend his funeral. "No need to fuel the rumor mill," she said. "They're just dropping an empty box anyhow." It seemed that the undertaker had become smitten with Miss Nellie as well. No one knew what really happen to Wilbert's body – except Tommy, and he wasn't talking – but a shooting star zipped across the sky above Rocky Ridge almost every time Miss Nellie gazed up into the night sky.

*

Falling Rocks had lost a true character, but a radiant, new energy emerged through four teenagers, and breathed new life into a sleepy, little town that balanced the scales of existence. There was much more to Falling Rocks than met the eye. That new energy was young and wild though. And Miss Nellie was worried. Charles had snapped back to reality, and Sally broke his controlling grip on her. She spent nearly every minute of her free time hounding after Miss Nellie since they had come off of the mountain. But Sally still accompanied Charles to his senior prom later that spring, and Andy did not understand.

Andy was a mash of teenage hormones and emotions, and he was only one heartbeat away from being unstable – maybe a little more like his brother than anyone noticed. Miss Nellie couldn't even have Andy and Sally near each other without a distracting tension, which mostly ended up in a full-blown argument.

And Mikey—he disappeared regularly—running through the mountains like a wild man, and driving his mother to the very edge of insanity. It was risky for a human to fraternize so often with a Sasquatch, but Mikey denied ever seeing his friend again. His eyes said otherwise though.

"He's not coming back," Jeff would say every time Mikey come up missing. Miss Nellie tended to agree, or about half expected him to show up seven feet tall and covered in hair.

Miss Nellie felt the pressure to move her young apprentices forward…at least one of them. But which one? Not a decision to be made in hast, but she was running out of time. She could feel Enki's influence about, and she was pretty sure it was with Shorty. He had moved out of Andy's house, but drove past every night on his way to the Hotel. And every time he passed through Plum Hollow, the wind whispered and the crystal mask glowed from under his coat on the truck seat. Miss Nellie had caught him already, his truck parked along the road, and him snooping around through the burnt rubble of the old haunted house – Wilbert's home place. If Shorty found the invincible, crystal sword hidden under the icy waters of Blue Hole…

*** 

Eventually Miss Nellie put Sally to work and loaded her arms up with a couple of taped-up shoeboxes that needed safely stored away. The boxes were full of Wilbert's things – the deed to his house, deeds to the Rothstone tract and his home place in Plum Hollow, his will, and other keepsakes. Sally leaned back with the heavier than expected boxes while Miss Nellie rummaged through her pantry, opening a narrow door in the very back corner. Sally's eyes gleamed and her dimples cut into her cheeks. She knew where they were going. Miss Nellie lifted a battery-powered lantern from a shelf, and they both descended a treacherous grade of steps and disappeared into the dark tunnel.

Neither spoke a word as they chased the black mass through the tunnel, and turned left toward the shelter door, allowing the darkness to close in on them from behind. Miss Nellie cranked on the hatch door while Sally patiently waited, her arms aching, but too excited to care. Finally the heavy door screeched open.

Inside, Miss Nellie sat the lantern on a shelf, and pushed aside an array of books with her forearm, allowing a nook on the table for the hefty shoeboxes. Sally pried her fingers from the bottom of the boxes as Miss Nellie struck a match and gently nudged the wick of each candle mounted on the candelabra. Thin wisps of pungent smoke swirled about the room above the dancing flames as they stretched higher and brighter.

Miss Nellie turned toward the steel cabinet and began twisting the face of the combination padlock. To the right, to the left, back and forth she spun the dial while quietly mumbling something under her breath, as if she were relying purely on luck to open it. But, as entertaining as she was, Sally's eyes were pulled back to the table. The books were of some age and well used, but nothing like the others still on the shelf along the wall. The one that had been shuffled to the top even had a Little Cove Public Library sticker on its binding. It was a deep red, with black, gothic-like designs pressed into the cover, and though upside down in Sally's view, the words Mythology and Folklore, ornately drawn in a dull gold, seemed to come to life under the wavering candlelight.

Sally couldn't resist and picked up the book, turning to the first of several bookmarks. She expected to find the legendary Bigfoot inside, but shuddered when the book unfolded to a full page rendition of a hairless giant with a hammer-like club and only one piercing eye. The page to the right was entitled, 'Cyclops.' She quickly flipped through the pages until the book fell open again - the Kraken. Sally's brow flattened with confusion and rapidly increasing anxiety as the candlelight danced across the glossy, full-page artwork. Again she flipped through the book, finding fairies, dwarves and elves. And near the end, even leprechauns. The last page flipped to the left, revealing the library checkout sleeve glued to the back cover...and the book was long, long overdue.

Sally sifted through the remaining pile of books on the table, finding a few more from the library, several from bookstores that Sally never heard of, and who knew where the rest came from? And among this bizarre collection of literature, Miss Nellie found interest in the legends of Atlas and Hercules, King Arthur and Excalibur, the Spear of Destiny and the crystal skulls, the Fountain of Youth, and the great city of Atlantis to name a few. There was a thick book about ancient architecture, covering every pyramid from Asia to Europe, Africa to the Americas, and places like Stonehenge, and Machu Picchu. One book focused solely on the Bermuda Triangle, and there were even a couple of informative books geared toward younger generations on Stingrays and scuba diving.

Without warning the padlock loudly clicked open, and Miss Nellie proclaimed, "Ha!" Sally smiled as she moved out of Miss Nellie's way, leaving the books behind and glancing over the maps that covered the other side of the table as she went. Miss Nellie turned with one shoebox, placing it on a shelf in the steel cabinet. Sally leaned in for a closer look in the dim light.

The first was a topographical map...well, several smaller, more detailed maps, cut and taped together perfectly to make one large, square map that hung over the edge. And right in the middle, drawn in red marker, was a triangle, with a notch in the one side toward where the map identified as Rothstone Park. Sally leaned in closer yet. The red lines seemed to follow the contour lines of the map, like the triangle was a real land mass. Three red lines intersected at a red dot in the middle of the triangle, and each line passed through the corresponding corner of the triangle, stretching out across the map. One line stopped at a red X, and according to the map, somewhere south of Falling Rocks, maybe near Blue Hole. The other two lines were bare, one stretching to the north east across endless farm country dotted with small towns, the other cutting due west over nothing but mountains.

Sally became aware that Miss Nellie was standing on the other side of the candelabra, by the last shoebox, and she was quietly watching. Sally abruptly stood upright, and nonchalantly moved her eyes across the table, refusing to notice Miss Nellie's attentiveness. Her eyes stalled on a folded up, black, poster-sized paper that Sally quickly identified as a constellation chart. Miss Nellie had been drawing on that as well, apparently with a white crayon, and though mostly folded underneath, it was clearly the same triangle, with only one line showing, ending on a star belonging to another constellation.

Miss Nellie slid the last box over the edge of the table and into her fingertips, and she turned toward the cabinet again. Sally leaned over the second map. It was a much wider angle, but easily recognizable as the East Coast. And again, Miss Nellie had been adding her personal touch. The Bermuda Triangle was outlined in red at the bottom, and little blue arrows tracked north through the Atlantic, following the coastline – possibly marking the ocean currents. There were two red X's. One was well inland, and, without closer inspection, marked home. The other marked the headwaters of the Chesapeake Bay, at the mouth of the Susquehanna River, and the word 'battle' was written to the left, across Maryland. And to the east, written in red, 'Atlas' floated in the light blue waters of the Delaware Bay, with a trail of red A's drifting to the north along with the blue arrows of the ocean current. It must have all meant something, but nothing to Sally.

Suddenly, something furry slid in over the map, right in front of Sally's face, causing her to squeak as she stumbled back from the table.

"Oh I'm sorry, sweetie," Miss Nellie said as she pulled out her chair, and eased her old, tired bones down for a rest – yet another reason why she couldn't afford to wait any longer to pass on her legacy. But Sally's eyes wouldn't leave... whatever it was... that looked like deer hides, rolled together and bound by thongs of rawhide. And sitting on top of a spiral notebook. Eventually Sally broke her stare from the thing on the table, and looked at Miss Nellie, cracking a nervous little smile.

"Have a seat, dear," Miss Nellie said as she pulled out the second chair.

~*~*~*~*

Also by Michael Henry

*****Inside the Devil's Pocket*****

*Decades ago, a chain of events began deep in the Appalachian Mountains that will terrorize the country for ages to come. John Bayley emerges from the aftermath to seize his place in history. For generations before his birth, John was bred from evil. Evil rears its child with the cruelest of human nature, and John is molded into a spiteful, master manipulator. Unaware of his destiny, John chooses to become a minister.*

*John's golden tongue raises him to idol status. His newfound power becomes an addiction and he is willing to do anything to feed it. John's mind loses sight of the truth. unable to judge himself, he believes that the is the right hand of God and destined to destroy the world using unthinkable means. John accomplishes the impossible and wreaks havoc across the countryside until the remnants of good stand against him.*

*Desperation and bloody sacrifice crumbles John's empire even faster than it rose. The predator quickly becomes the prey. John runs for his life, refusing to accept his heritage every step of the way. Abandoned and out of options, John can no longer hide from his true destiny.*

*Does mankind triumph over evil, or is John just another link that tightens around our soul?*

Available from A-Argus Books
www.a-argusbooks.com

21986545R00157

Made in the USA
Charleston, SC
09 September 2013